THE
MITFORD
TRIAL

ALSO BY JESSICA FELLOWES

The Mitford Scandal
Bright Young Dead
The Mitford Murders

Downton Abbey—A Celebration
The Wit and Wisdom of Downton Abbey
A Year in the Life of Downton Abbey
The Chronicles of Downton Abbey
The World of Downton Abbey

THE
MITFORD
TRIAL

JESSICA FELLOWES

MINOTAUR
BOOKS
NEW YORK

Published in the United States by Minotaur Books, an imprint of St. Martin's Publishing Group

THE MITFORD TRIAL. Copyright © 2020 by Jessica Fellowes. All rights reserved. Printed in the United States of America. For information, address St. Martin's Publishing Group, 120 Broadway, New York, NY 10271.

www.minotaurbooks.com

The Library of Congress has cataloged the hardcover edition as follows:

Names: Fellowes, Jessica, author.
Title: The Mitford trial / Jessica Fellowes.
Description: First U.S. Edition. | New York : Minotaur Books, 2021.
  | Series: The Mitford murders ; 4
Identifiers: LCCN 2020037491 | ISBN 9781250316837 (hardcover)
  | ISBN 9781250316851 (ebook)
Subjects: GSAFD: Mystery fiction.
Classification: LCC PR6106.E398 M593 2021 | DDC 823/.92—dc23
LC record available at https://lccn.loc.gov/2020037491

ISBN 978-1-250-31684-4 (trade paperback)

Our books may be purchased in bulk for promotional, educational, or business use. Please contact your local bookseller or the Macmillan Corporate and Premium Sales Department at 1-800-221-7945, extension 5442, or by email at MacmillanSpecialMarkets@macmillan.com.

Originally published in Great Britain by Sphere, an imprint of Little, Brown Book Group, an Hachette UK company

First Minotaur Books Trade Paperback Edition: 2021

10 9 8 7 6 5 4 3 2 1

THE
MITFORD
TRIAL

PROLOGUE

18 June 1933

Outside, the horizon had been lost to the darkness, with sky and sea both black as the underside of a dead man's eyelids. No stars shone and the moon was hidden behind the clouds. Only the white foam that curled away from the sides of the ocean liner revealed movement, as the prow forged through the water.

Inside, on deck B, in the drawing room of cabin seventeen, a man stood by a mirrored drinks cabinet and stared dully at the bottles before him. They hadn't been sailing many nights and already most of them were half-empty. He poured a slug of whisky into a glass tumbler that he couldn't be absolutely certain was clean. On the gramophone player, a woman was singing a song about her lover going away. The room was comfortable enough. It could have been the front room of any mock-Tudor house in the suburbs but for the smell of the sea and the occasional lurch of the ground beneath his feet. On the sofa was a pillow and a folded blanket. There was a woman merely yards away, on the other side of the thin wall,

1

clattering in the bathroom, and soon she would sleep in the comfortable bed.

Curtains were drawn across the French windows – as grandly described in the brochure – leading out to a narrow balcony, large enough for a table and two chairs, where the cabin's residents could enjoy watching the sunset with an expertly mixed cocktail. It wasn't mentioned in the brochure, but there was also enough room for a person to hide, bent down in the corner.

The man sat down on the armchair that faced into the room, away from the pitiless dark beyond. He was tired, he had drunk too much, fought too much and knew he had lost too much. He'd made mistakes and felt too old to put them right. Besides, he'd already tried, and failed.

He heard the door to the cabin open, but it was out of sight and he couldn't be certain whether someone had come in or was leaving. He wondered briefly if he should get up and check, and that was the last thing he thought before he dropped his glass, as pain blew through him and blood filled his mouth.

PART ONE

CHAPTER ONE

~~~~~~~~

15 October 1932

When the morning arrived, Louisa Cannon, as she still was, lay for a while between the sheets, looking up to the ceiling as she studied the contents of her mind. She had slept deeply in an unfamiliar bedroom and wondered now if this was perhaps not a good thing. Weren't nerves expected, possibly even necessary? A display of excitement and trepidation for what lay ahead was conventional, even if one was hopeful and optimistic. Yet Louisa was sure that she felt completely calm and safe, as if she knew she had been away too long and was at last on her way home. At that moment she heard noises on the landing, a shuffling of feet and fervent whispers beyond her door. Louisa smothered her laughter as the brass doorknob turned slowly and a voice of protestation was hushed severely. She saw three sisters standing in the doorway, looking at her with huge eyes, the smallest girl hopping from foot to foot with her usual impatience.

'It's all right,' said Louisa. 'You can come in.'

'Nanny said we weren't to disturb,' the tall blonde said. 'But I knew you wouldn't mind.' This was Jessica, known to all as Decca, fifteen years old and with a determined set to her mouth, hardly different in temperament from the three-year-old with long curls Louisa met when she arrived to work for the Mitford family. Then, there had been five young sisters and one brother; the youngest, Deborah, had not yet been born. She came up now to Louisa's bedside, her blonde hair cropped to just below her ears, and handed over a piece of folded card.

'I pressed some cornflowers for you,' said Debo. 'Something blue.' She smiled shyly and Louisa smiled back.

'Thank you, Miss Deborah. I shall keep them in my pocket and they'll bring me luck. I suppose I had better get up, there's somewhere I've got to be, isn't there?'

The younger girls giggled at that, told her Nanny had made breakfast and they were going to go next door, to see their muv and farve, Lord and Lady Redesdale, the former of whom was likely tapping his watch as they spoke. The eldest of the three had said nothing throughout but watched Louisa with a steady gaze.

'Miss Unity?' Louisa reflected that while the other sisters wore their hearts – and their tempers – on their sleeves, Unity tended to the more unsentimental approach. As a small child she had often retreated alone to corners, and when she spoke it was usually to Decca, in their own secret language.

'Do you really love him?' she asked simply, her eyes still fixed on Louisa. But Louisa was able to reply with a steadfast look of her own.

'I do.'

Unity nodded solemnly and left the room, ushering her sisters before her.

Louisa savoured her breakfast with Nanny Blor, elderly now with her red hair faded to a rusty grey, though stalwart and bustling about the place as comfortingly as ever. Afterwards, Louisa put on her only 'new', a steel-coloured silk hat with a silvered veil. She pinned it carefully and was buttoning her coat up in front of the mirror in the small hall – she was staying in the mews cottage at the back of the Mitford's London house in Rutland Gate – when the front door banged open noisily. Nancy and Tom, the first and third in the line-up of siblings, came rushing in, bringing some of the cold October air with them.

'Lou-Lou,' said Nancy affectionately, kissing her on the cheek. She was only a little younger than Louisa and not yet married herself, though she had been nothing less than generous when Louisa had told her about her engagement. 'Don't you look divine.' She shot her brother a look, nudging him to approve the compliment.

'Yes, yes,' said Tom. 'Very good indeed. Marvellous hat.' He was tall, dark and handsome, like a hero in a romantic novel, and, Louisa knew, had women all over Europe longing for him to ask them to dance. With Louisa's father long dead, she had nervously asked Tom to walk her down the aisle. Her mother wasn't even coming up from Suffolk for the wedding, feeling too frail to do so, even if she was happy for her daughter. Although Louisa had been a maid of some kind for them over several years, the Mitfords were as close to family as anything she had. They maddened her half the time, but she felt she owed something of her happiness to them and she'd wanted them to be a part of her wedding.

Nancy fidgeted in her bag and pulled out a lipstick. 'Here,' she said and advanced on Louisa. 'The finishing touch.'

Louisa submitted and allowed Nancy to apply the red colour to her lips. She even accepted dots of scent at her wrists and behind her ears, too.

'Now shall we go?' said Louisa. She felt a flutter in her stomach and, with it, a slight wash of relief. All was as it should be.

Nancy went next door, as she was going to share a taxi with her sisters Unity, Decca and Deborah, while their parents were driven by the second oldest daughter, Pamela, who had a passion for motoring and whose pride and joy – other than the herd of cows she managed for her brother-in-law – was her dark green Austin 10. Their other sister, Diana, would be making her way separately with her own two young boys, Jonathan and Desmond, from her house in Cheyne Walk. Diana's husband, Bryan Guinness, was down at their country house, Biddesden, as he more or less had been in recent months. There were rumours of an impending divorce but nothing officially declared, and Louisa knew better than to ask the question.

Lord Redesdale had lent Louisa his car and driver, and it was only as the man in the peaked cap held the door open for her that she realised she had never sat in the back seat of a car before. All at once she felt shy, and remained silent for the journey to Chelsea Town Hall, Tom beside her. In those minutes, Louisa missed her father terribly; his brusque manner had ineffectually masked a genuine love for his family and she ached to be able to reach out for his hand, callused with work, soot permanently beneath his fingernails. She wondered if she had made a terrible mistake arriving in this grand car. She hadn't meant to pretend she was something she wasn't, it had just seemed like a glamorous and fun thing to do, and generous of her previous employers to offer it. But perhaps she should have taken the bus, as she normally did to go anywhere. She *liked* the bus, she thought with a lurch of sickness. Then, as the car slowed down to park beside the pavement on the King's Road, yards from the blue door she was soon to walk through, Louisa spotted Guy Sullivan, her future husband, as he hurried along. He happened to look at the car she was in, then through the window and, for the briefest second, they caught each other's eye. It was supposed to be bad luck to see each other before the wedding, wasn't it? She leaned back slightly, but Guy grinned at her, the bright sunlight reflecting on his round spectacles, his long, lean frame poised as if in haste to marry her, and she knew she had never looked forward to anything so much as being his wife.

Afterwards, the wedding party crossed the road to go to the Pig's Ear for what Nancy kept insisting was 'the wedding breakfast' but which Louisa knew was sandwiches, tea and beer. She and Guy had paid for everything themselves; there would be no champagne. But she was more than fine with that and as she stood beside Guy, before their friends, her cheeks were beginning to hurt from all the smiling. The thin gold ring was on her left hand, and Guy held onto her right, squeezing it often as he turned to look at her.

'I can't believe it has finally happened,' he said. 'Louisa Cannon, my wife.'

'Mrs Sullivan to you,' she teased, prompting another kiss from her delighted groom.

'Oi, oi, there's quite enough time for all that later on.' A beaming Harry Conlon, the best man, tugged at Guy's arm. 'Wasn't there something about a cake and speeches first?'

Harry's wife, Mary, pretty and heavily pregnant, ticked her husband off. 'When they're ready and not before.' She whispered to Louisa, 'I think he was more nervous than Guy. Absolutely terrified he'd lose the ring. He's never had stage fright like it before.'

They shared a conspiratorial look over at their husbands – their husbands! – before Mary walked off to find somewhere to sit down.

The pub was crowded. Though they had wanted only a modest wedding party, there was all Guy's family – his parents, his three brothers and their wives, plus assorted cousins and small children – and all of the Mitfords. Plus a sprinkling of friends: Jenny, who had grown up on the same Peabody estate as Louisa, but whose beauty had married her into the upper class, was over from New York for a brief spell with her husband Richard; Luke Meyers, Louisa's friend from the time she had spent working for Diana as her lady's maid, who was now working in Munich as a correspondent for *The Times*; and one or two others of Guy's childhood friends – neighbours from the street he had grown up on. That would have been enough guests, but it was Guy's colleagues who had filled up the room. Policemen, Louisa had discovered, liked to celebrate one of their own, and as Guy had worked through the ranks from constable to detective sergeant for the CID, plenty of them had claimed him. There were uniformed juniors and plain-clothed seniors, all busily ransacking the egg and ham sandwiches, and repeatedly toasting the health of the new Mr and Mrs Sullivan.

Louisa pulled Guy over to a table in the corner, on which stood a white cake of three tiers, a long knife beside it. There was a clinking on glass and the room fell quiet. Louisa took a step to the side, gently pushing Guy's hand away.

'Go on,' she whispered.

She saw Guy resist the urge to polish his specs, picking up his glass of beer instead. He raised it slightly.

'My lords, ladies and gentlemen,' he began, 'my wife and I—'

He was interrupted by a roar from the room, the policemen calling out his name before he silenced them again with a wave of his hand. Louisa spotted Lord Redesdale looking about him with bemusement.

'My wife and I are very happy to see you all here. Before we cut the cake, I'd like to thank a few people who've made the day possible.' He went to pull a piece of paper out of his pocket but, as he did this, the door of the pub banged open and several heads turned around to see a young messenger boy come in.

In the momentary silence they heard a Cockney accent ask: 'Is this the Sullivan wedding? I've been told to find the groom.'

There was an embarrassed murmur as people parted to allow the boy through. The boy's eyes darted around the room and he pulled his cap further down on his head before he shuffled up to Guy, who watched him approach, his notes still in one hand, his drink in the other, as if caught out by the music stopping in a children's party game.

At least, thought Louisa, the part in the ceremony when anyone could object to the marriage had passed.

The boy stood before Guy with a piece of folded paper in his hand and there was another dance as Guy realised he had to start moving, so gave Louisa his notes and drink, and took the note. He read it, then looked out to the sea of expectant faces. Louisa couldn't detect what their mood was other than a mixture of exasperation and curiosity.

'It's from the commissioner,' he started, and Louisa saw

all the policemen lean forward a fraction. 'The rally for the British Union of Fascists has begun and the crowds are bigger and more rowdy than expected. Everyone is needed. All leave is cancelled.'

He looked at Louisa and mouthed, 'I'm so sorry,' but before she could even respond, everyone's drinks had been put down and the men were rushing out. There was the occasional call of 'Sorry, mate,' but on the whole, she knew, this was what they were made for, this was why they did what they did. Nor was the summons a surprise. Guy had warned her of the possibility, only two days before – too late to postpone the wedding.

Louisa took Guy's hand. 'You'd better go too.'

He kissed her on the lips. 'I'm sorry, Mrs Sullivan.'

She gave a small smile. 'I'm a policeman's wife, aren't I? We'll have our supper together tonight, at home.'

Home, for now, was with Guy's parents. His father was ill and needed almost constant care, and Guy's mother hadn't the strength to do it all alone. Louisa and Guy had discussed it and decided to stay on until some other solution presented itself. Louisa didn't mind too much – it was a neat and cosy house, and she had next to nothing by way of furniture of her own. This way, they could save and find somewhere they wanted. As for a honeymoon, that was only ever going to be a train to Brighton and one night in a hotel on the seafront. They would have to do it another time. There was no point in fussing, it couldn't be helped.

Luke came over as soon as Guy had left and gave her a kiss on the cheek. 'You look beautiful, darling,' he said. 'I thoroughly approve of this colour on you.'

'What are they doing?' In a corner, Louisa had noticed that

Lord and Lady Redesdale were in an animated discussion with their daughters Nancy and Unity.

'I gather the girls want to join the rally too, lend their support to Sir O,' said Luke. 'I think their Muv and Farve are trying to say no, but you know what it's like trying to refuse those two something they want.'

Louisa knew only too well. Even so, she felt a pull of disappointment. 'Does no one want to stay and help me celebrate my marriage?'

Luke raised an eyebrow. 'Don't be petulant. It doesn't suit you. And besides, I'm here, thank you very much. I count for at least forty policemen.'

'Yes, you do. Sorry.' She knew she was being silly. Guy's family were still there, and there was plenty of food to get through. She wished she didn't mind about the Mitfords as much; somehow, she always let her expectations get the better of her and she kicked herself for it.

The only person in the room who had the good manners to look ashamed was Diana. Though still married to Bryan, everyone knew that her lover was Sir Oswald Mosley, the founder of the BUF and the instigator of the day's rally. Louisa had heard Diana declare her undying love for him as Sir Oswald told her he felt the same, but that he would never leave his wife. Diana's usual cream-and-rose complexion had a dark flush, and she kept her gaze away from Louisa as she handed her boys to Nanny Blor, apologising that her own Nanny Higgs was on leave. In the next moment she had fled the pub. Walking quickly through the door after her was a man Louisa didn't recognise. He wore a grey trench coat and a hat with a wide enough brim to hide his features, and he didn't give a backwards glance as he hurried out. He carried neither newspaper nor briefcase. Perhaps a plain-clothes detective who had been slower off the mark than the others.

Those bloody Mitfords, she thought, they've dictated my day again.

CHAPTER TWO

A s a detective sergeant for the CID, Guy no longer wore a uniform, but nor did he usually attend to police duty in a suit with a white carnation in his buttonhole. He thought about removing it, then decided that he wasn't going to let his work interfere any further in his wedding. Louisa had packed up the room she'd been renting a few doors down, and Guy was determined to carry his bride over the threshold of their bedroom that night. What's more, he'd do it in his best suit with the flower in its rightful place.

All the policemen had been warned and therefore already knew that they were to report directly to their superiors at a meeting place by St Martin-in-the-Fields. Some of the uniforms jumped on passing buses, others joined taxis hailed by more senior ranks and a few rounded up foursomes to take in their cars. Guy was scooped up by DCI Stiles, who, as per usual, looked more elegant than the groom, with a Savile Row suit and his silver hair slicked back, not a strand out of place.

'Sorry about this, Sully,' said Stiles as they clipped along the King's Road together.

'Not to worry, sir. Can't be helped.'

'Least you've got a missus now – there'll be dinner on the table when you get home.'

Guy gave a polite laugh. He didn't like to point out that as he'd never left home, there had never been a night when dinner hadn't been on the table. His mother insisted on the importance of 'something hot' even though he was now thirty-two and was the last of his brothers, by a long chalk, reliant on her maternal care. Tonight, though, Louisa would prepare his dinner. He didn't even know if she could cook, but he knew he'd eat it all up, even if it was boiled tripe, and tell her it was delicious. He was determined to be a good husband. Even if he had failed at the first hurdle: absent from his own wedding party.

Guy shook it off and concentrated on the matter in hand. 'What's the form, sir?'

Stiles stopped at a black Daimler, the standard-issue motor car for senior officers, but this one had a pale pink cushion on the driver's seat. Stiles saw Guy look at it.

'I get a stiff back,' he explained.

They got in and two uniforms who had been walking close behind got in the rear seats.

'Indicate right, would you?' Stiles asked, and the policeman sitting behind him rolled down the window and stuck his arm through. Stiles pulled the car out and, when they were purring along, filled them in on the afternoon's event.

'As you know, we got word a few days ago that Sir O was planning this rally. It's the first of its kind and we don't properly know what to expect, but if we've all been called in, then I'd say the numbers are bigger than anyone thought.'

'What sort of numbers?' asked Guy.

'Anything over five thousand, I'd say. We were prepared, but for less than that. There are uniforms out there and a few plain clothes keeping an eye out for any irregular activities on the side. This is worrying. I don't like the idea of that many people thinking the BUF has got something to offer them.'

'Sounds all right to me, if you ask, guv,' said the man who'd pulled his arm back in again. 'Macdonald's a shower, isn't he? A traitor to the Labour party. We need a real leader, someone who believes in the Brits and the working man.'

Stiles looked at the man severely in his rear-view mirror. 'I wasn't asking you, Kershaw.' He looked at the road ahead and braked in time to let a young woman holding a small child cross the road. 'You boys in the back, report in at the church and you'll be told where to go. Sully, I want you to get to the back of the crowd. Watch out for anything suspicious. Anyone taking advantage of the crowd situation, whether it's pickpocketing or starting a fight.'

'Yes sir.'

'We need to know who these people are.'

'Yes sir,' said Guy automatically. Then: 'Why, sir?'

Stiles gave a sigh. 'A politician might give you a different answer, but I think they're troublemakers. Bored young men, most of them, sorry they missed out on the war.' He gave Guy a sideways look. 'They shouldn't be. They were the lucky ones.'

'Yes, sir.' Guy coughed. The shame of not fighting had never left him, even if it had hardly been his fault. He'd been disallowed on the grounds of his extreme short-sightedness. But where he had been lucky, his brothers were each called up and one of them never came home.

Guy looked outside as they drove along Pall Mall, in the

shadow of the great cream slabs that housed gentlemen's clubs, men snoozing in armchairs, egg stains on their ties, blissfully unaware of the vast numbers of police swarming into this corner of London. The weather was dry, bright, a little chilly – a perfect day for his wedding, he had thought that morning. Perfect, too, for anyone who had an idea of turning out to a public gathering. Rain was enough to dampen the political ardour of most, but there was none today. Yet the streets looked quiet, bar the usual Saturday shoppers and strollers walking between St James's and the National Gallery, or even dropping down from the seedy streets of Soho. There were policemen hurrying along and Guy saw one or two civilians notice them, saw the alarm on their faces as they wondered why there were this many.

Stiles pulled his car into a dead end after the corner at Haymarket and all four got out quickly, but Guy could feel straightaway that there was no hum of a crowd in the air. There was nothing in the air at all beyond a cold breeze that made his neck feel stiff.

The uniforms ran off ahead, while he and Stiles marched in step, both with their long strides. They said nothing as they walked, their ears pricked for warning signals. But none came. Only as they turned into Trafalgar Square did the scene present itself – and not as they had expected. There were far too many policemen; anyone would have thought it was a gathering of constables and sergeants. They slowed their pace as they approached what was a peaceful crowd. Flummoxed by the quiet, truncheons were stealthily replaced in their holsters and the uniforms stood around the edges of the people who were collected in the square. Their faces were turned in one direction: a man in a dark suit and white shirt, standing on a plinth beneath Nelson's column, coal-black hair combed back and a full moustache, talking with great animation.

Stiles stopped and put his hands in his pockets, raising his eyebrows. 'We've been had,' he said.

'Sir?'

But Stiles said no more, gesturing that Guy should follow him, and they ducked into the crowd, making their way closer to the man on the plinth. It was only when they were near that Guy realised it was Sir Oswald Mosley. He knew who he was, but not for the usual reasons – Guy was not interested in the minor machinations of politicians – but because Louisa had told him about the man that Nancy called 'Sir Ogre'. He was Diana's lover, though the pale woman standing close to him now, with two boys of around ten and twelve years old, was definitely not Mrs Guinness. Eight men in black shirts and dark grey trousers flanked them on either side, arms folded while their darting eyes belied their confident stance at the sight of all the police pouring into the square. Of the people watching, there were a few women here and there, like rogue poppies in a wheat field, but for the most part they were young men, in grey shirts and flannels, and only a few wore jackets. Guy wondered if they left their houses that morning in shirts and trousers? It seemed a strange decision, especially with the threat of a change in the weather at this time of year. Unless it was a collective choice, a uniform of sorts. That thought put Guy on edge, somehow. Uniforms on police and soldiers, even for firemen and nurses, were reassuring. On civilians, he wondered what they were trying to say and suspected it was more defence than protection.

There was a movement between some people on the right of Sir Oswald, and Guy saw him register it with a brief flicker of his black eyes: Unity Mitford, her thick fair hair sticking out stiffly beneath her hat, her face expressionless but for parted lips as she gulped in big breaths. Behind her, standing awkwardly, shielding herself behind her statuesque sister, was Diana, her expression clear for all to see: total, unadulterated admiration.

Sir Oswald's voice rose in volume; his jabs with pointed fingers were even more forceful. Guy tried to listen to what he was saying but couldn't latch onto anything that made sense. Each sentence seemed disparate from the previous one, a series of instructions or exhortations to his followers, acknowledged by raised voices and the occasional clapping of hands. One thing was clear: Sir Ogre saw himself as a leader, the only one who could take the people out of the chaos and disorder that surrounded them. This made Guy laugh – everyone was standing quietly and listening, and they were surrounded by the well-organised ranks of the London Metropolitan Police. He quickly shut up when one or two of the folded-arm brigade turned their fierce gaze upon him.

Guy whispered to Stiles, 'What do you think happened?'

Stiles gave a small shrug. 'Who knows? My guess is that either someone from the BUF tipped off the police because they were expecting bigger numbers and didn't want any fights, it being the first gathering outside, or one of their objectors wanted to rattle them and sent a false message to Scotland Yard.'

'We must fight for the freedom of our speech,' Mosley was saying. 'We will resist the Communists who would inflict their vile oppression upon us. We will not give an inch. If they fight, then yes, my friends, we will fight back.'

At this, as if it were a signal, the guards unfolded their arms and Guy felt the crowd move, though whether it was forward or backwards he couldn't say. The flankers were agitated, their elbows jutting, their heads flicking to the side at the merest prompt. They looked ready for a fight. A cry went up near the front of the crowd, close to Mosley, followed swiftly by three or four voices shouting indistinctly. Hecklers, presumably, and only to be expected.

Mosley continued talking, but his gestures were edgy, his stance retreating into himself. The woman beside him pulled her boys in closer; her nervous smile had disappeared altogether. From various points in the crowds, a chant formed until the few objectors were singing loudly and in unison:

Hitler and Mosley, what are they for?
Thuggery, buggery, hunger and war!

Things descended into mayhem at speed then, as the fascists turned on the chanting men and women, fists flying and yells of indeterminate curses roaring above. Mosley stopped talking and Guy observed him gather his family around, before they were marched through the crowd and out to, presumably, a car that waited for them. Guy tried to find the Mitfords, but they, too, had vanished.

Stiles pulled at Guy's arm. 'Leave this to the uniforms,' he shouted. 'Follow me.'

As they pulled out of the serried ranks, Guy realised that most of the men were leaving with them. Only a few had chosen to stay behind and fight. He guessed that that was what they'd been after all along. Was that what Mosley had wanted, too? Guy hoped not, but it was an obvious tactic: create disorder and then be the one to create the order out of it.

Back at the car, Guy felt the oppressive tension fall away, and in spite of the chill air, he was sweating beneath his shirt. As if he had forgotten the fact and only now remembered it, Guy turned to Stiles.

'It's my wedding day, sir. I'd like to get back to my wife.'

Stiles smacked his hand on Guy's back. 'My lad, I'm sorry about what happened. But I don't think we've seen the last of those bastards. It's just as well we know what we're up against.'

'Sir.'

Stiles gave a wry smile. 'Now's not the time for lectures. Off you go. Good luck. I'll see you on Monday morning.'

Guy looked at his watch. Only ninety minutes had passed since they'd left the party. Fingers crossed Louisa would still be at the pub. He would fetch her and, hang the expense, they'd take a taxi to the station and catch the train to Brighton. He knew she had a small suitcase packed and ready, and he didn't need much beyond a toothbrush and razor. In a matter of hours, he would hold her close to him beneath the hotel bed sheets and the rest of the world could disappear. He would get back to rescuing it next week.

CHAPTER THREE

23 May 1933

Louisa knocked on the side door of 26 Rutland Gate. The day before, a letter had arrived from Nancy asking Louisa to call in on a 'matter of urgency', without specifying what the matter was. Guy had teased that it was probably no more than a request for a seamstress, and Louisa had agreed. Even so, she could not help but answer the summons. Standing now, by the side door, she told herself that she was only there because she wanted to say hello to Nanny Blor first, not because she was avoiding the front entrance. She was no longer a servant but a married woman and almost-trained court stenographer, perfectly entitled to walk up the steps and knock the brass ring firmly. But she didn't do it.

The door was opened by a young kitchen maid Louisa didn't recognise, who admitted her readily. On asking, it turned out Nanny Blor was out with Debo, the youngest sister, and wouldn't be back for an hour. Instead, after a few minutes Louisa was summoned up the stairs to the library. As she came in, she saw that Nancy was sitting on a comfortably stuffed sofa, a tray of tea things before her already. The room was generously named: only one wall was lined with books, as Lord Redesdale was known in the family to have no interest in them. The story was that he had read one book before the war and thought it perfect, giving him no reason to make the attempt again.

It was warm, even for the month of May, yet Louisa knew the windows would have remained open by six inches even if a storm were blowing outside. It was the Mitford way. She had been connected to this family for such a long time now in one fashion or another, since 1920, and had known Nancy since she was a young girl of seventeen, barely emerging out of the nursery. Louisa herself had been but three years older, escaping a rogue uncle and a life in London that she had no longer wanted. Working as a nursery maid for Lord and Lady Redesdale had been more than a refuge: it had been her salvation. Through them, and their seven children, she had been witness to a world beyond the one her parents had decreed she should remain in. She knew now she had ambition, education and a social standing that while still firmly working class, allowed her and Guy to imagine a future that was different to that of their parents. Their children, should they be lucky enough to have any, would probably have a life even brighter and better.

All this, nonetheless, did not stop Louisa from feeling a certain habitual servitude around any of the Mitfords and she caught herself hesitating a fraction when Nancy asked her to sit down. Of all the sisters, Nancy was the one Louisa knew best. The eldest of the seven siblings was an astute observer of those around her – as Louisa had realised after reading her first novel, *Christmas Pudding* – but less inclined to give away her own intimate feelings. She was perhaps the most fun of them all, the

24

most daring and the most gregarious, but she could be spiky, and Louisa had developed a thick skin against Nancy's infamous teases. Yet there was an ease between the two of them, too. After all, she and Nancy practically found their way into adulthood together and there wasn't much she didn't know about her, even if Nancy knew less about Louisa. They hadn't seen much of each other since Louisa's wedding more than six months before, and she had no idea what this summons was about.

'Lady Mosley has died,' said Nancy, after she had poured out the tea and given Louisa a slice of fruitcake.

'Oh,' was all Louisa could think to reply. She wasn't sure what response Nancy was hoping for.

'Naturally, Diana is devastated.'

Louisa tried to work this one out. Lady Mosley was either Sir Oswald's mother or his wife. Would either one's death devastate Diana?

She must have shown her bewilderment on her face because Nancy put her cup and saucer down and said, with some impatience: 'Diana's divorce is about to go through. The last thing she wants is anyone thinking she is pleased about this.'

'Yes, I see,' said Louisa. She wasn't sure she did.

'And between you, me and the doorpost, I expect she worries about Sir O's attention wandering. Now she's no longer his mistress, he may find her less of a thrilling conquest.'

How repulsive, thought Louisa. 'Mmm,' was all she could manage, taking a bite of the cake to distract from her inability to say anything to this.

'Anyway, the point is, Sir Ogre will have to be the grieving widower for a while, even if I admit he does seem genuinely upset. He and Diana have to be kept apart while her divorce goes through, so Lady Redesdale has suggested taking her away on a cruise for a few weeks.'

'That'll be lovely for them.'

Nancy gave a mock shudder. 'Beastly things, being on a ship all day, no land in sight, unable to get away from ghastly Mr and Mrs Frightful-Bores as you walk around and around the deck. No, thank you. But it seems a good solution to the current predicament. Lady R wants to take Unity too. Unity is begging to go to a finishing school in Munich and they can deposit Decca in Paris on the way, as she'll be there for a year. In short, the old Heart-of-Stone is having an about-turn and giving them a fond farewell.' She picked up her cup again. 'Not that the thought ever occurred to her about me. I was practically pushed out of the door at the first chance.'

It hadn't been like that, but Louisa gave her a sympathetic look. Louisa had lost her closeness with her own mother after she left home. She knew her ma had been happy to see her daughter moving on in the world, yet it had separated them, too: Mrs Cannon felt unable to ask her daughter about the new things that preoccupied her, and Louisa worried that her decision to do things differently had been hurtful towards her parents' own choices. It meant that they spoke about little beyond the weather and some shared memories.

'I can't go on the cruise because someone has to stay behind to keep an eye on things. Lord Redesdale spends almost no time at Swinebrook any more but is here in London, snoozing in a leather armchair in his club the whole day long.'

Swinebrook was Nancy's name for the house that Lord Redesdale had built. They had all loved Asthall Manor, the place where Louisa had first gone to work for them, and she couldn't blame them for missing it. The new place was, by all accounts, as aesthetically pleasing as a dog kennel, and as hospitable. Nanny Blor had told Louisa that her jug of water for washing in the bedroom often froze overnight in the winter.

'Which means someone had better go down there now and then to check Nanny Blor and Debo aren't languishing alone,' continued Nancy. 'Besides, I can't go swanning off, I have to earn my living these days. I'm still writing dross for *The Lady*, but they do pay and allow one to have more than two evening dresses in the wardrobe. And I can't leave Hamish behind.'

Nancy's five-year engagement to Hamish St Clair Erskine showed no sign yet of coming to its natural conclusion. Whether that was marriage or a break-up was anyone's guess. Louisa knew what the family wanted for Nancy – and it wasn't to see her walk down the aisle towards him.

Louisa had eaten all her cake some time ago and was appalled to feel her stomach rumble. She'd worked through her lunch hour in order to leave early to make this appointment with Nancy. She thought perhaps she would stop off at the butcher's on the way home and surprise Mrs Sullivan by cooking everyone's supper that evening.

'Lou-Lou?' Nancy clicked her fingers. 'You went off somewhere else there.'

Louisa snapped into focus. 'Sorry. You were saying?'

'I think you should accompany my mother on the cruise. I know you're not Diana's lady's maid any more, but perhaps as a sort of paid holiday you could be one for Lady R for a few weeks? It's simply too much to ask for her to manage Diana, Unity and Decca. You know how they can be.'

Louisa looked out of the window; the sky was overcast and

people walked past pulling their collars up against a wind that appeared to have got up.

'I believe they're taking the train from Victoria to Paris, then on again to Venice, where they'll meet the boat. It stops at various places in Italy and Greece before it comes back to Venice three weeks later for the Orient Express home. What do you say?'

Louisa regarded Nancy's pleading expression, her well-coiffed curls that framed a heart-shaped face, her silk shirt and light woollen skirt, her fashionable square heels. She thought of her own shabby coat hanging in the hall and a hat that hadn't been replaced for three years (she couldn't wear her wedding hat every day). Louisa had avidly pored over books of maps and paintings in the Asthall library when she first went to work for the Mitfords, dreaming of what she would do before she began to think of settling down with a family of her own. The fact was, for all of the changes in the world in the last decade alone – the Amy Johnsons who co-piloted planes and Roald Amundsens who explored the Arctic – the chance to go abroad for any length of time, in a degree of comfort, was beyond reach for the likes of her. The Mitfords had taken her to Dieppe, and she had been to Paris and Venice when Diana's lady's maid. She yearned to feel the warmth of the Mediterranean sun on her face again but she bore the guilt of Guy's salary reduced by the cost of her training.

'Thank you, Miss Nancy, it's kind of you to think of me,' said Louisa carefully. 'But no, I'm afraid I can't. It would be a wonderful opportunity for someone but not, this time, for me.'

She was as polite as she could be, but she had to be firm. Louisa wouldn't ever be a servant again. Never, not for a thousand pounds a day, not for all the olives in Italy.

CHAPTER FOUR

~~~~~

After Louisa had turned down Nancy's request, there had been an awkwardness between them that could not be quickly resolved, and Louisa made her excuses. She left through the front door, the same maid showing her out, and as Louisa descended the steps she saw a maroon-coloured motor car pull up. A Jaguar? She was never too sure of cars, but it was what she knew anyone would call 'a beauty'. Diana was in the passenger seat, dressed in black, a black slouch hat pulled down to shield most of her face, but there was no disguising her now-famed beauty. The driver was a man Louisa recognised as Diana's friend Cecil Beaton, a raffish type who took endless photographs of their crowd, often printed alongside Nancy's anonymous party reports for the *Tatler*. Not wishing to see Diana today, given the conversation with Nancy, Louisa hurried off down the street. As she did so, she noticed another car pull up a hundred yards on. This driver looked familiar too, but she couldn't be sure if she knew him or if he had the sort of face that could have belonged to a number of men. He returned her glance, but he did not show that he knew her and she thought she must have been mistaken as she hurried down to her bus stop at Scotch Corner.

At Hammersmith, Louisa got off earlier than usual, making a detour to the butcher's only to find that it was shut. Early closing on a Wednesday. She hadn't realised. The thought flashed through her mind that her mother-in-law wouldn't have been caught out in the same way. Perhaps Mrs Sullivan had been doing more than her fair share of the cooking. After all, she spent her days looking after her fading husband, an exhausting and never-ending task. Louisa sympathised. In spite of her training and the licence it gave her to get out of the house, there was a monotony to the family's routine that she wanted to interrupt. Determined to see the thing through, Louisa went into the grocer's instead and picked up two tins of corned beef, potatoes, carrots, a cauliflower and half a pound of Cheddar cheese. A treat. Mrs Sullivan might have some of these ingredients at home already, but she wanted Guy to know that she had planned and prepared the supper herself to give him something special. Or as special as she could make it, anyway. Half the problem was that all those years with the Mitfords had eroded what little ability she'd had to cook, what with Mrs Stobie sending up every meal to the nursery. Diana always hired extremely competent cooks too, giving the servants a taste for fine food. When living alone, Louisa had subsisted off toast and tinned soup.

But opening the door of the brick terrace, Louisa heard shouting from the front room and stopped. Something told her that she should interrupt, before she heard something she wouldn't want to hear. Still, she hesitated, her ear at the door.

Mrs Sullivan's voice was shrill. 'I notice she's quite happy to call herself your wife when it suits her. Not so much when it comes to her duties.'

Guy's reply was quieter, firmer, nevertheless edged with exasperation. 'It's 1933, Ma. Wives don't have duties.'

'I don't see why not,' his mother fired back. 'When I married your father, I was happy to cook and clean. I was proud to be Mrs Sullivan.'

'Louisa is proud.'

'Oh no, it's not good enough for her, the honest work of a housewife. She has to go out to work, doesn't she?'

'Ma . . . '

'Even then' – Louisa could picture her mother-in-law wagging her finger at her son, a good six inches taller than her – 'she *says* she's going out to work, but she's not bringing any money in! She's *training*. You, poor boy, must support all four of us—'

'That's enough . . . '

Louisa decided she agreed, and pushed the door open.

Mrs Sullivan glared at Louisa and, without saying hello, walked into the kitchen, where she could soon be heard banging pots and pans as she took them out of the cupboard. Guy, flushed, looked at Louisa sorrowfully.

'Why are you home early?' She was annoyed to have been caught with her bag of shopping, as if he'd see how the magic trick worked.

Guy looked in the direction of the kitchen, where the sound of the tap running at full steam could be heard. 'I got a telephone call from Ma.'

'A telephone call?' The house didn't have a telephone. It would have meant Mrs Sullivan going to the post office or walking three streets away to use the phone box. Neither of which seemed likely unless it had been a dire emergency. Louisa almost dropped the shopping as a thought occurred to her.

'Your father? Where is he?'

'He's fine. At least, he is now.' The last of the fight puffed out of Guy and he slumped into the chair by the fire, swept clean of its ashes, the grating efficiently blacked. 'He's upstairs now, but he went missing earlier. Ma had gone next door to talk to Mrs Ratchett and she thinks she must not have closed the door properly. She was going frantic looking for him and telephoned me rather than calling the police.'

'You are the police.'

Guy took his glasses off to clean them. 'Yes, I was able to tell Stiles what had happened and he was most understanding.'

'Where was he, then? Your dad?'

'In the pub, nursing a pint of bitter. An old pal of his recognised him and stood him the drink. If you ask me, he was enjoying feeling like his old self again. But it rattled Mother, she was frightened by it and . . . '

'What?' Louisa kneeled down beside Guy and put her hand on his arm. 'I heard something when I came in. You can tell me.'

'No, I shan't. Fear makes people angry. Whatever you heard, she didn't mean it.'

At that second, there was a loud crash that sounded like a wrecking ball coming through the kitchen window but was probably only a roasting tray dropping on the tiled floor.

'I see.' Louisa leaned back slightly on her heels. Her thighs were aching and the room was too warm. She thought of the cheese sweating in its brown paper wrapping.

'She's old, she's tired and she's afraid. She doesn't know

what's going to happen to Dad; doesn't know what will happen to her when he goes.'

Louisa knew he was right, but she felt humiliated. She gestured to the shopping bag, which had slumped over, the cauliflower peeking out of the opening, like a tease, threatening to roll out through the front door and into the freedom of the streets. She knew how it felt.

'Look. I've bought supper. I was going to cook it for you tonight, as a surprise. A treat.'

Louisa saw Guy consider his reply, which irked. 'Thank you. You don't have to make these gestures. I know when your training is done you'll earn good money. I am proud of you.'

She knew he meant it.

'It's only ... ' He glanced at the kitchen door. 'I'm trying to keep the peace here.'

'You want me to apologise to her?'

'No. Yes.' Guy took her hands. 'Talk to her. She likes you, you know she does.'

'I've done my fair share of hard work.' She was defensive, but Louisa thought of her own mother, her back straining under the loads of laundry she carried from the big houses she worked for, the sheets that would be strung up in their front room.

'I know you have,' said Guy. 'Like I said, I'm proud. I married you because I believe in you and I know we want the same things. I'm sorry we have to live here, with my parents. I know that's hard on you. I promise we'll be a family of our own, soon.'

Louisa took her hands from him and stood up. Her thighs were burning. 'Is that what this is all about?' She looked at him as if trying to read behind his eyes. 'I don't want to have a baby.'

33

She stopped. It wasn't quite what she meant, but she knew it was too late.

'You don't want children?' Guy stood up too, somehow taller and thinner than ever, a balloon with no air.

Louisa looked at him sadly. 'I do, Guy. I do want children, but not now. I don't see the rush, that's all.'

'You're thirty-two years old.'

'Does that make me over the hill?'

'No, my darling, no it doesn't. But it makes it more difficult.' Guy was whispering now, though Mrs Sullivan had at last had the tact to close the kitchen door. The row was no longer about her. 'I want us to be a family. That's all. I love you.' He pulled Louisa towards him and she didn't resist, but she didn't put her arms around him either. She felt flat, and sad.

'What if I can't?'

'Then we'll be together and we'll love each other. But I'm sure you can.'

He kissed her on the forehead and Louisa closed her eyes.

CHAPTER FIVE

⌒⌒⌒

The following morning, Guy left the house at seven o'clock as usual, kissing Louisa goodbye in the kitchen, where she was finishing her toast and marmalade. He bore his usual cheerful demeanour and they had chatted lightly about the case he was on – a burglary interrupted by the house's owners. Louisa listened and asked questions. When she heard the front door close, her shoulders slumped a little. It wasn't that she had changed her mind about any of the fundamentals of her life, far from it: she loved Guy, she wanted a family with him, she looked forward to a long future together. It was only that she was unsure how she could get them both back on the same path again. For weeks there had been a feeling of discontent that she couldn't shake, a feeling that only dissipated when she sat at her desk at the London School of Stenography.

Sitting on the top deck of the bus, Louisa leaned her forehead on the cool of the glass window, admiring the occasional late bursts of blossom she could see below. Every year it happened, and every year it charmed anew. The clouds of pink and white that settled on the trees, transforming the greyest streets in London to something out of a child's drawing. She thought again about Nancy's offer yesterday but gave it only the briefest reflection. She was grateful to the Mitfords for everything they had done for her, but she owed them no more.

By the time Louisa got off at her stop outside the school in Fulham, she was feeling a little more light-hearted. She resolved to try again with supper that night for Guy, perhaps see if they couldn't get out of the house for a walk, to talk through how they were going to map out their future. There was time to complete the training, get her feet under the courtroom table, as it were, and after she'd had a baby or two, she could go back to work. Stenographers were allowed to be married – it wasn't like the police service. She thanked her lucky stars that she hadn't got into the police when she'd tried a few years ago: she'd have had to choose between her career or Guy. In some ways, that meant thanking her roguish uncle Stephen, who had led her down the wrong side of the pavement and gained her a minor record or two, enough to have her police application rejected. But she didn't like thinking about Stephen and she wasn't sure she could go as far as to thank him for anything, even that.

Besides, she knew she could look at the road she'd travelled since then with pride. She gazed across the street at the stenography school – nothing more than a terraced building with its name engraved on a gold square plaque at the side of the door. Yet this was enough to represent freedom and a future for her. Glancing left and right before crossing, Louisa saw a man further along on the opposite side, apparently reading the collection times on a postbox. He was wearing a trilby hat and a dark suit, in itself unremarkable, but there was something about his profile, plus the suspicion he was watching her, that unsettled Louisa. Ignoring him but feeling him there, like an actor who has mistakenly made himself visible in the wings before coming on the stage, she walked across and quick-stepped up to the front door of the school. It was only as she pushed it open that she remembered where she had seen him: in the car parked near the house at Rutland Gate yesterday, shortly after she had finished her interview with Nancy. It must be a coincidence, or he was another man altogether. She dismissed it and went through the entrance.

At lunchtime, Louisa usually went to a greasy spoon down the road with Tessa, but today she told her that she needed to swot up on the technical terms they'd been learning. There was a test the next week, so it was only half a lie. If this man was still there, she'd ask him who he was.

When Louisa went out, the sunshine after the gloomy classroom making her squint, she hesitated on the step and looked up and down the road, almost disappointed to realise that he was nowhere to be seen. Perhaps it had only been a coincidence. Or she had mistaken two men as the same. She walked on down to the café anyway, holding her book in one hand, her grey handbag in the other.

The café she favoured on North End Road, Gerry's, was like any other to be found on almost every high street in Britain. The windows were permanently steamed up and a smell of stale, hot fat mixed with tobacco hit as soon as you opened the door. Tables were screwed to the floor and wiped down frequently with a filthy rag by the waitress, Kay, who reliably looked as pleased to be working there as a pig would to find itself in an abattoir. At any one time, several places would be occupied by men who spoke little but concentrated on shovelling their fried eggs and ham into their mouths or reading the newspaper as they smoked their postprandial cigarettes. It was, however, one of the few places a woman could eat alone, and though she suspected the daily diet might not be the healthiest of choices, Louisa took it in exchange for the chance of solitary peace. Everyone in there ignored her and she liked it that way.

Today would be different.

Louisa settled into a seat close to the wall, her back to the window, opened up her book before her and gave her usual order to the waitress: a mug of tea – milk, no sugar – two fried eggs, fried bread, a ham slice and fried potatoes. Apart from the occasional noise from the kitchen and a shouted order between Kay and the ambitiously titled Chef, there was little to distract and she set to revising *ab initio* and *sub judice*. When a shadow crossed her table, she assumed it was Kay about to put her plate of food down and she pushed her book to the side, only to realise that the man she had seen in the car yesterday and on the road today was now sitting down in the seat opposite. He removed his hat and undid the buttons of his suit jacket, looking steadily at her all the while as if he already knew her. She thought about protesting that the seat was taken, but she knew he'd know it was a lie. And besides, she was curious.

'Hello, Mrs Sullivan,' he said. 'Sorry to disturb your lunch hour.'

She assessed his face. A long chin, straight nose and near-black eyes, his skin had the yellow tones of one that had been tanned for many years then faded in British winters. His voice was posh but soft, not domineering. A memory flashed up: the man in the pub in the trench coat.

'Was it you at my wedding?'

He didn't answer this. 'I'm Iain, that's all you need to know.'

Kay came over and put the plate down, giving Iain a quizzical glance, but as she was not one prone to much intellectual curiosity, she soon pushed off after he'd asked her for a cup of black coffee.

He gestured to her food. 'Please, don't let me stop you from eating. Do you mind?' He pulled out a silver cigarette case and opened it without waiting for her answer.

Louisa picked up her knife and fork, only it seemed her appetite had deserted her completely. She tried a mouthful and gave up.

'Could you let me know what this is about? Otherwise, I'd better get back to my classes.'

'You're not needed back for forty minutes. Your routine is predictable, apart from last night when you stopped off at the grocer's on the way home. And you were surprised to find the butcher's shut.'

That startled her. 'You were following me?'

Again, Iain didn't answer the question, instead continuing to smoke his cigarette. When the waitress brought his coffee, he put in three spoonfuls of sugar and said: 'Too long spent in foreign climes has given me a sweet tooth.' It was to be the only time he explained himself about anything. 'Mrs Sullivan, are you aware that there are serious threats to the security of our country right now?'

This was an unexpected question.

'No, I can't say I am aware.'

'You should be. A bright woman like you, don't you read the newspapers?'

Louisa decided this was rhetorical.

He carried on. 'Hitler's Nazi Party has been in power for four months. In that time Herr Hitler has threatened to reject the Disarmament Conference, withdraw from the League of Nations and has publicly disavowed the Treaty of Versailles. He has opened a concentration camp for political prisoners, which appears to be a fairly loose term. They have also taken over Bavaria.' All the while Iain spoke softly, yet she was in no doubt that he spoke with authority. 'Be in no doubt: Germany is preparing for war.'

Louisa picked up her mug to take a sip of tea, but she was trembling and she thought she might drop it.

'When a country is preparing for war, they will do their best to infiltrate the political systems of others around them. Perhaps to convert them to their cause and avert war, perhaps to pretend that they are for peace, perhaps to weaken their potential enemy's armies. Whatever it is, we have to be on alert and guard ourselves against it.'

Louisa felt her legs shiver. Iain leaned a little towards her.

'Mrs Sullivan, I fought in the last war. The last thing that I want is for any of our young men today to fight in another. Everything that we can do to avert this must be done. The question is: are you in?'

'Am I in what?'

'Are you willing to help our country avoid war?'

Louisa had been at a distance from the Great War. She'd been a young girl in London, at school, then working with her mother, a laundress. They'd worked for families who had lost sons, she'd seen their grief. There had been rations, and she knew Guy had lost a brother, but it was the officers she'd seen begging in the streets that was the most distressing. Wounded, sometimes blind, sometimes missing a limb, they'd sit with their pitiful signs asking politely for food and money as people rushed past them. Everyone wanted nothing more than to get back to normal, they hadn't wanted to be reminded of the catastrophic error their country had made in getting involved in what, so she understood, began as hardly more than a minor skirmish in Austria. No, she didn't want another war.

'What exactly are you asking of me?'

Iain's voice took on a brisker rhythm. 'I believe you have been asked to accompany Lady Redesdale and her daughters on a cruise.'

She almost burst out laughing. 'Yes, but what's that got to do with anything?'

'We need you to go on that cruise.'

We? Who was we?

'The British government, Mrs Sullivan.'

She hadn't even asked the question out loud.

'We need you to keep a close eye on Mrs Guinness and her younger sister, Miss Unity Mitford. Take note of any unusual movements, any meetings they have, that sort of thing. The details will be forthcoming nearer the time.'

'But that's ridiculous. What on earth have they got to do with war?'

Iain signalled to Kay for the bill. 'I'll get this,' he said, gesturing to Louisa's uneaten lunch. 'They are members of the British Union of Fascists. That's not the whole explanation, but that will do for now. In the meantime, please accept the position and I will meet you again.' He had said this almost as an aside, concentrating more on pulling a money clip out of his pocket and peeling off a pound note.

'But I don't want to work for them again. I'm training as—'

'Yes, yes, we know. You can pick that up later. This is more important. *Far* more important, Mrs Sullivan.' He got up and left the money on the table. 'She can keep the change. I'll see you in a few days' time. Oh, and one thing – you cannot tell anyone about our meeting or your reasons for accepting the position, not even your husband. Especially not your husband. I'll know if you do.'

Louisa remained in her chair for several minutes until she glanced at the clock on the wall and realised she needed to hurry back to her class. It felt ridiculous enough to question whether it had even happened, but the pound note was on the table and it definitely didn't belong to her. That was that, then. She had a few days and then she'd meet Iain again, at some time and place of his choosing, no doubt. Could she do this? It would mean keeping a secret from Guy, something she'd never wanted to do. But this request – command? – was bigger than either of them. She was being asked to serve her country. If she was ever forced to lie to Guy, she would do so only if it was to protect him. Maybe she wasn't the same kind of wife that their mothers had been, nor did she regret that, but she had to believe she could love him, yet still do the things she wanted to do. Because she had to admit this: she did want to do it.

CHAPTER SIX

～

Having sent a note to Nancy to say that she had reconsidered the offer and would like to accept if it still stood, Louisa was quickly summoned back to Rutland Gate. As she had been asked to arrive at eleven o'clock in the morning, she had given up the idea of attending her training that day and sent in a note warning them of her absence. She didn't need to lie and say she was ill, as after all she was a paying client, not a schoolgirl. But she felt the weight of guilt lie heavy on her chest nonetheless. Unless it was weight for a different reason: apprehension at immersing herself back in the Mitford world when she had – foolishly – congratulated herself on leaving them for a life of marriage and a career, a life she had thought would put them if not quite on an equal footing, then no longer that of master and servant. Yet here she was, metaphorical mob-cap on her head. Resolutely, as if not to undo the good work of her previous exit, Louisa knocked this time on the front door. The maid who opened it betrayed no judgement but took her into the morning room, where Louisa was greeted by a formidable line-up: Lady Redesdale, Nancy, Unity and Tom.

Louisa was no longer the trembling nineteen-year-old in a scrappy dress and hastily polished boots that she had been when she first met the matriarch of the Mitford family, but in the presence of her former employer she sometimes found that hard to remember. Lady Redesdale was not an unkind woman, but she kept her distance in all senses of the phrase, and her Victorian manner was deliberately designed to keep the likes of Louisa in the dark as to what made her blue blood pump through her veins. Whether Lady Redesdale liked Louisa was, at best, not any of Louisa's business, at worst, irrelevant. What Louisa did know, which her daughters often did not affect to know, was that Lady Redesdale cared for them a great deal. She had never demonstrated this through anything so common as kisses and cuddles when they were babies (they got these, in spades, from Nanny Blor) but through her attentiveness to their development. Lord Redesdale had objected to his daughters going to school, but the governesses his wife hired were engaged to teach a progressive system, and this only after Lady Redesdale had herself taught the girls how to read, as well as the basics of English history. As her children had grown older, Lady Redesdale held dances for them and managed house parties, sometimes in the teeth of her husband's short-tempered objections, and even sat up until the small hours waiting for them to climb back in through the ballroom windows when they eventually returned from whichever nightclub they had escaped to earlier on. (Not that she knew that last part.)

'Lady Redesdale, Miss Nancy, Miss Unity,' said Louisa, acknowledging each in turn with a nod.

None of them stood when she entered the room and she waited now for one of them to beckon her to a chair. It didn't happen. Tom was already standing, leaning on a mantelpiece, the other hand in his pocket. He nodded when Louisa looked towards him. Nancy had told Louisa that Tom had half the princesses of Europe trailing after him. Even given the exaggeration, it was believable.

Nancy broke the icy smiles. 'Lou-Lou, it's divinely kind of you to help us in this way.'

Lady Redesdale sat up a fraction straighter. 'Cannon—' she began, but Nancy immediately interrupted.

'It's Sullivan now, if we're to use surnames at all. Don't you remember? Lou-Lou is married.'

'I can't call her Sullivan,' said Lady Redesdale. 'I'll never remember it.'

Louisa wondered if she should wave helpfully, remind them that she was in the room.

The matriarch turned to Louisa. 'It's quite wrong, but I shall have to call you either Louisa, which makes you sound like a kitchen maid, or Cannon, which is more correct but makes you sound unmarried. Which do you prefer?'

'Louisa is fine, m'lady.' Some might think she was an acquaintance if it was overheard on the ship, even though she knew she was kidding herself if she was already looking for ways not to be seen as a maid.

'Louisa,' Lady Redesdale began again. 'Nancy is convinced that I cannot cope alone. I am not of the same opinion. Nevertheless, the fact remains that Mrs Guinness is now without a lady's maid, having moved into her house in Eaton Square ...' She broke off and Louisa saw the faintest flicker of pain as she took in another breath. 'There is an idea that with all three of us needing jewellery fetched from the safes in the evening, help with our luggage and tickets—'

Unity interrupted this time. 'Don't go on. Louisa knows perfectly well what to do. And besides, the lady doth protest too much.' She turned to Louisa. 'The real reason Lady Redesdale objects to you accompanying us is because she thinks every time you come near us, another murder happens.'

Lady Redesdale pinched her mouth, but her daughter ignored this and carried on. 'It's not true, is it, Louisa? There were *years* when you were with us when no one got murdered at all.'

Nancy and Tom burst into a fit of laughter at this, but Louisa was appalled. She opened her mouth to say something, though she wasn't sure what she could say.

Nancy flapped her hand and, through her snorts, managed to get out a protest. 'Honestly, Unity. You must learn some social graces.'

Unity looked perplexed. 'What's wrong with what I said? It's true, and anyway, Louisa knows us well enough by now.'

'Quite,' said Lady Redesdale, doing her motherly best to restore order while managing to neither agree nor disagree with her children. It was a diplomatic skill necessary in a family of nine. Lord Redesdale's tactic was simple: absolute authority. (Until 'the thin end of the wedge' was reintroduced and soon the situation would revert to whatever had prompted his fury in the first place.)

Louisa shifted on her feet and this brought Nancy's attention back into focus. 'I've told you the plan, the train to Venice and so forth—'

'Are you not doing the river cruise through Germany?' interrupted Tom.

Nancy held out a hand to silence him. 'You're not in court now. Don't ask difficult questions.' She explained to Louisa:

'Tom's been called to the bar. His chambers is Four Paper Buildings at Temple. Lord Redesdale can't quite believe he's got a son that works.'

Tom snorted at this and his mother gave him a sharp look.

Louisa tried to ignore the excitement she felt at the thought of this trip. She was going as a secret agent. She had to keep that uppermost in her mind. It was not a holiday; she did not want to be apart from Guy.

'Yes, you did tell me,' said Louisa, not involving herself in the argument with Tom. 'The trip sounds wonderful.'

'Oh, it will be,' Unity started to say, her face, usually unreadable, now animated.

'Have you got a passport?' demanded Lady Redesdale.

'Yes, m'lady. It was arranged when we went to Dieppe some time ago.'

'That's settled then. We'll pay you six pounds a week and you may bring a suitcase and a vanity case for your own things. If you could come here on Sunday afternoon at half-past two, we will travel together to Victoria to catch the train for Paris. We'll need two cars, and I'd like you to be in the taxi with Miss Unity and Miss Jessica.'

'Will that be all, Lady Redesdale?'

'That will be all, Louisa.' She brushed something invisible off her skirt and the interview was over.

47

CHAPTER SEVEN

The following day, Louisa returned to the London School of Stenography. A part of her hoped she'd somehow been mistaken about what Iain had been asking her to do, or even that she'd dreamed him up entirely. Then she could tell the Mitfords she wouldn't be travelling with them after all, and she could resume her normal life. Uneventful and safe. Guy was a policeman, that was enough drama for anyone.

Yet when she pushed open the door of Gerry's Café at lunchtime, she was strangely relieved to see Iain sitting there. He gave her the briefest of glances she understood to mean she should sit at a separate table. Thankfully, she had put her class friends off again. She knew they were beginning to think her offish, but she reasoned she'd be able to explain eventually. After she had ordered her usual from Kay, keeping her eyes away from the ubiquitous filthy rag tucked into the waistband of the waitress's apron, Iain stood up and Louisa saw he'd left the coins on the table to pay his bill. He put his hat on and walked towards the door, dropping a piece of folded paper onto her table as he walked past. Louisa quickly took it and opened it on her lap. No one was looking at her, but she felt nerves flutter in her stomach. All it said was: *Hammersmith Bridge, 5 p.m.*

Louisa tore the paper up into several pieces and put them into an almost empty coffee cup, where they quickly absorbed the remaining liquid. There was an insouciance to the way Iain simply assumed she would be available at that time that should have infuriated her. Supposing she had made other plans? But he knew she would cancel anything. The fact that she had returned his glance and gone to sit at another table, then passively waited and accepted his note meant she had already let him know that she was signed up to whatever he asked of her. It was arrogant and thrilling.

At five o'clock, Louisa was on Hammersmith Bridge, looking out over the river. It was a view that never failed to prompt her love of London. Though she had been entranced by the beauty of the countryside when she had first gone to work for the Mitfords, it was the vast anonymous scape of the city, and the river that wound through it, that lashed itself around her heart. The sun was not yet sinking but shone warm on her face, the deepening yellows a reminder of the summer that was not too far away now. She was on high alert, feeling like a cat on a brick wall, waiting for the mouse to come – or was it the other way around? – when she sensed Iain standing beside her.

'Well done, Mrs Sullivan,' he said. 'You have already pleased us.'

'I wasn't trying to please you,' Louisa replied. 'I was merely carrying out what appeared to be orders.'

'Even better.'

There was a brief silence while Iain seemed to take in the

view and they both watched a narrowboat pass out from under the bridge. A woman sat on the deck and looked up at them. She waved, but neither of them waved back and Iain turned around.

'What do you know so far?' he asked.

Louisa told him of the travel plans, the time they would be departing and what she had been told of the route.

'That aligns with the information I have,' he said with satisfaction.

'How do I know you are who you say you are?'

'You don't,' said Iain equably. 'Truthfully, I'm not.'

'What?'

'Iain is not my real name. But that doesn't need to concern you. You'll simply have to take this on trust. All you need to know is that these orders come from the British government. We're a small department but a vital one, and I expect we'll grow in size. There will be further opportunities for ambitious women such as yourself. Our man at the top is particularly keen on women agents.'

'Why?' Louisa was intrigued by the phrase 'our man at the top'. Who was that? The prime minister? The King?

Iain curled his top lip. 'Who knows? Thinks they're more reliable, sharper. I suggest you prove him right.'

'How will I contact you?'

'You won't need to do so often, but I'll give you an address to which you can send a telegram, if absolutely necessary. If we need to get hold of you on the ship while it's at sea, we'll find a way to do it. It's not dangerous work. We simply need you to keep an eye on Mrs Guinness and her sister, then report back on your return. Mosley is a person of interest, as are the people close to him. We want to know what connections he's making in

Europe. It will probably all come to nothing, and that will be to the good, frankly. He's a loathsome man with no commitment to any political ideas other than the ones that he thinks will put him into power.'

'Will he get into power?'

'I doubt it. Mosley's an anti-Bolshie, he's got that going for him, as do all the fascists. But he could feed Hitler's chances of success and we don't want dictators in Europe, especially not in Germany.' He took out a cigarette but didn't offer her one. 'You don't need all this detail. Keep an eye on those women and let me know if you see anything that raises your suspicions.'

'This whole conversation is suspicious, if you ask me.' Louisa tried a joking tone, but Iain didn't smile. He only lit his Player's and walked off, leaving her to watch his retreating back and the traffic as it poured over the bridge away from her.

CHAPTER EIGHT

⟡

The train for Paris was leaving Victoria station at five o'clock in the afternoon. It was a Sunday, and Guy was able to come see Louisa off, but she wasn't certain that this was necessarily a good thing, not for him. It was bittersweet to have him on the platform: nobody had ever been there for her before, nobody to leave behind that would mind her going. She wished only that her going didn't feel so definite, even terminal, when they both knew she would be back in a few weeks. He looked terribly sad as he stood there, and she fought an impulse to run back, grab her suitcase and throw herself into his arms.

Instead, Louisa stood on the step of the third-class carriage and beckoned him towards her. In his hat and suit – he'd worn it because he knew he'd have to shake Lady Redesdale's hand at some point that day – he looked handsome. It was a funny thing, but since they'd married he'd become more and more good-looking in her eyes. She wondered if it was because she hadn't allowed herself to look at him properly in that way before, or whether it was because she had traced all his contours with her fingertips and knew what lay beneath those clothes, that he could stir an excitement in her. She knew how much he loved her and that made her feel protective of him, too. He was hers, and she wasn't about to let him forget it.

'Come here, Guy,' she whispered.

He checked the platform. Lady Redesdale, Diana, Unity and Jessica boarded their first-class carriage further up the train. Lord Redesdale and Nancy came to wave them off but departed fairly quickly, with Nancy saying she was going to take the 'poor old human' off to luncheon at the Ritz so that he could drown the sorrows of his absent wife and daughters in champagne. He hadn't looked especially sorry but had cheerfully taken his leave, muttering something about his dogs and a fishing trip when Lady Redesdale started to remind him of instructions for the servants.

Louisa's coat was unbuttoned and she pulled Guy closer, put his hands on her waist, then tipped her head up so he could kiss her. When they broke apart, he was smiling.

'I'll have another, please,' she said.

'The guard will blow the whistle in a second,' he said, but he bent down once more.

'I love you, Guy Sullivan. Don't you forget it. And I'll be coming home to you soon.'

'Promise?'

'Promise. And you do the same. Don't go getting distracted by any of those young policewomen, you hear?'

He shook his head, though they both knew this was a joke. Then, his hands still firmly on her, he spoke again, a worried crease on his brow. 'I still don't understand why you're doing this. Is it because you think you need us to be apart for a while?

Tell me what I need to do to make things better, Louisa. I don't think I could stand it if I lost you.'

She took his hands and held them. The guard blew the whistle. 'It isn't you, Guy. It's something I need to do. I'll come back and I won't be going away again. Come on, now.'

There had been more than one conversation about this upcoming trip, in each of which she had done her best to reassure Guy, telling him that she had accepted the offer from the Mitfords because it would earn good money. In sorrow, she realised his insecurities remained.

With seconds to go, she took an affectionately chiding tone. 'It's not for long.'

The guard blew the whistle again, and this time Guy stepped back and closed the door. Louisa leaned out of the window and waved to him until steam and distance meant they could see each other no more.

The train journey ahead was not going to be a difficult one. The carriage attendants would unpack the overnight cases. Other than helping the Mitfords change for dinner, Louisa would not lay eyes on them until they arrived in Paris the following morning. Louisa had done the journey a few times before, when she had worked as Diana's lady's maid during the early years of Diana's marriage to Bryan.

Arriving the next morning in the warm sunshine, Louisa felt heat and happiness seep into her bones. The air already carried the weight of its high temperature, as if the paving stones had been slowly cooking for weeks. Lady Redesdale and her daughters were booked in for two nights at the George Cinq hotel, with Louisa on a put-up bed in Unity's room. Over those few days, Diana filled her suitcase with dresses she had ordered some time before and Lady Redesdale bought Unity a few token items for the cruise and checked the arrangements made for Jessica's stay. There was an unsentimental farewell between the sisters: each, in their own way, thought Louisa, knew the thrill of the freedom that Jessica had gained, limited though it was by the instructions to go outside only with one of the rather elderly women who taught at the finishing school.

After Paris followed their second long train journey, which took two days and two nights, the landscape speeding past the window in a blur of green and blue.

As thrilling as the journey was, Louisa was electrified by their arrival at the dock in Venice, where the *Princess Alice* awaited them. Its appearance was every bit as glamorous as she hoped it would be, with rows of portholes in the gleaming white hull and two enormous funnels at the top, soon to be billowing steam. Along the top rail stood a line of smartly dressed crew in their starched uniforms. Crowds of people were there, both the passengers as they boarded, with their best hats and coats on, porters scurrying with trolleys to carry the huge cases on, and a swathe of well-wishers there to wave them all off.

Louisa watched it all, enthralled. It was as if she had stepped into a newsreel or a Hollywood picture and none of it felt quite real. In her pocket she held a piece of paper, folded twice over, on which was written: 308 *Hood House, Dolphin Square, London*. All she needed now was a reason to send a telegram to that address, using the code she had been taught by Iain. She both hoped and dreaded that she would have cause to do so.

CHAPTER NINE

The *Princess Alice* was one of the newest ships in the Empire Line collection and the interiors showed off much in the way of silvered trim and mirrored walls, as well as several modern conveniences of which its owners were very proud. There was an electric lift that went directly from deck C – the deck from which passengers boarded and disembarked at the ports – up to deck A at the top, where the first-class restaurant and sun deck were found. Below deck A were the first-class suites, ballroom and casino, which could be accessed only by stairs, before reaching the second- and third-class accommodation, the crew's canteen and cabins and, the lowest level of all, the engine and boiler rooms.

On their first night, tired from the excitement and travel, the four of them had barely taken in their new surroundings before retiring to their rooms for an early night. Diana, who had some experience of travelling at sea – 'in yachts, quite different,' she had crowed – advised that they all spend several hours horizontal at the start of the journey, a tip to help them find their sea legs.

Louisa had requested that she have her own cabin, which had caused some huffing and puffing at first – most servants slept in a dressing room in their mistress's staterooms, which gave them automatic access to the first-class entertainment and dining decks.

'So much more convenient,' Lady Redesdale had said. But Louisa had stood her ground. She knew she would need to make notes for Iain and she could not risk Unity finding her pocketbook. So she told them she was too old and too married to share a cabin, and it transpired that Lady Redesdale had the clout to ensure Louisa's access to the first-class decks when she was with them.

The arrangement included a telephone in Louisa's cabin, and whenever Lady Redesdale, Diana or Unity required her help, they could call her on it and summon her to deck B, where their three suites were situated. Lady Redesdale's cabin had an inner door that led through to Unity's, but Diana's was further along the passage. Even with the impending decree absolute, Bryan had insisted on paying for her passage, so hers was the only suite of the Mitford party to have a separate drawing room, with Constable imitations hanging on the walls and a balcony large enough to take breakfast outside. Not that she would: Diana had enjoyed her boiled egg and soldiers in bed since the first day of her married life.

Down in deck D, Louisa's third-class cabin was small, with no window and a bed that she had to pull down from the wall, but she was glad to have her own washbasin. She hung her clothes up carefully and put her framed photograph of Guy on a narrow shelf. It had been taken on their wedding day and he had removed his glasses for the picture, his eyes squinting slightly as he focused on the photographer. The bed linen had the well-worn sheen of hundreds of hot washes and the thin blanket was an unappealing grey colour, but the room was cool, a relief from the unfamiliar heat outside. In any case, she wasn't planning to be in her cabin much beyond sleeping there.

This was prescient. The next afternoon, having returned to her room after luncheon to find a comb (Unity had left hers behind), she had barely come through her door when the telephone rang, a loud, jangling noise. The operator did not wait for Louisa's assent to take the call but merely told her it was Lady Redesdale on the line and Louisa heard the clunk as the connection was put through.

'Hello? Hello?'

'Yes, m'lady, it's Louisa here.'

'Oh, come up, would you?'

The line went dead.

Louisa walked up the flights of stairs – at least she would get fit on this trip – and opened Lady Redesdale's cabin door after a brief knock. Inside she found her mistress and Unity standing over by the writing desk, staring at a white card. An empty envelope lay on the blotting pad.

'We've been invited to drinks this evening by the captain,' said Lady Redesdale. 'It's a bore, but I suppose we can't refuse.'

Unity took the card out of her mother's hand. 'You'll need your tiara.'

'Not unless it's white tie, I won't.'

Her daughter had already lost interest in the subject of her mother's jewels and was focusing again on the card. 'It's Captain Schmitt,' she said to Louisa, as if reading the name for the first time. 'A German captain. Do you think he'll be *very* good-looking?'

58

'That's certainly not something for you to be thinking about,' her mother intercepted briskly. 'Louisa, would you go to the purser's office and fetch my jewellery case. You'd better bring Mrs Guinness's too. We'll need to start dressing in half an hour now we have the wretched drinks. Unity, you can wear your yellow dress.'

'I don't know why you insisted I brought it. I look like a child in it.'

'You are a child. Don't argue with me and go and get yourself ready. If Louisa has time she can help you with your hair.'

At seven o'clock, all three of them had left their cabins, dressed in their frocks and jewels, and Louisa had stayed behind to tidy Lady Redesdale's cabin. Unity's had, in a few short hours, already taken on a state of permanent disarray, just as her bedroom was at home, driving Nanny Blor to despair with scraps of paper everywhere and things always going missing. Stockings would be dropped on the floor with no thought as to who might have to pick them up, hair grips would apparently vanish into thin air, and sweeps under the bed would regularly net a haul of blunt pencils, pocket mirrors, combs, ribbons and discarded books. Louisa put away the last of Lady Redesdale's things and put out her nightdress before she looked at her watch. Supper would not be served in the third-class canteen for another half an hour. She could tidy Unity's room too, but something in her resisted it, and anyway, there would be a maid arriving soon to prepare the cabins for the night. Instead, Louisa thought she would attend to Diana's cabin. It wasn't strictly necessary either, a maid might even be there already, but Louisa could feel that folded piece of paper in her pocket as if it were a heavy stone. She gave the room a final glance and left, closing it behind her.

She had turned towards Diana's cabin, away from Unity's, and perhaps it had been because her head was lowered, or perhaps the lights were dimmer in the passage, but whatever the reason, Louisa bumped heavily into a woman standing at a cabin door, jiggling at the handle.

They both started to apologise and Louisa was about to move off when she noticed the woman was crying. She was exceptionally pretty, even with the tears streaking her mascara, with a heart-shaped face and a slight figure beneath her cream satin dress, which had a nasty red wine stain on the front.

'He won't let me in,' she sobbed.

Louisa didn't like to ask who had locked the door, but she didn't need to.

'Joseph,' said the woman, agitated now. 'Please, don't do this.'

Louisa hesitated but the door remained resolutely locked.

The woman let go of the door handle and covered her face with her hands. 'I'm sorry,' she said, muffled. 'We haven't been introduced and this is terribly embarrassing.'

'Please don't worry,' said Louisa, seeing at once the mistake the woman had made. 'I'm not staying in these rooms. I'm a lady's maid.' The words still caught in her throat. She wanted to say: 'Not *just* a lady's maid', but she could not.

At this, the woman's hands dropped down and Louisa could see the relief bloom. 'Then you probably have a magic trick to help me with this?' She gestured at the stain. It wasn't large, but it was noticeable.

'I'm sure there's something we can do. Come with me.'

They hastened along the narrow corridor, and Louisa opened Diana's room – she had keys to all three cabins – and beckoned the woman in.

'Thank you so much. I'm Mrs Fowler. What's your name?' Her voice carried no hint of either regional dialect or aristocratic breeding, it gave no clue as to where she had come from, only where she was now. Attractive, fashionably dressed and embarrassed.

Louisa answered Mrs Fowler's question, making sure she spoke soothingly as she dabbed at the stain with some white wine from the drinks' tray in Diana's drawing room. They adjusted a brooch to cover the worst of it, then Louisa left her in the bathroom to fix her face. In a few moments, Mrs Fowler came out and there was no trace of the distress remaining.

'I can't thank you enough,' she said. 'I had better return to the party now or it will be over. Whose room is this, by the way?'

'Mrs Guinness,' said Louisa, knowing the effect this would have.

'Oh.' Louisa saw the shame return to Mrs Fowler, and tears sprang to her eyes again.

'Please don't worry. I won't say anything to her.'

Mrs Fowler shook her head. 'No. I couldn't stand it.'

'Truly, it's fine.'

'You'll keep my secret?'

'Of course.'

Reassured, Mrs Fowler departed. But Louisa couldn't help wondering whether the secret was something bigger than a stained dress and a locked door.

CHAPTER TEN

L eft alone in Diana's cabin, Louisa tidied the bathroom – Mrs Fowler had helped herself to the powder puff and a red lipstick – then summoned the courage to do that which she had planned before she'd met her fellow passenger in distress. She was at least safe in the knowledge that even if a maid were to come in, even Diana herself, she wouldn't look suspicious. She had been hired, after all, to look after Diana's wardrobe, take shoes to be cleaned and jewels to the purser's office, where they were locked in a safe. There was nothing at all out of the ordinary about her straightening the books on her bedside table or the papers on the bureau. But still Louisa's heart hammered like a woodpecker the whole time. She may not have been guilty of anything underhand – yet – but she wasn't convinced she looked innocent. Her cheeks felt hot enough to fry eggs. Nor was she even sure what she was looking for. Iain had said they were interested in any relationships Diana might be forming with European fascists, but the more Louisa considered this, the more ridiculous it seemed. Sir Oswald Mosley had met Mussolini, she knew, but Diana hadn't.

She opened a drawer in the bedside table and saw there were a sheaf of letters bound with a red ribbon. Louisa recognised the handwriting: she had come to dread the arrival of these letters when she had been a lady's maid to Diana only the year before. Diana sat next to Mosley at a dinner party at the beginning of 1932, eighteen months ago, and it wasn't long before it was clear to anyone close to her – if not, sadly, to her own husband Bryan – that she had developed a full-blown crush on him. Louisa was sure things were kept above board and proper for several months, but there had been lots of notes and hastily arranged meetings, apparent coincidences when they had both turned up at the same party. Increasingly, Diana chose to stay in London rather than accompany Bryan to their country house at the weekends. That was when Louisa noticed the repetition of a certain hand-writing on the envelope, and how its arrival on the breakfast tray signalled a change of plans by Diana, a different party that she was going to attend. She'd be late home on those evenings, full of unstoppable admiration for 'Sir O' and his ideas that were going to save Britain from the quagmire of the Depression. Barely six months after Diana met him, she was calling him 'the Leader,' and six months after that she had left Bryan.

Looking about her first, Louisa took the letters out of the drawer. She couldn't hear anything, but then everything in the cabin was deadened by the thick carpet, and the passage outside was carpeted too. She considered standing by the door of the cabin so that she could quickly be alerted if anyone arrived, but she wasn't sure she could dash across the room to put the letters back and close the drawer by the time the handle had stopped turning. What if she took *one* out and read that first?

Since Louisa had first come into the room, the sun had set

and now it was almost completely dark outside. She realised she was standing in a room with almost no light, and that *would* look suspicious. Holding one letter, she put the others back in the drawer, then went around the bedroom and the drawing room, turning on the lights. She was steady on her feet and had been surprised at how little one was aware of the fact that they were sailing at sea but for intermittent rolls that gave Louisa the same sensation as a lift just before it stopped, a mild feeling of one's stomach arriving later than the rest of the body. What with that, her heart on overdrive, the heat and the stuffy atmosphere, Louisa felt nauseous, and when she looked down at the letter she saw that her sweaty hands had smudged the ink. She was standing in the middle of the drawing room wondering what the hell she was going to do about it when she heard the main cabin door close with a heavy clunk. There was a short hallway and whoever it was would emerge in a few seconds. Quickly, she stuffed the letter into her pocket and bent down over the coffee table, as if she were rearranging the large books on it.

'Sorry, miss, I didn't realise anyone was in here.'

Louisa closed her eyes in grateful prayer and stood up straight. She turned around and saw a young cabin maid, dressed in the Empire Line's colours: a plain navy dress with red piping on the hem, cuffs and collar, a white apron, a white cap – old-fashioned, neat and reassuring. The girl herself was lovely looking: a button nose, blue eyes and dark hair, a sprinkle of freckles.

'That's all right,' said Louisa. 'I was finishing in here; you can take over. The bath needs cleaning.' Nerves were making her peremptory.

'Yes, miss.'

The maid left the room and Louisa heard the taps running.

She had better go and have her own supper before she was required to help Lady Redesdale prepare for bed.

The crew canteen was relatively quiet – most of them were either working in the restaurants and bars or preparing the first-class cabins for the night – and Louisa was grateful to collect her cottage pie and sit alone at a table. As it was below deck, there were no windows and the overhead lighting felt too bright for eight o'clock in the evening. She was sure her skin must look sallow and she could feel damp patches under her arms. She missed Guy. He would be at home now, with his parents, having helped his mother clear up their supper. Afterwards he'd sit in the chair his father used to occupy and read the paper, perhaps chancing a go at the crossword. Louisa and Guy usually did it together and the memory of their joshing over a simple clue that they couldn't get made her feel lonely. The idea that she was carrying out work to protect the interests of her country seemed laughably far-fetched now. She must have misunderstood Iain and got caught up in a misguided, overblown sense of her own importance.

With a jolt, she remembered that she still had Diana's letter in her pocket. A lover's letter from Mosley. The likelihood that it would contain anything of interest to anyone, let alone to Iain and whatever secretive body he was working for, was absurd. To read it would be nothing more or less than a prurience, a nosy-parker read of a privately expressed sentiment. With nothing in it that threatened the country's security, reading the letter was most likely illegal.

Louisa had broken the law before. Not for a long time, and only when under the pressure of her uncle, who had threatened violent retribution if she failed to do as he instructed. Those criminal records may have been minor, but they had been enough to prevent her from gaining a much-wanted place on the police training scheme. 'If you've done it once before, you could do it again' had been the clear implication behind the polite but firm refusal to admit her to the Metropolitan Police Force.

What if it turned out that they were right?

Louisa took the letter out of her pocket and looked at the smudged ink. It was bad, but nothing that she couldn't explain away. The boat gave a roll and her stomach rose and fell, but it was the kick of adrenaline that she felt the most. It gave her – she had to admit it – a sense of pleasure.

CHAPTER ELEVEN

B ack in her cabin, Louisa sat down on the edge of her bed
and stared at the envelope that did not belong to her. It had
been opened, of course, so there was no need for steaming, if
that was even something that worked. It wasn't something she'd
been tempted to do in the past. Louisa thought about Nanny
Blor's exhortation to the children whenever they were caught
hiding around corners or behind doors, trying to eavesdrop
on their parents or the servants: 'Listeners ne'er hear good of
themselves.' It was unlikely there would be anything about her
in this letter, but she nevertheless had the foreboding that no
good would come of reading it. Before she could think about it
any more, Louisa took it out.

The letter was short, only two sides, written from Sir Oswald's
country house, the address embossed at the top, and dated only
two days before they had left London. His writing was skittish,
hard to read at first, with slanting letters and oversized dashes.
She had to adjust her eyes almost, until she could be sure of
making out the words correctly. The first few lines were of

loving reassurance, and Louisa read these quickly, deliberately not taking in the detail so she could pretend she was not seeing anything too intimate and irrelevant to her commission. There were only three sentences she noted, buried in the middle of his flowery lover's words.

Louisa copied these sentences down in her notebook:

I shall shortly be taking a trip on the Continent, not alone, and forgive me, my darling, for not giving you the exact details, but for reasons that will become clear, it is safest if I don't. Believe me, though you may think it to my advantage, it is absolutely to ours and our vision for a great future, one which enables not only our happiness but that of our country's. I shall write again soon, to your first Poste Restante, and explain further.

'The Continent' could mean France, Italy or Germany. To say that it could lead to Britain's happiness could only mean a political motive. Whether it would turn out to be of interest to Iain, the next letter presumably would tell.

At half-past ten Louisa was still in her cabin reading, half-waiting for a summons from Lady Redesdale, when the telephone rang. It was Diana, asking her to come up: she'd decided to throw a small party and she needed Louisa to help hand around the drinks.

Her body had started to warm and relax as she'd lain on her bunk; with some effort she swung her legs off and stretched, splashed a little water on her face and made her way up the flights of stairs to Diana's suite. Even as she walked the long corridor, she could hear the hubbub coming from B-13, and when she went through the door, the cigarette smoke and music took her instantly back to the sensation of walking into the Forty club in Soho. Diana knew how to throw a good party.

There must have been about thirty men and women crammed into the drawing room, all talking loudly and, it seemed, impatiently brandishing empty glasses at a tanned young cabin steward. Diana acknowledged Louisa's arrival with a finger pointed at the drinks cabinet and carried on talking to a man who looked like the captain of the ship. If Unity had hoped for a romantic fantasy with Captain Schmitt, she must have been disappointed: he was about sixty years old with a paunch that his smart white uniform could not disguise.

Louisa slid through the crowd to the steward. 'I'm here to help you,' she said.

'Thank you, miss.' He didn't even manage to catch her eye but remained focused on his task, pouring out martinis into glasses that were held by women with fingers that could barely be seen beneath their clustered rings, thick with diamonds and emeralds.

There was an open bottle of champagne on the side. Louisa picked it up and started to fill the coupes of those closest to her, then found another bottle and pushed herself back into the party, looking for empty glasses that needed refilling. It was hard to move as she was barely acknowledged by the guests, and often she would stand there, mutely, for some half a minute or so, her bottle tipped at an enquiring angle, while the man before her carried on with his interminable anecdote. It occurred to Louisa that she should use her notebook to write down some observations in it. Any one of these people might turn out to be useful further down the line when it came to reporting back to Iain.

The guests were a motley assortment of ages and chic: some wore their riches and style with the lightest of touches – as Diana did – while others may as well have written out their bank balance and pinned it onto their backs. Lady Redesdale was sitting on a sofa, looking tired but gamely keeping up conversation with an elderly gentleman wearing a jacket that appeared to have been doing him service since King Edward VII was on the throne.

A gramophone player was crackling out a Fats Waller record and Louisa could see some of the bodies swaying a little unsteadily as they moved their hips to the jaunty beat. It felt late and Louisa thought longingly of her bed, but there was a heightened, celebratory atmosphere, as if everyone had determined to set the mood of the voyage as they meant to go on.

It was then that Louisa saw Mrs Fowler in her cream dress, looking less sharp around the edges than she had a few hours earlier. She was standing close to the gramophone's speaker horn and was holding a cocktail in one hand while the other cupped the ear of the steward as she whispered something to him. He had his head bent slightly as if in concentration, but his eyes were looking around. Whatever the exchange was, it was brief, and Mrs Fowler straightened herself up and took a sip of her drink when the steward walked off. She caught Louisa's eye and there was the merest suggestion of a shared secret in her half-raised eyebrow. Before Louisa could begin to wonder what Mrs Fowler was hinting, an older man, thin-lipped and pallid, with grey hairs in his full moustache, came and held her by the elbow. He started talking to her and there was something urgent and private in the way he did this. Louisa looked away. She felt she had seen something, but she couldn't say for certain what it was.

The bottle of champagne she was holding was empty and she returned to the bar area to find another. The steward was there too, busying himself with clearing the dirty glasses and rearranging the decanters of vodka and gin. He was no more than nineteen or twenty years old, with a head of thick, honey-coloured hair, and his movements were nervous, as if he'd had an electric shock and hadn't recovered.

'Do you need a break?' asked Louisa. 'I'm sure I can hold the fort for a while.'

He looked up at her, his face blank, his thoughts a million miles away.

'Do you?' Louisa repeated.

His eyes gave the quick darts around she'd seen him do before. 'I do,' he said, 'but I'd better not.'

'I'm Louisa Sullivan, I'm travelling with Lady Redesdale and her daughters as a lady's maid.'

He flushed at that. 'Sorry, miss. You shouldn't have been handing out the drinks. Blythe North was supposed to come and help, but . . . '

'Don't look so worried. It's not your fault, and besides, I don't mind too much. It's funny, watching them all.'

They both turned around and looked out at the party. A few people had left and there was more space in the room now, but those who remained behind were either dancing in close-knit formation or touching each other as they spoke with exaggerated gestures and laughter.

Louisa turned back to the boy. 'What's your name?'

'Jim.'

'Have you worked on this ship long?'

He picked up a cocktail shaker, unscrewing the top, preparing to mix another. 'Three years. I grew up in Southampton, always saw the liners in the docks, fancied giving it a go.'

'You must have seen a lot.'

'I have, miss. Been all over. Seen some stuff. Truth be told, you see the boat most of all.' He was pouring out a measure of vodka now, skilfully not spilling a drop, in spite of an unexpected roll in the boat. 'On my day off, all I want to do is lie on my bunk and sleep.' He gave a shrug. 'Sorry. You don't want to hear all that.'

Louisa smiled. 'No, I don't mind. It's a bit lonely for me on this boat, in a way. It's nice to have a conversation.'

Jim looked at her, alarmed. 'I've got a girl.'

Louisa was confused, then she laughed. 'Oh my goodness, I didn't mean it like that. I'm married.' She wondered how he could think it – she had to be at least ten years older than him. Perhaps she should be flattered.

He laughed too. 'Nice to meet you then, miss.' He gestured to the crowd. 'Better get some more drinks out. Hopefully they'll go to bed soon.'

'Yes, hope you're right. I'll take this then, shall I?' Louisa picked up the champagne and stepped away, heading for a group of people she could see in the corner, but before she got there, she felt a touch on her arm.

'Mrs Fowler.' Louisa addressed the woman she'd met earlier, adopting a formal tone she felt was correct for the situation. 'Would you like some champagne?'

Mrs Fowler's red lipstick had smudged slightly on her lower lip and Louisa could see beads of sweat around her hairline. She put her face only inches from Louisa's. 'What was he saying to you?'

'Who?'

'*Jim*. Who else could I mean?' Her words slurred and Louisa tried to lean back. She could smell the gin on Mrs Fowler's breath.

'Nothing particularly. We were introducing ourselves.'

Mrs Fowler dropped Louisa's arm and emptied the last dregs in her glass, holding it out for Louisa to refill. She didn't seem to mind that she was asking for champagne in a martini glass. 'Good. I thought he might have been making a pass.'

Louisa was about to say he'd hardly make a pass at someone so much older, but she stopped herself. It wasn't appropriate for someone in her position to say to a passenger on the *Princess Alice*. And besides, she had the sensation that Mrs Fowler would not appreciate the comment. Louisa was older than Jim but younger than Mrs Fowler; women did not always want to be reminded of their age. Perhaps Mrs Fowler hoped Jim would make a pass at her. Stranger things had happened.

Thankfully, Louisa saw Diana beckoning her over, so she made her excuses and went over. Diana was standing with a sulky-looking Unity and a tall blond man in a sharply cut suit.

'It's time Miss Unity went back to her room. Would you take her, please, Louisa?'

Unity didn't acknowledge Louisa but instead snapped back at Diana, 'I can see myself to my cabin perfectly well.'

Diana put her hand on Unity's shoulder and lowered her voice, though she was – deliberately? – still loud enough for the man to hear. 'Farve won't allow you to walk to the end of the road alone. I hardly think I can let you wander around a ship unaccompanied at this time of night.'

'It's no more than the length of a corridor,' Unity replied with a pout, but she knew the argument was lost. 'Goodbye, Herr von Bohlen,' she said to the man, holding out her hand for him to shake it.

'Goodbye, Fräulein Mitford,' he replied, firmly. 'I am sure we shall meet again.'

Unity was all smiles. 'Oh, we shall.' She turned to Louisa but didn't say another word, only threw her sister a final, furious glance and stalked out towards the cabin door.

Louisa's heart sank a little. A furious Unity was a well-worn, tiresome experience, though at least she could get to her own room soon after. Tomorrow they would arrive at their first port and she was eager to taste the air of Italy and send a postcard to Guy, to pretend for a moment that she was on a carefree holiday.

CHAPTER TWELVE

~~~~~

The morning after the party, Louisa was awake early, eager to get out onto the deck to watch their approach to land. They had been at sea for two nights, long enough for the thought of solid ground to appeal. It had been a little over a week since she had left London and seen Guy. Wrapping up in her grey wool coat, she went outside and walked along the port side to the prow, marvelling at the warmth that lay beneath the chill dawn breeze. The sun had only recently risen and the light was edging the horizon like an angel's halo. Louisa could see smatterings of terracotta-coloured houses on the thickly forested hills, with an impressive villa near the coastline, its window frames painted white and a roof of russet red tiles. The deck was quiet, no bustle as yet of passengers walking up and down, calling out to fellow diners they'd met the night before or avoiding those to whom they already owed a poker debt.

Louisa walked up to the railings and leaned on them, and was soon lost in nothing more than the simple enjoyment of watching the white foam roll on the water and feeling the reassuring weight of the ship as it moved. After a few minutes, she realised she had better go and get her breakfast as it wouldn't be long before Lady Redesdale would be up and making plans for the day ahead.

On the brief walk back to her cabin last night, Unity had told Louisa that she hoped to persuade her mother to ask Herr von Bohlen to join them on the planned excursion around Livorno port. Louisa couldn't see why Lady Redesdale would agree to this, but perhaps there was no real reason to say no, either. Unity was eighteen – nearly nineteen – years old and had been brought out as a debutante the year before; it was, on the face of it, desirable that she should be courted by a suitor or two. On the other hand, Louisa suspected that Lord and Lady Redesdale had been burned by their decision to allow Diana to marry Bryan Guinness when she was nineteen: that marriage was ending in divorce barely four years later. Lady Redesdale maintained that Diana was too young and Bryan too rich, but the couple had been adamant and, at first, had seemed happy, producing two baby boys in quick succession. It hadn't been long before Louisa noticed Diana's boredom with Bryan's loving, but cloying, atten-tion. When Diana met Sir Oswald, the slight wobbles in her marriage had turned into full-blown collapse.

As Louisa was thinking about this, she was looking out to sea and was dimly aware of a couple that were on the other side of the prow, also leaning on the railings and enjoying the view. Only now she realised their voices were raised and if they were on the further side closer to the cabins, they might be in danger of waking people up. Louisa looked across and saw it was Jim, the bar steward from the party, and a young woman. She looked again and saw, yes, it was the pretty maid who had been in to clean up Diana's room the day before. They had not noticed her and only had eyes for each other, if not in a loving way.

Louisa turned her head back to the water only to find that, without trying, she could not help but hear their row.

'You're at the beck and call of that bloody woman,' shouted the maid.

'I'm my own man, be in no doubt of that, you b—' The next words were lost to the wind, which was probably no bad thing, thought Louisa. '...ought to be grateful for the cash.'

The maid said something in return. Louisa could hear only sounds being spoken but not the words, before Jim called out: 'Blythe, don't, you know I—'

Blythe. Jim had mentioned her name to Louisa before, the maid that was supposed to be helping out at Diana's party. It might have been the cause of the argument. Louisa stole a glance. They made a handsome couple and it must have been common enough for romance to bloom between members of the crew, but it must make it sticky if you fell out and still had several weeks left of working together. Louisa did not wish to eavesdrop any more, and took the longer route back to the doors leading inside so as not to let them know she'd overheard. She had the feeling that even if there wasn't much information to gather for Iain, this was going to be a situation that gave her plenty of glimpses into other people's lives.

A few hours later, Louisa was with Lady Redesdale, Unity and Diana, waiting in the foyer of deck C as the ship's crew prepared the gangway for their exit onto dry land. Herr von Bohlen was not with them, but Louisa had been told they would be meeting him, with his companion, at the local museum, recommended on the ship's daily newsletter. The *Princess Alice Bulletin*, a printed sheet of paper that was slipped under every cabin door in the morning, also informed that Livorno was one of Italy's largest seaports, close to Florence, and that the weather would be fair, with temperatures reaching a high of seventy-three degrees.

A crowd gathered at the doors and when they were finally opened, the people pushed out with a surge and a rise in their chatter as if they were being released like doves from a box.

For a while Louisa and the Mitfords walked along a seemingly predestined route until they reached a warren of smaller streets and found that their fellow passengers had more or less fallen away. Viridian hills lay beyond, contrasting beautifully with the terracotta-coloured buildings of the town. The heat lay on the cobbles so still and thick, Louisa felt as if they were pushing the air with each step.

'I need to find the central post office,' said Diana, as they slowed their pace and started to peer into the Italian shop windows. 'I told Nanny Higgs that the boys could write to me care of the *Poste Restante* here.'

'They're three and two years old – how can they possibly write?' demanded Unity.

Louisa noticed Diana's colour change, but she answered peremptorily. 'They can't. Nanny Higgs does it for them, but it's good to get them into the habit. She'll ask them what they want to say to me and so on.'

Lady Redesdale said nothing to this. Louisa wondered if they were thinking the same thing: it wasn't a letter from her children that Diana would be hoping for but from Sir Oswald. That made her remember the smudged letter she had in her cabin and the promise it had made to explain why he was taking a trip abroad. Louisa wanted to see any new letter Diana received, too.

After asking a couple of people in loud, slow English where the post office was, a charming young Italian man with perfect British diction told them the directions. It was only a few minutes' walk and when they arrived they saw there was already a queue, mostly made up of passengers they recognised from the ship. Halfway along the line was Mrs Fowler. Diana made a beeline for her.

'Ella,' she called out and the woman turned around. She had resumed her composed good looks and was wearing a chic pale blue duster coat and round gold-rimmed sunglasses.

'Mrs Guinness.'

'Oh, do call me Diana.' Diana had sidled up to Ella, much to the muttering consternation of the people immediately behind her, but no one told her to get to the back of the line. Diana's bearing was far too regal to permit that sort of suggestion.

Unity and Lady Redesdale followed Diana, standing close by, pretending they weren't queuing, but when Ella reached the counter, Lady Redesdale leaned across and asked if she couldn't get her ten stamps for England, handing over several lira notes. The post mistress handed most of them back, along with coins for change, and Lady Redesdale thanked her, as well as politely acknowledging the others in the queue, efficiently cancelling any protests they might otherwise have made.

Diana received three letters, one of which she hastily put in her pocket. 'Nanny Higgs and Bryan,' she said in a satisfied voice as they walked out. 'Shall we find some lunch now?'

The fact of Bryan still being in love with her, despite the impending divorce, was well known. Louisa felt a pang of pity, but it wasn't his missive that drew her interest. She forced herself not to look at Diana's pocket concealing the letter she wanted to read. Knowing she would have to find a way to steal it and read it, without Diana realising, was going to distract her until it was done.

Ella came outside with them. She had nodded to Louisa but not spoken to her.

'You're lucky,' she said to Diana. 'I'd love to hear from my youngest boy, but he's at school and they only write once a week, and sometimes he can't be persuaded to do even that much.'

'Where is he?' asked Lady Redesdale.

Louisa knew this was a loaded question: the answer would immediately bracket Ella in a position that would place her as either 'one of them', or not.

'St John's in Poole,' Ella replied innocently.

'Oh? I don't know that one,' said Lady Redesdale, and Louisa saw Diana's look of irritation with her mother. Had she planned a friendship with Ella? If so, it wouldn't last beyond the length of the voyage now there could be no pretence about the social gulf between them.

'We need to be at the museum in one hour and twelve minutes,' said Unity, checking her wristwatch.

'Well, then. Let's go here,' said Diana, gesturing to a café with tables outside and an olive-skinned waitress standing in the doorway bearing a clutch of menus. Diana's hair was shining blonde in the sunlight and her happiness was evident. Louisa was certain that was down to the envelope in her pocket, not the two in her hand.

'It's too hot outside,' her mother interjected. 'We'll go in. Would you like to join us, Mrs Fowler?' Her tone was neutral;

there was no way of knowing if she hoped Ella would say yes, or not.

'If you're sure it's all right, I'd love to.'

'It's only luncheon,' replied Lady Redesdale, and led the way inside.

It was cool and dark after the blazing sunshine, and they stood and blinked a little in the doorway. The waitress had gone ahead and was laying down menus on a table in the far corner. It was empty inside but for an old man at the bar with a small glass of cloudy liquid, and two men close to the back wall.

Ella took Diana's elbow and said in a low voice, 'I've remembered I promised my boys an Italian toy each. I'd better go.'

Diana, not understanding, answered more loudly, 'Please don't, it's not our only stop, there will be more shops. I'm eager to find out more about you.'

At this, the two men looked around and Louisa recognised the one with the moustache – he was the one who had been talking in an urgent manner to Ella the night before. He stood and walked over to the group but didn't acknowledge anyone but Ella.

'What are you doing here?'

She braced herself, straightening her back and lengthening her neck. 'It wasn't planned, dear. May I introduce you? Lady Redesdale, Mrs Guinness, Miss Mitford.' She turned to the women. 'This is my husband, Joseph Fowler.'

He bowed his head in their direction. 'How do you do?' But he offered nothing further, drawing his wife around by her shoulder and inclining his head to hers. 'I'm in a meeting with Sir Clive. I don't think it's appropriate.'

Louisa looked across at his table and saw the man he was with.

He was half-standing awkwardly, a napkin in one hand; it was clear he had expected to be introduced and his manners were far too good for him to sit back down again until the female party had done so first. He was in his early fifties, she supposed, with slicked-back dark hair greying at the temples, and although his suit was undeniably cut to flatter, with a navy dotted 'kerchief peeking out of his top pocket, his face was broad and misshapen, with a crude nose, thick lips and bushy eyebrows that threw shadows over his eyes, which were small and dark, yet somehow inviting. Caddish or charismatic? As if in answer, Iain's advice came swiftly to the surface: she was to strive to notice detail without imposing supposition upon facts. Easier said than done, she was now realising.

Ella broke away from her husband. 'I'm so sorry, Lady Redesdale. You'll have to excuse me. There's an errand I must do before we are back on the ship. Enjoy your luncheon and I hope to see you all soon.'

Without looking back, she walked into the sun and her husband sat down again, to resume his meeting with Sir Clive.

After lunch, when Louisa and Unity left slightly ahead of the others to keep the appointment that had been made with Herr von Bohlen at the museum, only Sir Clive acknowledged their departure with a raised hand.

CHAPTER THIRTEEN

⁓

The museum in Livorno was eventually found in a side street after Louisa stopped to ask for help from three strangers. Each time, Unity jiggled impatiently and accosted Louisa for the new instructions, reminding her that they were due to meet Herr von Bohlen in six minutes, then three minutes, and finally that they were late.

'We're almost there, Miss Unity. I can't make it happen any faster.' Louisa was exasperated. Unity was well out of the schoolroom, wore red lipstick and had once been drunk on champagne. But she had never been anywhere without a chaperone, still spoke in her secret childish Boudledidge language with her sister, Jessica, and, certainly in the company of her mother or Nanny Blor, reverted to girlish behaviour as easily as rice pudding slipped off her spoon and down her throat.

'Do I look all right?' Unity asked for the umpteenth time. She was wearing her best, most fashionable day dress, cream with red buttons off-centre from neckline to hem, which landed mid-calf. A narrow cut, the belt was cinched too tight and made her tummy pouch below 'like the udders on one of Pamela's Jersey cows', Nancy had said when the dress had its first outing in London. Unity lacked the easy chic of her older sister, Diana, with wrinkles in her stockings and creases in her jacket, and if she wasn't concentrating, her mouth pulled down at the edges.

'Perfectly fine for a museum outing,' said Louisa, knowing she was being disingenuous but refusing to be drawn in otherwise.

Unity sighed at this, but they were walking quickly and soon they were at the wide wooden door of the Museo della Città di Livorno, and just inside, waiting in the cool of the marbled hall, was Herr von Bohlen. He had an admirably athletic figure, visible in a suit that Louisa recognised as expensive, and greeted Unity with old world manners, though he could not have been more than twenty-five years old. Louisa he ignored; he must have been briefed that she was merely a chaperone.

'If you please, I would like to introduce my companion,' he said, in a noticeable German accent, though his delivery was smooth. A man of similar age but much shorter, with a countenance that revealed neither pleasure nor displeasure, removed his hat and gave a small bow to Unity. 'This is Herr Müller,' continued von Bohlen. 'Shall we go through? I have taken the liberty of purchasing your tickets. Will Lady Redesdale and Mrs Guinness be joining us?'

Unity gave a dismissive wave of her hand. 'They'll be along later. We don't have to wait for them, they can get their own tickets.'

'Ah, but Fräulein Mitford, I have purchased their tickets also. I will leave them at the desk.'

He went to the ticket office to leave instructions, while the three of them remained waiting for him silently. When he returned, the group set off, heading for the first room indicated on the guide, from which von Bohlen read aloud. Unity, usually ready to challenge any instruction given by her parents or sisters, agreed to each of his suggestions. The museum had some early Roman relics on display and though Louisa was fairly interested, she soon realised that her role was to stand a few steps behind as Unity and von Bohlen inspected and discussed the pale stone artefacts. Both Louisa and Herr Müller appeared to be employed in the same capacity and both spent their time listening to the conversation conducted, proffering no thoughts or ideas of their own. Not that their opinions were sought. The thought crossed Louisa's mind that Herr Müller's mission may well have been very similar to her own. The Nazis presumably had a secret service.

Even with two silent companions following their every word and movement, Unity was utterly without guile. Herr von Bohlen was to be left in no doubt as to her allegiances. Each question he asked her was answered, but so too were a thousand unasked queries. By the time they had reached the second room, with its modest display of seventeenth-century religious paintings, Unity had told her new friend about her parents, her sisters and her brother, her desire to go to Germany, to learn German and to study German history and culture.

'You are almost more of a patriot than me,' he laughed at one point.

'Oh, but I think I probably am,' Unity replied seriously. 'My parents want me to go to Paris to learn French, but I have already told them that Germany is the future, not stupid old France.'

'And what, Fräulein, makes you think that Deutschland holds

the key to the new world? After all, we have been destroyed and outcast by our European neighbours for some time now.'

They were standing before a painting in which Jesus was lying outstretched on a golden rock, bleeding from his wounds on his hands and feet as a young woman tended to him, a cloth in her hand and a pail of water by her kneeling figure.

'Resurrection,' she said. 'I believe the Germans will be reborn from their suffering and be stronger and more powerful for it.'

'You have been reading some interesting theories,' was von Bohlen's comment, and though he did not wink, Louisa felt he had only resisted with an effort.

Unity smiled. 'Perhaps,' she admitted. 'But I do believe it, too. I've also been reading about your new leader, Herr Hitler. He sounds . . . ' she searched for the word, ' . . . inspiring.'

'Indeed?' Von Bohlen raised an eyebrow. 'I must say, I approve. He is a true patriot. He believes in Germany for Germans and he will be the one to lead our country to strength once again.'

Louisa felt Müller straighten beside her. She wondered if he was standing to attention at the mention of his country's leader. What was it Iain had said to her about him? That he was a dictator? She knew that Lord Redesdale would not have a German name mentioned in his house: 'Damned Huns'. But then his generation had fought in the war and his own brother had been killed in Flanders. Unity knew nothing of life before the war, could not remember a time when peace and prosperity seemed to stretch ahead in an Edwardian haze of goodwill and confidence, its monarchy as solid and immutable as marble chess pieces. Today, the Depression showed few signs of ending, with daily newspaper reports of the mile-long queues for bread in America and much of Europe, though the Mitfords and their

86

circle seemed immune to it all. They had carried on their dances and house parties, Diana's wardrobe had remained resplendent, and cocktails had been drunk. Louisa knew money had been lost by the Guinness family, but they had such a lot of it, it had apparently not made too much difference.

She'd allowed her mind to wander and only now realised that Lady Redesdale and Diana had come rushing into the room, disturbing the quiet atmosphere with their hurried movements and exclamations of thanks to von Bohlen for buying their tickets.

'Wolfgang, it was too kind, but we're terribly grateful,' said Diana, and Unity bristled.

He gave another of his stiff, small bows and extended his hand to catch hers and kiss it. 'It was no trouble at all; I am delighted to be of service.'

'*Danke schön*.' Diana giggled. 'This is my mother, Lady Redesdale.'

The ritual was re-enacted, but Louisa thought Lady Redesdale less enamoured by the elaborate charm, withdrawing her hand quickly after he had raised it to his dry lips. He briefly introduced them to his companion, who did not step forward but merely inclined his head.

The enlarged group moved sedately around the museum, with Unity and Diana on either side of Wolfgang, and Lady Redesdale keeping a slight distance, peering more closely at the paintings and artefacts, spending more time reading the information cards beside them.

Diana was quick to establish her credentials, telling Wolfgang of her 'close friendship' with Mosley, as leader of Britain's own fascist party.

'He went to visit Mussolini in Rome last year,' she told him.

'Sir Oswald was terribly impressed with everything *Il Duce* has achieved.'

Wolfgang held his hands behind his back as he walked beside Diana, like a visiting dignitary. 'I understand he is most impressive.'

Unity was holding a copy of the museum guide and Louisa saw that tiny rips had been made all around the edges. Lady Redesdale waylaid herself – deliberately, it seemed – by an arrangement of Roman household items from the first century BC, and Unity leaned into Wolfgang, keeping her eye fixed on her mother.

'I've joined the BUF.'

Wolfgang looked quizzical.

'The British Union of Fascists. Sir O's party.' Her whisper became more hurried, more urgent. 'It's marvellous. He's absolutely tremendous. As soon as you hear him, you cannot help but join him.' She stopped and took a breath. 'I'm sure you understand. You know, with Herr Hitler.'

'You are a perceptive young woman,' said Wolfgang. 'I should be interested to meet this Sir Oswald and discover what it is he is planning for Great Britain.'

Diana flashed Wolfgang one of her more brilliant smiles. 'I'm sure that can be arranged. Are you planning to be in London?'

Louisa fixed this conversation to memory as she listened: it would be noted down as soon as she could discreetly do so. What would Diana arrange for this German, so interested in British fascism?

'I was not, but perhaps, Frau Guinness, I will make some plans in due course.'

Unity was less able to hide her glee at this than her elder sister.

'Not all your fellow countrymen are this sympathetic. Must you be careful to whom you discuss this matter?' Wolfgang asked.

'Oh, I don't know,' said Diana airily. 'It depends on the circles you move in. All our friends are anti-Bolshie. Fascism is the only real choice to make if you have half a brain.' She stopped, as if tired of the subject. 'Now, we had better push on. There are shops we must go to and I would like to catch up with Mrs Fowler.'

Louisa thought she detected a small reaction from Wolfgang to Mrs Fowler's name but couldn't be certain if it was good or bad.

'Absolutely. I have had more than my fair share of your delightful company. Perhaps we might meet tonight? There are cocktails, I believe, being served in the Blue Bar for the first-class guests.'

'Yes, we'll be there,' said Diana. She signalled to her mother, and to Louisa, and the four of them left the cool of the museum and entered the blazing midday heat and bustle of the market streets.

CHAPTER FOURTEEN

The port town of Livorno was mostly clustered on a hillside, and it was a weary Lady Redesdale who dragged behind her daughters and Louisa after two hours of their darting in and out of various shops that sold things designed to please tourists, and no one else. It didn't help that she had to also constantly navigate between Diana, who had the money to buy whatever she pleased, and Unity, who had no more than pocket money. Louisa had no lira in her possession yet couldn't help but admire the linen and lace, the painted plates, the traditional dresses made miniature for babies, the porcelain trinkets and the postcards of donkeys. Diana picked up toys for her young sons, Jonathan and Desmond; Lady Redesdale bought a linen table-cloth; while Unity dithered over a carved wooden sheep – 'for Decca, it's just like her pet lamb, Miranda' – and a set of Bakelite napkin rings for Nancy, 'to tease Muv with'. Lady Redesdale's resistance to napkins was legendary, having begun as nothing more than an economic measure with the laundry when she had lived in London as a new bride.

Eventually, even Diana could not ignore the pale look that had come over her mother and suggested they stop at a café in the square, to sit in the shade and drink fresh lemonade.

'You've never had anything this delicious,' Diana insisted, when her mother tried to protest that she wanted to return to the ship. They sat down at a table, their shoes dusty from the arid pavements, their paper bags of shopping bundled on another chair, and ordered the *limonata*. It arrived in a tall glass jug and Louisa drank it gratefully, the sour tang and the sugary drops crystallising on her lips.

As she was putting her glass back down on the table she happened to glance at a shop doorway that was almost out of her sightline, on a side street that led off the square. She couldn't see what the shop was beneath its smart black awning, but it wasn't that which had drawn her attention. It was Mrs Fowler, looking far happier than when she had left them earlier in the restaurant; she looked almost giddy, in fact, having exited the shop with quick steps and turning around as if she was dancing a waltz. Louisa then saw the steward from the party – Jim, wasn't it? – emerge from the same shop, carrying several large bags and packages. He seemed more hesitant, looking about him. Nor was he wearing the civvies Louisa might have expected, the sort of thing that Guy might wear by the coast in the summer, but a cream suit that was spanking new, shiny brown leather brogues and a panama hat that sat, it had to be said, at a jaunty angle to set off his good-looking face.

Unity spotted them too and called out, 'Mrs Fowler!'

Ella looked around and when she saw their party she blushed a deep red that was obvious even in the shadow of her wide-brimmed hat.

Diana waved her arm to them. 'Come and join us.'

Lady Redesdale leaned towards her older daughter. 'Are you sure that's suitable?'

'Don't be stuffy, Muv,' said Diana. 'Louisa, would you fetch another chair?'

Louisa got up and picked up a nearby chair, but as she carried it over, Ella had almost reached them and put out a hand to Louisa, indicating that she should put it back down.

'I'm sorry to do this again, but I can't stay.'

Jim waited at the corner of the side street and the square, looking uncomfortable with the unwieldy parcels.

Diana looked over at him, then at Ella. 'I say, what are you up to?'

Ella gave a shake of her head. 'Nothing at all. Joseph needed some new clothes and, as he was busy with his meeting, I asked the cabin boy to help me out.'

'It looks as if *he's* wearing the new threads.' Diana was laughing.

Lady Redesdale hid her disapproval behind a large gulp of lemonade.

'Oh, well, they're the same sort of measurements, you see, so I asked him to try the things on. You know how it is in these foreign shops, you can't rely on them to give you the right size.'

Louisa had only met Joseph Fowler briefly, but she was fairly certain he was a good few inches taller than Jim.

'I see,' said Diana, but she arched her back as she regarded Ella.

'Anyway, we had better get back to the ship. Jim is on duty soon and I had better not get him in trouble with the first officer. You know how it is.'

'Not really,' said Diana, a smile still teasing around her mouth.

'Don't mention it to Joseph, will you?' Ella said, looking at each one of them. 'It's a surprise. It's his birthday soon.'

'When is his birthday?' asked Unity.

'What?'

'When is his birthday?' she repeated, cow-like eyes looking up at Ella.

'Soon,' said Ella firmly. 'Now, I must be off. So sorry to miss you again. I'll see you on the ship later?'

'Naturally,' said Diana. They watched Mrs Fowler walk away, Jim scuttling after her down the side street. 'What do you think that was all about?' she mused when they had disappeared.

'I'd prefer that you didn't discuss it in front of your sister,' said Lady Redesdale.

'Muv, I'm almost nineteen years old.'

'You are not married.'

'Diana was married at my age,' Unity fired back. Louisa almost expected her to perform her old childhood trick of disappearing under the table when the conversation went the way she didn't like.

'Yes, well.'

Diana sat up at this. '"Look at how that turned out" – is that what you meant to say?'

Her mother said nothing to this but placed her hands carefully on her lap.

Louisa looked at her watch. 'It's time we got back to the ship, too, if you would like time to bathe and change for dinner.' Trying to resolve the bickering between Lady Redesdale and her daughters was the least enjoyable aspect of her work, and usually the least successful. Predictably, Louisa's comment simply turned the antipathy in her direction.

'I will decide when we return to the ship,' snapped Diana, but her mother interceded gratefully.

'I think it would be better for all of us if we retired from this heat,' said Lady Redesdale, standing as she spoke. 'Louisa, come with me, if you would. Unity, you too.' No mention of Diana. The message could not have been clearer if she had written it on a note and put it in a bottle.

As it turned out, Lady Redesdale had been struggling more than they had realised. When they returned to the cabin, she complained of a violent headache that soon turned to a migraine. It was decided that she would spend the evening lying on her bed in the dark and silence, while Louisa would chaperone Unity to the cocktail party that was being held in the Blue Bar that evening. Louisa had brought one suitable dress, cut close to her slim figure and made of dark orange velvet. It was made by neither seamstress nor couture but bought from the ready-to-wear department at Selfridges. Guy had told her she was the most beautiful woman in the room when she wore it. She held onto that memory when neither Unity nor Diana commented on it but continued to fuss over their own dresses and jewellery, complaining that it was 'frightfully difficult' to maintain standards on the ship and make one's dress look different on three separate occasions. At last they were satisfied and at seven o'clock they all made their way to the party.

As usual, there were around sixty people in the room, dressed in black tie and sipping dry martinis.

'The same dreary bunch every time,' complained Diana as they walked in. 'I've remembered why I don't like cruises.'

'Why come on this one, then?' said Unity.

'Because I've got to keep away from the Leader while the divorce goes through, idiot.'

She must have read the letter from him by now. It didn't seem as if he'd said anything in it to improve her mood. Would it be in the bedside drawer, tied up with the others? Had Diana noticed the missing letter? Louisa hadn't yet found an opportunity to return it. Every time she thought about the letters she had the same lurching sensation as she did when looking down from a great height.

Diana had gone quiet, and Louisa couldn't help but feel a little sorry for her. She didn't like Mosley, nor the fact of Diana's leaving Bryan, who she thought was a good and decent man, and it was all the more puzzling when Mosley's reputation as a philanderer was ironclad.

Nancy had told Louisa that one night he had confessed to his wife all his affairs during their marriage. 'Thirty infidelities in twelve years, and those were the ones he admitted to,' she had told Louisa in her urgent whisper, reserved for the best gossip. 'And Cimmie apparently said, on hearing this long list of names, "But they're all my friends." No wonder she died soon after.'

At any rate, Louisa thought, the likelihood of his having completely changed his ways was minimal. Perhaps the letter had made Diana question the wisdom of giving up so much for Mosley.

Louisa looked around the room. After only a few days, the faces were already familiar. Ella Fowler was talking to the man her husband had been having lunch with earlier, Sir Clive. He was leaning in towards her and his manner seemed flirtatious, but Ella was an attractive woman – he could hardly be blamed. Her husband, Joseph, was sitting down – the only person in the room who was – holding a full tumbler of whisky. She hoped it had been mixed with soda water or he'd be drunk by the time he got to the bottom of the glass. But the surprise was when she saw Wolfgang von Bohlen, standing beside his companion, Herr Müller. Unity saw them at the same time and gave an audible gasp.

'Louisa, do look. He's in uniform. Have you ever seen a more handsome man?'

Indeed, it was a uniform. Black, with knee-high leather boots over his trousers, a belt, a leather strap that crossed over his torso and a striking red and white armband with a symbol on it.

Unity had followed Louisa's eyes. 'It's a swastika,' she said, 'the emblem of the Nazi Party. It's funny because I was conceived in Swastika.'

'What?'

Unity smiled. 'It's a place in Canada. Where Muv and Farve went prospecting for gold. They didn't get any, of course.'

'Hmm,' said Louisa. Something about it unsettled her. Perhaps it was no more than Unity's reaction to Wolfgang in his uniform, a combination of naivety and sexual ardour that sat uncomfortably side by side.

A waiter came up holding a tray of martinis. Unity took one and Louisa, swept along, took one too.

'I see,' said Unity, 'you've come out to play.'

Louisa looked at her glass, as if surprised to see it in her hand. 'Just the one.'

'That's what they all say.'

Diana had left them and gone over to talk to Ella.

'Let's go and join them,' said Unity. 'I ache to talk to Herr von Bohlen, but I'd better wait for him to come to me, don't you think?'

Louisa had taken her first sip and felt the heady rush of gin. It was not unpleasant.

'Yes. Better that.'

They walked over, but Louisa stood to the side. It was not her place to join the conversation, and besides, she was not used to such strong drink. She needed to gather herself.

Ella introduced Sir Clive Montague to Unity while Diana grabbed a second martini from a passing tray. Louisa had seen her like this before, when her youthful impetuousness overrode her usual elegance. It didn't usually lead to much good.

CHAPTER FIFTEEN

~⚬~

The Blue Bar had large glass doors that led directly onto the deck, wide open tonight as it was such a warm evening, even with the ship travelling at speed through the dark sea. Louisa was grateful. It was crowded with guests, and though there was not the same heightened excitement as the first night of the cruise, there was still a lot of loud chatter and cigarette smoke in the air. She positioned herself to catch a breeze that was coming in, while she stood and listened to the conversation between the group before her: Ella, Diana, Unity and Sir Clive Montague. The introductions had been made, but Diana, it was clear, was not going to indulge in the small talk that the guests usually made when they first met.

When Sir Clive asked Diana if she had been on the *Princess Alice* before, she replied abruptly, 'No, and I shan't think I'll do it again. Three weeks of no plays, no nightclubs and the same people at the same table for every luncheon *and* dinner.' Belatedly, she seemed to realise what she had said. 'I don't mean to be rude.'

Sir Clive laughed at that, a rumble that came from deep in his chest. 'The trick when meeting the same people is to draw something different out of them each night. That's what makes these trips compelling for me.'

'How do you do that?' Unity asked with genuine interest.

'Well, my dear,' said Sir Clive, who didn't have a moustache but looked as if he should have one and should be stroking it, 'you simply ask questions. Ones that people tend not to expect to have to answer.'

'Why did you ask Diana if she'd been on the ship before, then? *Everyone* asks that question.' A fair point from Unity.

Louisa took another small sip of her martini and awaited the answer.

'One can't leap into the deep waters of another's soul. You must take some gentle laps in the shallows first.'

'You're gaining their trust, in other words,' said Diana, who looked piqued in spite of herself.

Ella had been watching them as she finished her half-full glass in a single mouthful. 'I need another drink,' she said. 'Isn't it time to go into dinner now?'

'Shortly,' said Diana, turning back to Sir Clive. 'Tell me, why are you in the business of diving into the deep waters of people's souls? It sounds like dangerous work.'

'I'm an investor,' he replied congenially. 'One must always, however, invest in the person, not the business. Businesses come and go, but the people may reward over a lifetime.'

'Not my husband,' snapped Ella.

'Oh?' Louisa saw Diana scent something juicy. 'Tell me more.'

Sir Clive demurred. 'It has been charming to meet you and your sister. I do hope we will encounter each other again. For now, if you will excuse me, I had better go to dinner. I do believe they are about to sound the gong.'

He walked away and Diana raised her eyebrows. 'I say, Ella, you must tell us what that was all about. It was maximum behaviour.'

Ella gave a sigh. 'He sank a lot of money into one of Joseph's projects – some education centre attached to Blenheim Palace, of all places. But the other investors didn't come through, and it was called off. By the time my husband realised, Clive's money had already gone, spent on producing the plans, wining and dining councillors and god knows who else. Now he wants it back.'

Listening to this, Louisa suspected Ella had drunk one martini too many. It was all very indiscreet. Everyone hung on her words.

'Naturally, Joseph doesn't have it. He hasn't got a chance of repaying a penny. It's no coincidence Clive's on this ship. It's how we met him in the first place and he's been trying to chase down Joseph for months. He must have found out he'd be on here now. Someone's in his pay, but I don't know who.'

Louisa knew this wasn't the story that Iain was after, but she was drawn in nonetheless. Who on the ship was passing information about the Fowlers' whereabouts to Sir Clive?

'What will happen if Joseph doesn't come up with the cash?' asked Diana.

Ella rolled her eyes. 'I don't know and I don't care. He's been asking me to soft-soap him, but I don't see why I should. I think I'll divorce Joseph soon.' She took a step back, a slightly wobbly one, knowing she'd pulled the pin out of a grenade and needed to get out of the way of the explosion.

'Oh darling, I'm doing that now and it's ghastly. Are you sure that's the only way out?'

'I've done it once before.'

Now she had Diana.

'*Have* you?' Diana clicked her fingers and a waiter came over. 'Two martinis, dry. Quickly.'

Ella gave Diana an impish grin. 'Joseph is my third husband. I married when I was eighteen, first of all, and went with him to England—'

'Where did you go *from*?' Unity interrupted.

'British Columbia. I grew up there.' The drinks arrived and Ella took one. 'But he was killed in the war. In the meantime, I had joined an ambulance unit that worked behind French lines. I was awarded the Croix de Guerre with Star and Palm for my bravery.'

Diana raised her glass as if to toast the achievement. 'Go on.'

'After the war, it was . . . hard. You were probably too young to remember, but everything felt different and we were all too sad. I married an American – a captain – and we moved to his hometown, but we separated almost as soon as our son was born. We shouldn't have been together a week; we were never going to last a lifetime.'

'What did you do then?'

Louisa was grateful to Diana for her questions, while she herself stood motionless in the shadows, her martini barely touched.

Ella looked around, checking perhaps that Joseph was not in earshot. 'I worked as a pianist and a songwriter, but I had my boy to look after. Eventually, I made my way back to British Columbia, hoping for some help from my family. Huh. Some hope. Then I met Joseph. You know the rest, or can guess it. And now, here I am. On a ship somewhere in Europe, pathetically longing for a crumb of affection from a cabin b—' She stopped and put her hand to her mouth. 'Oh. I've said too much.'

Unity's face was disapproving. 'I think everyone has gone into dinner.' They looked around and saw the room was almost empty.

Louisa stepped forward, a jolt registering with Ella as she did so. She spoke as if she hadn't heard a word, in her role as the perfect maid. 'We'd better go through. Are you ready, Miss Unity?'

'Yes, we're ready.' Diana had taken Ella's arm, like a gentleman chaperone. 'You stay with us, Mrs Fowler. I think there's more to hear.'

Louisa did not believe that Lady Redesdale would approve of Unity hearing more about Mrs Fowler's desire for affection from someone who was not her current husband, but, as ever, she was helpless in the face of Diana's determination.

Joseph Fowler, however, was not.

As they walked out of the room, Louisa became aware of movement at the periphery of her vision. She thought at first it was the moonlight reflecting off the glass of the French windows that led out to the deck.

'Ella,' Joseph called out without shouting. His wife turned around, her arm still hooked through Diana's. 'Were you about to go into dinner without me?'

'Mr Fowler, it's entirely my fault, I was practically forcing your wife—' But Diana was not able to go on. Joseph had walked over to them at speed and, with a smack of his hand, propelled his wife's arm away before he grabbed it, his fingers pressing hard into her soft skin.

Louisa felt the anger rise in her faster than the bubbles in a soda syphon. Diana and Unity had been silenced; Ella was apologising in gulps that could have been either fury or shame, or a messy mixture of both.

'Let her go.'

Louisa spun around and saw Jim, the cabin steward she'd served the drinks with only a few nights ago. Jim, the cabin steward she'd seen dressed in a smart linen suit and carrying several shopping bags for Ella.

Joseph dropped Ella's arm and she started to rub it, not looking at either her husband or Jim but at some vague spot on the carpet.

'How dare *you* tell me what to do.'

'Mr Fowler, I only ask that everyone is calm.' Jim held his palms out in a placatory manner, but Louisa saw the determination in his face.

'I'll do what I want. I'm the first-class passenger here. You are merely our cabin boy and you need reminding of the fact.'

With that, he leaped forward and threw a punch at Jim, landing on his jaw, but the sound was dull, rather than a crack. They banged into the side of the bar, knocking off several glasses that had been left behind by the guests going into dinner, which fell and smashed into one another, shattering into tiny pieces that flew around the floor like a galaxy of distant stars.

By this time, Diana and Unity had backed away until they were almost at the door, and Louisa had moved to Ella's side, ready to protect her.

Jim wrestled Joseph to the ground, where they struggled on the broken glass and spilled dregs, and all the women could see was a flailing of arms and legs, with each one either crying out or grunting, until someone – a man, thought Louisa briefly – ran in and pulled Joseph off, leaving Jim on the floor, bloody scratches on his hands and one on his face. Everyone was behaving hysterically now, but Louisa had been stilled by something else altogether. She knew the man who had rushed in.

It was her husband, Guy.

CHAPTER SIXTEEN

'**G**uy.' Louisa stared at him. 'What are you doing here?'
He was panting slightly, gripping Joseph in a policeman's hold, both hands behind his back. Jim was picking himself up off the floor, brushing off the broken glass and gingerly inspecting his hands, the blood streaking. No one dared even to whisper. Unity and Diana watched it all with the wide eyes of children in the front row of a pantomime.

'I wanted to surprise you.'

'You certainly did that.' She tried to rearrange her face, not look as if she was displeased, because she wasn't, but she had been caught completely off guard.

'Let go of me, I tell you,' said Joseph, breaking the thin ice that was threatening to frost over them.

Guy kept hold of his senses as best he could. 'Not until you have assured me that you won't be throwing any more punches this evening.'

'I'm an old man,' Joseph said heavily. He did look old then, a greying face of disappointment, his moustache drooping. 'I don't want to fight.'

Jim, the comparison inevitable, looked young and fit, his white uniform stained with drink. He looked at them all, bewildered and afraid, and then ran off, pushing past Diana. A bartender had already begun to clear up the glass. Ella watched Jim go but remained where she was standing.

Diana and Unity loosened their stance, as if breaking from a game of musical statues. 'I think we had better go into dinner ourselves. Louisa, we'll call up later when we need you,' Diana said quietly. 'Mr Sullivan, it's a pleasure to see you again.'

They would be disconcerted, Louisa knew. It was possible Lady Redesdale would disapprove. No. It was definite she'd disapprove. Oh, what did Louisa care anyway?

Guy had released his grip on Joseph and Ella had started to walk away with him.

'Hello,' Louisa said to her husband. 'Shall we start this again?'

Guy let out the breath he'd been holding. 'Yes please.'

Louisa took Guy's hand and led him to the deck outside. There was nobody about, as everyone was at dinner, and the moon shone heavy and full above them. It was warm, yet Louisa shivered slightly. She moved close to her husband, who wrapped his arm around her as they leaned on the balcony, watching the phosphorescence on the waves that plumed out from the fast-moving ship. For a few minutes they did nothing more than enjoy the sensation of their bodies together, the sea air, the night.

Louisa's curiosity punctured the stillness first. 'Why are you here? When did you get here? And how?'

He kissed the top of her forehead. 'I missed you. It's as simple as that. It wasn't difficult to find out where the ship was stopping, and I got the train down. Stiles was understanding and gave me the time off. It helped that we had arrested and charged the man we'd been looking for.'

'Can you stay long?'

Guy shook his head. 'Only two nights. I'll have to leave at Rome, get the train back. But I thought it was worth it to see my girl.'

'It is. Thank you,' she said and leaned up for a proper kiss.

Reassured and settled, they went to supper. Louisa entertained Guy by describing the personalities she had come across on the ship. As well as Mr and Mrs Fowler, with their extraordinary history, there was the cabin steward, Jim.

'Any idea why they had that fight?' Guy asked.

She hesitated, wary of spreading rumours of immorality if they weren't true. On the other hand, a case had to be examined from all angles.

'I think Mrs Fowler is having an affair of some sort with Jim,' she admitted. 'In Livorno, when I was with the Mitfords, we saw her with him, and he was wearing clothes she'd clearly bought him. She tried to say he'd been helping her with finding the right size for her husband ... '

Guy shook his head. 'These people. But we don't know that her husband knows.'

'No. But it's not a happy marriage, whether or not she's cheating on him.'

'Mr Fowler threw the first punch. Doesn't that mean he suspects Jim of being his wife's lover?'

'I'd say so,' agreed Louisa.

'What do you know of him?'

'Jim? Not much. He works in the first-class cabins. We both handed out the drinks at one of Mrs Guinness's parties. He's a young lad, hoping to see the world by working on the ship.' She pushed the somewhat tasteless chicken onto her fork. 'He was polite enough. I was surprised when that fight started. I wouldn't have said he was the type.'

Louisa told Guy that the Fowlers were far from the only oddities on the ship. There was Captain Schmitt, with his penchant for parrots.

Guy interrupted. 'Don't tease.'

'I mean it,' said Louisa, laughing. 'You'll see him later and know I'm right. He wears a parrot brooch next to his medals and I swear I saw him wearing a tie with parrots on it.'

It felt good, being with her husband, eating and talking together. Why had she been so quick to accept the assignment from Iain? Louisa thought maybe she still had some growing up to do. She suspected that when things had become difficult at home, she had leaped at the first opportunity to get away. She wouldn't do it again. Guy deserved better than that. She looked up at him, his open face, his round glasses on his fine nose. He'd looked almost boyish when she first knew him, but she liked the years that had settled on him since then.

'What about the Mitfords? Have they been behaving themselves?' asked Guy.

'Yes,' said Louisa, relaxing now. 'Not too bad at all. I don't pretend to understand them sometimes, but I know them so well they don't surprise me too much.'

'Has Mrs Guinness been in touch with Sir O?'

'Why do you ask?'

Guy gave a small shrug, a forkful halfway to his mouth.

'She's divorcing. I suppose I'm just being a nosy policeman. I'm intrigued as to what's going on there.'

Was Guy on the same mission as her, for Special Branch? Was that why Iain had instructed her not to talk to her own husband?

'No. I don't know. That is, she wouldn't tell me even if she was.'

If the letter had been in her pocket, instead of her own bed-side drawer, it might have set fire to her skirt. She knew she was being evasive, but she had to move Guy away from the subject.

'What other people are staying on here? What sort are they?' Guy was pressing the point. Or perhaps she was being paranoid.

'A mixture, so far as I can tell. Not the sort that Lady Redesdale would usually sit at a table with, judging from some of the expressions on her face. She complained that everyone laughs too loudly on this ship.'

Guy's eyebrows lifted above his specs. He didn't understand snobbery. If he was going to make a distinction between people it was where their moral compass lay. His work gave him plenty of opportunities to judge that and Louisa knew there were times when he found it hard to maintain his general optimism about the human race.

She told him then about the others: Sir Clive Montague, who had lost a fortune with Joseph, how smitten Unity was with Wolfgang von Bohlen, a man who went everywhere with a silent companion, Herr Müller. The elderly woman whose name she didn't know but who walked six dachshunds around the deck on a continuous loop for three hours either side of luncheon, every single day. Rumours of a famous ballerina on the ship, Daisy Lipstadt, as yet unseen. The mother, father and two young girls of ten or so, who always wore co-ordinating colours: that very day the mother and daughters had worn yellow dresses and he a yellow tie and socks. And then there was the waiter with shell shock, jumping out of his skin every time a cork was popped.

Guy listened to it all attentively. 'You've been observing closely,' he said. 'Anyone would think you were a detective.'

'There's not been much else to do,' she replied, conscious that she was being a little edgy.

'Maybe. But I know you. You can't help yourself.' He smiled, then yawned. 'Sorry, it's been a long day.'

Louisa leaned over and touched his arm. They'd finished eating and the room was nearly empty, as the various workers had been called away to deal with the evening's goings-on.

'You're tired. I still have to work. Why don't you go to my cabin and sleep?'

'Have you your own?'

'Yes, it's only got a bunk in it, but I have it all to myself. What did you book?'

'The cheapest thing I could find – and there weren't too many options in any case. Not much more than a notch above a hammock in the mess, I think.'

'You're practically a stowaway.'

'So long as I can stow away with you, my darling, that's fine with me.'

Guy stood up and Louisa followed suit. She gave him her cabin key from her pocket, together with directions, and promised she would be back with him as soon as she could be.

CHAPTER SEVENTEEN

❧

Having seen Guy off and had something to eat, Louisa faced the rest of the night renewed. She needed to get to the upper deck to see Lady Redesdale, a few flights away, but she made quick work of the dimly lit passage the crew and servants used to move speedily through the ship. At the last door, she came out right by an exit onto the deck and decided to take a final peek at the stars.

Almost as soon as she had pushed the heavy door open, she heard a woman sobbing. Electric light from the portholes and occasional bigger windows was thrown onto the deck in shafts, but in between was pitched into darkness. Louisa looked along, following the sound, and saw Ella, crouched down on the wooden boards, having pushed herself against a flat white wall. Her face was in her hands and the sobbing had not subsided. Hastily, Louisa went over to her and kneeled beside her, not daring to put her hand on Ella's back but having her palm hover there instead.

'Mrs Fowler? It's Louisa Sullivan. Can I do something to help?'

Ella looked up at her. Tears had streaked her make-up and blotched her cheeks. It wasn't all that easy to see the beauty that Louisa knew was there. More distressing than the streaks and the blotches was the pain and fury in her eyes.

'That bastard.'

Louisa looked around but they were alone. It was cold outside, no hint of the warm currents that the earlier evening had carried on the air.

'Let's go inside, Mrs Fowler.' Louisa spoke firmly.

Ella looked at her and there was a flash of fear, then she dropped her head down and pulled her knees in tighter. Louisa felt exasperated. The *dramas* of these people. They had money, houses, freedom. Why did they have to go and complicate things? She sighed and tried again. In spite of all that, she felt sorry for Ella too. Her husband was not a nice man and that couldn't make up for any riches.

'Come on.' Louisa took one of Ella's arms and started to stand, trying to pull her up at the same time. Ella was heavy and resisted at first, but then put a hand on the floor and weakly pushed herself up, mumbling under her breath as she did, swearing indiscriminately. Once she was standing she smoothed her palms across her face as if erasing the mess there. She closed her eyes briefly, which made her wobble slightly, and when she opened them again she looked at Louisa with intent.

'I love him,' she slurred. 'I love him so much. No one understands it and no one will believe it. Not even him.'

'Your husband?' asked Louisa, knowing as she said it that that was not who Ella meant.

'No, not that stupid man.' Ella motioned with her hand as if he were crawling up to her at that second and she were swatting him away. 'Jim. I love Jim. I love him. Ha.' She started laughing in such a way that Louisa knew it threatened to turn to tears quickly.

Louisa dug in her pockets for the handkerchief she knew she must have somewhere – once a nursery maid, the habit was hard to lose – while Ella continued half-muttering, half-shouting through snot-nosed sobs about how much she loved Jim and hated her husband, how she was going to leave him and run away with the cabin boy. Louisa finally brought the hanky out and told Ella to be quiet, while she dabbed at her face with a corner of the white cloth.

'Shhh, Mrs Fowler,' she said gently, soothingly. 'It does no good to talk of things now. You're tired and you need to rest.'

'I can't rest, he'll do something to me in my sleep. He wants me – *his wife* – to go to bed with Sir Clive.'

That stopped Louisa. Her own uncle, Stephen, flashed into her mind, unbidden and unwanted. Dragging her from her bed in the middle of the night. A door closing. A belt unbuckled. She had escaped in time but the fear had driven her far from home. If this was what Ella was being put through, Louisa would not judge her actions.

'He can't pay that money and he wants me to go to . . . to go to . . . ' She hiccuped then and finally gave up. By this time, Louisa had wiped away the worst of the mess and had one arm around Ella's waist, another gripping her shoulder, steering her back inside. It was a tricky manoeuvre with the heavy door, but they managed it eventually. Louisa decided they would use the crew's corridors to get as close to Ella's cabin as possible, in order to avoid the risk of bumping into anyone she knew.

Unfortunately, it didn't work.

CHAPTER EIGHTEEN

G uy was on his way to Louisa's cabin, feeling light on his feet in spite of his long day, not to mention the nerves that fluttered in his chest ever since he boarded the first train at Victoria, which had been only three days ago but felt much longer. It wasn't that he didn't trust Louisa, or that he didn't have faith in their marriage, but he had been afraid of her reaction to his sudden appearance on the ship. He couldn't shake the feeling that there was something she was hiding from him, but was at a complete loss to explain what it could be. Guy was confident the mystery wasn't a lover – she wasn't that kind of person and he knew the intimacy they shared was real. The only thing he could think was that the Mitfords had made a request of her that she was too embarrassed for some reason to confess to him. Which was absurd. Louisa should know he adored her, would forgive almost anything. Still, she had appeared happy to see him, once she'd got over the surprise, and he was looking forward to her coming back to the cabin later and the two of them being forced to share such a narrow bed. Yes, he was looking forward to that very much indeed.

Although Guy had every intention of walking straight to the cabin and lying down to wait for Louisa, he wasn't feeling tired at all, and when he remembered that there would be a bar on the ship that served good whisky . . .

Ten minutes later, Guy was at the back of the smoking room, lined with rows of leather books on dark wooden shelves and with a blue cloud of cigar smoke that hung below the ceiling. There seemed to be only men in the room, guests and stewards. There was a quiet hum of chatter and soon Guy, his single malt whisky in hand, felt soothed. Now that he was here on the ocean liner, a spectacular vessel in itself, and had found Louisa, he could enjoy these few days as a well-earned holiday. Tomorrow they would still be sailing – they weren't due to dock in Rome until the day after – and he planned to stand on the deck with Louisa in the full blast of hot sunshine, gazing out at the wide blue sea, where they could talk about their future. He hoped that once this cruise was over and she was back home with him, they could start to live as a family, maybe even move out of his parents' house if he found someone to help his mother. He knew Louisa needed to work, too. Seeing her on the ship, hearing her astute observations, watching her react to the demands of the Mitfords and deal with them skilfully, had reminded him that Louisa was a modern woman. She needed the challenge and stimulus of a career. He would support her from now on.

Lost in this thought and with his whisky almost finished, at first Guy paid no attention to raised voices from the opposite corner of the room. After a few minutes, however, when it had turned to shouts, his policeman's instinct kicked in.

The room was not large, yet it was tricky to decipher what was happening when the walls were dark and the candles on the tables were throwing flickering shadows. Heads turned in the direction of the noise before all at once there was an almighty bang and several men jumped up as a body fell onto the floor, pulling a table and glasses down with it.

Guy ran over, slightly hampered by the edges of chairs that were in the way like thick branches on a forest path. By the time he got there, only seconds later, the body – a man, thankfully alive – was being hauled upright by the other guests in the bar. None of them were, it had to be said, the most athletic of guests, though one could only admire their derring-do. With red faces and a great deal of puffing below their handlebar moustaches, the men were holding onto a figure that was startlingly familiar: Guy had pulled him away from a fight only two hours before.

'Mr Fowler?' asked Guy.

'What of it?' Joseph slurred. His head lolled slightly as his arms were held fast.

Guy considered pulling out his detective sergeant's badge but felt, in the circumstances, it might be too much. What he was dealing with were overzealous, mildly drunk guests and an embarrassed man. Guy saw there was a second entrance into the bar, through which Joseph had fallen. Even in the low light, it wasn't hard to see that Joseph had been in a fight – his second of the evening. One would hope that was out of the ordinary, even for him.

Guy raced to the door, but whoever the other man was, he had already made a hasty retreat into the shadows. Joseph, his arms released, was still trying to catch his breath, and gave himself a helping hand by knocking back the remains of a glass of what looked like water but was almost certainly neat gin.

With silent permission from Guy, the other guests drifted

back to their chairs. The drama, such as it had been, was over, and they had important discussions to finish about plummeting shares and rising demands of their mistresses.

'Mr Fowler,' Guy repeated. 'Would you like to sit with me for a while?'

Joseph regarded Guy and gave him a cursory look from head to foot. 'Whatever would I talk to *you* for?'

'It seems to me that things must be on your mind.'

There wasn't much more than a grunt in reply to this. Yet Guy sensed, in the absence of another answer, that there was a tacit admission to the suggestion. Guy sat down and gestured to the seat opposite him, at the same time summoning a steward.

'Could you bring a pot of coffee, please?' he asked.

Joseph started to say that he didn't want any, but his voice trailed off. Reluctantly, he sat down heavily in the chair. There was a light thrown onto his face and Guy saw that he had deep grooves running along his forehead and thin papery skin stretched over his cheekbones, though his hair was dark with only a few silvered streaks. He must have been approaching seventy years old and though he'd kept a slim figure, there was a weariness to the way he moved his limbs that was more than the weight of the alcohol running through his veins.

'Who are you anyway?' Joseph said.

'Guy Sullivan. I'm Louisa's husband.' Joseph looked blank at this so Guy continued, 'She's the lady's maid to Lady Redesdale.' This prompted a gesture of recognition. 'I decided to join the ship for a few days.' Guy knew that if he wanted to prompt a confession he'd need to lead the way with one of his own. 'I missed her. We're fairly newly married.'

'You're not young,' said Joseph, bluntly.

'No, not so young. It . . . well, it took a long time to persuade her that she wanted to be with me.'

The steward came over and set down the coffee pot with two cups, a small jug of cream and a bowl of dark brown sugar crystals. He poured out the coffee, then left. Joseph stared at the cup before him but didn't pick it up.

'Mr Fowler,' carried on Guy, 'I know you don't know me, but I'd like to help you avoid any further aggravation on this ship.'

Joseph let out a bark at this. 'You'd have to push my wife overboard in that case.' He practically threw the coffee down his throat and the sobering effect seemed to give him a jolt. 'I don't know why you're sitting here with me. There's nothing to be done. I've lost everything. I've been humiliated and kicked in the teeth when I'm down.' He gave a bitter laugh. 'I'm not even going to be able to pay the bill on this bloody boat when I leave, now *Sir* Clive' – the title was pronounced with heavy sarcasm – 'has refused my offer.' He looked at Guy earnestly. 'My wife is a beauty. He's a fool.'

Guy was uncertain as to how these statements connected at first, then he realised that in Joseph's mind, one plus one equalled three. At least the pugnaciousness seemed to have gone out of him.

'My mother always said not to make any big decisions when tired,' said Guy. 'I think it's time you went back to your room, Mr Fowler. If there is anything I can do for you, I'd be happy to talk to you tomorrow.'

Joseph shrugged at this, but there was no light in his eyes. 'Fine, fine,' he said. 'I'll go. But I can tell you: it's not going to look any better for me in the morning.'

CHAPTER NINETEEN

⚘

Louisa and Ella stumbled up the crew stairway together, the occasional footing lost on a step by Ella, with Louisa holding grimly on. Both had their heads down, watching the way in the low light, which is why they didn't notice a man standing quietly by the door that led out to deck B.

As they were halfway up the stairs, slowly but steadily making their way up, Ella finally seeming to sober up, they heard a cough. Not the cough of a sore throat but that of a signal. There was an immediate shuffle from further up the stairwell before Louisa heard a voice that she recognised calling out: 'What? What is it, Müller?', followed by a stamping about of heavy boots. Unity.

Ella quickly recovered herself and looked at Louisa. They shared an expression of wide-eyed surprise.

Louisa hurried up more stairs and saw Herr Müller standing there, avoiding her approach. His face was as implacable as usual, if lacking even the shred of friendly neutrality she had seen before. Louisa had left Ella a few steps down, clinging onto the banister rail that was screwed into the wall. Unity's head appeared from around the corner. Her lipstick was smudged, her hair disarrayed and she was pulling at her skirt. It didn't require detective skills to guess what she had been doing – but with whom?

'Miss Unity?' Louisa said.

Unity stared at her and chose the tack of fury. 'What are you doing here? And is that Mrs Fowler with you?'

Louisa was taken aback by this. She looked at Müller, hoping for – what? Reassurance that she was not the one at fault here? But this was not the conversation that was going to break his habit of a lifetime: he would not be getting involved.

'Yes, this is Mrs Fowler. Miss Unity, who are you with?'

Unity had shaken herself back into composure, albeit with smudged lipstick, and a redness on her chin that was starting to glow. 'That's none of your business,' she said, crossly.

'Lady Redesdale—'

'Please don't tell Muv.' Unity pushed past Müller and ran to Louisa, gripping her arm. She whispered into her ear, 'Please, don't say anything. I'll go back to my room now and won't leave it again. I promise.'

Louisa knew it was a ridiculous situation. Unity was old enough to drive a car. But her parents did not like her to walk a hundred yards along the street alone, take a train by herself, or even walk without a chaperone along the corridors of the *Princess Alice* when it was close to midnight. But Unity had broken so many rules tonight, one more couldn't make much difference.

'You had better get back to your room fast,' was all Louisa would say, deliberately withholding reassurance that she would be a keeper of secrets. She didn't agree with the tight reins the parents put on their daughters – from her experience, it only led to them kicking with ever more violent force at the walls that closed in on them – but it was not her place to say so.

Unity went back up the few steps and exited through the door. Müller did not follow her but instead went around the corner and up another flight of stairs, following whoever had been causing Unity's dishevelled appearance. Louisa could make a good guess as to who that was and it made her nervous.

Pulling back into focus, Louisa took Ella's arm again. This time they made better progress and within a few minutes were at her cabin door. Ella fumbled in her clutch bag and brought out the key, handing it to Louisa, a slight tremor passing through her fingers. Swiftly, Louisa opened it, and it was only once they were on the other side of the heavy door that they realised there were raised voices coming from the drawing room.

The Fowlers' cabin was smaller than Lady Redesdale's or Diana's but laid out in a similar fashion. There was a short entrance that led into a drawing room with French windows leading out, presumably, to a balcony – the long curtains had been closed. Ella rushed through into the drawing room, Louisa close behind her, and this time they saw Jim and Blythe, frozen and silent, winners in a game of musical statues.

Though stilled, they had not managed entirely to cool the heat of their argument. Blythe's face was flushed and Jim's jaw was pulsing with tension. Whatever they had been arguing about, it was more than a professional disagreement about how to polish the glass.

Ella spoke in a low voice, controlled yet threatening to tip into hysteria. 'Get out of here.'

Jim started to move, but she gripped his arm. 'Not you. *Her.*'

Blythe started to say something but stopped herself. Avoiding Louisa's glance, she ran out. The door banged shut.

Ella, still holding Jim's arm, turned to Louisa. 'What are you still doing here?'

Startled by the menace in her tone, Louisa chose not to ask her why but left quickly, too.

Outside the cabin, Louisa looked along the passage. It was lit by low electrical lights in the ceiling, more than enough to show the way in an emergency. It was completely silent – the carpets and thick metal doors that hung in every entrance and exit made sure of that. She had been distracted for too long and it was possible that Diana would have been telephoning for her, wondering whether Louisa would turn up to help her undress and ready for bed. It was surely too late now, she'd weather a ticking off in the morning. Lady Redesdale, she hoped, would be in deep sleep thanks to her migraine, and Unity . . . well, she'd cross her fingers for now that Unity had done as she was told. Louisa had no desire to knock on Unity's door and prompt either a waspish denial or a confession. It could wait until the morning when she would have calmed down.

But when she turned the corner she ran smack into Blythe. The young woman must have been waiting for her. Before Louisa could ask what Blythe wanted, she started to talk as if her lid had come off.

'It's not what you think. He loves me, I know he does. She won't let him go, and he's tried, I know he's tried.'

'Who?' Louisa shook her head. 'No, don't tell me. I don't think I want to know. I think you should go to bed. Things always look better in the morning.'

'Jim,' said Blythe impatiently, answering the first question and ignoring the rest. 'Jim loves me. We're going to get married and open a hotel by the sea.'

'Good for you.' Louisa tried to push past Blythe, but her arm was held.

'He's weak, that's all. And she's got money, she keeps spending it on him. He feels sorry for her. Says her husband is a bully. But I don't believe it, I think she likes twisting my Jim around her little finger. She's got something coming, thinking that.'

'Blythe,' said Louisa firmly. 'None of this is any of my business. I don't want to hear it. I strongly advise you get some sleep.'

Blythe's face crumpled. 'I've got no one to talk to on this blasted boat,' she said. 'Not when *she's* here. I thought you were one of us. I thought you'd understand.'

Louisa took pity on her then, but she was tired and she wanted to lie down, with Guy. Knowing he was there and waiting for her was beginning to cause a physical ache in her chest.

'I'm sorry,' Louisa said. 'I'm sure it must be hard, but I can't help you. I've got to get on. Please, go to bed and get some rest.'

Louisa gave Blythe's arm a tap and walked away. She only hoped the maid would take her advice, but otherwise decided she wouldn't give her a further thought. In any case, it was unlikely that she'd ever have anything to do with her again.

CHAPTER TWENTY

21 *May* 1935
Old Bailey, Court Number One

Guy had sat in several courtrooms in his years as a policeman. Most notably when he worked as a constable for the railway police at the start of his career and been a witness at the inquest into the death of Florence Nightingale Shore. Later, as constable for the London Metropolitan Police, Guy was instrumental in finding the murderer of Adrian Curtis and had had to withstand intense interrogation by the defence lawyers at the trial. Alongside DCI Stiles, his boss in the CID, Guy attended numerous proceedings, whether as witness or simply to observe, with satisfaction, the sentencing of a criminal they had caught.

This was different.

For a start, it was Court Number One. In spite of its cramped size, it was the most notorious and intimidating of all the courts at the Old Bailey. If it was a theatre, it would be the London Palladium, the place where the most famous and infamous of criminals were tried. In the dock that Guy could see in front of him now, dominating the room, had stood George 'Brides in the Bath' Smith, Frederick Seddon and Dr Crippen. Who, of the *Princess Alice* murder case that he had helped bring to trial today, would find their own place in the grisly annals of criminal history?

Guy stopped himself from this train of thought, too similar to the tabloid articles on the case. There had been a disturbing amount of press attention, dissecting every stage of his investigation, hauling his name into an uncomfortable spotlight. People he'd been to school with and forgotten about for years had read Guy's name as the arresting officer and wrote to ask him for seats at the trial. He'd been appalled at the prurient nature of those he'd otherwise thought of as nice, unassuming characters.

The witnesses had yet to step into the courtroom and they'd already been judged and convicted by the public, not for any crime but for the slightest detail of their past deemed morally dubious or shady. Guy prided himself on sticking to the letter of the law, to facts and evidence. He felt, in this instance, alone.

Nevertheless, he had to put his faith in the law. Right now, the law looked impressive. On the front bench, off-centre, sat Mr Justice Hogan, his red face and bulbous nose framed by the long white wig of stiff curls. Beside him was the London mayor in full regalia, asserting his right to be present at the opening proceedings, a privilege he had rarely taken advantage of in the past. To the left of the judge was the witness box, currently empty, and behind that the twelve members of the jury. These ten men and two women had finally been arrived at after an arduous procedure where various chosen members of the public had had to be dismissed for having been too close to the crime, knowing too much in advance, too influenced by the newspaper reports or even, in one case, suspected of blackmailing a witness. Thankfully, the jury member had been flushed out before trial could begin, but it had meant another delay. It was one of the reasons the case was being held in London and not Winchester Crown Court. If not the only one. Guy suspected something of a West End transfer behind the move.

Directly in front of the judge sat the stenographers, and to their right, the counsel's rows. These were, for once, jam-packed, not only with the barristers leading the prosecution and defence, but also with their serried ranks of juniors, pupils and colleagues, not to mention close friends who had doubtless begged for a seat. It was, therefore, of no surprise to Guy to see Miss Unity Mitford there. Her brother, Tom, was one of the junior barrister team working for Mr Terence Manners, K.C., the leading defence lawyer. Guy had met him only briefly in the past, not enough to form an opinion on his character, but he had seemed quieter and calmer than his sisters. At the bench now he looked young, shuffling and reshuffling the papers before him, alongside a pile of three or four thick books.

Manners, in his long black gown and short wig, cut an imposing but not frightening figure. He reminded Guy of a kindly but firm headmaster, one who would indulge the pranks of schoolboys, but only up to a point. Before him, on his table, were several bound files thick with papers, and he was even at this last minute scribbling further notes and passing them back to his juniors.

Also present was the second defence counsel, Mr Vangood. He looked out of his depth, a provincial barrister more used to being a big fish in a small pond. Here he had the look of an understudy called onto the stage to take a lead role with only minutes to spare. His stomach protruded from the gape of his gown, revealing a pinstriped suit with waistcoat and a gold watch chain, which was either old-fashioned or pretentious. Judging by his drinker's nose and half-moon specs, Guy bet on the former.

Finally, there was the prosecution lawyer, Mr Burton-Lands. The oldest of the three, in his mid-fifties, perhaps, he had dark hooded eyes that seemed not entirely unsympathetic. Stiles had whispered to Guy that Burton-Lands had published a book on stamp-collecting as a young man, but whether this was meant in his favour or against him Guy couldn't ascertain.

On the other side of the dock were the press benches, crammed with the usual oily types, pencils behind their ears, while up above in the public gallery were numerous women of all descriptions squeezed in together, many dressed in what looked like their Sunday best, looking for all the world as if they were having a grand day out. Guy had heard that some had paid ten pounds for their spot, held by men who had slept in the queue outside the Old Bailey overnight. Their eyes were turned in a single direction: to the dock, where sat the two accused prisoners and their guards.

CHAPTER TWENTY-ONE

The telephone was ringing and would not stop. Louisa held the earpiece up, shouting into it, but it kept on ringing and no matter what she did – even pulling the cord out of the wall – its jangling sound penetrated into her ears until it seemed to vibrate her skull.

Guy shook her and she awoke. The telephone was ringing and she picked it up.

'Louisa?' It was Diana. 'Were you asleep? You need to come up here straightaway. Bring Guy, too.'

'What is it?'

'I can't tell you on the telephone. Come, as fast as you can.'

Louisa replaced the handset and rubbed her eyes. She switched on the bedside light and winced at its brightness. Guy lay on the bed, half-blind without his glasses, his hair messy and his broad chest still warm. He'd been asleep when she'd got in and she didn't think she'd ever known anything so nice as climbing into that bunk with him already there. Bliss was always brief.

'That was Mrs Guinness,' she said. 'She wants us both to go up there. Something's happened.'

Guy sat up and reached for his glasses, putting them on before he spoke. By that time, Louisa had already got out of the bed and was starting to pull on her clothes.

'What's happened?'

'She wouldn't say, but she asked for you to be there, too.'

'Me?'

Louisa knew they were both thinking the same thing. Whatever had taken place, Diana thought a policeman needed to be there. 'Yes, come on. We'll get no rest till we find out. She's probably gone back to her cabin and not realised she left her bag in the bar and thinks it was stolen.' Louisa was trying to lighten the mood but the truth was, she knew it would be more serious than that. Diana was not frivolous or forgetful. As to what it could be, she didn't know.

Louisa's own corridor was quiet, but as soon as they reached the back stairs, they could hear that there was more activity than was usual for so late at night. It was two o'clock in the morning, and there were sometimes drinkers still in the bars, or even a few dancers by the piano, but something in the air made Louisa uneasy. Up on deck B, Louisa led Guy swiftly to the passage along which lay the cabins of Lady Redesdale, Unity and Diana. Here, several people were swarming about, some in striped pyjamas, some in crew uniform, some in evening dress. There was anxious chatter at a high fever pitch and one woman was crying, a man rubbing her back, ineptly comforting her. Louisa and Guy pushed past as quickly as they could, making their way to Diana's cabin. Louisa knocked and the door was opened by Unity, wearing a navy cotton dressing gown, her hair wrapped in a silk turban, her mouth pale and straight, devoid of its usual red lipstick. She said nothing but stepped aside to let them both in.

In the drawing room, Diana was sitting on the sofa, also wearing a dressing gown, but one which could have passed muster as an evening dress for a dance at Buckingham Palace, with a feathered brooch pinned at one shoulder and matching satin slippers with a small heel. Her face was clean but drawn. In spite of her youth and beauty, she was grey around the gills, thought Louisa, recalling an expression of her mother's.

'Joseph Fowler has been attacked,' said Diana. 'Horribly.'

Louisa felt as if an invisible hand had pushed her in the chest.

'Do you know who did it?' This was crucial. If it was an unknown attacker, there was someone on the ship who was – potentially – extremely dangerous.

'No,' said Diana, oblivious to the consequences of what she was saying. 'Ella was too hysterical to tell me anything. I'm not even clear as to whether she found him or someone else did.'

'Where is he now?'

'I suppose they must have some sort of sick bay on a ship like this.'

'Where was he attacked?' Guy had stepped forward and Louisa could see that his instinct had taken over, all other formalities to be ignored.

'Presumably where he was found. In his cabin.'

Louisa and Guy exchanged a glance. She stayed quiet.

'Where is his wife?' Guy asked.

Diana lit a cigarette and blew out the first puff of smoke. 'She called from her cabin so she must be there. I'm not unsympathetic, it's ghastly, of course. I simply don't want to get caught up in this.' She looked up at Louisa, furious. 'The Leader does not need this; he will not like it.'

'What did you do when she telephoned?' asked Louisa. Unity had walked around behind them and sat down on the opposite sofa; she lit a cigarette too. Louisa could feel the smoke settle on her hair and clothes.

Diana closed her eyes briefly, opening them again to talk. 'She wasn't making any sense on the telephone. She said she'd done him in, then she said he'd done it, naming no names. She was slurring, she sounded mad. I thought she was drunk or sleepwalking or something. I went down to her cabin, but then I saw . . . ' She broke off. 'I saw him in the chair, bleeding from his head. It was horrible.' She looked at Guy. 'Almost as soon as I got there, others rushed in, and I left. I didn't want to be in that room. I got back here and called Unity, then you.' She looked at Louisa. 'I needed company.'

'Why did you say Mr Sullivan needed to come too?'

'Because I don't want to have to be the one to talk to Mrs Fowler. I'd like Guy to do it. He's a policeman, isn't he?'

Louisa smarted at the use of his Christian name, the casual demotion of his rank from detective sergeant.

Guy started patting his pockets. He said quietly to Louisa, 'I don't have my notebook on me. Where can I find paper and a pen?'

She kept her attention on Diana but pointed to the desk in the corner of the room.

'What? For heaven's sake, are you taking notes? I told you: I don't want any part of this.' Diana stubbed out her cigarette, only half-smoked.

Guy turned from the desk, holding a pad of writing paper in

his hand, a pencil in the other. 'I have to,' he said. 'You might be a witness; you could have seen something important.'

'Why? You saw the man earlier, he obviously gets himself into fights. He'll get patched up, then he'll be back to his normal, awful self, won't he? It's not as if it's a murder investigation.'

'No,' said Guy. 'But if it turns into one . . .'

Unity stood up then, alarm on her face. 'Why are you saying that? Why?'

'It's best to be prepared,' was his reply.

Unity sat back down heavily. 'Muv is not going to like this at all,' she muttered.

'Mrs Guinness,' said Guy. 'I'm going to go to the Fowlers' cabin now. I will need to talk to you again about the telephone call and what you saw.'

Diana looked at him balefully. 'I'll get some sleep first, in that case. Louisa, telephone down for some hot milk, would you?'

Louisa and Guy locked eyes. She hoped this wasn't going to ruin their short time together, but she already had a sinking feeling that it would.

CHAPTER TWENTY-TWO

~~~~~~

This time, Guy used his badge. Thankfully, he never took it out of his inside suit pocket, so although he had dressed in a hurry, it was with him. He held it out as he walked into the cabin that Louisa had directed him towards, further along the same passage as Diana's. The guests in the hallway had started to drift away now, the remaining few in danger of revealing themselves as ghoulish tourists in dressing gowns.

The door to cabin B-17 was closed – all the doors on the *Princess Alice* swung shut automatically – but not locked. Guy pushed it open and stepped into a narrow entrance, with a further door opposite; to his left the entrance carried on, leading presumably to other rooms of this suite. It was cluttered with several coats and hats hanging up and shoes that were ineptly lined up against the wall. To his surprise, Guy could hear jazz music playing loudly. Quickly, firmly, Guy opened the door into the drawing room. Immediately he blinked: all the lights were on, making it bright enough that his eyes ached, but it did at least leave nothing to hide.

Guy took in the scene, trying to nail down as many details as he could in a few seconds. On the left-hand wall was a second open door that he assumed led to the bedroom, or bedrooms, and a bathroom. The room was comfortable and stylish, grander than anything in his own house but more modest than Diana Guinness's stateroom. Opposite the door he'd walked through were floor-to-ceiling curtains, dark yellow with a flower print, parted in the middle, and through the gap he could see only darkness on the other side of a clear panel of glass – French windows leading to a balcony, he assumed. In front of the curtains an armchair, the impression of a body that had been sitting in it still visible on the cushions. To the left of the chair there was a muddy-looking damp patch on the cream carpet that he wanted to inspect more closely. Otherwise, everything was in its place.

The real problem was the people swarming everywhere, all over the crime scene, talking in low voices, their eyes darting around. Mostly young men in white uniform so far as he could see. No one seemed to respond to his having entered the room until he caught the eye of a maid, her skin as white as the frilled apron she wore. She looked away quickly and turned towards a figure that Guy knew he should have noticed sooner.

This was Joseph Fowler's wife, he was sure, having seen her earlier, after the first punch-up of the evening, leaving with the older man to go to supper. She was no longer in her evening dress but in coffee-coloured satin pyjamas that had a dark stain on one of the trouser legs; her hair was unkempt and she had a glass of whisky in one hand. Most surprisingly of all, she seemed to be dancing – swaying – around the room, talking loudly and incoherently to no one in particular. As he watched, she grabbed the arm of one of the white-suited crew members and appeared to be trying to kiss him, the man putting his hands on her shoulders and trying to talk to her calmly. All this happened in a matter of seconds.

Standing by the armchair – his shoes too close to the stain on the carpet – also watching Mrs Fowler, was the man that Guy knew must be the captain. He was in full uniform, including the cap with its gold badge on the front. Guy walked over and stood a little to his side, hoping to make the captain move away from the incriminating spot on the carpet.

'Excuse me, sir, are you the captain of this ship?'

The man turned to Guy, his pockmarked skin weathered, his blue eyes faded to the colour of a winter's morning. 'What is it to you?' He had a German accent, but it was not strong.

'I'm DS Sullivan, I'm with the CID of the Metropolitan Police. I gather there's been an incident.'

The captain looked over at where Mrs Fowler was swaying by the gramophone player. There were loud squeaks as she scratched the needle on the record and he winced.

'Captain Schmitt.' He put out his hand for Guy to shake, but his eyes narrowed. 'Yes, there has been an incident. How is it you are here? Did you know this was going to happen?'

'No, sir, it's coincidence. I'm staying on your ship for a few days because my wife is here, working as a lady's maid for Lady Redesdale. I joined at Livorno and was planning to leave at Rome. Captain, can you tell me – are we further than twelve miles from land?'

'Considerably further; we cannot dock for another thirty-two hours.'

'And my understanding is that the man who has been attacked, Mr Joseph Fowler, is British?'

'*Ja*, that is my understanding too.'

'In that case, if there is a line of inquiry to pursue here, it falls under the jurisdiction of the British police. If there is no one else here, I think I had better take charge. Will you agree?'

Captain Schmitt nodded. He gestured to a crisply dressed young man beside him. 'This is the first officer, Mr Logan. He will assist you in any way you need. If you will forgive me, I must return to my post.'

'I will need to talk to you later,' said Guy.

'Absolutely.' The captain left, and on his signal three members of the crew followed him.

Guy knew he needed to talk to the maid and Mrs Fowler, but the likelihood of her telling him anything that would make sense was vanishingly small. He turned to the first officer, but before he could say anything, another man came into the cabin and walked straight towards Mrs Fowler, who put her arms around his neck, the remaining few drops of whisky sloshing out of the glass.

'Doctor,' she mumbled, 'doctor, I need you.'

'Mrs Fowler,' said the doctor, carefully removing her hands but keeping hold of her.

Guy went towards him and showed his badge. 'I'm Detective Sergeant Sullivan—' he started, but the doctor waved at him to stop.

'Mrs Fowler is in no state to say anything. I'm taking her to her bed and giving her morphia to calm her down.'

Mrs Fowler leaned heavily against the doctor as he said this. 'I did it, I did it,' she was saying. 'He's been killed.'

Guy was alarmed, but he wasn't going to stand in the doctor's way. The two of them walked through the door to the bedroom, the maid following behind.

CHAPTER TWENTY-THREE

There was no one in the room now but Guy and the first officer, who was standing by the drinks cabinet, undoing and redoing the button on his blazer. He stood a little straighter as Guy walked towards him.

'Mr Logan,' Guy began, then hesitated. 'Is that how I address you?'

'Yes, sir.'

'I don't know the ins and outs of ships – you'll have to forgive me if I say anything out of line. I need you to get rid of everyone in the passage outside – but carefully and taking note of their names in case I need to question anyone. Also, please make a note of the names of the crew who were here earlier with the captain. Has anyone touched anything in here?' He wanted to be professional, but he knew he was failing to keep the nerves out of his voice.

'I couldn't say for certain, but I don't think so, sir.'

'Do you know anything of the condition of Joseph Fowler?'

Logan touched the tip of his nose nervously. 'I believe he is unconscious, sir. He's in the ship's sanatorium. The doctor will know more.'

'He will, but he is occupied for now. I'd like you to call through for me, please, and ask the nurse for a report. Thank you,' he said, and when Logan hadn't moved: '*Quickly* now.'

Alone, Guy set to work as best he could. He had no fingerprint dusting powder, no blood-testing kit, no assistants. Without moving the curtains he looked through the glass, but it was dark outside and he could only make out the railings of the narrow balcony, with a small white iron table and two chairs.

Back in the room, the patch beside the armchair looked muddied, but further along he saw small spots, darkened to a deep rust red, missed by whoever had tried to clean the rest. He thought there might have been two or even three different spatter patterns, meaning Mr Fowler had been struck at least as many times on the left side of his head as he sat in the armchair, perhaps from behind. An empty tumbler was also by the chair, tipped on its side. Otherwise, there was little to tell a tale. It was the usual innocuous interior of the more expensive of the *Princess Alice*'s cabins, with cream carpet and printed blue wallpaper. The only jarring note was the folded blanket and pillow on the sofa.

Logan came back into the room as Guy became aware of a woman's voice: Mrs Fowler in the bedroom, or perhaps the maid. He needed to speak to them soon.

Logan confirmed that Joseph Fowler was alive but had not regained consciousness. Guy asked him to stand guard and ensure that no one came in. The second doorway in the drawing room, which he guessed led to the bedroom, also went through to the narrow passage, continuous from the front door. Someone could come in through the front door of the cabin and, by turning left, reach the bathroom and bedroom without needing to go through the drawing room.

Guy looked inside the bathroom, which had a light on over the sink. The walls were either glass or mirror, with black and white tiles on the floor and around the sides of the bath, everything gleaming. On the side of the sink was a cabinet with three drawers, with a mirrored box on top that contained a messy collection of what he assumed was Mrs Fowler's cosmetics. A wet flannel was scrunched up in the corner of the sink, there were streaks of grey on the soap and the toothpaste had its top off. She was not a natural housewife, perhaps.

He pulled back the bath curtain and saw that there was a sopping-wet man's waistcoat and jacket draped on the taps. Guy recognised these as the ones Joseph Fowler had been wearing earlier that evening.

Guy knocked on the bedroom door, which was closed. Within seconds, the young maid he had seen earlier peered around it. Guy could hear a low groan coming from behind her.

'I'm sorry, miss, but I need to speak to Mrs Fowler, if she's awake?'

The maid glanced behind her. 'She is awake,' she said, sounding as if she wasn't certain about this.

'I'm a detective with the CID,' explained Guy. 'I am taking control of an investigation into the attack on Mr Fowler. I need to know if Mrs Fowler saw anything.'

The maid spoke in a whisper that could barely be heard. 'She's in no fit state. She's been saying such terrible things, sir.' She looked at the floor as she spoke. 'Telling me *she* did it, then that it wasn't her, it was … well, I don't know who, sir. She seemed to start saying "sir", but who knows what she meant by that. She's not very clear.'

The maid stepped forward and pulled the door behind her a little. 'It's been a dreadful night, sir.' She trailed off at the repeat of the title and looked uncertainly at Guy.

Poor thing, he thought. She'd come to work on a ship to see the world, probably expecting to do nothing more complicated than any job requiring a feather duster.

CHAPTER TWENTY-FOUR

22 *May* 1935
Old Bailey, Court Number One

The prosecution counsel called Blythe North as their witness. She came in with her head bent down and when she spoke to take her oath, she was quiet enough for Mr Justice Hogan to be forced to ask her to speak up. She wore sombre clothes and little make-up, but something in the way she carried herself made Guy think she had designed herself to be noticed. She was strikingly pretty, with dark hair and a figure wrapped in a narrow cream coat that brought to mind starlets who traded on their 'girl next door' looks. No girl who looked like that had ever lived next door to anyone he knew.

Guy had met Blythe on the ship, but in the chaos of the attack and its aftermath, he had not noticed any of this. The marvel was how she had turned herself about completely – he almost might not have realised that the cabin maid he had interviewed then and the woman in the witness box now were one and the same.

Stiles leaned across to whisper, 'I hear she's landed a part in a play at the Haymarket that opens soon.'

Ah. That explained it.

Mr Burton-Lands asked Miss North to recount the facts of her whereabouts on the fated evening. This time her diction was beautifully clear and confident. She was an actress who knew how to respond to her director.

'I was working as a cabin maid on the *Princess Alice*. I had been employed by Empire Line for eight months.'

'One of the cabins you were assigned was that of Mr and Mrs Fowler?'

'Yes, I was the maid for ten of the cabins on the port side of the deck.'

'Where were you on the night in question?'

'I was preparing the rooms for the night. I did them while the guests were at dinner, switching some of the lamps off and turning down the covers, tidying up if needed.'

'At what time did you reach the Fowlers' cabin on that night?'

Blythe's voice remained steady. Guy could not help but admire her steeliness.

'About eleven o'clock. For the Fowlers, I would do the usual tasks but also put out a pillow and blanket on the sofa.'

'Why did you do that?'

'I believe it was because Mr Fowler slept there.'

Mr Burton-Lands turned his attention to the jury. 'Mr Fowler did not appear to share the bedroom suite with his wife but slept on the sofa.' Point made, he returned to Blythe. 'Were you alone as you worked in cabin B-17 that night?'

'No. Mr Evans was also working in there.'

'What was he doing?'

'He was clearing up the drinks cabinet, washing and polishing the glass.'

Mr Burton-Lands then faced the jury and, as if he was asking them the question, said: 'And what happened to interrupt your work?'

'Mrs Fowler came in, earlier than expected.'

'Earlier? How did you know her routine?'

'They always took the same cabin and I'd been their maid before,' said Blythe. 'We always prepared their cabin last and usually she would return from dinner at about half-past ten or thereabouts. Occasionally to retire to bed, but more often to powder her nose before leaving again to join one of the parties that were happening on the ship.'

'Was Mrs Fowler usually with her husband when she came back after dinner?'

'No. Once or twice she mentioned that he had gone to the smoking room for a cigar.'

'Did she say where he was on this night?' Mr Burton-Lands' demeanour was entirely calm.

'She was distressed when she came in and said there had been an argument. I didn't hear much more than that for she told me to leave.'

'Had you finished your work?'

'No, but there was no staying. She wanted me out of there.'

'Leaving only her and Mr Evans in cabin B-17?'

'Yes,' said Blythe, dropping her head.

Mr Burton-Lands swept a glance over the men and women who were sitting in the press benches, each of whom was writing furiously. A great deal of what he said was likely to end up being quoted under large headlines tomorrow. It could put pressure on a man.

'Were you aware of any relationship between Mr Evans and Mrs Fowler?'

'Yes,' said Blythe, her voice barely louder than a whisper.

'Did you speak to your fellow worker, Mr Evans, about it?'

'I tried, because I knew he'd get in trouble with the captain if it were ever discovered. But he told me it wasn't my business and I had to stay out of it.'

'Did he express any intention of ending the relationship?'

'No, sir.' Blythe turned the jury. 'I knew she was trouble—'

'Objection.' This came from Mr Vangood, Jim's defence counsel.

The judge barely looked up but raised his hand. 'Objection upheld.'

'Continue,' said Burton-Lands, gently.

'Mrs Fowler came back from her dinner, with Lady Redesdale's lady's maid, and dismissed me from the room, and as hers had been the last cabin I needed to do, I went straight to my own. I was tired and looking forward to some sleep.' She gave a wan smile as if she was just as tired today. 'I lay on my bunk and only managed to take my shoes off. That sometimes happened. The maids did long hours on the ship.'

Blythe kept talking. Guy wished she'd get to the point.

'I was woken up by the telephone in my room and it was Mrs Fowler. I couldn't absolutely make out what she was saying. She sounded ... ' Blythe gave a glance at the woman in the dock. 'Drunk, sir. She was crying and telling me to come to the room quickly.'

'What time was this?'

'I think it was half-past midnight. I couldn't say for sure. I only knew I didn't think I'd got much sleep. I splashed some water on my face and put my shoes on and hurried down there ...' Her voice petered out.

'I'm sorry, Miss North. I know it is hard to talk about. A minute or two more, if you would. What did you find when you returned to the cabin?'

Blythe's eyes filled with tears. 'Mr Fowler, he was ... I thought he was asleep, he was in the armchair, and his head was back. I heard him sort of moaning, and then I saw ...' She hiccuped slightly. 'He had a towel wrapped around his head and it was covered in blood. I saw blood on the carpet.'

Mr Burton-Lands let her pause for a moment, but no longer. 'Please tell the court everything you can remember.'

'Mrs Fowler was pulling off his jacket and his waistcoat, she was shouting, and she gave them to me and told me to rinse them out.'

'Why did she tell you to do that?'

'To get the blood out. It stains if it sets, but cold water, quick as possible, gets it out. And she told me to scrub out the blood on the carpet. She was saying something about her boys, how this would destroy them, she didn't want them to see this.'

'Her boys?'

'I assumed she meant her children.'

'They were not on the ship, were they?'

'No, sir. I believe they were left at home with a nanny.' She turned to the jury. 'You hear a lot when you're a maid. People often forget you're even in the room.'

'Did you do as she asked?'

'Yes, but I couldn't clean the carpet properly, she was hurrying me up. I was confused; I wasn't sure if I should be doing it or not.' She looked up and seemed to think, as if she was going to say more, but then didn't.

'Had she called a doctor?'

'I think she must have done. He arrived less than ten minutes after I did.'

Mr Justice Hogan put his hand up. 'We'll stop there, Miss North. The court will adjourn for luncheon. We shall resume in an hour.'

CHAPTER TWENTY-FIVE

W alking away, Guy gathered his thoughts: Joseph Fowler
had been struck on the head, with what he did not
know; whether Mrs Fowler had called the doctor or the maid
first, he couldn't be certain, but the doctor arrived some time
after Blythe; yet why did the doctor take so long to arrive? Guy
would have to ask him about that. In the doctor's absence, Mr
Fowler's head had been wrapped in a towel and his jacket and
waistcoat rinsed out. A bloodstain on the carpet had also been
partially scrubbed out. Mrs Fowler then called Diana and told
her what had happened, and asked her to come – why? After the
doctor, the captain and some of the crew arrived at the cabin.
Instead of being stricken and bereft, Mrs Fowler appeared to
have thrown something of a party in her pyjamas, getting drunk
on whisky and playing records on the gramophone. Now she
was drugged by morphia and talking incoherently in her bed
about having done the deed herself, or possibly that it had been
committed by 'sir' – did that mean 'Sir Somebody' or a 'sir', as
Guy himself would be addressed? He couldn't gauge what class

she was – he'd detected an accent, probably American – and therefore it was possible she would address any senior man as 'sir'. Louisa had mentioned that there was a Sir Clive on the ship, that he had lost a fortune on Joseph Fowler. Was that it? He'd have to dig for those details.

Speculation wasn't useful right now. What he needed to know was who had been in the room when the attack happened. In short: who were the likely suspects if there was anyone other than Mrs Fowler present? Who had been first on the scene?

Mrs Guinness.

After hurriedly telling Logan to remain at his post and to fetch him immediately from Mrs Guinness's suite if there was any immediate change in the situation, Guy marched along the passage and knocked on her door. Louisa opened it, but instead of letting him in, she stepped outside and held the door almost shut behind her.

'She's fallen asleep,' she said.

'I need to talk to you, Louisa, and Mrs Guinness.'

'What's happened?'

'I will tell you, but there's too much to explain and I can't shake this feeling that I need to make my investigations now, as soon as possible.'

'Investigations?'

'Yes. Whatever happened to Joseph Fowler, he didn't walk into a door, to say the least. Are you sure Mrs Guinness can't talk to me now?'

'Well, I . . .' Louisa turned and pushed the door open. 'Take a look for yourself.'

Guy stepped in and gingerly looked through the second door into the drawing room. Diana was stretched out on the sofa, a blanket over her, her golden hair loose and on the cushion she had pulled beneath her head. There was a light snoring noise.

'It will have to wait, then.' He couldn't keep the frustration out of his voice. 'Did she say anything to you earlier?'

Louisa shook her head. 'She was more concerned about the news of her being on the ship when this happened affecting the Leader's reputation in some way. But if Mr Fowler survives this attack, I doubt news of it will get out, don't you?'

'I've no idea. What about Miss Unity? Did she see anything?'

'I don't think so. She's gone back to her cabin to sleep. She was reluctant, but I persuaded her. She doesn't like to miss any drama.' Louisa took Guy's hand. 'I'd better stay here, try to move Mrs Guinness into bed, then I'll come and find you.'

He recognised her tone: she wanted him gone. He knew he should ask her about having been with Mrs Fowler earlier, but he decided he would find a better moment. Instead, he gave Louisa's hand a squeeze and walked back to cabin B-17.

CHAPTER TWENTY-SIX

G uy returned to the bedroom. Forewarned, Mrs Fowler
was sitting up on the bed, though not in it. She was in
the same pyjamas, with a matching coffee-coloured dressing
gown over the top and her toenails painted a dark red. Guy
was reminded of the spots of blood on the cream carpet in the
next-door room. Her face had been washed, leaving her pale,
but in spite of the dark hollows beneath her eyes, her good looks
were vivid. She clutched a heavy glass of clear liquid and started
when Guy came in, spilling a drop on her stomach.

'Mrs Fowler. I'm Detective Sergeant Sullivan.'

She said nothing; her eyes reverted to their glassy stare. The
maid stood up as if to leave, but Guy stopped her.

'I'll need you to stay, Miss North.'

She nodded miserably and sat back down.

Guy took out his notebook. 'Mrs Fowler, as the attack on your
husband happened at sea, it falls under the jurisdiction of the
British police, and the captain has agreed that I should make
any necessary inquiries. Mr Fowler is seriously unwell. If there's a

slight chance that this is going to turn into a murder investigation, then it's vital to get as much information at this stage as I can.'

At this, Ella looked up sharply, her eyes focusing on Guy with an alertness he'd not seen before. 'Murder?'

'Not yet, Mrs Fowler, and I hope very much it doesn't come to that, but if it does . . . ' He trailed off, attacked by guilt that he may have made more of this than he should have done. Was his ambition getting the better of him? Guy didn't have a chance to pursue this line of thought because Ella started raving.

'Oh God, oh God. He lived too long. I did it, you know I did. I did it. I did it with a mallet. It's hidden. You won't find it.'

'Mrs Fowler . . . ' Guy didn't know whether to write this down or try to calm her. She was intoxicated, that much was clear: no statement she made now would stand up in court. Nevertheless, he needed to ask her what had happened because if there was an attacker loose on the ship, he needed to be found.

The maid stood up, hovering and uncertain. He didn't give her a signal one way or another. Truth was, he was uncertain, too. Meanwhile, Mrs Fowler carried on, waving her glass around, drinking from it and mumbling, incoherently for the most part, with the occasional phrase shouted out more clearly.

'Mrs Fowler,' Guy said as firmly as he could, as if trying to waken her out of a semi-conscious state. 'Can you tell me what happened this evening?'

She started trembling then and dropped her now empty glass onto the bed. 'He told me he wanted to die; he *dared* me to kill him. I picked up the mallet and he told me I hadn't the guts to do it.' She looked up at Guy, her eyes wild. 'If I'd had a gun, I'd have shot him. I tell you, I would have.' Then she buried her face in her hands and gave a loud sob. 'Is he dead, is he?'

151

'No, Mrs Fowler, he isn't. He may yet live. He could tell the tale.' Would she understand the threat behind this? Would it *be* a threat to her?

'Oh God.' She lay back and closed her eyes, and this time the maid did not wait for Guy to tell her what she could or could not do and started to pat a cold flannel on Mrs Fowler's face, calling her name urgently, but Mrs Fowler would not be roused.

The maid looked back at Guy. 'Do you think she did it?' she whispered.

Guy gave no answer to this in voice or gesture. Mrs Fowler wasn't going to give him the coherent replies he needed.

Having instructed the maid not to leave Mrs Fowler's side, Guy went back out to the drawing room. First Officer Logan was still standing at the entrance. He confirmed that he had received no telephone call to indicate a change in Joseph Fowler's condition but was concerned that the doctor wouldn't call through.

'I'm sorry,' said Guy, 'but I'll need you to go back there and ask them. If he looks like he's regaining consciousness, I must know. Press this point on the doctor, would you? I'll stay here until you return.'

Left alone, he scanned the room again. Mrs Fowler had talked about a mallet. If that was here, there was a chance he would find the weapon and, as any policeman knew, that could lead directly to the culprit – whether it was Mrs Fowler or not. He knew that he had Mrs Fowler's admission, but it wasn't clear-cut – she'd said to him, and Mrs Guinness, that 'he' had done it, hadn't she? – and this instability of hers worried him. He needed hard facts.

Before Guy could get started on a forensic assessment of the scene there was the sound of someone coming in through the hall. He went to the door expecting to see Logan, but it was Louisa. She kissed him quickly and looked at him with concern.

'Mrs Guinness has gone to bed at last. She didn't say any more about what she saw earlier. Will you tell me what has happened? You look washed out.'

'Do I? I'm tired, that's all,' he said.

'May I see?' She started to walk through into the drawing room.

'Louisa, careful. That is, it's a crime scene. There were people everywhere when I got here; I got them cleared out. I was about to try to make a proper note of what's what.'

'Do you think things have been moved?'

'It's possible.'

She walked through but stopped almost as soon as she had crossed the threshold. 'Was that blood there?'

'Most likely, and someone has tried to wash it out.'

They gave each other a meaningful look.

'Where is Mrs Fowler?' asked Louisa. 'Do you know her part in this, if any?'

'No.' Guy cast his eyes in the direction of the other door. 'She's in the bedroom and she's not in a good way.'

'No, I shouldn't think she is.' Louisa started to move through the room slowly, as if avoiding cracks in a pavement.

'Have you been in here before?' asked Guy.

'For less than a minute. I happened to bump into Mrs Fowler earlier this evening and brought her back here, but she dismissed me as soon as we got here.'

'Why didn't you mention this?'

'There hasn't been a moment, has there? It's not as if I knew it would be important and you were asleep when I got into bed.'

Guy couldn't argue against this. 'Tell me: when you saw her, what was her mood?'

'She was upset. She'd had a row with Mr Fowler and she wasn't very clear, but she seemed to suggest that he wanted her to do something awful ... ' Louisa trailed off, embarrassed to spell it out.

'To do what exactly?'

'To go to bed with the man he owed money to, to clear the debt somehow. She didn't want to do it.'

'I should hope not,' said Guy, eyebrows raised.

Louisa gave him a world-weary look. 'It happens. I got the feeling it wasn't because she was morally against the idea, though I suppose it could have been. I think it was more to do with her affair with Jim.'

'Of course,' said Guy, 'there was that fight in the bar earlier. Perhaps it continued later and got out of hand?'

Before they could discuss it any further, there was a timid knock at the door and Logan came in.

'Sir?'

'Come in. What's the report?'

'The doctor says it's not looking good, sir. He's lost a lot of blood and they can't see him regaining consciousness. It's a matter of hours, he says.'

Guy ran his hands through his hair. 'Right. Would you mind staying by the entrance? If anyone wants to come in, ask me first.' Guy turned to Louisa. 'In short, then, in a few hours it's a murder inquiry.'

'Oh God.' She looked unsteady and he put his arm around her shoulders. 'He wasn't a nice man, I don't think, but I wouldn't have wished this ending on him. They have a son, a six-year-old boy. I think there's another boy, too, from her previous marriage. What will happen to them?'

'I don't know, but perhaps those boys are the reason we need to find out the truth.'

'We?'

Guy kissed her on the cheek. 'Force of habit. But as we're both here, I don't see why not? I'd like you to assist me, if you can. You see things I miss. We could be unbeatable together, don't you think?'

She gave a small smile, but she cast her eyes away as she did so.

CHAPTER TWENTY-SEVEN

An hour later, Louisa was curled up on the sofa fast asleep, the pillow that had been intended for Joseph Fowler under her head. It was four o'clock in the morning, and though the ship's interior was warm, Guy felt a cold shiver run through him, a combination of tiredness and the expenditure of nervous energy that had been propelling him for the last few hours. His stomach rumbled; supper seemed like a long time ago and breakfast even further away. If he could have a cup of hot coffee he could keep going easily. Not much chance of that, somehow. He'd searched for the mallet all over the sitting room, not that there were many places to look: under the sofa, in the drinks cabinet, behind some books on a shelf. Then he had tried the hall, such as it was, with its coats hanging up and a couple of cupboards for shoes. Finally, he had looked in the bathroom again, but that had yielded nothing of interest beyond Joseph Fowler's sock garters and Ella's numerous face creams. (Though the jacket and waistcoat were still sopping wet – why had they been rinsed out in the bathroom and not sent to the laundry?)

If the confession about the mallet was true – it struck him as an odd thing for Ella to have had to hand; he needed to find out where it had come from – it must have been thrown overboard. He made detailed notes about the position of the furniture, the blood spatter, the damp patch, the spilled drink. He tried to imagine all the different questions DCI Stiles would ask about the situation and answer them as comprehensively as possible. There was someone – Guy was uncertain of his rank – keeping guard outside, and the maid was asleep in the chair beside Mrs Fowler, who was also sleeping, but fitfully, judging from the jerks of her body he'd seen when he'd put his head around the door. If she was the person who had attacked her husband, he didn't think she'd be doing the same to anyone else tonight. Perhaps he should rouse Louisa and get them back to the cabin: a couple of hours' kip might be in good order.

It wasn't to be.

Logan came in, his young and handsome face rubbed away by the ordeal of the night. 'Sir, can you come with me? Something's happened that I think might concern you.'

'What is it?'

'There's a report of a man . . . It's someone who appears to be hiding in a place they shouldn't be. Given the events of tonight, I thought—'

'You thought right, Mr Logan. Thank you.'

Throwing a worried look at Louisa, Guy decided it was best to let her carry on sleeping – with luck she wouldn't wake before his return – and closed the cabin door firmly behind them.

In the dead of night, the ship was eerily quiet and calm. Logan led Guy hastily along the carpeted passage that seemed to stretch on for miles. Guy had spent some time looking for Louisa when he had arrived the day before – could it be only twelve hours he had been on this ship? – but he had the distinct feeling that he had barely scratched the surface of what was there. It felt, to him, as large as the *Titanic*, though he hardly dared think the name, let alone say it out loud, like actors superstitiously never saying 'Macbeth' backstage. But the solidity of it, the vastness of it, the semi-conscious knowledge that there were ballrooms, luggage rooms, boiler rooms, kitchens, mess rooms, a smoking room, tennis courts, hundreds of guests and even more staff, all somehow floating, even *sailing* through miles and miles of deep, freezing water with land not even a speck in the distance ... it was difficult to comprehend.

Even as Guy had been thinking all this, Logan had maintained his fast pace, and now they were walking down several flights of stairs, with Guy picturing large sharks with gleaming white teeth on the other side of the metal hull. Eventually they reached what felt like the bottom. It was dark and noisy with the sound of clanking engines and hissing steam. There were workers visible, though not many – they had barely seen a soul on the way down – and they looked dirty, sweat patches on their backs and fronts, wide black trousers with grease stains, their hair slicked back.

'Is he in here?' Guy said, then realised he had to shout. He repeated himself more loudly.

'We think so – noises were heard,' Logan shouted back. Then he stopped and leaned in more closely to Guy, in order to talk at a more normal volume. 'We find stowaways in here sometimes. Someone reported a person they couldn't identify.'

'Vulnerable?'

Logan had started to move away. He leaned back. 'What?'

'You said they were hiding somewhere they shouldn't be?'

'Yes,' Logan agreed. 'It's dangerous in here. You've got to know where you can go safely. Only a selected few know about this place.' He said, with emphasis: 'It's not somewhere to chase a man.'

'Right. I understand,' said Guy. He felt exposed too, like a soft-shell crab. 'Is there someone who can help us?'

Logan didn't reply to this. He had picked up his fast pace again and Guy knew that too much time had been lost already. They were winding their way through tight spaces, between hissing metal pipes and containers that were piled and twisted around them like sleeping dragons, until they reached a darker, cooler corner. Guy tried not to think about the fact that if the boat sank, they'd be the first to drown, nor did he have any idea how to find the stairs back out of there.

Logan stopped and a man came out of the shadows. Guy's eyes, poor at the best of times, adjusted slowly as he tried to make out more than what appeared at first to be all sinewy, shining muscles and skin. The man said nothing but indicated they should follow him. He disappeared into the darkness but in less than a second had opened a door, revealing light, and gone through it.

Guy followed behind Logan and found they were in what looked like a narrow passage, dimly lit, with another door at the far end. He couldn't tell if it was locked or not, but it looked solid and most definitely shut. It was warm but not oppressively hot, and when he turned slightly to the right, Guy realised that what he had at first taken to be a wall was metal shelving that held boxes of various shapes and sizes, each one with a large number painted on the side.

'The ship's toolkits,' said Logan quietly.

There was a vertical gap in the middle of the metal shelving and Guy saw that the wall was several yards further back. They heard a scrape of metal and they all looked at each other.

'Hello,' Guy called out, trying to keep his voice light and friendly. As if anyone hiding behind several metal boxes in the depths of an enormous ship's boiler room was playing a child's game, waiting to be found so they could all go and eat ice-cream afterwards.

'You need to come forward. You're not in any trouble.' *Yet.* 'We think you might be able to help us.'

There was no sound. Guy had identified the thing of which they had to be afraid: in those toolboxes could be found any number of potentially fatal weapons. If the man hiding here had been the same one who attacked Joseph Fowler earlier, leaving him for dead, who was to say what he might do to anyone else, or even himself, if cornered, with a rope-cutting knife or a thick iron spanner in his hand. Guy was trying desperately to size the situation up and take control when there was an almighty crash, and something heavy fell on him. There was a sharp pain on the side of his head, then nothing.

PART TWO

CHAPTER TWENTY-EIGHT

When Louisa woke in the Fowlers' cabin it took a second or two to remember where she was. She had fallen fast into a deep sleep and coming out of it made her briefly dizzy. Someone had turned off the overhead light, but the large lamp on the console table was on and she winced at its brightness. Slowly, Louisa wiped her face with her hands, catching a small gathering of spit at the corner of her mouth, smoothed her hair down and pulled out her dress, which had wrinkled and bunched around her thighs. There was the heavy silence in the cabin that had almost become familiar, the weight of noiseless air and dense water that surrounded the ship. She looked at her watch: it was almost five o'clock in the morning. The sun had not risen yet, but it wouldn't be long. Where had Guy gone to?

She wondered if she ought to tell Iain somehow about what had happened last night. It wasn't connected to Diana or Unity as far as she knew, but she felt confused as to whether she was supposed to tell him only about them or anything that could potentially be of significance. She ought to tell him about Unity and Wolfgang, though. He was an SS officer, wasn't he? Louisa exhaled loudly and sat up straighter, as if she had been startled by the sound. Oh, *where* was Guy? She had a vague feeling that she shouldn't leave the cabin, but remain as a sort of guard. On the other hand, she didn't want to stay.

A tiny sound came from beyond the wall behind her and reminded Louisa that Ella Fowler was in the bedroom. This was her opportunity to look closely. She might see something that Guy had missed. There had been a lot of people in here, he'd said – they may not have realised that it was a crime scene that needed to be protected. Things might have been unwittingly moved or brushed aside. At the thought of this task, all of Louisa's senses simultaneously sharpened. She tasted the bitter dryness of her mouth, absorbed the light and shade of the room, smelled the vase of lilies in the corner and heard the thick silence. She ran her hand over the stiff linen covering on the sofa and pushed herself up to standing. As quietly and efficiently as she could, she scanned every inch of the room, then went down on her knees to look underneath the sofa, revealing only an abandoned cocktail stick and a used tissue. The paintings on the wall did not conceal secret cupboards and the mirror definitely only worked one way. She started to feel foolish, as if she had thought herself in real life and realised it was only a set with props. Even the books on the shelves were artfully placed, with titles that didn't go together and that no one would ever read: *Great Golf Courses of Germany* and *The Flora and Fauna of Mallorca*. One cupboard didn't open and only after a minute or two did she realise it wasn't locked but had a fake door – there were no hinges.

She tried to take note of the things that were real. The

impressions on the armchair that showed where Mr Fowler had been sitting when he was attacked. The damp, dark red patch on the carpet, looking more like paintwork in a farmyard. There were fashion magazines on a low table that had been scattered and an upset glass.

All the while, the dawn slowly started to crack on the horizon, the light gradually fading up through the gap in the curtains that shielded the French windows to the balcony. Why was there a gap in the curtains? Louisa knew they would have been closed for the night by the maid who came to prepare the room for the evening. If either Ella or Joseph had wanted to go onto the balcony to take in the sea air, they would have opened them wide, then closed them when they came back in. The narrow open strip puzzled Louisa and she stared at it as the sun's cool morning rays turned the sky from dark violet to pink and orange. The handle for the door was visible in the gap and Louisa knew the French windows opened from the middle, but they slid to the side rather than opening out. There were shutters on the outside but Louisa had registered that the maid never closed the ones for either Lady Redesdale or Mrs Guinness. Perhaps they were only intended for use during storms.

Louisa stepped towards the glass and looked through it to the narrow balcony outside, but it was empty bar a small table and two chairs. She jumped, startled, when the door behind her opened abruptly and she heard someone walking in. She turned around and knew she looked guilty, as if she had seen something she shouldn't have, but the young man before her did not seem to notice.

'Miss,' he said, 'I've been sent to fetch you and send you down to the sick bay. It's your husband.'

Fear tipped over her like a bucket of cold water. 'What do you mean? What's happened?'

The cabin steward, innocent in his pressed white uniform, looked afraid. 'I don't know, miss, sorry. I've been told to find you and tell you to get there quickly. It's on deck E, next to the engineers' mess. If you take the crew staircase, you'll reach it quicker. I've been told to stay here, to guard the room.' He looked at her again. 'Sorry, miss.'

He didn't need to say any more, or if he did, Louisa didn't hear it. She had fled the room and was running towards the crew staircase, deck E and her husband as if his life depended upon it.

CHAPTER TWENTY-NINE

～～

G uy was awake when Louisa came into the room. The lights
were low and there were two single beds with only one
occupied, by her husband. She saw him try to shift himself to sit
upright, but immediately she put a hand gently on his shoulder,
to let him know to rest. With her hand still there, she asked the
doctor what had happened.

'He had a sudden blow on the back of his head, I believe. It
was a nasty shock and he was knocked out for a minute or two,
but I daresay he will be fine now. You'll need to watch out in
case he gets a headache later and let me know if he does as it
could be a sign of concussion. Otherwise, he only needs to rest.'
Dr O'Donnell's thin face was beginning to look in need of a
shave and strands of hair kept falling into his eyes. It had been
a long night.

'You poor darling.' Louisa turned to Guy. 'Do you know
who did it?'

'I don't think it was deliberate,' answered the doctor. 'He was
in the boiler room – a piece of machinery fell on him.'

'Ow,' Louisa couldn't help exclaiming. 'What were you doing down there?'

Guy lifted his head a little and spoke hoarsely. 'Trying to find someone. There'd been reports of a man hiding out in the boiler room and, given what had happened earlier, there was a feeling that I ought to be involved.'

'Did you find him?'

Guy sank back into the pillow. 'I don't know. You need to ask Mr Logan.' He screwed his eyes shut and opened them again. 'Doctor, when may I get up, do you think?'

The doctor looked at his watch. 'It's a little before six o'clock in the morning. I'd say you'll be fine for breakfast at eight. But I do not want you overdoing it.' He smoothed his hair back impatiently. 'I need to try to rest too. I'll be back later.'

'Wait, what about Joseph Fowler?' asked Guy.

'He's still alive but only just, I'd say. The nurse is under strict instructions to find me if anything in his condition changes.' With that, he left the room, closing the door behind him.

'I've only got a couple of hours myself,' said Louisa. 'Lady Redesdale will want me at eight. Tell me what you need me to do and I'll do it.'

Louisa ran through the list in her mind again and decided that the first thing she absolutely *had* to do wasn't on there. She needed to contact Iain. Although he had instructed her that it was likely anything she had to tell him could wait until her return to London, he had given her an address for a telegram in case anything needed to be urgently relayed. Louisa decided that the events of last night were something Iain needed to know. He had instructed her to report on anything unusual, after all. Tucked into the side of her brassiere was the small piece of folded paper with an address in elegant writing. Louisa went to the telephone room, where the woman at the desk sleepily asked her for the name and address of the recipient: Miss Vita Lowning of 23 Dolphin Square. In the telegram, Louisa could not spell out any details, merely send a coded message that he had told her to use beforehand. It meant that, if he could, he would find a way for her to be contacted so that she could tell him, or a trusted messenger, whatever it was she thought he needed to know. At the time, Iain had stressed that this was only to be used if it was absolutely vital.

Louisa's heart beat as she arranged for the considerable cost of the telegram to be billed to Unity's cabin. She'd have to sort out any problems with that further down the line; hopefully it would be sent to Lord Redesdale. Was she right? Was it something Iain would need to know about? The only thing that could be worse would be if she didn't tell him and he was angry with her for it. That decided the matter.

'Yes, miss? What's the message?' asked the telephonist, inspecting her fingernails at the same time.

'Please send: *Clouds gathering. Stop. Twenty-four-hour forecast. Stop. From C.*'

The telephonist raised an eyebrow. 'That's it?'

'Yes,' said Louisa, 'that's it. As soon as you can, please.'

Next, Louisa went to find Mr Logan. Guy had told her he was the first officer, so she assumed that the best place to find him might be the captain's office. When she went there, however, the door was firmly shut and though she pressed her ear to the door, she could hear nothing inside. As she was wondering what to do next, a middle-aged man in crew uniform approached.

'Can I help you, madam?'

She couldn't help bristling slightly – did she look old enough to be a 'madam'?

'I'm looking for First Officer Logan,' she said. 'It's a police matter.'

'Are you a policewoman?' The man couldn't keep the surprise out of his voice.

'Yes ... that is, no, I'm not. But there's a policeman on the ship, injured, and he's asked me to find Mr Logan, to ask him something.'

'That funny business, I suppose,' said the man, chummy now. It was a ship, after all – gossip spread faster than burning petrol. 'I heard they caught someone. They're being held in the ship's cell, cabin E-131. It's starboard side. Do you know what side that is?'

'Yes,' said Louisa, disheartened at the thought of all those stairs again. 'Thank you.' She started to walk off but turned back. 'Do you know who they caught?'

The man tapped the side of his nose with his finger and looked around them in an exaggerated manner before standing up straight and laughing. 'No idea, miss. You get stowaways and all sorts on a ship like this. If you ask me, it's a miracle something like this hasn't happened sooner. Or maybe it has and they've hushed it all up.' He tapped his nose again. 'You need to watch out for them, they hide all sorts of secrets you couldn't even guess at.' Then he winked and walked off.

They? Who did he mean? Louisa was spooked. Did he know something or was he stirring up trouble, taking advantage of the disturbed atmosphere on the ship? Was it possible that Iain had sent Louisa onto the ship to follow Diana and Unity, while knowing there were other dangers aboard?

There was only one way to find out.

CHAPTER THIRTY

I n the violet darkness of the early morning the ship stirred
to life. The guests were largely still in their cabins, some of
whom had been disturbed by the events on deck B, but most of
whom were sleeping off large dinners and strong drinks from
the night before. The ship would not dock until the following
morning and there were few reasons to hurry out of bed. But the
staff were busy, cleaning the common areas, laying the tables in
the restaurants and swabbing the decks, one of the few authen-
tically ship-like activities that went on. Through the portholes,
Louisa saw that the dawn had almost broken; the calm sea was
gunmetal grey, the sky a clear blue. Seeing the morning made
her realise she'd hardly slept, and her dress felt grubby. She'd
have liked the time to nip to her cabin to change.

Having made her way around most of the ship in the few days
she'd been there, Louisa had come to understand something
of the logistics of how the cabin numbers were arranged, and
how the passages and stairwells were interlinked, so without too
much trouble she found Cabin E-131, the ship's cell. Standing

outside the cabin was another man, younger this time, in a white uniform with fewer gold stripes and buttons than the captains and senior crew members bore.

'Excuse me,' said Louisa, 'can you tell me where to find First Officer Logan?'

The man stayed rigidly upright, as if he were standing guard outside Buckingham Palace. Without moving his head to face her, he said, 'Cabin E-132.'

'Thank you,' said Louisa, puzzled. She felt like a child in a fairy story, being sent hither and thither by talking woodland creatures to find the gingerbread house. She knocked on the door, the man's eyes quickly glancing away when she looked up at him, and it was opened by another man in uniform, who looked weary but not hostile.

'Mr Logan? I'm Mrs Sullivan, the wife of DS Sullivan, who I believe you met earlier ... '

'Come in.' He stepped back and Louisa followed him into what was a small cabin with no bed, only a desk and a chair. There was an interlocking door at the side, which she presumed led to E-131. 'How is he? That was a nasty bang to the head he got.'

'Fine, thank you. The doctor says he can get up for breakfast in a couple of hours, but he's not to overdo it. I've come down because my husband was eager to know what happened last night. As am I.'

'Please, won't you take a seat?'

Louisa sat down and realised too late there was only the one chair. Now Mr Logan would be standing and talking to her, which felt awkward, but it was too late to stand up again.

'I do hope you will forgive me for having called your husband to the situation, but it seemed necessary at the time and I think we were proved right.'

'Yes, Mr Logan, I do understand the difficulty of these things.' She felt calm and grown-up now. It was some time since anybody, other than Guy, had spoken to her as an equal and worthy of respect. It made her warm to him quickly while also making her feel self-conscious.

'There were reports of someone in the boiler room and, more seriously, in the tool room, which sits beyond it and which few staff are even aware of. As you can imagine, it contains some expensive and specialised equipment. We know that there are crew who sometimes feel the need to get away for a little while and this is – unofficially – tolerated. But the tool room can be accessed only by unlocking a padlock, and there is a list of people who are given the code to do this. Furthermore, anyone who goes in there must sign a record that is hanging outside the door, and inside, a logbook for any tools that are removed. In short, it is a highly supervised area.'

'I see.' Louisa's neck was starting to ache from looking up at Mr Logan. He seemed to notice this and perched on the desk casually, reducing both the gap and the formality. She breathed out.

'The thing is, Mrs Sullivan, I don't have much experience of handling criminals. We have had the occasional petty thief on board. Most memorably, an elderly lady who stayed in first class and was fond of pocketing light bulbs. Perhaps you'll understand if I was hesitant to apprehend a man who had been responsible for a brutal attack on one of our guests only hours before.'

Louisa understood.

'I fetched your husband and we made our way down to the

boiler room. It's a hot and dark place, not the most pleasant of places to work, and it's possible that the heat was overpowering. It may have made your husband weaker than usual.'

Louisa saw he was trying to excuse any possible shortcoming on Guy's part and she liked him for it. It was a gentlemanly thing to do.

'When we entered the tool room, we could hear there was a man in some distress in there, and items had been thrown. I imagine he was feeling cornered and under attack. Our concern was for him to cause no further damage to the equipment, or to himself or any of us. But he pushed over a shelving unit and a large, heavy box fell on DS Sullivan and he was instantly knocked out. Mr West, a fellow crew member, and I attended to your husband to check that he had not been badly hurt, and in the commotion the man – whoever he was – ran out.'

'He ran out? Then where is he?'

'That's just it, Mrs Sullivan. I don't know.'

'You don't know? Who is in Cabin E-131, then? With the guard standing outside?'

'Nobody. The room is empty. But the last thing I need is anyone knowing we have an escaped assailant on the ship. I thought it best if guests believed he had been caught.'

'You mean, there *is* an escaped assailant on the ship?'

Mr Logan stood up, the informality of his perching on the desk now too much at odds with the horror of what he had described. 'Yes, Mrs Sullivan. We are taking measures—'

'What measures?'

'We have informed certain key members of the crew, who are on the lookout.'

'But isn't it likely that the man you are after, if he went to the

175

tool room, is a member of the crew?' As she spoke, Louisa knew she had the answer already.

'Yes, I expect you're right,' said Logan. 'I'm an idiot for not thinking of that. What do I do now?'

'I know the man you're looking for,' said Louisa. 'All you have to do is find him. I don't think he acted alone, and there's someone I need to go and see while you do that.'

CHAPTER THIRTY-ONE

23 *May* 1935
Old Bailey, Court Number One

The barrister walked back to his bench. He did not hurry but shuffled his papers a little before looking back to the judge. 'I should like to call the first witness for the prosecution: the first officer for the *Princess Alice*, Mr Greg Logan.'

Guy watched as Logan walked through the courtroom and into the witness box. He placed his hand on the Bible and, in a clear voice, promised to tell the truth. His uniform and cap gave him a military air, though this was completely false. Guy knew that Logan had joined the ship as a young boy of fifteen and risen through the ranks, as he was dependable, efficient and patriotic.

Mr Burton-Lands asked Logan to state his name, rank and address before opening the questioning. As his own witness, this was not going to be an interrogation, yet Guy could not yet ascertain why Logan had been brought in first. It soon became clear.

'Mr Logan, could you please tell the court the circumstances in which you first met Mr Jim Evans.'

'It was five years ago, 1930, in Southampton. There was a recruitment day for various positions open on Empire Line cruises, and I had been asked to conduct some of the initial interviews. Mr Jim Evans presented himself that morning. As I remember, he was one of the first in the queue, early in the morning.'

'What position was he after?'

Mr Logan gave a short cough into his fist. 'He wanted any position that would be made available to him, sir. He was only fifteen years old and already one year out of school.'

'Had he any previous employment?'

'There was one reference, from a man who had employed him as a general labourer.'

'Was it a good reference?'

'Excellent.'

Mr Burton-Lands looked pleased at this, which bewildered Guy. This was a witness for the prosecution. Why was he apparently emphasising the good, even excellent, character of the accused?

'What were your first impressions of Mr Evans?'

Mr Logan appeared to recollect. He had a handsome face and, with his snow-white suit, there couldn't have been many who could have resisted his charms.

'He was clean and eager, willing to work hard and at any labour. He was immature, I could see that, but I sensed he wanted to get away from his domestic situation.'

'Did you suspect he was running away from something?'

'No, sir. And in subsequent conversations he explained to me that his mother had died when he was young, he had never known his father and had been brought up by his grandmother.

178

He was afraid of falling into bad company in the docks and wanted both employment and discipline.'

'And travel?'

Logan smiled. 'All sailors want that, sir.'

'In three years, did Mr Evans prove himself an able employee?'

'Yes, sir. He was reliable, never off sick and always returned to the ship when required.'

Guy looked at the jury: they were all listening carefully. It was the start of the case, they were always attentive then. It was why it was important to bring out the most effective witnesses first.

'Is that not the norm?' enquired Mr Burton-Lands with a half-smile.

Logan coughed again and gave an apologetic look to the jury. 'We strive for the best on the *Princess Alice*, but it has been known for younger members of the crew to be somewhat distracted by exotic temptations, sir.'

'Still, Mr Evans pleased you. He worked hard. Did he rise through the ranks?'

'Not at any great speed. He began as a pot-washer in the kitchens, then was made a busboy in the crew canteen, and from there to waiter in the second-class restaurant. He was promoted to cabin steward two years ago after applying for the position and has remained there. It's not unheard of, but it might have been hoped that he would invite promotion in his last six months.'

'But he did not?'

'No, sir. We – that is the second officer and myself – felt that he lacked the maturity or education to go further at this stage.'

Mr Burton-Lands turned to face the jury. 'He lacked the maturity to go further at this stage,' he repeated directly to them, then he turned back to Logan. 'Can you explain your-self further?'

'It's hard to put an exact reasoning upon it, but he seemed still more like a boy than a young man. He requires precise instructions, which he follows to the letter, but he rarely takes it upon himself to extend his responsibility.'

Mr Burton-Lands turned to the judge. 'No further questions, your honour.'

CHAPTER THIRTY-TWO

The minutes had been slipping by fast and Louisa needed to go to see Mrs Fowler before Lady Redesdale awoke. Guy had said it was important that someone spoke to her soon, in the crucial early hours when her memory of the night before would be at its freshest. Not to mention that he still needed to find the weapon of attack. There was a hollowness in her stomach and she felt almost nauseous from hunger, but she would have to hang on for a little longer.

Back on deck B, Louisa hurried along the passage that now felt as familiar as a childhood home, the effect intensified by the fact that all the passages in the ship looked the same – mile after mile of dark red patterned carpet with evenly spaced doorways and lights along the cream textured walls that narrowed in the distance. Her light-headedness made her feel as if she were in a disturbed dream and in the seconds before she found door B-17, her chest tightened from the claustrophobia of it. Nodding at the young cabin boy who was standing by the door, Louisa let herself in with a gentle knock. There was nobody in the drawing room and the lights were all still on, though the room was otherwise dim, a single shaft of sunlight coming through the narrow gap in the curtains. Whether it was a domestic instinct or something else, Louisa decided she would turn the lamps off and draw the curtains, though she wouldn't tidy anything up. There was absolute silence in the cabin and she briefly wondered if she should make her presence known, then decided that whoever was with Mrs Fowler knew that only permitted persons were gaining access and if they were catching some sleep they could have a few minutes more. Louisa went first to the curtains and pulled them apart, only to be briefly blinded by the sudden brightness of the Mediterranean sun. When she opened her tightly squeezed eyes again, flashes of light danced about. When they cleared, she saw something that made her gasp.

The balcony was small but oddly shaped, with the sides angled, the space mostly occupied by two heavy wrought-iron chairs and a table, the type commonly seen in modest country gardens. What Louisa had seen behind the chair on the left, wedged in the corner, was a wooden mallet with the unmistakeable stains of blood. Checking behind her, Louisa stepped outside and picked it up carefully by the long handle. It couldn't be left outside in case rain came and washed away the evidence. As it was, it was a miracle that the sea had been calm in the night. Louisa wondered how it could have ended up in the corner. Perhaps the culprit had intended to throw it overboard and not realised that it had landed there. In the light it was visible, but it would have been easily missed when it was still dark. Or someone could have deliberately put it there, planted the mallet in a place that was hard but not impossible to find? Why, she could not guess at yet, but it was a possibility to be explored.

It was too large to put in her pocket, and too conspicuous to carry around with her. Gingerly, Louisa looked for somewhere to put the weapon and decided it would be best hidden in the drinks cupboard, which could be locked. Louisa put the key in her pocket: she would give it to Guy as soon as she saw him. The thought that this block of wood had almost killed someone made her shudder. The mallet had to have come from the tool room, but had it been taken deliberately, knowing what it would ultimately be used for? Ella's confession to the attack had been almost dismissed by her and Guy because of her drunken condition. But the close proximity of the weapon gave it more credence, particularly when tied to Ella's affair with Jim. Evidence, she could say. The responsibility of this conclusion weighed heavily upon Louisa.

There was a stirring from the bedroom and Louisa started. It no longer seemed wise to conceal her presence. She stepped into the hall and knocked gently on Mrs Fowler's bedroom door. Blythe opened it.

'Louisa?'

'Blythe. I didn't realise you'd be here.'

Blythe's washed-out face told the tale. 'I didn't have much choice. She called me last night and I've been stuck here since. I've not slept a wink while she's been tossing and turning, calling out things I can't make sense of.'

'I'm sorry.' She was. It can't have been pleasant and it was, after all, well beyond the call of her duty as a cabin maid. 'Does the housekeeper know you're here?'

'No, and I'm supposed to be back on shift soon.'

'I expect things are in a muddle for everyone,' said Louisa, biting her tongue. She didn't want to leave Blythe alone with Mrs Fowler, but she couldn't risk explaining why. 'Can I talk to anyone for you? Find someone to take over?'

'Thank you. Mrs Kelway is Head of Housekeeping. If you find any other maid, you could ask them to take a message to her.'

'I'll do that. I need to talk to Mrs Fowler first, though.'

Blythe's eyebrows pulled together. 'You?'

'DS Sullivan is incapacitated. He asked me to see how she is.'

'She's asleep.'

'You mentioned she's been calling things out. I'm sure she won't be sleeping well, and anything she can remember now could be vitally important. Has she said anything about what's happened?'

'No, not exactly.'

Louisa knew she had to pull rank. True, she had no real rank to speak of, but needs must. She had to do this for Guy. Possibly for Iain. Which meant, for king and country. At which point she told herself not to be ridiculously self-important.

'She has said something then?'

Blythe leaned forward a little and lowered her voice. 'She keeps saying something about Sir Clive.'

'What is she saying about Sir Clive?'

But Blythe's brief show of confidence had been dispelled. 'Nothing. She's saying his name, no more than that.'

'I still need to talk to Mrs Fowler. Perhaps now would be a good time for you to go to find the housekeeper? I assume she'll need someone to cover your duties this morning.'

Blythe hesitated in the doorway and Louisa felt the tension

between them as a standoff, but the younger woman relented quickly. 'Yes, I'll do that.'

Louisa watched her walk around the corner and waited for the sound of the door closing before she knocked gently and went through to Mrs Fowler.

CHAPTER THIRTY-THREE

The woman Louisa hoped to talk to was in the bed, lying on her side, her eyes open and staring at the blank wall beside her. There was a window in the room, but the curtains were still shut and only a faint haze of sunshine showed around the edges. There was a small lamp on the dressing table, which gave out the only light in the room. Prone, Mrs Fowler did not acknowledge Louisa's entry into the room and she felt like an intruder. After all, she had no real right to be there, no legitimate power. But she did want to find out what had happened – for Guy, and maybe for Iain, too. What she was doing might have been questionable, but it wasn't illegal.

Was it?

'Mrs Fowler,' Louisa called softly. 'It's me, Louisa, Lady Redesdale's lady's maid.'

'I know who you are,' said Ella, her voice firmer than expected. 'Why are you here? Where's Blythe?'

'She's gone to talk to the housekeeper. I'm sure she'll be back soon. I'm here because my husband is DS Sullivan.'

Ella's head turned sharply. 'A policeman?'

'Yes, you met him earlier, but it would be understandable if you didn't remember.' She edged slowly towards the bed and did not dare sit down in the chair but hovered, bent at the waist a little. 'He's investigating what happened last night but has been briefly ... ' She tried to hold Mrs Fowler's gaze. 'He's unwell himself. He asked me to talk to you.'

'What good will it do?' She slumped back onto the pillow and pulled it down, curling herself up.

'Anything you can remember will help. I know it's been a terrible night ... '

'How is Joseph?'

Louisa hesitated. 'I'm sorry to say that it's not looking good, Mrs Fowler. He's still unconscious.'

Ella let out a howl of – what? Fury? Pain? Despair? Louisa couldn't tell, but the visceral sound disturbed her and she nearly ran from it. It was the last noise she had expected to come from the wretched heap in the bed.

'Go away, go away. *Go away,*' shouted Ella. She pushed herself up with her hands and faced Louisa. 'I did it. I did it and I will pay the price.' Her eyes red, she spoke hoarsely and with feeling. 'Everything is destroyed, don't you see? Leave me, please, I beg you, just leave me. I only want to be alone.'

Louisa put one hand on the bed. 'Mrs Fowler? How did you do it?'

There was no coherent response. Ella had gone face down into the pillow and was muttering into it, her words stumbling. Louisa felt panicked, at a loss as to what she should do next, when there was a knock at the door and it opened. She straightened up and saw Dr O'Donnell come in. He did not acknowledge Louisa but immediately went to Ella.

'Mrs Fowler? Mrs Fowler?' He spoke in a no-nonsense tone, one hand on her shoulder, until she sat up on her knees. Louisa couldn't see her face, but she watched as the doctor spoke to her tenderly. 'Mrs Fowler, I'm going to give you some more morphia. Would you like it?'

'Is that a good idea, doctor?' The words were out before Louisa could stop them; she had been about to extract a confession, she was sure of it. Did the doctor realise? Was there a reason he wanted to keep Ella quiet?

The doctor gave Louisa a cold glance and bent over his patient.

Like a child accepting a sweet in return for stopping tears, Ella mouthed a silent 'yes', her face streaked, her mouth parted. She lay down on her bed, mute and pathetic. It moved Louisa more than anything. The doctor administered morphia and soon Ella's eyes were closed, her breathing heavy. When it was all done, he started to walk out of the room, and indicated to Louisa that she should follow.

'I've arranged for a nurse to come and sit with her,' he said. 'She'll sleep now for some time, I hope.' He rubbed his eyes and when he opened them again Louisa could see they were spent of all light. 'The truth is, I think her husband is about to die and she hasn't the strength to cope with the news yet.'

'I see,' said Louisa, not knowing what the correct response to this should be. Sorry as she was for Ella and Joseph, she was more concerned for Guy. 'And my husband, DS Sullivan? How is he?'

The doctor gave a thin smile. 'He's fine. There are no signs of concussion. You can go and see him, take him to breakfast. I expect you'll both need your strength. I need to get back to Mr Fowler.'

With that, they both parted, leaving only the young cabin boy standing at the door.

CHAPTER THIRTY-FOUR

24 May 1935
Old Bailey, Court Number One

The newspapers made quick work of reporting on the previous day's cross-examinations and, over fried eggs and bacon at the café down the road from the Old Bailey, Guy had heard the chatter of the men and women around him as they took on their own roles of judge and jury on what was being called 'the ship murder trial'. It was, without question, the sensation of the day, and although part of him could not help but feel some professional pride at his involvement, he also felt a dread, the knowledge that his part in it would be analysed by the world as closely as they picked apart Ella's outfits that she wore in court. This could be the case that saw his career sink or swim. The irony in that gave him no pleasure. In the courtroom, he could do no more than watch and hope for the best.

'The court calls Dr William O'Donnell for the defence,' said Tom Mitford.

Guy realised that Nancy was in the court, tucked away

in a far corner in the back row of lawyers. Strictly speaking, only those with professional connections to counsel or the case should sit there, but it was well known that in certain trials, family members would be granted special favours. She looked as if she would break into song from pride at watching her brother.

A man in his late fifties, slim and with only the merest flecks of silver in his hair, took the stand. He looked like a ship's doctor in a romantic film, thought Guy. Handsome enough to distract a young honeymooning bride from any physical discomfort.

Dr O'Donnell confirmed that he had received a telephone call from the Fowlers' cabin at about quarter to one in the morning and it had taken him fifteen minutes or so to get there.

'Could you tell the court what you saw?'

The doctor touched his silk tie before speaking. 'Mr Fowler was on the armchair but in a loose position, his legs stretched out before him. A blanket had been spread over him. He was wearing his evening trousers and shirt but no tie, waistcoat or jacket. There was a bloodstained towel wrapped around his head, and his head was covered with blood, which was clotted and clinging to his hair, so that I could not make any proper examination immediately.'

'What condition was Mrs Fowler in?'

'She was excited and seemed to be intoxicated.'

Guy heard a giggle from the public gallery, but a sharp glance upwards from Mr Justice Hogan silenced it.

'Did you speak to her?' Tom asked his questions as he looked down at his papers. Nervousness?

'Yes, I asked her what had happened, and she said, "Look at him: look at the blood. Somebody has killed him."'

'What did you do then?'

'I thought it was a case that required immediate attention. I telephoned through for a nurse and two of the crew to come as quickly as possible with a stretcher.'

'Did Mrs Fowler discuss anything that had happened that evening before you arrived?'

'Yes, she said she and Mr Fowler had had dinner and made a plan for their visit to Rome when the ship next docked. She said that Mr Fowler was happy about it. She drew my attention to the fact that he had given her a passage in a book to read about suicide.'

'Did she say how she came to find Mr Fowler?'

'Yes. She told me she had gone to bed after returning from supper alone, as Mr Fowler had stayed at the bar for a further drink. She said she had been aroused by a cry or a noise, I am not sure which, and that she ran into the drawing room, found Mr Fowler lying back in his chair, and on the carpet by him a pool of blood and his artificial teeth.'

Tom was pulled up short by his statement. The artificial teeth detail. Guy had forgotten that would be coming up. Even he could guess what would fuel tomorrow's headlines now.

'Please tell the court what happened next.'

'Using a stretcher, Mr Fowler was transported to the sick bay, which contains a basic operating theatre. It was a longer jour-ney than anyone would have liked for a man in his condition, but there was no other way around it. He was unconscious, but we ensured he was still breathing. It was necessary to shave Mr Fowler's head to find out the extent of the damage, and we saw three distinct, separate wounds on the back of the head. I knew then that this would be a matter for a criminal investigation.'

'Did you telephone the police?'

'No, there was no official police presence on the ship. I telephoned the captain, Captain Schmitt, who I believe immediately made his way to the Fowlers' cabin.'

'Had you met Mrs Fowler before this evening?'

'Yes, she had taken several trips on the *Princess Alice* and I had given her morphia relief in the past. She suffered chronically from chest trouble.'

'Had you seen any sign that she might be a drug addict?'

'None whatsoever.'

'Were you concerned that the morphia she received from you was excessive in its amount?'

The doctor's head jerked up at this question. 'Absolutely not. I measured and monitored the doses carefully.'

Tom took a slip of paper that had been passed up to him from the front – a note from senior counsel. He read it and continued his questioning. Nancy was still watching him as adoringly as a mother watching her child in a nativity play.

'I want to ask you if you know anything about her and her previous life. Did you hear at any time that Mr Fowler had threatened suicide?'

'Yes, he had told it to me once, and Mrs Fowler had also told me of his remarks.'

'Speaking generally, how would you describe her temperament?'

'Uneasy and very excitable. Occasionally, I was witness to her drinking too much. She had also confessed to me that Jim Evans was her lover.'

'Did you not report this to the captain?'

'It was a confidential conversation – I could not.'

There was a whisper of a reaction to this, but Tom moved swiftly on.

'Did she take you into her confidence further with regards to Jim Evans? And could you tell us when such conversations took place?'

'Yes, she spoke to me only the day before the attack. She told me that she believed Evans must be taking drugs and that he had tried to procure more drugs when the ship was docked at Livorno. I saw Evans because Mrs Fowler asked me to see him to find out what drugs he was taking.'

'Did you ask him?'

'Yes. I was concerned as a fellow employee of the ship, and as a doctor. I saw him the next day—'

'To clarify, the day of the attack?'

'Yes. I asked him if he was taking drugs and he said, "Yes, cocaine." I asked him where he got it and he told me he found some cocaine at home and it gave him pleasant sensations and so he carried on.'

'Did you warn him?'

'Yes, and I offered him help if he wished to give it up.'

Mr Justice Hogan leaned forward then. 'Did he accept your offer?'

'No, my lord.' The doctor's hands moved to his tie once more, but he gave it only the merest of adjustments.

'How many times did you see Mrs Fowler over the course of her trips on the *Princess Alice*?' Tom had resumed his questioning.

'I would say almost daily for each trip she was on. I believe she was on the ship six times in three years. Possibly more.'

'And you have said that you have never treated her for drug-taking?'

'I have said so and I say it again now.'

'Was she an extraordinarily excitable woman?'

'At times.' There was no emotional expression in the doctor's face. Guy supposed they saw and heard all there was to life in their surgeries, as his colleagues did in the police cells.

'I am not suggesting by these questions that in a state of excitement she did what she is accused of, but I want to know what sort of atmosphere there was between the married couple. To what did you put down these sudden fits of excitement?'

'Sometimes too much alcohol; other times, if there was any upset or if she was cross.'

'Nearly all temperament?'

'No, illness. The condition I attended her for was one of pulmonary tuberculosis.'

The judge interrupted again. 'Being a person suffering from tuberculosis, did you recommend any alcohol?'

'No.'

Mr Justice Hogan allowed a note of impatience. 'Did you advise her about alcohol?'

'Yes. My advice was to lead a quiet life and practically give it up.'

After a polite pause, Tom took up the cross-examination again. 'Did you believe Evans when he said he had been taking cocaine?'

'I suppose I did. He told me he had tried to get some when he had last been home and had failed.'

'Did he tell you where the money came from?'

'No, and I did not ask him.'

To this final answer, Tom turned to the judge. 'No further questions, my lord.'

He sat down and Guy wondered if he was the only one to notice a bead of sweat trickle down Tom's cheek before it was quickly mopped away by a starched handkerchief.

CHAPTER THIRTY-FIVE

As she was not too far away, Louisa quickly went first to Lady Redesdale's suite, but she was thankfully still in a deep sleep. It was only half-past seven and Louisa thought it would be safe not to return until nine o'clock; Unity and Diana would be certain to remain in their rooms for even longer. Reassured, Louisa went to find Guy, but by the time she reached the sick bay he was already standing outside the door, his shoes and jacket back on.

'I was hoping you'd come and find me,' he said. 'I couldn't lie there any longer but wasn't certain what to do next.'

'How are you feeling?' asked Louisa, tender towards her husband. She reached up behind his head. 'Oh, that is a lump. You poor thing.'

Guy felt it himself and grimaced. 'Yes, it's a little sore.' He bent down and gave her a quick kiss on the cheek. 'Thank goodness you're here. Tell me, did you manage to do those things?'

'Yes, there's a bit to report. I know the doctor said to get breakfast, but I don't think there's time . . . '

With both of them in need of fresh air, they walked outside onto the deck, where the warmth of the sun and the salty breeze revived them.

Leaning on the railings, Louisa told Guy about the mallet and gave him the key to the drinks cabinet, as well as Ella's apparent confession.

'And there was blood on the mallet?'

Louisa confirmed there was.

'Then there's a strong chance that Mrs Fowler *is* telling the truth in her confession,' said Guy. 'Is someone standing guard at her room?'

'Yes, I sent the maid, Blythe, to get rest, and the doctor said he was arranging a nurse to sit with her. But he gave Mrs Fowler another dose of morphia, so she won't be going anywhere for a while.' Louisa felt very thirsty, her mouth was dry. 'Why is she also talking about someone else having done it, though? The "sir" she mentioned, I mean.'

'Blythe told me that too,' said Guy. 'Do you know who that could be?'

'Sir Clive,' Louisa recalled, quickly. 'She said Ella was saying his name, though no more than that. He's the man to whom Joseph owed money, remember . . . '

'I'll need to talk to him,' said Guy. 'Anything else?'

Louisa revealed Mr Logan's admission that whoever had been hiding in the tool room – and pushed the shelves onto Guy – was still loose on the ship.

'Does he have any idea who it was?' asked Guy.

'He mentioned that everything has to get signed in and out, and few members of the crew even know of the existence of the room. The mallet surely came from there. I think it was Jim.'

'You're right,' said Guy. 'There's motive and he's crew. If he didn't have authorised access to the tool room, he could have known about it.'

There was the distinct feeling of movement around them. A few of the guests would be getting up now and both Louisa and Guy knew that gossip about the night before would soon be whispered over tea and toast, from table to table, cabin to cabin, deck to deck.

'If there's no one in that cell, then Logan won't still be in the office next door,' said Guy, thinking out loud. 'We'll have to ask the captain where he is. But we need to see the logbook for the tool room as soon as we can.'

'But whoever attacked Mr Fowler won't have signed the mallet out, will he?' said Louisa.

'No, but they may not have taken it from the tool room themselves. Or they may have taken it for a perfectly legitimate reason, only for it to be fatally used later.'

Something about the way Guy was taking charge was attractive. Louisa had almost forgotten how much she liked watching him at work.

'You look tired, my love. Why don't you go to our cabin for a bit, then we can meet again later?'

'I couldn't feel less tired,' said Louisa. It was true. Her blood seemed to be pumping through her veins at twice the normal rate; she felt light-headed.

'I'm going to go and see the captain and track down that register. If Jim's name is on there, I'll bring him in for questioning.'

'You'd better ask the captain for a room to conduct interviews.'

'Yes, you're right, good thinking,' said Guy. He put a hand

affectionately on her shoulder. It felt strong and warm. 'Now, please. Go and change. You've got work to do, too.'

'How will I find you? I'll see to Lady Redesdale and the others, then I'm sure to get some free time.'

'I'll leave a message for you at the purser's office.'

Brisk, full of purpose, Guy left Louisa and she made her way to her cabin. Once there, she had a wash, changed her dress and brushed her hair. She knew that Guy meant for her to have a catnap, but she didn't want one, and she knew the danger of it turning into deep sleep if her body realised how tired it was. She was itching to get a response from Iain, but that would be at least a few hours more. It was time to return to her post as Lady Redesdale's lady's maid. Nor could she forget her commission: she still needed to read the letter that Diana had picked up from Livorno, if it was the follow-up that Sir Oswald had promised.

When Louisa arrived, a maid had already brought up Lady Redesdale's breakfast and she was sitting up in bed looking refreshed. Sun flooded the cabin, with not a single cloud in the azure sky to blot the view.

'Ah, Louisa, you're here.'

'M'lady.'

'I feel much better now. Could you knock on Miss Unity's door and tell her to come through?'

'Yes. Before I do, I wonder – did you hear what happened last night?'

Lady Redesdale turned to Louisa, trying and failing to cover up an aghast expression on her face. Louisa instinctively knew this was not because of any horror over the events of cabin B-17 but because she had initiated a conversation. And if a maid, even a lady's maid, had initiated a conversation, it was almost certainly one that Lady Redesdale didn't wish to have.

'Oh dear. My daughters,' she said with a sigh, spreading butter generously onto a piece of broken-off toast. 'What have they done now?'

'It's not Miss Unity,' Louisa said, banishing the image of Unity on the stairs. That would have to be dealt with separately. 'And Mrs Guinness has only a minor part in it. No, it's to do with Mrs Fowler and her husband. I thought you should know as it's likely the entire ship will be talking about it by the time you get outside.'

Briefly, without going into any upsetting details, Louisa explained to Lady Redesdale what had happened. Then she had to tell her that *she* was involved.

'What on earth are you talking about, Louisa?'

'My husband is here, m'lady . . . ' She trailed off.

Lady Redesdale's silent response told Louisa all she needed to know of what her employer thought about that.

'As Mr Fowler is British and we are out at sea, the crime falls under the jurisdiction of the British police. Which means he has taken charge of the investigation.'

'That is most tiresome. But why should you be caught up in it?'

Louisa looked at her blankly before she realised it was a serious question. 'I'm his wife.'

Lady Redesdale put down her knife with a slight clatter on the plate. 'A wife has no need to interfere in her husband's affairs. I should say it's far better if she stays well away from them. I may say that the position works equally well in reverse. I have never asked for Lord Redesdale's involvement in my own business.'

That certainly was true.

'Lady Redesdale, I shall still honour my duties to you, Miss Unity and Mrs Guinness. Any assistance that I offer to DS Sullivan' – no harm in reinforcing his rank, thought Louisa – 'will not interfere with that.'

'Hmm, well. It's not as if we're completely helpless, and it must be distressing for Mrs Fowler.' Lady Redesdale ate the last of her toast and dabbed at her mouth with the napkin. 'If you could take the tray away, Louisa, I'll get up. My migraine has gone, thank goodness. I'll wear the light blue skirt and jacket today, with the cream silk shirt.'

'Yes, m'lady,' said Louisa, calculating that she could be away from the room within the hour and would make brisk work of it with the other two.

CHAPTER THIRTY-SIX

〜

When Louisa went through to Unity's room, she was taken aback to see her up and dressed, sitting by the window and looking out at the vast body of water that lay around the *Princess Alice*. If one was lying on a raft looking for land, the situation would feel quite hopeless.

Unity leaped up when Louisa entered. 'There you are. I've been simply longing to get out of here. Is Lady Redesdale up?'

'Yes, her migraine is gone.'

At this news, Unity's face fell. 'Damnation. Sorry. I meant . . . I was hoping to go and find Herr Wolfgang, you see. I thought he might ask me for a stroll on the deck.'

Louisa decided not to respond to this but set about tidying some of Unity's things in the cabin.

'Would you ask Lady Redesdale if you and I could walk on the deck? Then we might bump into him.' Unity had not put any cosmetics on her face and she looked fresh and young.

Louisa thought of the tall, blond man in his SS uniform and something of the image made her inwardly shudder.

'Miss Unity, as you know, that's not my—'

'Oh, hang your duties, Louisa. I don't see why my parents shouldn't approve of the match. He's an aristocrat, an Olympic sailor. He's even in the army, a special division, and he's told me that his father is frightfully pally with Hitler. Herr Hitler! I do long to meet him. Tell me what is wrong with any of that.'

Louisa decided there was no longer any point in playing the part of the acquiescent maid. 'He's not an Englishman, that's what's wrong. You know how Lord Redesdale feels about foreigners.'

'Well, he's a stupid old human. The war was forever ago. Everyone's forgotten about it. I don't see why he can't.'

To this Louisa merely raised an eyebrow as she folded a cardigan and put it in a drawer. Unity slumped in her chair and started kicking at the table leg mindlessly.

'You haven't asked about what happened last night,' said Louisa, changing the subject to one she wanted to discuss.

Unity perked up at this. 'I can't believe I quite forgot. How is Mr Fowler?'

'It's not good. He's unconscious and not expected to recover.'

'Poor man. Who did it to him? Diana had the most ghastly shock with that scene last night. She said she would telephone me when she woke up. Has Mr Sullivan spoken to her yet?'

'That's a lot of questions,' said Louisa. 'Mr Sullivan is working on the case now. I'd like to try to find him soon. I've been assisting him a little. Would you come with me?' This wasn't Louisa's first choice, to take Unity with her, but after what she had seen on the stairs, she was taking no chances in leaving her alone.

Unity widened her eyes. 'That *is* unorthodox. What would

Lady Redesdale say?' Then she broke into a wide smile. 'Absolutely I'll come with you. Can we go this minute?'

At the purser's office, Louisa found a message from Guy telling her that he would be in D-326, and she could go and find him there. Unity stayed close to Louisa's side, unable to resist looking out for Wolfgang, pointing out various places where he might be – the dining room, the smoking room, the deck – until at last Louisa stopped stock-still on the stairs.

'Miss Unity, you are going to have to stop trying to make arrangements with Herr von Bohlen. Lady Redesdale is never going to agree to it.'

'Are you going to tell her what you saw last night? Or what you *thought* you saw. It was perfectly innocent.' Unity's shoulders were braced.

'I shan't, but I'm not entirely sure that I'm doing you a favour.' Louisa turned her back and carried on up the stairs. This time Unity followed quietly.

When they reached D-326, the door was ajar. Louisa knocked and heard Guy's voice tell her to come in. Before she could stop her, Unity had followed Louisa in. This was a cabin that belonged to someone, with a half-drunk bottle of whisky on the side and books on a low table by a winged armchair. It was not a generously sized cabin, but it had a lived-in, homely feel. By the window was a table that had been cleared of everything but an ashtray, with two chairs on either side of it. Guy and Logan were standing by the chairs.

'Miss Mitford,' said Guy, in acknowledgement.

'Hello, Mr Sullivan. What's going on in here?'

'This is First Officer Logan and he has kindly lent me his cabin to pursue inquiries.' Guy answered patiently, but the pressure was building. Louisa knew he needed to prove to himself and his superiors at home that he could handle this investigation.

'Miss Mitford understands the need for discretion,' said Louisa, resisting the urge to cross her fingers as she said this. 'Has anything changed since I saw you?'

Guy looked at Logan, who took up the cue. 'We've decided to ask each head of department to call a meeting. Cabin stewards and maids will be asked to report on the guests in their rooms. We need a head count of everyone on the ship.'

'And then you can tell who is missing,' said Louisa.

'Why? Who is missing?' Unity stepped closer to Guy. He looked to Louisa, who indicated that he could tell Unity the truth.

'That's it: we don't know for absolute certain. But someone is hiding on this ship.'

'A stowaway?'

'That is a possibility,' said Logan. 'Please do not be concerned. We're absolutely certain that there's no danger to anyone.' He didn't look as certain as he sounded.

Unity regarded them all for several seconds. 'I don't see how you can be so sure. It's obvious that whoever you believe to be running around loose on this ship, hiding and goodness knows what else, is the man who attacked Mr Fowler. How are you to know he won't attack someone else?'

Guy looked pained at this, but Unity was still rattling on.

'I have the perfect answer. You should tell Herr von Bohlen about this.'

'Who is Herr von Bohlen?' asked Guy, curiosity getting the better of him.

'He's in the *Schutzstaffel*, the Nazi police force. Not just anyone can get in, which means he's frightfully clever, too. I'm sure he could catch your man in the blink of an eye. Rough him up too, if you liked.'

'Miss Mitford, I do think . . . ' But Louisa couldn't finish the sentence. She was too appalled to be able to spell out exactly what she thought. Did Unity not understand the depravity of what she had just said? She faced her husband. 'Is there anything I can do to help?'

'Yes,' said Guy. 'I need to talk to Sir Clive Montague, but it would be better if you could bring him here, rather than me. It would be more discreet, if you understand my meaning.'

Louisa was about to reply in the affirmative when Unity turned to her.

'Do you imagine Lady Redesdale would be more pleased with this idea than my taking a stroll on the deck with Herr Wolfgang?'

There was no answer to this. Instead, Louisa said goodbye and left the cabin, with Unity close behind.

CHAPTER THIRTY-SEVEN

'**S**hall we go and find Herr von Bohlen?'

Louisa and Unity were walking away from Guy's newly appointed interview room, making their way up the central staircase to deck B. Louisa's life as a servant had always involved frequent trips up and down stairs, but never quite like this. Unity was dressed in a belted white linen dress with a sky-blue cardigan – she looked as pretty as she ever might, but there was no softness or charm to her demeanour. She was blunt and heavy, the caveman's club to Diana's samurai sword. The one thing that could be said for her was that you weren't left guessing at Unity's meaning when she talked. Whether it was naivety, ignorance or impatience on her part, she was never coy. Louisa knew if she asked the question, Unity would answer. If she didn't want to say anything, she would be silent. Either she talked and told you, or she said nothing: there was no nuance in between.

'Why?'

'Because I want to see him and because he can help track down whoever did it,' Unity said, slightly breathlessly.

'I'm not going to cut across DS Sullivan's orders,' said Louisa, 'and he's asked us to find Sir Clive Montague.'

'Fine.' This was followed by a familiar look: Unity sulking.

Louisa was aware of a change in the atmosphere of the ship. Voices were hushed yet there was no silence. Everywhere she looked, she saw people whispering to each other with urgent rhythms, scandalised looks on their faces. Rumours would be spreading fast about who had done what to whom, and there were most likely about ten different versions of the story circulating around the passengers and crew already. Hysteria would build; they needed to find Jim. He couldn't have gone far – unless he had gone overboard. Louisa's heart pounded at that thought.

Logan had given Louisa the number for Sir Clive's cabin, B-38, portside, the other side to the Fowlers and Mitfords. There was a palpable sense of a clock ticking down, as if it were embedded in her chest, her heart thudding with the second hand. The ship was due to dock at Rome the very next morning, less than twenty-four hours away. If Jim was still missing then, he would have a good chance of escape. She realised, too, that as well as the whispers, there were more crew visible than usual, standing by exits to the decks or at the stairwells. Each one on heightened alert, checking their watches too frequently, their eyes darting from left to right. It was enough to make anyone feel paranoid.

Unity tugged at Louisa and whispered into her ear, 'Do you think the killer is walking around the ship, weapon in hand, ready to strike again?'

Louisa hoped no flicker of fear showed in her own face. 'Of course not. If he's got any sense at all, he'll be hiding somewhere, laying low.'

'How do you know it's a man?'

'I don't, but it's more likely, I'd say.' Not looking where she was going, Louisa bumped into another passenger, a portly man with a red face and even redder hair. 'Beg pardon, sir,' she said.

'You need to be careful, miss,' he said, excitement flushing his cheeks even more. 'They're looking for an armed man, you know. Dangerous type, could be anywhere.' He waggled his comical eyebrows and sped off.

Louisa thought she heard a chuckle as he departed. She despaired of the human race sometimes.

Two more corners at speed and they arrived at B-38. Louisa knocked on the door.

'What are you going to say to him?' Unity mouthed.

'I'll think of something,' Louisa replied, but she wasn't sure at all.

Nobody came to the door. Louisa knocked again. Unity pressed her ear to the wall but shook her head.

'I can't hear anything.'

'Perhaps he's gone to breakfast.' Louisa stood by the door, at a loss as to what to do next, knowing that every second wondering was a second wasted.

They were about to walk away to the dining saloon on deck A, when there was a click at the door. Sir Clive, immaculately dressed as always, opened it.

'Miss Mitford.' He looked at Louisa, questioningly. She noticed that he hadn't put the cufflinks in his shirt yet.

Louisa knew how this worked: she couldn't talk to Sir Clive because she hadn't been introduced. Nor would she be, as a lady's maid. As imperceptibly as possible, she nudged Unity.

'Sir Clive,' said Unity. 'I do apologise for disturbing you.'

'Not at all. How can I help?' As he said this, he stepped outside, pulling the door almost to behind him.

Unity looked at Louisa helplessly but pressed on. 'I expect you've heard what happened last night?'

Sir Clive glanced quickly at the empty passage. 'Yes, I have.' He seemed to refocus on Unity. 'Are you ... involved in some way? Can you tell me how Mrs Fowler is?'

'No, I'm not involved. That is, not really. Mrs Fowler is well, I believe.' Unity was stammering and Louisa thought she had better step in, introduction or no introduction. Nothing was normal this morning.

'Sir Clive, would you come with us, please? Mrs Fowler is, naturally, disturbed by the events of last night. Her husband is very unwell. There is an investigation underway—' She froze. From the cabin had come the sound of something – or someone? – falling down. A clatter, followed by a dull thud. Sir Clive did not react.

'What was that?' Unity went to look behind Sir Clive, but he held firmly onto the door.

'Probably some books falling off a shelf,' he said tersely. 'Keeps happening, every time the ship rolls. I don't know why they bother putting books in the cabins at all.'

The ship hadn't rolled. They may have been out in the deep seas, but the water was completely calm. Someone was in there.

'Sir Clive,' Louisa began again, 'I can't really explain now, but please would you come with us? Your help is needed.'

'I can't see what I have to do with it.' He turned to Unity. 'Forgive me, my dear. I'd like to assist if I could, but I'm afraid the matter has nothing to do with me. Will you send my regards to your sister and mother?'

With that, he opened the door and started to slip in, but Louisa grabbed his arm.

'Sir Clive, there's a policeman on the ship and he insists on talking to you. Don't you think it would be much easier if you could come with us now? There won't be any gossip if you're walking with us, but I fear people already recognise my husband.'

That made him stop. 'Your husband?'

'Yes, I am here as Lady Redesdale's maid, but my husband is DS Sullivan of the CID.' She relaxed her grip on his arm, knowing she had him now. 'Shall we go?'

Sir Clive knew when he was beaten. He closed the door and together the three of them walked away and down the steps to the interview room.

CHAPTER THIRTY-EIGHT

24 May 1935
Old Bailey, Court Number One

Mr Manners called Sir Clive Montague to the stand. Guy had been tipped off that he would be appearing next and knew it would cause a stir in the public gallery: anyone with a title always did. He couldn't help feeling that there was a general sense that toffs deserved a hard time in court, even if they weren't the ones in the dock. As for his own feelings towards Sir Clive, Guy's were mixed. While he was a gentleman in manners and appearance, there was something about him that was shadowy. Guy had never managed to shake the feeling that he was hiding something, however helpful and charming he had been during the investigation. It was entirely possible that he *was* hiding something, but that it was nothing to do with the case that Guy had been trying to solve. But perhaps the skill of the barrister's cross-examination, the formality of the judge in his robes and the presence of ten men and two women jurors would bring Sir Clive's secret out into the open.

Sir Clive climbed into the witness stand, his large bulk seeming to fill it completely, like a bull in a pen, and yet the care he had taken over his appearance with his carefully combed hair and his immaculately trimmed and polished nails made him almost touchingly vulnerable.

'For the court, please confirm your name, age and place of residence.'

'Sir Clive Leinster Montague, fifty-three years, of 42 Cadogan Square, London, and also of Maudlen Park, Derbyshire.'

'Thank you, Sir Clive. We appreciate your being here and will make it worthy of your time,' said Mr Manners rather obsequiously, thought Guy. 'Could you please tell the court something of your professional background?'

'I trained as a lawyer then went into the City, I'm afraid.' Guy saw Nancy smile at this. 'I was lucky and made money before the war. Since then, I've invested in property and land.'

'Have you been a successful man, would you say, Sir Clive?'

'I've been lucky enough to have seen some success, yes.'

'And yet your fortune is not limitless, is it?' Mr Manners delivered this with a smirk. But Sir Clive appeared to take no offence. Presumably, they had worked out this line of questioning in advance.

'As with many other unfortunate people, I lost a great deal of money in the crash of 1929. However, it was not all of my capital, and I have simply had to make more careful investments in the years since.'

'I see.' Mr Manners cleared his throat and changed his stance. Guy recognised this now as the barrister's trick for indicating that a slightly new line of questioning would now be pursued. 'Could you please tell the court how you came to know Mr and Mrs Fowler.'

Sir Clive briefly faced the jury and gave them a polite nod, as if he had been introduced to them at a cocktail party. 'We were fellow guests on board the *Princess Alice*. I believe I first met them at one of the captain's cocktail parties in 1931, towards the beginning of the year, on a cruise from Southampton to Venice. It is one of my favourite trips and I always get the Orient Express home.'

'Quite.' Mr Manners' response was dry.

Guy, and no doubt the counsel, was conscious of a reaction in the public gallery. Casual journeys from Venice on the Orient Express were not common currency for most – did Sir Clive not know this or was he deliberately painting a picture of a cultured and wealthy man?

'What was your impression of them?'

'I liked Mrs Fowler a great deal, immediately. She was attractive and charming, a good conversationalist, a marvellous singer. I found her husband a less socially agreeable character, but it was evident that he had genuine talent as an architect, an area that I naturally find interesting.'

'Because of the nature of your investments?'

'Yes.' Sir Clive glanced briefly in the direction of Ella Fowler in the dock, but quickly refocused on Mr Manners.

'Eventually, you came to invest a substantial amount of money in an architectural project of Mr Fowler's. Can you describe how that investment came about?'

'We had met on the ship several times and I had discussed much of Mr Fowler's career with him; we shared an alignment when it came to our views on buildings and landscapes, the future of architecture and so on. When he first told me about the invitation by Blenheim Palace for him to compete for a bold new vision for a farm and educational institute, I was intrigued.'

'Mr Fowler did not, then, ask you for money straightaway?'

'Not at first, no. He was more cunning than that, flattering my ego, hoping that I might be more susceptible to his proposals later. I am embarrassed that I fell for it.' Sir Clive gave a coy smile in the judge's direction, who ignored it.

'What was your investment for, exactly?'

'It was for the initial pitch. To win such a commission means not only that a project is financed, it means acclaim and a strengthening of a reputation, which should lead to further work. We envisaged becoming a partnership thereafter. My money was for the costs of the surveys, the drawings, the wining and dining of councillors who would need to approve the project, et cetera. It's fairly standard stuff but expensive. Few architects, certainly those without a firm of their own, can afford to do it without an investor.'

'Was Mrs Fowler aware of your financial agreement?'

'I believe so, though it was never a topic of conversation between us. I must say that I would find it hard to credit her husband with the habit of involving her in his work affairs. Once or twice he mentioned that it was best for her not to know how much money he was bringing in as, he said, "she would only start asking for more".'

'Well, yes,' said Mr Manners, with an eyebrow half-raised. 'Some of us know the feeling.'

There was a titter from the gallery and the judge looked up from his notes.

'Keep to the point, Mr Manners.'

'Yes, my lord. Sir Clive, we know that Mr Fowler did win the commission for Blenheim Palace, but that the project collapsed a few months in. You therefore lost a great deal of money—'

'A great deal.'

'But you understood that this was simply the way of business?'

'I am a man of experience.' Sir Clive seemed to stifle a cough, then saw a carafe of water and a glass before him. He poured himself a glass, and it seemed to Guy as if the whole court stopped to watch Sir Clive slowly pour the water, then take a few sips, as if it were a deliberate part of the proceedings.

'Relations between yourself and Mr and Mrs Fowler remained cordial?'

'Naturally. We continued to see each other as fellow guests on the *Princess Alice*. As I have said, I enjoyed the company of Mrs Fowler and saw no reason to discontinue.'

'Sir Clive, when did you become aware that Mrs Fowler was conducting a love affair with a member of the crew on board the *Princess Alice*?' Mr Manners asked this as dispassionately as he might have asked Sir Clive to confirm the date and whereabouts of his place of birth.

Sir Clive, however, was less comfortable. The cough threatened to stick in his throat once more. Again, he took sips of water. 'I think towards the end of 1932, around October, on a cruise between Cannes and Barcelona. Mrs Fowler told me directly of the affair and the unhappiness it was causing her.'

'Were you shocked?'

'A little. But I am a man who has lived a number of years and travelled widely. I'd be a fool to think such things do not occur. Mostly, I was sad for my friend.'

'How so?'

This was the juice in the orange, thought Guy. The entire court was utterly still.

'The signs had been there that her marriage was not a happy one. I believed her to be a woman of great character, certainly deserving of a good life. But I could see she had sought refuge in the wrong places, and this was not being borne out by her lover's apparent ill treatment of her.'

'Of what did she complain?'

'She told me that Jim Evans, her lover, was leaning on her heavily to give him money to buy cocaine.'

Guy could have tapped a cue for the ripple of low voices that this statement started.

'What was your suggestion to Mrs Fowler?'

'I told her that she should report Jim Evans to the captain and ensure his dismissal from the ship.'

'Did she follow your advice?'

'She said that she would but, much to my great sadness and regret, she did not.'

'Thank you, Sir Clive. No further questions, my lord.'

CHAPTER THIRTY-NINE

For the long walk from deck B to deck D, neither Sir Clive nor Louisa said a word. Unity, however, kept up a constant stream of chatter, which was most unlike her. Fortunately, she didn't talk about the attack but instead reiterated a long list of reasons why she found Herr Wolfgang and his homeland so fascinating, so courageous and extraordinary. Quite apart from her infatuation with Wolfgang, Unity must have been nervous, and Louisa felt guilty that she had brought her charge into the middle of a rather unpleasant situation. On the other hand, she didn't see what choice she had. A brutal attack had happened on a ship: it could be said that all of the guests and crew had been unwittingly drawn into it, each one to varying degrees affected by the awfulness of it, unable to escape it because of the harsh reality that they were in the middle of a body of deep water. And that was before anyone realised that the person who had committed the terrible act was loose on the ship.

What Louisa needed to do, urgently, was tell Guy that some-one needed to get into Sir Clive's cabin to find out what was what. She knew the sound she'd heard wasn't books falling on the floor. The question that kept circling in her mind was: why would he hide someone? And given there was only one person hiding on this ship, and it had to be the person who had attacked Joseph, why would Sir Clive hide them? Someone who had attacked a man he, Sir Clive, had done a business deal with? One he had lost money with, in fact.

Ah.

Could Sir Clive be protecting the attacker because he had set it up, to avenge himself for the debt?

Louisa wanted to turn around and run back to Sir Clive's cabin, but she had to keep on walking as if nothing had changed and she bore no suspicion or knowledge about anything.

The walk started to seem oppressively long and repetitive. The ship felt too warm and the whispers between the guests started to echo so that she could hardly tell what she was hearing and what was reverberating in her own mind. By the time they reached the interview room, Louisa thought she might faint. Without waiting for a reply to her knock, she nearly fell into the cabin and walked fast to Guy. Sir Clive and Unity followed behind, he now looking distinctly uneasy, Unity at last biting her tongue.

Guy started at their entrance, then took one look at his wife and seemed to understand.

'Sir Clive Montague, I assume? Thank you so much for coming here. I won't keep you long. Please, take a chair. I'll be with you in just a moment.'

Sir Clive, looking as if he had seen the ghost of his Christmas past, sat down as Guy hustled Louisa and Unity back out of the cabin. He closed the door behind them.

Louisa spoke in a rush. 'I think Sir Clive is hiding someone in his cabin. You need someone to go down there quickly. It may already be too late.'

'There's no one to send. Logan called the other officers to do a head count of crew and guests, to establish who is missing. I'm on my own here.'

'Then you will have to go. It will take too long to find someone else.' Unity said this, and Guy and Louisa stared at her as if they'd forgotten she was there.

'You're right,' said Guy. 'It has to be me. If it's the man who attacked Joseph Fowler, he could be dangerous. You'll have to stay here and watch Sir Clive. I doubt he'll go anywhere.'

'No, but what if he suspects that you've gone to his cabin? He's a big man. I doubt either of us could hold him back.'

'I keep trying to tell you, we need Herr Wolfgang,' said Unity.

'No,' said Guy and Louisa in unison.

'I'll have to lock him in,' Guy decided. 'We'll go back there together. Miss Unity, please could you go to the captain's office and try to find someone who can come and stand guard here. I'll take the chance he won't batter the door down. They're heavy beasts even if he tried.'

'I'm not supposed to go anywhere alone ... ' Unity started, then stopped. 'Oh, hang it. Yes, I'll do it. Where shall I meet you?'

'Come back here. Either way, I hope we won't be long,' said Guy grimly.

Louisa knew she was deserting her Mitford post, but only because her husband needed her more. Him and Iain. She needed to know as much as she possibly could about what was going on and hoped she'd hear from Iain soon.

Guy took a key out of his pocket and locked the door. He did

221

it as quietly as possible, but there was no mistaking the distinctive clunk as the bolt slid in. None of them waited to hear if Sir Clive had noticed.

This time, there was no careful trot through the ship. Louisa led Guy to the back stairs, free from the sight of guests who might otherwise be alarmed, where they ran as fast as they could up to deck B and along the passages to Sir Clive's cabin. The door was closed.

'Is it locked?' whispered Guy.

'I didn't see him lock it,' Louisa replied. 'Perhaps he needed to make sure that whoever was in there could get out.'

Guy nodded. Louisa kept her eyes fixed on him.

'I'm going to go in first,' said Guy. 'You stay at the door.'

He pushed it open and stepped in. Louisa followed but did as instructed and stayed just inside the doorway, having shut it quietly behind her.

She could see at once that it was one of the smarter cabins, more like Diana's than Unity's. Sunlight flooded through the large windows and the walls were covered in an embossed blue paper, a match for the Mediterranean skies beyond.

Guy moved noiselessly on the thick carpet, while Louisa looked down the narrow hall that must have led to the bedroom and bathroom, possibly a dressing room, too, but nothing unusual revealed itself. For the longest minute she could not hear nor see anything of Guy, but felt only her blood pumping around her ears, like waves crashing on a stony beach. And then she heard the raised voices of two men, shouting – but in confusion, not anger. Daring herself, she moved towards the drawing room door and looked through.

Guy put his hand out to stop her, but he didn't look afraid.

She leaned further forward and looked around the corner. Crouched behind the sofa, with his back to the wall, was Jim Evans. He had dark sweat patches under his arms, his face was grey, his eyes wide with fear.

'I'm sorry, I'm sorry,' he said, over and over to them. 'I didn't know what to do; I didn't know where to go.'

Louisa walked further into the room. There was nothing to be afraid of, but there was everything to ask.

CHAPTER FORTY

'**G**et up.'
Jim, trembling, slowly started to rise but remained behind the sofa, pressed as close to the wall as he could be. Louisa remained at the doorway, while Guy stood, his tall frame broader and stronger than she'd ever seen, deliberately imposing his strength upon the wilting hideaway.

'I'm going to need you to come with me, answer some questions,' said Guy.

'I don't know anything, I promise I don't. I . . .' He ran out of the little courage he'd managed to muster. His head bowed down, he leaned back, almost unable to support himself on his feet.

Louisa took a step forward. 'Jim.'

At the sound of his name, he looked at her, like a willing dog.

'Why are you in here?' Louisa kept her voice soft.

Guy gave her a glance, but she refused to meet his eyes. She knew it wasn't her place to interrupt – he was the policeman. But instinct told her that Jim was terrified and might respond better to a gentle enquiry.

'I didn't know where else to go. When I saw what had happened, I knew they'd look for me, and I was right, wasn't I? He's right here.' Jim pointed to Guy. 'He saw me earlier, saw the fight with Mr Fowler. I'm the accused, aren't I? And now I've gone and hid, and you'll never believe me now. And, oh God. I knew it would come to this and I told her to stop, I told her . . . ' He ran out of air, wiping his face with the crook of his arm.

This time, Guy signalled to Louisa to carry on. She stepped further forward, almost at the sofa now, Jim still behind it, still pressing back as if he hoped he could disappear into the wall.

'Who did you tell to stop, Jim?'

'I don't know,' he mumbled, head back down again.

'Mr Fowler has lost consciousness. The doctor thinks he has hours left to live.'

'Christ, man. I knew he was in a bad way, I saw the blood. That's why I had to get out of there.'

'When did you see him?' Guy had spoken.

'I heard the row, but I didn't know what had happened, I didn't know it was that. And then I went in and I saw him . . .' Jim looked at them both now, pleading. 'I had to get out or everyone'd think the wrong thing. I bet you're thinking it now. Aren't you?'

'Who was Mr Fowler having a row with?' asked Guy, dipping his head, trying not to lose eye contact with Jim.

But he clammed up at this question. Shook his head. 'I don't know, I don't know. I couldn't, no.'

'You need to come with me now,' said Guy.

'What's going to happen to me?'

Guy didn't answer that. Instead, he walked around and took

225

Jim's arm – there was no resistance – and the three of them left the cabin and returned to the interview room on deck D.

The return journey felt long. Not only because of the silence between the three of them but because it was soon apparent that rumours spread faster than they could walk. Guy had beckoned a member of the crew stationed at one of the stairwells and told him to find First Officer Logan and report that he was needed urgently at the interview room but was not to go inside until DS Sullivan had arrived.

The young worker looked at Jim, in his steward's uniform, and gestured with his thumb. 'He the one they're after, then?'

Guy refused to answer the question, but the damage was already done. The man ran off and by the time they had gone down two decks, it was clear he'd started the Chinese whispers. Nobody pointed their fingers, but they didn't need to: looks were accusatory enough.

When they reached Logan's cabin, he was standing there, with Unity and Diana.

Louisa hurried over and pulled the sisters away. 'What are you doing here?'

'Diana saw me walking by myself after I'd been to see the captain and jumped on me as if I was the fifty-two bus.'

'I could tell she was hiding something,' said Diana. 'And you, Louisa. What are you hiding? What's been going on this morning? Everyone is acting in the most extraordinary manner.'

'Perhaps we had better go back to your rooms,' said Louisa.

'I don't want to go there.' One of Unity's infamous sulks had arrived in its usual sudden manner. 'For once, something exciting has happened and you want us to hide away?'

'It's not exciting,' said Louisa. 'A man has been viciously attacked and is almost certain to die. It's tragic.'

'Keep your wool on, you know what I mean. I don't see why we should be kept away from it, is all. Besides, Diana was practically at the scene, she might be of use. DS Sullivan needs to talk to her, doesn't he?'

Diana bristled. 'I was not at the scene. I was called afterwards and I left as soon as I could. I know nothing of any of it and only wish this whole ghastly business had never happened. I need to talk to the Leader. In fact, that's what we're going to do right now. Come with me, please, the two of you. We'll go to the telephone office and ask them to send a telegram.'

Louisa looked behind her, but Guy, Logan and Jim had gone, presumably into the cabin. She would have to find out later whether Jim had said anything further to incriminate himself. It wasn't clear that he had done it, but it wasn't exactly indisputable that he hadn't done it either.

CHAPTER FORTY-ONE

There was a short queue at the telephone office by the time they got there. Louisa overheard snatches of their telegram requests: 'Leaving ship at Rome.' 'Book three nights in Paris hotel.' 'Returning in five days, tell the servants.' One attack had been enough to spook several of the guests. If they discovered it was a member of the crew who had committed the crime, they might start trying to swim for shore. Eventually, Louisa reached the desk, where she recognised the telephonist from before, a redhead who was most likely a regular reader of Hollywood fanzines with articles on 'Movie Star Lipstick Tricks'.

'Mrs Sullivan,' she said warmly, a strong Manchester accent quickly apparent. 'I've got a telegram for you.'

The sisters did not hide their surprise. 'Who would send you a telegram?' asked Unity.

'I haven't a clue,' lied Louisa. 'I do hope it's not my ma.' She took the envelope from the redhead, thanking her. 'Would you mind if I read this privately? If it's bad news . . .'

'Of course,' said Diana. 'No need to explain.'

Louisa moved off and stood by a window. The blue sea and sky still stretched out around the ship, empty and clear, meeting at the horizon like a neatly stitched waistband. She opened the envelope carefully, prising it with her fingernail, wanting to avoid any tears. The message inside had been written quickly in pencil on the ship's own telegram card, taken down from the tapped-out Morse code. Not that the language into which it had been translated did not also need to be decoded.

`AUTHORITY GIVEN · THIRD OFFICER`
`W WELLESLEY · IMMEDIATE ACTION REQUIRED ·`

There was no sender name, only the address in Dolphin Square, enough to make it clear to Louisa who had sent it. Who was Wellesley? What had been authorised? She turned the card over, seeking further clues, but it was completely blank. Louisa put the card back in the envelope and folded it in half so it would fit in her skirt pocket. Just in time – Diana and Unity were heading towards her.

'Was it your mother?' Unity did not look concerned, merely curious.

Louisa was caught off guard. 'No, it wasn't.'

'Then who was it from?'

Louisa was saved by Diana. 'It's not actually any of your business, Unity. We'll go to the upper deck now. I need the air. It feels terribly stuffy in here.'

Diana marched ahead with great long strides towards the central staircase, Unity and Louisa keeping up behind. Diana's natural elegance, shown off to perfection by her couture wardrobe, reduced all other beings around her to goblin-like figures.

At least, that was how it felt. All three were stopped when a middle-aged woman in a cheap-looking violet dress interrupted Diana on the stairs.

'Mrs Guinness?'

'Yes?' Diana smiled at her, friendly but guarded. She did not, as a general rule, talk to strangers without an introduction.

'I know about you and Sir Oswald Mosley,' the woman began, talking in a voice that was just loud enough for a few other passengers to turn their heads.

'I'm sorry, I really don't—'

But Diana got no further. The woman drew herself back, then jutted forward and spat into Diana's face.

'You're both disgusting,' she said, each word a poisoned dart, before turning away and hurrying down the stairs as fast as her lumpen figure would allow.

There was a horrified silence for a few seconds as they watched the woman disappear around the corner, and then Diana was gasping like a fish out of water. Unity and Louisa ran to her, shielding her, handing over a handkerchief so she could wipe her face.

'Quickly, Mrs Guinness,' said Louisa, urging her to move on, away from the scene. Something in the atmosphere of the ship had soured; enough, at any rate, to allow the woman to believe she had the freedom to attack.

Diana held back until they were out of sight of anyone else, then she burst into tears. 'Why would that woman do such an awful thing?'

Unity was patting her sister's face with a fresh handkerchief.

Diana pushed Unity's hands away. She stopped crying almost as soon as she had started and stiffened her back. 'Because I am married still, that's why.' She closed her eyes briefly. 'I knew something like this had to happen at some point. It's almost a relief for it to be done. It's over now. I think I'd like to lie down for a while, if you don't mind.'

'Of course, we'll walk you there,' said Louisa, feeling rather disturbed herself. She also still needed to get into Diana's room to find the letter. But she was thwarted once more.

'No. I want to be alone.' Unity started to say something, but Diana put her finger on her lips. 'You are to say nothing of this to anyone, especially not to Muv. Do you understand?'

Unity nodded miserably.

'I will see you at luncheon,' Diana said firmly and walked away without looking back.

CHAPTER FORTY-TWO

⚜

In the so-called interview room were Guy, Sir Clive Montague, Logan and Jim. Guy had noticed Sir Clive and Jim exchange concerned looks, but neither of them said anything to each other. The cabin was not a generous one; it would be impossible to interview the one without the other hearing every word. Nor could he interview them at the same time. Being on the ship might have broken certain protocol, but he could not risk doing anything that meant evidence presented at a trial would be dismissed.

'Mr Logan, would you please take Sir Clive back to his cabin and stay with him? I'd appreciate it if conversation remained at a minimum.'

Logan agreed and began to walk towards Sir Clive, but the older man stood, indignant.

'What is going on? I may remind you that you have charged me with nothing, nor will you. I am willing to help you with your inquiries, but I will not be moved around this ship like a guilty prisoner.'

'Sir Clive,' said Guy, as calmly as he could. 'I'm sure a gentleman like you understands that we are at the beginning of what is almost certainly about to become a murder inquiry. I am the sole policeman on this ship and must proceed with every caution. I would appreciate your co-operation.'

There was some muttering to this, but Sir Clive did not object any further and shortly left the cabin with Logan.

Guy turned to Jim, who was shaking, the colour drained from his face. There was a sour smell of sweat coming from him and his blond hair looked dirty, falling lankly on his forehead. Most of all, he looked very young and afraid, a baby bird that had fallen out of its nest.

'Sit down, please,' said Guy, gesturing to one of the chairs by the table.

Jim did so, hands on his lap, trembling.

'I'm going to ask you some questions now about your movements last night.'

Jim made no response to this, but his eyes flicked from the door to the tabletop. Now and then a noise would come from the hall, a bump or loud voice, and Jim would flinch.

'Before we go any further, my name is DS Sullivan and I'm with the CID branch of London's Metropolitan Police. I did not come to this ship in any official capacity, but given that the attack happened at sea, I have the jurisdiction to conduct an inquiry. We met, as you will no doubt remember, yesterday evening when I broke up a fight you had with Mr Joseph Fowler in the Blue Bar. How did that begin?'

Jim looked out of the small window at the sea. 'I don't know.'

Guy put his pencil down. 'Jim, you can either make this difficult for yourself or easy. I suggest you make it easy and tell me straight what happened, or you're going to be leaving this ship and walking directly into a prison, which you won't be leaving for many years, if ever. Tell me what happened, if there were any mitigating circumstances, and you might have a chance of feeling the sun on your face.

'Let's start again, shall we? How did the fight in the bar begin?'

Jim looked out of the window again while he spoke. He never managed to meet Guy's eyes when he was talking.

'He thought he'd seen me say something to Mrs Fowler when we were in the bar. It made him angry. I told him to let go of her arm.'

'Had you said anything to her?'

There was no verbal response to this, only a small shrug of his shoulders.

'Had you made him angry before?'

'I don't know. I don't think so.' He raised his voice a fraction. 'I don't care much for him. He doesn't deserve her. I didn't care what he said to me, so long as he was leaving her alone.'

'Her? Mrs Fowler, you mean?'

Jim nodded.

'Were you having an affair with Mrs Fowler?'

'Sort of.'

'What do you mean, "sort of"?'

Jim rubbed his eyes with his thumbs. 'We did at one time, for a bit. Only on the ship, when she came on it. She was nice to me, she bought me things.'

'Flattered, were you?' Guy was scoffing.

'Something like that.' Jim crumpled a little further, his back soft.

'Why didn't her husband deserve her?'

'He's a bully. She was frightened of him.'

'Did you see him bully her?'

'Once or twice, but I didn't need to see it to know it was going on.'

Guy couldn't tell if Jim was being simple or obstructive. He needed to push harder. Someone knew what had happened last night, and he was going to make that someone tell him. But he'd have to be stealthy about it.

'After the fight was broken up, what did you do?'

'I was on duty. I went back to work. I had rooms to get ready for the night. I'm the steward for the first-class cabins, the odd numbers between one and twenty, starboard side.'

'I believe the altercation in the bar occurred at around half-past seven,' said Guy, referring to notes he'd made earlier. 'You were then seen in cabin B-17, belonging to Mr and Mrs Fowler, at around half-past ten, when Mrs Fowler returned from dinner. Correct?'

'Yes.'

'Between half-past seven and half-past ten, you were working in the cabins on deck B, were you?'

'Yes.'

'What happened when Mrs Fowler returned to her cabin?'

Jim's eyes moved from the door to the window, looking anywhere but at Guy. 'I don't remember exactly.'

'Can you remember who she was with?'

'She was with Lady Redesdale's maid. Louisa. I don't know why. But she wasn't there long; Mrs Fowler told her to leave as soon as they'd got in the room.'

'What sort of state was Mrs Fowler in when you saw her then?'

Jim clasped his hands together, then wiped them on his trousers. 'Upset, I suppose.'

'Why?'

'I think she'd had an argument with Mr Fowler at dinner.' He stopped and put his hands on the table, supporting himself as he moved nearer, shifting his chair closer, too. 'Is she all right? I want to see her.'

'That's not going to be possible,' said Guy.

'Whatever she said to you, don't listen. She didn't do it.'

'Who did?' Guy was wary. If this was confession or conspiracy, he couldn't tell yet.

Jim shifted again, sat on his hands, looked out of the window.

'Mrs Fowler and I were ... ' He stopped, took a breath, then carried on. 'We had started to, you know ... But we heard the door go. She told me to hide on the balcony.'

Guy was not there to judge, only to gather facts. Even so, the baseness of people perturbed him sometimes.

'They had an argument, a big one. I heard it. He was screaming at her, things he'd said before. That he wanted to die, that she was a ...' There was a hesitation that went on too long for Guy.

'A what?'

'A *slut*. She was screaming back at him; she'd had too much to drink. Nothing new there, either.'

Guy waited, but Jim didn't say any more. He prompted: 'What happened then?'

Jim shook his head. 'I can't say. I need to see her first.'

'As I've said, that isn't possible. You're both witnesses.'

'Fine.' Jim looked out of the window again, stared at the blue. Then he turned back to Guy. The trembling had stopped, the colour had returned to his cheeks a little. He seemed calm. 'I did it. I did him in, with the mallet.'

'Where did you get the mallet from?'

'It was in the cabin. I'd borrowed it, from the tool room, yesterday morning. I didn't get it for . . . that. I got it because there was a loose nail in the floor, and I forgot it was there. I was meant to return it.' He took a shaky breath. 'It was in their cabin, it was just there.'

'What did you do with it?'

'I hit him with it.'

'How?'

'What do you mean, "how"? I hit him on the head. Didn't you see the blood? There was . . . there was such a lot of blood.'

'How many times did you hit him?'

'I don't know, I wasn't counting. Twice? Four times? Enough. Enough to do it.'

Guy folded his arms and fixed Jim with a cold stare. 'And when did you go to the tool room?'

Jim frowned. 'I just told you, didn't I? Yesterday morning.'

'I'm not talking about when you borrowed the mallet. I mean when you were hiding there – when you pushed the shelves over, doing me an injury.'

'That wasn't me,' protested Jim.

'Then who was it?' Guy had to restrain himself from physically shaking Jim. It was lucky for them both that there was a knock at the door, and before Guy could reply it had been opened by a young cabin steward.

'Apologies, sir. I was sent urgently to tell you that Joseph Fowler has been pronounced dead.'

Guy stared at him blankly, his mind racing, then pulled himself together. 'Thank you. You may go.'

The door closed and Guy stood. 'Jim Evans, I'm arresting you on suspicion of the murder of Joseph Fowler.'

CHAPTER FORTY-THREE

W hen arrested, Jim said nothing, only nodded and stared at
the empty tabletop. Guy called through to the telephonist
and, after a short discussion, was put through to the bridge, the
ship's command room. When the call was over, Guy felt a surge
of pleasurable anticipation rush through him. It didn't always
happen in his line of work, but when he had a hunch that he
was on the brink of solving a case, the gratification was intense.
Shortly after, there was a knock at the door and Guy instructed
whoever it was to enter.

'Third Officer Wellesley at your disposal, sir,' said the man
who came in.

Guy tried to find a distinguishing feature about him – a policeman's habit – but it was difficult: he was of average height and
good looks, in his thirties, Guy guessed, unsurprisingly kitted out
in a crisply ironed white suit with navy and gold trim. There was,
he supposed, meant to be a look of the military about the crew,
but Guy was sure none of them could have been trained much
beyond a salute to the captain when the ship set sail.

'Thank you, Mr Wellesley. Could you please take this man, Mr Evans, down to E-131 and stand guard outside the door until I give you further instructions.'

'What's in E-131?' asked Jim, half-standing. The smell of sweat had got stronger.

'It's the ship's cell,' said Guy. 'I'm afraid you're going to have to stay there until we reach the shore. It's not the last you've seen of me, however. I will need to interview you again about what happened last night, but there are other things I need to attend to straightaway.' He turned to Wellesley. 'Take him now. Either I or First Officer Logan will be down to see you later.'

'Yes, sir,' said Wellesley. He leaned towards Guy and spoke in a low voice. 'Do I need handcuffs, sir? Only I'm not sure there are any.'

'No,' said Guy. 'Keep him walking beside you. He's under arrest and there's no land in sight. I'd say he'd be a fool to run, wouldn't you?' But he raised his eyebrow warningly at Jim as he said this.

With Wellesley and Jim gone, Guy hurried back to B-17 to see Ella Fowler. The atmosphere in the ship was very different to that which he had first felt on arriving the day before. The high ceilings and gilt that decorated the rooms on the first-class decks had intimidated him less than twenty-four hours ago. Now they seemed like cheap movie sets, nothing more than a tawdry mask for the base traits of human nature. All he wanted was to spend time with his wife. It was depressing to realise that, even out on the deep blue sea, the failings of men and women would interrupt his plans as much as they did on the streets of London. And yet, he couldn't deny the part of himself that found this work satisfying, too.

It was almost luncheon; his stomach was rumbling, but he couldn't stop. As he rounded a corner he spotted the welcome and lovely sight of Louisa, walking ahead with Unity Mitford. There was someone else with them, too, a tall, blond man. Guy double-stepped his pace and caught up with them.

'Guy,' said Louisa, caught by surprise. All four stopped walking. They were halfway across a foyer, the hub that led to various entertainments for the first-class guests – the tennis courts, shuffleboard, table tennis and so on. It was not busy today, but most of the guests walking through were dressed in jaunty sports outfits. Unity, big-boned in her green skirt and cream sweater, did not fit in with the others. The man, however, had the look of someone who had swum fifty miles every day for the last year, with broad shoulders and a tan that set off his slicked blond hair.

'Miss Mitford,' said Guy, acknowledging Unity.

'Hello, Mr Sullivan. This is Herr von Bohlen.'

The man put out his hand for Guy to shake.

'Good day to you, Mr Sullivan.'

'Mr Sullivan is Louisa's husband; he's a policeman in London,' said Unity to von Bohlen. 'It's the most extraordinary good fortune that he happened to be on the ship, for poor Mr and Mrs Fowler, you see.'

'*Ja*, I do see.' Wolfgang gave Guy a thin-lipped smile.

'I'm not sure about luck today. I'm sorry to say that Mr Fowler has died,' said Guy.

Louisa's hand went to her mouth. 'That means . . . '

'Murder.'

The German blanched beneath his tan.

Unity's face betrayed confusion. 'Are you sure, Mr Sullivan? That seems awfully dramatic.'

'I'm very sure,' said Guy. Louisa was right, these people lived in another sphere. 'In fact, while you are here, perhaps I might ask: were you at dinner in the same dining saloon as Mr and Mrs Fowler last night?'

'Yes,' said Unity. She arched her back slightly, and gave Wolfgang a sidelong glance.

'Did you happen to notice their conversation at all?'

'Yes, their table is not too distant from ours. They were frosty, from what I could see. I wasn't surprised, given the earlier altercation in the Blue Bar.'

'Hmm.' Guy nodded. 'Thank you. That at least confirms what another witness has told me.'

'Where were you going?' asked Louisa.

'I need to see if Mrs Fowler knows yet, and if not I will have to tell her. What about you?'

'We were just on our way to luncheon,' answered Unity, though the question had not been directed at her. 'Wolfgang – that is, Herr von Bohlen – is hoping to join us. I want Mrs Guinness to hear about his fascinating work for the *Kraft durch Freude*.'

'Please, Fräulein Mitford, it is not so fascinating for everyone.'

'Oh, but it is. Mr Sullivan, you would appreciate this, I'm sure. *Kraft durch Freude* means "Strength Through Joy". It's another of Hitler's brilliant ideas: holiday camps for the German workers. All those millions of people who have been through the terrible Depression, which he has lifted them out of, can now be rewarded through holidays. And Herr von Bohlen is on this ship taking notes because there's going to be a *Kraft durch Freude* cruise ship and Hitler wants to know how to make it a really good one. Imagine!'

Guy looked properly at von Bohlen. 'You know Hitler?'

The German frowned. 'Not so well – a little. He is a busy man. My father knows him better. It is how I received the commission.'

'I see,' said Guy, not knowing quite how to follow this up. He knew who Hitler was, of course, and knew the dissension in the newspapers – an antipathy he shared. There was a general feeling that Hitler was an aggressive leader, but was the better choice when no one wanted the Communists to take over Germany. Fascism was a price everyone was willing to pay. That was the measure of what he understood, but there was probably more to it than that. Unity, at least, seemed very sure what she thought about it all.

'Will you be joining them for luncheon?' Guy asked Louisa.

'No. I will take Unity to the dining room, then I have an errand. After that, I can come and find you. I'll come to Mrs Fowler's, shall I?'

'Yes, thank you.' Guy thought his wife impressive and beautiful at times like this, an oasis in the desert where kindness was as rare as water. He was not looking forward to his next task, but he had better not delay it a minute longer.

CHAPTER FORTY-FOUR

In the dining room, the tables were packed with guests, in spite of it being only a quarter to one. The men wore cream linen suits, with several sunburned necks glowing red above the collars, while the women were in pastel-coloured cotton dresses with belts to cinch in their narrow waists. Waiters darted in the aisles and the sun shone blithely through the vast plate-glass windows. Light bounced from polished silver knives to pearls that hung heavily in the creased bosoms of the *Princess Alice's* most favoured guests.

Lady Redesdale remained seated as she saw Unity approach, but there was no mistaking her disturbance at her daughter being accompanied by a man. Louisa had a small speech prepared to explain why Wolfgang had joined them, but it wasn't necessary. He stepped smartly before the matriarch, seated like a queen on a throne, and executed a neat bow with his head.

'Lady Redesdale, I hope you can forgive the intrusion. I was to dine alone today and your daughter kindly suggested that it might be possible for me to join you instead.' He seemed to pause briefly, in case Lady Redesdale sought to jump in with declarations that that would be an excellent idea. She did not. He continued, 'Naturally, it is rather out of the order of things, but it seems today is, in so many ways.'

Still, there was no response. Even Diana was looking at her mother now, as if wondering whether she had turned into a pillar of salt.

Wolfgang took a step backwards. 'I understand it is an imposition. Forgive me.' He started to turn away when Lady Redesdale finally spoke.

'No, stay. We shall ask them to lay another place.' She raised a hand and a waiter came running over. The instructions were given and, like a conjuror's trick, another chair was found, the places adjusted, a napkin and cutlery laid on Lady Redesdale's right.

Unity took her seat opposite her mother, between Diana and Wolfgang. She could not keep herself from smiling, even when Lady Redesdale gave her a severe look.

'Louisa, I find I am missing my glasses. Would you please fetch them for me?'

'Certainly,' said Louisa, trapped in the request.

At least Lady Redesdale's cabin was not so far from the dining room; she would make the trip as quickly as possible. Guy would not be with Mrs Fowler for very long, she assumed, and she still had to find Third Officer Wellesley, whoever he was.

She fetched Lady Redesdale's reading glasses – they'd been left lying on the desk beside the passenger list – and returned to the Mitfords in under ten minutes, panting slightly. The guests in the dining room were now settled, the first measures of wine had been poured, and hungry faces were largely hidden behind the menus. When sailing, luncheon and dinner took on the seriousness and timing of a religious ritual. The choosing and eating of the several courses was not something to be undertaken lightly, but with careful consideration and appreciation. There wasn't much else to do during those long hours at sea.

Lady Redesdale and her daughters, however, were not choosing their consommés or dithering between lamb chops or lobster but listening intently to Wolfgang. Louisa approached the table slowly, not wishing to rush past the guests deep in thought but also wondering what he could be saying to hold all three of them in such rapt attention. Unity and Diana looked pale and concerned; Lady Redesdale, as usual, revealed little of her inner thoughts.

' ... marvellous for Sir Oswald Mosley to have the company of his late wife's younger sister on the motoring trip around France. Not to say her love and admiration, which is said to be extensive.' His eyebrow, which Louisa could have sworn was plucked, arched with amusement.

'Her love?' Diana said, faintly.

'Of course, you are a good friend of Sir Oswald's, are you not? I presume you knew his late wife, Lady Cynthia?'

'Not as such, no. We met a few times.' Diana's voice was in danger of disappearing into the air like smoke.

'Ah, well. She was a fine woman, I am told, and I should think it is quite the right thing to keep it all in the family. The late Lady Cynthia was a Curzon, as you know. This is a prestigious noble family, great lineage, *ja*? It is absolutely correct to ensure this line continues if he is to become the next leader of your marvellous country.'

Louisa could slow her walk no more. She approached the

table and laid the glasses on Lady Redesdale's left. Diana's eyes were blurred with tears, though none had dropped onto her cheek.

Unity's reaction was typically direct. 'But the Leader's sister-in-law, the younger one, that's Baba Metcalfe, isn't it? Fruity's wife? I mean to say, she's married. They can't possibly be carrying on. Did you say they were on a motoring trip? Diana, did you know about this?'

Wolfgang held his hands up. 'Please forgive me if I have said anything untoward about your good friend. This is simply something I was told. I meant only a little light conversation.' He gave an apologetic laugh.

'Who told you?' demanded Lady Redesdale.

'I could not say for absolutely certain. It is one of those things one hears, you know. There are mutual friends we have in common, between Sir Oswald and his British Union of Fascists, so much admired by many of my colleagues in the Nazi Party.' His face was one of conciliatory agreeableness. 'I have spoken out of the line. Let us talk of other things.'

Lady Redesdale snatched up her glasses without acknowledging Louisa. 'Yes, I think we had better choose our luncheon.'

Back outside the dining room, Louisa wondered what all that had been about. Was Wolfgang trying to gain favour with Diana and Unity, implying he knew people who were admirers of Sir Oswald, close to him, even? Was it possible he knew of Diana and the Leader's love affair? Though intimate friends and family were aware, it had been kept a secret as far as possible and nothing was in the newspapers. Of course, the attack on Diana that morning showed that rumours had leaked. Louisa couldn't feel sorry for Diana either way. Sir Oswald was not a man Louisa could find any compassion for, in either his politics or his private life. Diana had to be a blind idiot to get involved with a man like that.

More pressingly, all of this meant that Louisa didn't have enough time now to find Third Officer Wellesley. She needed to go to B-17 and see if Guy was there. Ella might now know of her husband's death. The question was: had she caused it?

CHAPTER FORTY-FIVE

Guy hurried down to Mrs Fowler's cabin. Starving, he snatched some bread rolls off a trolley in the hall. It looked as if someone's breakfast had been cleared away, so he hoped he hadn't technically stolen off another's plate – a fine predicament for a policeman – but he couldn't see himself sitting down to a leisurely lunch today. At the door of B-17, the crumbs brushed off his suit, he knocked gently, then stepped inside. Things looked as he had left them not so long ago. The muddied bloodstain on the carpet was more disturbing now that the man who had bled was no longer.

He was about to walk through the doorway to Ella's bedroom when Blythe came in. She looked grey and wrung out; hardly surprising, given her lack of sleep. Guy knew he wouldn't look any better himself. Even so, he was surprised: he was sure Louisa had told him that Blythe had been sent away, with the doctor arranging for a nurse to sit with Mrs Fowler.

'She's asleep,' said Blythe, before Guy could even ask the question.

'Right.' Guy could feel his brain slowing down, in need of rest. 'I think I had better wake her up, I'm afraid.'

Blythe perched on the arm of the sofa. 'Even if you wanted to, you couldn't.'

'More morphia?'

Blythe nodded.

'Has the doctor been here?'

Blythe didn't reply to this, only looked at the floor.

'Miss North, do you mean to say that Mrs Fowler has self-administered morphia?'

Blythe kept her eyes down.

'I see.' Guy put his hands in his pockets and exhaled loudly. He walked over to the French balcony door and put his face in the sun. The warmth and the light was almost as good as the bread he'd snatched earlier. 'Why are you still here?' Guy asked.

'I don't understand ... I thought she wasn't to be left alone?'

'Mrs Sullivan requested that you get some rest; either the housekeeper or the doctor was going to send a replacement.'

Blythe shifted on her feet. 'Mrs Fowler knows me – I thought she'd be less alarmed if she woke to find me here.' There was an uncomfortable pause. 'Do you have news of Mr Fowler?' asked Blythe quietly.

Guy turned to face her. 'I'm afraid so. He died, about an hour ago.'

'Did he ever say anything, before he died? Say what happened, I mean?'

'I don't think so, but I haven't spoken to the doctor. Possibly he did.'

Blythe thought about this and then stood up. She walked

across to Guy, carefully avoiding the marks on the carpet. 'This means you're investigating a murder, doesn't it?'

'It does, Miss North. Are you able to help me with my inquiries?'

Blythe looked behind her, as if checking that Ella was not about to burst through the door. But there was no noise beyond the low hum of the ship's movement in the water.

'She did it.'

Guy felt Blythe too close to him; her breath was hot and stale. He did not want to step away, but he pulled himself up straighter.

'What did she do?'

'Mrs Fowler, she killed her husband. She did it with Sir Clive Montague because they want to run off together.'

'Did you see them kill Mr Fowler?'

Blythe's shoulders hunched in. 'No, but I know they did it.'

'Did you hear them plan to kill Mr Fowler?'

'No, sir. I didn't. But I've heard Sir Clive talking about how he loves Mrs Fowler and would do anything for her. He said it to Mr Fowler. I was in Sir Clive's bathroom, cleaning it, and he probably forgot I was even there.' Her face was sullen.

'Go on.'

'She'll say Jim did it, but he didn't. He had nothing to do with it. I know he's been ... with her in the past. She seduced him, with her money and her promises. But he's with me now and he wouldn't do anything to ruin that. We've got plans. We're not going to be stuck on this ship, we're not going to be cleaning cabins and waiting on people all our lives. There are opportunities out there and I mean to make the most of them.'

'Slow down, Miss North.' Guy put a hand on her shoulder. 'Perhaps you should take a seat.'

'No, I don't want to. I want you to believe me that Jim didn't do it.'

'That's all very well, but I'm a policeman. It's not a question of what I believe, it's a question of evidence. If you can give me any evidence that Sir Clive and Mrs Fowler plotted to kill her husband, then we can talk.'

Blythe's breathing had become ragged, but she stayed quiet.

'Can I trust you to go back to your cabin?'

'Yes.'

'Off you go, then.'

Blythe left, and Guy judged from the heaviness of her movements that she would sleep at last. After a telephone call to the doctor's office requesting a nurse to come and sit with Ella, Guy went through to see her.

The room was dark, the curtains drawn against the high sun, and the air was stuffy. Ella was no more than a shape beneath the covers, with slight movement to prove life. There was a stool beside the bed, which Blythe must have been sitting on, and various clothes draped over a chair in the corner. Shoes had been kicked off beside it, and an evening clutch bag lay on the bed, some of its contents out beside it: a cigarette box, a book of matches, a pocket diary. Guy picked it up and tried to read its contents, but the tiny writing, the dim light and his bad eyesight made it impossible. On the bedside table was a novel, *Lost Horizon*, three bottles of pills, a jar of face cream, a glass of clear liquid and a packet of mints. But these weren't what held Guy's attention – a single-use syringe did, and a tiny dark brown bottle with a metal lid that had been pierced. Morphia. That would account for Ella's deep sleep, but had she given it to herself, or had Blythe injected her? Once again, Ella could not be told of her husband's death, or her part in it. He would have to wait for her to waken to make the arrest.

Guy heard someone coming in through the door of the cabin and left the bedroom, exiting through the hallway. He'd return later. Whatever she had to face when she woke up wasn't going to be pretty; she may as well have her rest first.

Crossing to the other side of the ship, Guy found Sir Clive's room quickly. He knocked and Logan opened the door, pulling a pained face as he did so. Guy entered and immediately Sir Clive started complaining about being illegally held against his will, which he seemed to mind only marginally less than the fact that he had missed luncheon. Guy let Sir Clive blow off steam before he spoke.

'I apologise, Sir Clive, but I am investigating a murder inquiry—'

'What? Joseph Fowler is dead?'

Too late, Guy realised he had broken the news. 'Yes, I'm afraid so.'

Sir Clive sat down on a chair and put his head in his hands. 'Oh, God.'

'What was Jim Evans doing, hiding in your cabin?'

Sir Clive looked up. 'He was?'

Guy examined Sir Clive's face closely. He looked confused, and it seemed genuine.

'Are you denying knowledge of Mr Evans' presence in this room?'

'I am.'

'You are aware of who Mr Evans is?'

For the first time, Sir Clive shifted slightly on his seat. 'I am. He is a cabin steward.'

'One that works for the Fowlers,' Guy prompted.

'Yes,' agreed Sir Clive.

'You witnessed the fight between Evans and Mr Fowler in the bar?'

'Yes, I did. I don't see how that leads to him being in my room, or why I should have been aware of his presence.'

Guy knew when a suspect wasn't going to budge. He decided he would have to press the point later. 'Fine. Where were you between eleven p.m. and one o'clock in the morning last night?'

'I was here. I came back after dinner.'

'Were you with anyone in here?'

'No, of course not.' Sir Clive sat back in the chair and pulled out a slim gold cigarette case, turning it over in his hand but not opening it.

'No maid or other member or staff can vouch for you being here?'

'No. I suppose it doesn't look good for me, but I can't rustle up an alibi for you. I simply don't have one.'

'What did you do when you got here?'

Sir Clive sprang open the case and took out a cigarette, tapping it on the closed lid. 'I think I had another drink and sat in my chair, thinking things over. Not for long, then I went to bed. I read a few pages of my book, then went to sleep.' He pulled out his lighter and, after the click, took a drag. His demeanour, thought Guy, was not that of a guilty man, but his confidence was somewhat cocksure. Guy didn't like it, but he couldn't put his finger on why exactly.

'What was the first you knew of what had taken place last night?'

Before Sir Clive could answer there was a knock at the door. Guy signalled to Logan that he should answer it. Into the quiet of the room there came the confused tones of a man talking in a German accent, then apologising and finally leaving. Sir Clive stubbed out his cigarette and Guy thought he noticed a very slight tremor as he did so.

Logan came back in. 'That was Herr von Bohlen. He apologises for the disturbance; he will find you later.'

It took a second for Guy to remember why he recognised the name.

'How extraordinary,' said Sir Clive. 'I hardly know the man.'

Guy wondered why he protested so strongly. It was something else he would have to hope would become clear before the ship docked in Rome. Time was beginning to run out.

CHAPTER FORTY-SIX

⁓

The deck, this particular afternoon, was as busy as Green Park on a midsummer's day. All the passengers wanted to take advantage of both the clear sunshine to top up their tans, as well as the constant fervour of whispered rumours and conjecture that were running between them like mice on hot wires.

'The captain might as well have announced Joseph Fowler's death on the tannoy system,' said Unity as they walked along the port side of the ship, watching the news spread behind cupped hands from deckchair to sunbed.

Louisa was walking a step or two behind Unity and Wolfgang, who must have acquitted himself over luncheon, though not enough to be left alone with Lady Redesdale's daughter. For once, Louisa approved of the strict rules that meant Unity was supervised, even if she would rather have been with Guy. At least there was the fresh air to enjoy, something that had been sorely lacking since yesterday evening. She'd even managed to grab a bite to eat after a quick trip to the third-class restaurant, before collecting Unity.

Wolfgang laughed at Unity's quip. '*Ja*, it's true. The people are more excited by crime than they are afraid. The people enjoy fear, I think.' He tipped his head down lower towards Unity. 'Do you like to be frightened?'

Unity giggled. 'I like fairground rides, if that's what you mean. That terrific whoosh when you hardly know which end is up. But I suppose no one is too worried here because it's pretty obvious his wife did it. There's no axe murderer on the rampage.'

'No, just a mallet murderer.' Wolfgang laughed again.

Louisa froze. How did Wolfgang know a mallet had been used to attack Joseph? So far as she knew, it was still in the drinks cupboard of B-17, unless Guy had collected it and taken it elsewhere for safekeeping. Even then, how had news of it leaked out?

Unity gave Wolfgang a mildly aghast look at his remark. 'Please tell me, what is Herr Hitler really like? You've met him, haven't you? I wanted so much to ask you about him over luncheon, but I'm sorry to say my mother is not yet quite able to understand his brilliance. I'm sure she will, only not yet.'

'You do not have to explain to me. I know the difficulties your countrymen have, though it is very easy for me. Herr Hitler is a leader of the true sort. He understands what the people need and he delivers it to them. Germany has been suffering for too long from a lack of dignity and pride. That is all we seek to restore.'

'But Herr Hitler himself – tell me, is he shy? I somehow feel he probably is.' Unity's voice had taken on a higher pitch in her alarming eagerness.

'Yes, he is a modest man in society. As a leader of men, he is brave, as he must be. He has only simple tastes; he likes women to show their natural beauty. He eats simple food and he has faith in Germany to become great again for its

256

people. We have to rid the country of those who do not have the same faith.'

'Jews, you mean?'

Wolfgang nodded. Louisa had to bite her tongue to restrain herself from getting involved in this conversation. Unity had kept her membership of the BUF a secret from her parents and so rarely gave voice to the ugly side of her beliefs. It was hard for Louisa to hear them now.

'My father has been appointed chairman of the Reich Federation of German Industry by Herr Hitler.'

'That sounds frightfully prestigious.'

'It is,' said Wolfgang, nodding slowly. 'He has been tasked with removing Jews from the organisation. It is not so difficult to do this, most are in agreement. Besides, it does not matter whether anyone agrees or not. As chairman he is the decision-maker. Herr Hitler is most generous to my father and his family, but we are loyal to him. We will be rewarded.'

'It is so unfortunate that no one can do the same in England.' Unity spoke seriously now, removing herself from her flirtatious, girlish persona that she had switched on for Wolfgang before. 'Everything has to be decided by the people, and as we all know, "the people" do not know how to make the best decisions. Of course, when our own leader, Sir Oswald, is in power, all this will change.'

'You think he will be?'

'Oh, yes, I really do. Especially once he is married to Diana. She believes in the cause almost more than he does. They will be unstoppable together. She's so beautiful and clever, and very popular, I don't think anyone could resist.'

'Married to Mrs Guinness, you say?' Wolfgang gave his most

charming smile. 'Oh dear. Perhaps I should not have mentioned his current excursion with this Baba.'

Unity blanched. 'I wasn't supposed to tell you that. It's a secret, I mean. Diana's getting a divorce and then she will be with the Leader.' She put her hand over her mouth and widened her eyes, a cartoonish face of concern. 'Don't say anything, will you?'

Louisa felt a lurch in her stomach. The stew she had gobbled down might have been a touch rancid. She hiccuped and Wolfgang turned his head slightly, catching her eye. Was she imagining it or did he have a mischievous look about him?

He leaned down towards Unity. 'I will not tell a soul. In fact, there is something I shouldn't tell you, but we can exchange secrets, do you not agree?'

'Yes, I very much agree. What is it?' Unity picked up her walking pace a little, perhaps to put more distance between them and Louisa.

'We – that is, my family – we tell people that our fortune is in steel. And that is no lie. We have made a great deal of money. But the real reason our future lies with Herr Hitler is because he has entrusted us with his rearmament programme. It is not public knowledge as yet, we are ... ' He motioned buttoning his lip.

Unity's eyes widened. 'For war?' she mouthed.

'No, certainly not.' Wolfgang was firm. 'It is for Germany's dignity only. To let the world know that we will not be told by anyone else what we can and cannot do. Herr Hitler wants only peace. But he sees not why we should lie down and be walked upon like a worn-out carpet. The Treaty of Versailles was designed to humiliate and break us. But we deserve respect and to be on equal feet with the rest of the world. Don't you agree?'

'Yes,' said Unity. 'Yes, I do.'

Louisa was afraid now. What she had heard seemed far more dangerous than anything Iain surely supposed she would discover. Damn her work for Lady Redesdale. She needed to find Third Officer Wellesley and she needed to do it fast. But she also needed to tell Guy that Wolfgang knew about the mallet. Who should she talk to first?

CHAPTER FORTY-SEVEN

'**M**iss Unity.' Louisa ran up to her and Wolfgang and tapped her on the shoulder.

Unity did not look pleased. 'What?'

'I'm terribly sorry, but it's three o'clock and I need to return you to Lady Redesdale.' Louisa almost crossed her fingers. She hoped Unity wouldn't see through the fib.

'But I don't want to,' said Unity.

Wolfgang, however, did not attempt to dissuade Louisa. 'It has been a great pleasure, Fräulein Mitford,' he began, stepping back.

'I do wish you'd call me Unity.'

To this Wolfgang merely smiled, and Unity saw her time was up. 'Fine,' she said. 'But I don't recall my mother saying three o'clock.'

Louisa decided to minimise the extent of her lie by leading the way towards the staircase inside. Wolfgang had already discreetly gone down ahead of them. The two young women walked silently to deck B, Louisa able to do no more than pray that Lady Redesdale had retired to her cabin for an afternoon nap. She might be surprised to see her daughter return, but she wouldn't be displeased. It had only been down to the relentless work of Unity and charm of Wolfgang that they had gained Lady Redesdale's reluctant permission for a stroll around the deck after luncheon.

When they arrived, Louisa knocked on the door and then held it open for Unity.

'Aren't you coming in?'

'Sorry, Miss Unity. There's something I need to do. I'll be back shortly.'

Unity pulled a face, but it was clear she was more irritated by having her time with Wolfgang cut short to bother too much with Louisa's plans.

Hurrying off along the passage, Louisa wasn't sure where she was rushing to, exactly. She knew there must exist a captain's office of some kind where she could enquire after Wellesley. Her concern was that she needed to be discreet. The captain would wonder what a third-class passenger – a lady's maid – wanted with one of his senior crew. Nor could she pass it off as a request from Lady Redesdale or either of her daughters, as the captain would be bound to mention it to one of them, in the way that people always did when you most needed them not to. Buried in her indecision, she rounded a corner and ran straight into her own husband.

'Guy,' said Louisa, relief and concern colliding within her. He looked worn out, in need of a shave, grey shadows beneath his eyes, and his glasses could have done with a polish.

'Are you alone?'

'Yes, for once. I've shaken the Mitfords off,' said Louisa, holding his tie in her hand, pulling herself closer to him, needing the safety of his body heat.

He grinned. 'I came here to be with you, and it feels as if I've hardly seen you. Can you come with me now?'

She almost hesitated, before reminding herself that her priorities were clear: Guy first, Iain – and any of his cohorts – second. It had taken her rather too long to realise that.

'Yes,' she said, 'I can. Where are you going?'

'I want to check on Jim Evans; he's being held in the cell downstairs.'

'Cell? What, like a prison, with bars on the window?'

'Not quite, it's a small cabin with a guard standing outside. I don't think they need bars – what will they do, jump into the sea?' Guy checked over her shoulder and, seeing no one, bent to give her a kiss. 'Come on, I'll tell you what's happened as we walk.'

Louisa took him to the crew stairway and on the way he told her that he had interviewed Sir Clive and knew something was up, but he couldn't pin anything on him.

'He doesn't have an alibi,' said Guy, 'nor does he seem to be too worried about that. I can't tell if that's him throwing me off the scent, or if it's simpler than that.'

'That's he's telling the truth?'

Guy shrugged. 'Hard to remember sometimes in my line of work, but occasionally people are *not* trying to pull the wool over my eyes.'

'What do you think happened last night?' Louisa had too many things chasing their own tails in her mind: Ella in love with Jim, and her husband knowing about it; Jim and Blythe with their plans for a hotel by the sea; Joseph offering his wife to Sir Clive in lieu of the debt; and Wolfgang, somewhere in the muddle, but nothing to do with any of the rest of it except for Iain.

'I can't say for certain yet, but my guess is that when Mr Fowler returned to his cabin, he caught Jim and his wife. I think a row must have erupted and somewhere in that, Mr Fowler was struck by the mallet, either by Jim or Mrs Fowler. Jim then fled the scene, leaving her to clear up.'

'You think Mrs Fowler and Jim killed him together?'

'Yes, but I couldn't say if it was plotted. Possibly. The strange thing is that they are admitting guilt, yet they are both vague as to how they did it. Jim said at first that he heard an argument between Mr and Mrs Fowler, and when he came into the room, having been hiding on the balcony, he saw Mr Fowler had been struck on the head. Now he is saying that he is guilty, not Mrs Fowler, but he hasn't specified how, except to say he used the mallet. It could be a clever ruse to put me off the fact that it was a cold-blooded plan to kill him, or—'

'The truth.'

They had almost reached deck E and Guy slowed down. 'Given that he has confessed, I've arrested him. There's no doubt in my mind that he is very strongly connected to this murder. He's showing every sign of guilt. Only I can't pin down who struck the fatal blow.'

The mallet.

'Have you told anyone about the mallet?' asked Louisa.

'I've discussed it with the doctor, asked him if he knew whether the injuries sustained were compatible with the mallet, that's all. He seemed to think it was, but he's only a ship's doctor, not a forensic pathologist, more's the pity.'

263

'Anyone else?'

Guy shook his head, puzzled. 'No, why?'

'Because I was just walking with Unity and Herr von Bohlen, and he said—'

'Hang on,' interrupted Guy. They had come into the final passage now, and Louisa saw a man in a white uniform standing outside a cabin door. This time he was guarding a prisoner, not an empty space.

'Wellesley,' Guy called. 'Thank you. Has there been any trouble?'

Wellesley. It had to be the same one. Coincidence or deliberate? She was completely thrown by this and forgot that she needed to tell Guy about Wolfgang and the mallet.

She regarded the officer. There was nothing distinctive or striking about him, but that was probably desirable when it came to secret agents. The last thing you needed was them being easily identifiable. He was only a few years older than Guy, she guessed; hard to tell with the uniform and the erect bearing as he stood by the door.

'No trouble, sir,' said Wellesley. 'Sounded as if he was crying at one point. I wouldn't say he's in too good shape.'

'Right, well, thank you. I'd better go in and see him.' Guy turned to Louisa. 'Sorry, darling. We'll have to find each other again. We can always leave each other a message at the purser's office?'

'Yes,' said Louisa. 'We'll do that.' She hoped she looked innocent, that he didn't guess she was at that very moment hiding something from him. She wanted Guy to go so she could get on with it, get it over with, but he was delaying, hesitating at the door.

'Go,' she said at last. 'You need to know what happened.'

'Yes, you're right.' He gave her hand a squeeze and went through the door.

When the door had shut, Louisa faced Wellesley.

'The nightingale sang in Sloane Square,' she said.

'Its song made the trees blossom,' he replied. And she knew there was no turning back.

CHAPTER FORTY-EIGHT

⟨ornament⟩

L ouisa's palms felt clammy. Having established contact, she wasn't sure what was supposed to happen next. Fortunately, Wellesley took charge.

The passage was empty. Cabin E-131 had presumably been chosen for the fact that there was little reason for many guests or crew to walk past it. Wellesley moved away from the door and Louisa stepped with him.

'Did you know about me?' Louisa asked.

Wellesley nodded. His face was serious, but he didn't look unfriendly. Under any other circumstances, she'd have judged him to be a perfectly nice, harmless member of the crew. Now she couldn't help wondering if he was a trained killer. All this talk of murder was making her mind plunge to the darkest places.

'I don't suppose I can ask what you're doing on the *Princess Alice*?' she said.

Again, Wellesley replied silently, but this time in the negative.

'You have a message,' he prompted.

'I think I do.' Everything suddenly scrambled; she couldn't think exactly what it was that she had wanted to pass on to Iain so urgently. 'That is, I was going to tell him about what happened last night. It wasn't strictly the sort of thing he'd asked me to report back on. I'm here watching . . . ' She decided she had better not say the name. 'Someone else. But it seemed like the sort of event he may have wanted to know about. Just in case.' Her voice petered out, a leak in a cracked cup.

Wellesley said nothing. He continued to watch her, his eyes darting occasionally along the passage to ensure it was still empty.

'Anyway, I suppose you've told him. Or will tell him.' She was gabbling now.

'What makes you think that?'

'I . . . Well, if he wanted me to find you, I assumed it's because you're more senior.'

'Hmm.'

Louisa was starting to feel exasperated. She knew an agent had to keep his cards close to his chest, but how was she supposed to talk to him? It was like playing chess with someone when only they knew the rules.

'There is something else,' she began. 'I overheard a conversation just now, between' – she looked behind her and lowered her voice to a whisper – 'Wolfgang von Bohlen and Unity Mitford.'

Wellesley's head moved a fraction. If he was a Jack Russell, his ears would have gone up.

'He told her that his family is involved in a rearmament programme with Hitler.'

'Where were you when you heard this?'

Someone came into view, about fifty yards away, and Louisa

almost jumped out of her skin. It was only a cabin maid, carrying a mop and a bucket. She turned off into another connecting corridor before reaching them.

'I was walking a few paces behind them. Chaperoning Miss Unity.'

'Stop,' said Wellesley. 'It could have been a trick. He must have meant you to overhear. Do not say anything more about him while you are on this ship. Do not – I repeat – do not alert him in any way to your mission on here. You are in danger of disturbing a much more senior operation.'

Louisa was too frightened to reply to this. She hadn't even mentioned the mallet and dared not ask what Wolfgang's part in that might be.

'You had better go now. Your husband might come out.'

She nodded but didn't move. Her shoes might have been nailed to the floor.

'Go,' he instructed, and Louisa fled.

A few minutes later, Louisa was back outside on the deck, swallowing big breaths of the sea air, calming herself down. She was in over her head. If she had been at the bottom of the sea, it wouldn't seem as bad as the situation she was in now. She tried to disentangle the threads. If Wolfgang was in the business of tricking her, what might he be doing to Unity? She had to protect Unity, but her feelings about this were far from straightforward. She'd known the fourth Mitford girl since Unity was a small child, but she had always been a complicated character, prone to sulks and silences. Now her ardent love for fascism made her an even more difficult person to stomach. Diana was no day in the sun either. Anger overtook Louisa at having allowed herself to walk into a situation where she was spending time with these unlikeable women, away from her husband and stenography training, to be a mere servant, and now, on top of all that, also part of a sinister scheme involving the British government and fascists.

She kicked the side of the boat in fury and heard someone call out, 'Cheer up! It might never happen.' She was tempted to run up and toss him over the side.

After a few minutes she had recovered enough to decide that she had better focus on the one thing she had been sent to do: monitoring Diana and Unity. She was afraid to even spend time with Guy when he was trying to piece together the events of the night before. If she knew something about Wolfgang, she dared not say it to him. All she could do was try to stall his investigation until they got back to London. When the *Princess Alice* docked at Rome, she would telegram Iain, tell him that she was cutting her trip short, and return with Guy. The Mitfords could go to hell.

Calmer and with a plan, Louisa went back inside to make her way to Lady Redesdale's cabin, where she thought Unity would still be. She would go past the purser's office on the way and leave a message for Guy, to say she was at work and would meet him at their cabin at half-past seven. By then, Lady Redesdale and her daughters would be on their way to supper and she would have respite for a few hours. Perhaps she and Guy would even manage to sit down and have supper together themselves.

Walking through the connecting hall on deck E to reach the staircase she needed, Louisa happened to glance in another direction and saw the stocky figure of Herr Müller in conversation with Sir Clive. The normally taciturn Müller was gesticulating and talking at speed as Sir Clive listened intently. She saw them only briefly, and she was certain they didn't see her, but she did not dare to stop to check. It was them, she was sure of it.

And then she decided: what of it? If it was of importance, it wasn't of importance to her. She would be better off dismissing the sight as nothing more than two guests talking to each other. Wellesley was presumably already on to them, if there was anything for him to know about.

But like most itches one tries to ignore, it would return to the surface again and again, tormenting her resolve.

CHAPTER FORTY-NINE

I n cabin B-17, Ella Fowler was awake. The last effects of the morphia had worn off and she was stone-cold sober, ashen-faced and sitting on the sofa, looking at Guy with eyes as empty as the blue sky outside. He had told her that her husband was dead and he was arresting her on suspicion of colluding with Jim Evans to murder Joseph Fowler.

'Until the ship docks at Rome, you need to remain in this cabin, under supervision. There will be a guard stationed outside the door at all times.' Guy waited for a response, but there was none. 'When we arrive at Rome, you will be taken to a local police station for further questioning, if necessary, until arrangements can be made for you and Jim Evans to be transported back to England, most probably by train.'

Ella blinked and seemed to shake herself awake. 'With Jim?'

'Yes, you'll be kept apart but—'

'No. I mean, have you arrested him?'

Guy affirmed he had.

Ella's voice shook, though she spoke without hysteria. 'Why?

I've told you: I did it. He didn't do it, he had nothing to do with it. It was me. Don't you understand?'

'I can't say I do understand, Mrs Fowler. But I intend to get to the bottom of it before we arrive in Rome.'

'How is he? Can I see him?'

'I'm not at liberty to tell you,' said Guy, not knowing if this was strictly true or not. But they were two witnesses, at the very least. He wasn't going to tell one what the other was saying. 'And no, you can't.'

Ella lay down on the sofa and pulled a cushion beneath her head, drawing her knees up to her chest. 'You need to talk to that bitch, Blythe,' she said. 'Whatever path she's led you down, it's the wrong one. She tried to steal Jim, but she couldn't have him. She's out to destroy us both.' She pulled her knees in a little tighter and wrapped her arms around them. 'Why did you leave her alone with me? She might have killed me.'

'What do you mean?' asked Guy. He wasn't convinced by this show of vulnerability and accusation. It struck him, not for the first time, that people were all too prone to believe that they were at the centre of their melodrama when it was nothing more than a run-of-the-mill love triangle that would have run out of puff before long. That a man should be dead because of it was disproportionate – like a train crashing because someone spilled coffee on another passenger's lap.

'Mrs Fowler, are you making a serious allegation against Blythe North?'

Ella closed her eyes. 'I want my boys. Will someone tell me where my boys are?' Tears began to flow, spilling across the bridge of her nose, and soon there was a damp patch on the cushion.

Guy gave up. Whether it was morphia, or hysteria, or grief, or something else alto-goddamn-gether, he wasn't going to get anything sensible out of her. He had made his arrests; he knew what he believed to be right. All he needed now was to put together enough evidence that charges could be pressed as soon as they arrived back in London.

His second interview with Jim had yielded little more, either. Jim had been frightened and Guy suspected he was something of a simple man, pushed around by the desires and demands of both Ella Fowler and Blythe North. Whether they had driven him to murder was the question in Guy's mind. Could someone who was apparently not a nasty or scheming person be driven to kill someone in cold blood with a heavy instrument? Striking the blow not once but three times? Three times indicated intent to kill, or a 'frenzied attack', as the newspapers liked to call it. Joseph Fowler was not a man in the best of health, judging from his grey appearance, not to mention his general depression, and it may not have taken much physical effort to end his life. But even without his attempt to fight back, there would have been cries of pain, the sickening noise of the wooden mallet as it smashed open the soft skin of his head, then struck and splintered the bone, with the splattering of blood across the cream carpet. The killer had to have had a certain amount of determination. It couldn't be written off as accidental or a clumsy attempt to teach Joseph a lesson.

And then, the oddest thing of all, both Ella and Jim pleading guilty, not because they both did it but, it appeared, to prevent the other from being arrested. Why would they do that? Ella had two children, young boys who needed their mother at home, not languishing in a prison cell. Jim had plans for a life

273

with Blythe – if the maid was to be believed. Or had he thought Ella was going to keep him in style, remove him from his lowly work as a steward, possibly extricate him from his demanding and difficult relationship with Blythe? Even so, why would he have chosen last night to kill Joseph Fowler? A night when he had already been seen engaged in a fight with the deceased, in which punches were thrown. If there had been planning and intent, surely he would have waited and chosen another time. If he'd been clever, he'd have killed Joseph Fowler shortly before the ship docked at Rome, so he could make good his escape and flee to Europe. It would have been extremely difficult, if not impossible, to catch him if he had done that.

The pieces in the jigsaw that Guy had were not making a coherent picture.

Ella had now cried herself to sleep. Guy wished he could lie down and do the same. He would find Louisa, hope that the two of them could steal away somewhere quiet, talk it over. She might have some good ideas as to the motivations of these awful people. Louisa was always the solution for Guy.

CHAPTER FIFTY

~~~~~

Having left a message at the purser's office, Louisa decided to go to her cabin for a quick wash and a change of clothes. Her body clock felt completely out of sorts and she felt as if she'd been in the same skirt and shirt for days. Without looking at the time she couldn't tell how long it was since she had last eaten or when she needed to go to bed. It didn't help that unless one was outside on the deck, everywhere was either dark or lit by bright electric bulbs. She yearned for a cup of strong coffee, eggs on toast and a few crispy rashers of bacon, and yet it wasn't breakfast time, or even anywhere close to it. The ship rolled, and Louisa lurched with it. On the whole, she had been pleased to discover that she had sea legs, but occasionally one would be caught out by an unsteadying movement that tipped one's stomach to unlikely places. She had a moment of desperately wishing this was all over and they were back on land, on their way home. All she could do was remind herself that the ship was sailing, moving onwards, and eventually it would dock and they would disembark and this claustrophobic horror would be over.

As she was brushing her hair in front of the mirror, inspecting what she thought might be a new wrinkle at the side of her eyes, there was a gentle knock on her cabin door. She thought it had to be Guy and opened it, smiling, only to see Blythe standing there.

'Can I come in?'

Louisa held the door open wider. 'Yes, it's quite small in here . . .'

'I know, it doesn't matter. I have to talk to you.' Blythe pushed in and sat down on the narrow bed. Louisa put down her hairbrush and leaned against the closed door. She didn't feel unfriendly, but she did feel disconcerted. She knew Blythe would be pulling her further into the situation between Ella and Jim; she didn't want to get involved.

It turned out she was wrong.

'I've come to talk to you about Sir Clive Montague,' said Blythe. She'd managed to get some rest, by the looks of it, though the strain of the night's events still showed on her face. Her dark curls were drooping and though her skin was as smooth and white as porcelain, it only served to show up the grey shadows beneath her eyes.

'What about him?'

'I know your husband has talked to him about last night. Sir Clive will have told Mr Sullivan that he was in his room alone when . . . when Mr Fowler was . . . you know.' She gave a slightly exasperated sigh, as if Louisa was forcing her to say something she didn't want to admit out loud.

'Wasn't he? In his room alone?'

'He might have been; that's not really the point. What I'm trying to say is that your husband will believe Sir Clive knows

276

nothing about what happened to Mr Fowler, but he does.' Blythe coughed. 'Can I have some water?'

Louisa rinsed out a tooth mug and filled it with water from the tap. 'It's all I've got in here.'

'Thanks.' Blythe took a big mouthful and seemed to resettle herself. 'Sir Clive is in love with Mrs Fowler; he loathed Mr Fowler, even though they did business together. I think he thought he might persuade them to divorce and then he would marry Mrs Fowler. I don't know. They're strange people, and I can't understand why anyone would want to be with that old bag, but each to his own, I suppose.'

'I suppose,' Louisa agreed, to encourage Blythe to get to the nub of her story.

'Sir Clive paid me to look on the advance passenger lists and tell him when the Fowlers were coming on board the *Princess Alice*, so that he could be sure of staying at the same time.'

'Why?'

'At first it was so he could make sure of seeing Mrs Fowler. I didn't mind, seeing as I wanted that old witch distracted from my Jim. But then ... ' She let out another big sigh.

'Then?'

'I don't know the exact ins and outs of it, but Sir Clive invested in a business deal with Mr Fowler, and it went wrong. Mr Fowler owed him money and Sir Clive wanted it back. He thought the Fowlers were avoiding him, but he knew about Mrs Fowler and my Jim, he knew they'd want to come back on this ship, and he planned to corner Mr Fowler then.'

'Blythe, what exactly are you saying?' Louisa wanted to find out more, though she had a sense of foreboding that it was not her that should be hearing this, but Guy.

'I think Mrs Fowler and Sir Clive planned the murder. Don't you see? She would have persuaded Sir Clive that if she was widowed she would marry him, and I suppose she'd have inherited Mr Fowler's money, too. Sir Clive would have been paid back, if that was what he really wanted. Only she duped him. She doesn't want to marry Sir Clive at all, she wants my Jim. But I'll tell you something for nothing – she won't have him, neither.' Blythe stood up, a trembling hand holding the empty tooth mug.

Louisa spoke calmly; she didn't want Blythe getting overwrought. 'That's all very well, but is there any evidence?'

'Sir Clive and Mr Fowler had a fight last night.'

'No, that was Jim and Mr Fowler, in the Blue Bar.'

Blythe put the cup down and stood close to Louisa. She whispered: 'I know about that one. This was later, in the smoking room. Sir Clive hasn't told DS Sullivan about that, has he?'

'How do you know what Sir Clive and my husband talked about? They had a confidential conversation.'

'I know now, don't I? It was easy enough to guess.'

Louisa reminded herself that she could handle this, she wasn't out of her depth here. It was nothing more than a vindictive young girl trying to protect her lover. She only had to ask the difficult questions until Blythe realised she was the one who was swimming out of the shallows.

'Well, then, how do you know about the fight? What was it about?'

'I don't know what it was about. But my friend, Alfred, who works in the bar, he told me. He knows about Sir Clive and everyone knows who Mr Fowler is now. I mean, since he died, lots of the crew have put two and two together.' Blythe gave a smug smile.

'Even if they did fight, it doesn't mean Sir Clive killed him later, does it?'

'Then why didn't Sir Clive tell your husband? Why doesn't he want the police to know?'

'Fine,' said Louisa. This had gone far enough. 'I will talk to him. I think you'd better go now. But, Blythe ... '

'Yes?'

'Not a word to anyone else. I mean it.'

'I won't. I don't care about anyone else anyway, I just want to see Jim. I don't know where he is, even,' Blythe admitted at last, emotion breaking across her face.

'You will soon, but you understand everything has to be done properly, if the right person is to be charged with the murder.'

'Are you a secret policewoman or something?'

Louisa felt caught out and let out a nervous laugh, and could have kicked herself for it. 'No, what makes you say that?'

'I don't know. You just seem a little involved in it all.'

'You were the one who came to me.'

'Hmm.' Blythe tossed her head. 'Well, I've said it. I'd better get back to work. Find me, will you, when they've let Jim out? I need to see him.'

Louisa opened the door and nudged Blythe's back. 'I'll find you.' She wouldn't, but even so, she had better let Guy know what Blythe had said.

CHAPTER FIFTY-ONE

❧

24 May 1935
Old Bailey, Court Number One

Almost as soon as Mr Manners had sat down, Mr Vangood was up. In spite of his generous girth and heavy-lidded eyes, he sprang up with the agility of a jungle cat. These challenges were the lifeblood of the criminal barrister, and for this provincial gentleman, the chance to corner his prey in the Old Bailey was likely to be a career highlight. The court readied itself for a showdown.

'Sir Clive, could you confirm for the court your marital status, please.'

The judge looked up sharply at this but did not interrupt.

'I am a bachelor, sir.'

'You have never married?'

Sir Clive looked confused at this question but shook his head. 'No.'

Mr Manners was poised to object, but it wasn't yet clear what path Mr Vangood was going down.

'I put it to you, Sir Clive, that you had something of a prefer-ence for the company of Mrs Fowler.'

When Sir Clive replied this time, it was not with the same smooth tones he had used in his cross-examination with Mr Manners. 'I have already said that I found Mrs Fowler to be more of a congenial character than her husband.'

'You've also said you are, I quote ... ' Mr Vangood cast a glance at his notes, 'someone who has "lived a number of years". I think by that you were implying a certain worldliness, were you not?'

'Well, yes ... '

'And you went on to say that you would be "a fool to think such things do not occur". Were they happening with you, Sir Clive?'

'I'm not quite sure of your question.' The accused – for that was how it looked now – fidgeted mildly with a button on his jacket.

'Did you, or did you not, attempt to seduce Mrs Fowler yourself?'

'No, I most certainly did not.'

'Then why did Mrs Fowler tell Jim Evans that you had told Mr Fowler that if she were to lie abed with you, that you would relinquish him of his debt to you?'

'No. That's not quite ... ' Sir Clive stopped. He looked to the ceiling. He'd not said much, thought Guy, but he'd already said the wrong thing.

'Not quite what you meant, but almost what you meant, Sir Clive?' prompted Mr Vangood. 'I put it to you, sir, that Mr Fowler was in the way of your intentions with Mrs Fowler. That he was an obstruction to your desire to be with Mrs

Fowler and, having lent him money, which you knew would be lost, you now sought to use the debt as a sordid means to your own ends.'

'No, no,' Sir Clive's voice was raised. 'That's not how it was at all.'

'Not at all, or "not quite"?'

To this, there was no response from Sir Clive.

'On the night in question, the night on which Mr Fowler was so viciously attacked and left for dead, you were on board the *Princess Alice*, were you not?' Mr Vangood had put the knife in. Was this going to be the twist?

'Yes, I was. As were several hundred other guests, as you know.'

'Had you seen Mr and Mrs Fowler that evening?'

'Briefly, at a cocktail party in the Blue Bar before dinner.'

'Did you talk to either of them then?'

Sir Clive seemed to have recovered something of his confidence. He spoke more smoothly, more as he had when he had first taken the stand. 'I can't recall, but I don't think that I did.'

'Yet you definitely noticed them there?'

'Well, yes. There was a fight between Jim Evans and Mr Fowler. It was over quite quickly, but it was nonetheless very disturbing for those present.'

'Did you know why the fight had started?'

'No, I did not.'

'But you knew, as has been established in this court, that Jim Evans was Mrs Fowler's lover. Perhaps you presumed that either one of the men believed they were defending her honour in some way?'

'I suppose I must have presumed, as you say.'

Mr Vangood hitched his trousers up over his hips. They were a little shiny over the knees. 'Did you comfort Mrs Fowler as this fight was happening or in the immediate aftermath?'

'I did not. There were others present who appeared to reassure Mrs Fowler. Shortly afterwards, she went into dinner with her husband.'

'You were not dining with them on that occasion?'

'No, I dined at the captain's table.'

The judge looked at the barrister. 'Is this line of questioning going anywhere, Mr Vangood?'

'Yes, my lord. If you could bear with me for just one more moment.'

Sir Clive threw a look of gratitude in the judge's direction, but this was not acknowledged.

'After supper, what were your movements?'

'I had a glass of brandy in the smoking room as usual, before retiring to my bed.'

'At no other time that night, from going into dinner until you went to bed, did you have any interaction with Mr or Mrs Fowler?'

'No, I did not.'

Mr Vangood looked at the jury and one of the men patted his hair self-consciously, as if wondering whether the barrister had seen something there.

'So you did not have an altercation with Mr Fowler in the bar at half-past eleven that night that resulted in punches being thrown and both of you being restrained by the other guests there?'

Sir Clive was silent.

'I think I had better remind you, Sir Clive, that if you tell a lie in court that is later discovered, you may be charged with perjury. A serious crime that carries a serious punishment.'

Sir Clive drank some water before he spoke. The care he was taking to speak in a measured and calm way was clear. 'I believe that is correct. It was over in a matter of seconds and I never gave it another thought, perhaps because the news I heard the following morning was deeply worrying.'

Mr Vangood turned to the jury again, this time with a smile of satisfaction on his face.

'No further questions, my lord.'

CHAPTER FIFTY-TWO

I t was only as she was walking away from her cabin that it occurred to Louisa to wonder: how did Blythe know which was her cabin? Louisa had never told her. Perhaps it was information on those passenger advance lists that she had. Did all the staff get given a copy, or was it something that Blythe had had to get hold of in secret? The thought flitted across her mind that Blythe might have made a good agent for Iain, too. Then she shivered. What if she *was* another agent? No, that would be absurd. Even so, there was an awful lot of subterfuge going on. Had there been another fight between Joseph and Sir Clive that Guy wasn't aware of?

At that, the itch made itself felt on the surface: the conversation she saw between Sir Clive and Herr Müller. Was there a connection between Sir Clive, Wolfgang and Joseph Fowler? At the various parties and drinks, she was fairly certain she'd seen Wolfgang and Mr Fowler in the same room, but never talking. She was probably reading too much into it. Sir Clive might have been helping Herr Müller find his way somewhere; they could easily have been introduced at one of the captain's parties and knew each other enough to be friendly.

She didn't like Herr von Bohlen, though. And her instinct had been right on that: Wellesley was on this ship to follow him. Mention of the mallet made her even more uneasy, though he could have talked to the doctor. It might be an open secret if the doctor was indiscreet. Even so, she must make sure that Unity wasn't alone with him again. Lady Redesdale would agree to this easily enough. Unity's stubbornness would be the only hurdle, but Louisa would simply have to be a very efficient chaperone.

What she hadn't reckoned on was Diana.

When Louisa came into Lady Redesdale's suite she found the matriarch sitting on the sofa, Unity beside her, while Diana stood by the drinks cabinet, mixing herself a martini. It was a little early, but Louisa had noticed a certain relaxation of their usual rules while on the ship, and it was unsurprising if the events of the previous night had thrown all protocol out of the porthole.

'Louisa,' said Lady Redesdale without looking at her. 'I was beginning to think you had jumped overboard.'

'I do apologise, m'lady. What with last night—'

But she was cut off. 'I don't want to hear any more about it. As it is I can hardly face dinner tonight. All those ghastly people talking about it. I may not go at all, and plead another migraine. If that is the case, I will need you to chaperone Unity.'

'Of course.' What else could Louisa say?

'I'm having dinner with Herr von Bohlen,' said Diana, and there was a note of glee in her voice.

Unity's face turned a darker shade of thunder.

'Darling, don't you see? I'm doing it for you,' Diana cooed,

286

pouring the cocktail into a glass, the ice rattling. 'And also for the Leader, of course. As I do everything.'

Unity crossed her arms and stared at the floor.

Diana sipped her drink. 'Herr von Bohlen is sympathetic to the difficulties some of us face, when we believe in our cause. He knows how it feels; he says he's been through very similar experiences in Germany.' Though she faced her mother and sister, Louisa had the feeling the explanation was for her. She was stating her defence. 'His own sister was attacked by a group of Bolshevik thugs only a few months ago. I want to talk to him about how we can tackle this awful bullying when we need to in England. For when the Leader really is our leader.'

'I thought you said you were doing it for me,' said Unity, arms still crossed.

'Yes, I am. He might be very suitable, darling. Therefore I will sound out his credentials on your behalf.'

'No daughter of your father will marry a Hun,' said Lady Redesdale, then she glanced briefly at Louisa. She had reminded herself that there was a servant in the room. 'Nor do I like this talk of young women being beaten up for their beliefs. Please stop it, Diana.'

'Farve is absurd,' Diana retorted. Louisa wondered if this was her first martini. 'His own father barely listened to any music that wasn't written by Wagner. Unity's middle name is *Valkyrie*, for goodness' sake. It's only the damn war that makes him feel like that. The German soldiers he fought were a different generation – why must their children be punished for the sins of their fathers?'

'I am not discussing this now,' her mother replied quietly.

In response to this, Diana made a show of looking at her

wristwatch, an elegant gold Cartier bracelet that Louisa remembered had been a present from Bryan. 'I need to get ready. Louisa, will you come with me, please? You can come back and fetch Unity shortly. Herr von Bohlen is collecting me from my cabin.'

In Diana's bedroom, Louisa laid out the evening clothes – a pale grey satin dress, cut on the bias, worn with four long strings of pearls and a short-sleeved bolero in silver fox. She looked at the bedside drawer where she knew the letters were. Could she risk trying to read that letter while Diana applied her make-up in the bathroom? Louisa knew it didn't take her long – less than ten minutes – to draw her arched eyebrows and darken her eyes. She would finish with a red lipstick and a dab of Chanel No. 5.

As she prepared herself, Diana called out to Louisa from the other room, chatting informally, which wasn't usual. Louisa walked around to the drawer and slowly slid it open.

'What news of Mrs Fowler? Has Mr Sullivan talked to her?' Diana asked.

Louisa felt protective of Guy's investigation. She wasn't at all sure she could divulge terribly much. On the other hand, the gossip on the ship was of nothing else. Such speculation could be more damaging than any of the facts.

'Yes, he has. But I think she's in shock, unable to say much that makes sense.'

Louisa looked in the drawer. The letters were no longer tied up but were loose. It was going to take time to work out which one was the newest. The date would have to be after they had left London. Keeping one eye on the door, Louisa pushed the letters around, trying to see the postmarks.

'I'm not surprised. She was drinking like a sailor last night,'

Diana said with a light laugh. 'Mind you, anyone would with a husband like that. Not to speak ill of the dead.'

Louisa found this astonishing. A man had died. He had been a bully, an unhappy and bitter old man, but his wife had taken a young lover. Could anyone be so callous about such a harsh ending, even for one like him?

Apparently, they could.

Then she heard footsteps and quickly shut the drawer. Damn. Foiled again.

Diana came through, hair and make-up done, wearing her silk robe, ready to put on her stockings and dress. 'Don't look at me like that, Louisa. I know it was awful, but if one dwells on it too much it's going to ruin the entire trip. With any luck Muv will decide we can leave at Rome and go straight home. I miss the boys.' Her face changed and she quickly wiped away a tear before it had a chance to fall. 'I'm worried, too. What Herr von Bohlen said at lunch today about the Leader and Baba . . . How did he know? Does it mean the whole world is talking about them?'

Louisa busied herself with putting away the shoe trees. She wasn't used to Diana being like this and knew she couldn't give her the reassurance she sought. Her stupidity and naivety enraged Louisa: everyone knew the rumours about Sir Oswald. The numerous affairs, the constant flirtations, the caddish behaviour – to put it generously. For Diana to imagine that he would stop all that . . . She may as well have wished for flowers to turn away from the sun.

Diana fell into a thoughtful silence as she dressed and Louisa was grateful to have no more said on the subject. Just as the quiet was about to turn awkward, there was a smart rap at the door.

'Open it, would you?' said Diana. 'I'll just put my earrings in.'

Louisa walked through to let in Herr von Bohlen. Only, he didn't walk straight inside.

'Frau Sullivan,' he said quietly. 'I was hoping to see you this evening. I didn't know it would be so soon.'

This took Louisa aback. How did he know her surname? And why would he hope to see her?

'Is this to do with Miss Unity? I'm sorry I interrupted you both, but you must understand—'

Wolfgang put a finger to his lips. 'No, no. It is not about that.'

Louisa was silenced, and unnerved.

Wolfgang reached into his inside breast pocket, watching Louisa's face as he did so. He pulled out two white envelopes, showing her just enough of the writing on the front, with a familiar ink smudge.

It was the letter addressed to 'The Hon. Mrs Guinness' from Sir Oswald Mosley. The letter that Louisa had taken from Diana's bedside drawer and failed to replace. It had been in Louisa's cabin the last time she saw it. Now Wolfgang had it in his hand.

'Someone has been misbehaving, *nein*?' he said with a smirk, and replaced the letters before stepping past her and into the drawing room.

CHAPTER FIFTY-THREE

Two letters. Louisa had read one of them, of course, and had meant to find a time to put it back in Diana's room, but what with everything that had happened, she had failed. The second letter he held – it had to be the one that Diana had collected in Livorno. The one Louisa had been fruitlessly looking for, only moments earlier. The trip to the Continent that Sir Oswald had promised to explain was the trip with Baba that Wolfgang had indiscreetly mentioned at luncheon. Deliberately, she now realised, he had said it in front of her.

She'd been a fool.

Sir Oswald had written in that first letter that his reasons were for the good of him and Diana, as well as the country. If those reasons were political, Wolfgang could have his hands on information that endangered them all. She had failed in her mission.

Now Wolfgang had the letters in his possession and there were so many questions. Why? Why had he stolen them? How had he known where Louisa's cabin was, and how had he known there would be something to find? How could Louisa retrieve the letter and make sure it went back to Diana, before she noticed it was gone?

Most pressingly of all: why had Wolfgang chosen to alert Louisa to the fact that he had stolen the letter and read its contents? He could only have gone to her cabin because he knew there was something he was hoping to find. If not the letter – he could not have known she had it; Diana hadn't even noticed it was missing – then it could only be that he knew she was an agent and was looking for proof. A notebook or a scrap of paper with a code written on it. There was only one reason he would want to find something like that.

Blackmail.

Dread crawled into her stomach.

It had to be Wellesley who had told Wolfgang about Louisa. He was the only other person on the ship who knew. Iain thought he could trust Wellesley, but what if he was a double agent? Whoever Wolfgang was, if Wellesley was watching him, telling Louisa to stay away from him, then Wolfgang was under protection. Untouchable. He could be capable of anything without fear of retribution.

Even murder.

CHAPTER FIFTY-FOUR

The ship was due to dock in Rome in less than twelve hours. Guy knew that the local police had been alerted to the death of Joseph Fowler. A telegram had also been sent to DCI Stiles in London. There would be an undertaker ready to take the body and prepare it for its return to England. Embalming was needed, as soon as possible. Guy had made the mistake of going into the airless room where Joseph Fowler lay, to see if there were any clues on his body that he had missed; the smell of decomposition was already unmistakeable. The rotting flesh hit his nostrils and forcefully reminded him that he was dealing with the unlawful and tragic killing of a human being, someone who needed justice: a husband, a father. He hadn't been perfect, but who was? He was a man who had given in too easily to his carnal desires, but it seemed to Guy that it was only in pursuit of trying to keep his second wife happy that he had made fatal mistakes, taking on work and debt that he couldn't possibly manage. Who among them could say they would not do the same?

The Italian police would be waiting to imprison those whom

Guy had arrested and charged, if he had managed to do so. The expectations would be high. He was a detective sergeant in a force with an international reputation for excellence. But the pressing point was that once they were off the ship, the opportunity to gather further clues and information would be gone. There would be additional questioning of the suspects, but it would be Guy's reports on the ship that would direct the trial at court. There was no room for error, and that meant recording as many hard facts as possible rather than relying on supposition or assumption made after the ship had docked.

From seeing Joseph's body, Guy went to the purser's office and found the message from Louisa waiting for him, which told him that she would be working for Lady Redesdale until after seven o'clock, when she had seen them to the restaurant. He looked at his watch: it was a little after six.

Jim Evans had been arrested and charged, and was being held in E-131, guarded by a rotation of crew. No one was armed, and there was nowhere for Jim to run to, unless he threw himself overboard.

Ella Fowler, also arrested and charged, was being kept in her cabin, also under watch.

He should feel settled, but the nagging feeling that something wasn't right wouldn't leave him. He went over the facts in his mind. Ella and Louisa had returned from dinner to cabin B-17, where Louisa had been dismissed. She was witness to the fact that Jim Evans was in the room when they arrived, and still there when she left. Joseph Fowler had returned later, around midnight, shortly after Guy had seen him and the fight had been broken up.

These facts were certain.

After that, it got sketchy.

As far as Guy could see it, there were four op...

First, that Jim had left the cabin before Joseph arr...
when Ella's husband returned, there was an argument, w...
had led to her grabbing the mallet and hitting him over the
head with it three times, before she telephoned the maid and
the doctor.

Second, that Ella and Jim were interrupted by Joseph returning, there was an argument, and Joseph was attacked by both
Ella and Jim. Ella could have encouraged Jim to flee, while she
worked to clear up the mess.

The third scenario was that Ella and Jim were interrupted by
Joseph, Jim hid on the balcony, heard the row between Ella and
her husband, came out and found the bloodied body, knew he
would be a suspect and fled.

The fourth possibility was that Ella went to bed, and Joseph
returned to the cabin to find Jim there. The fight they had had
earlier in the evening broke out again, resulting in Jim attacking
Joseph with the mallet, fleeing and leaving Ella to discover her
husband's bloodied body. Given the amount of morphia she
seemed to take, as well as how drunk she was, perhaps it was possible that she wouldn't have heard anything until it was too late.

It was only from the point at which Blythe and the doctor
had arrived at the cabin that Guy could pick up the facts again
with any certainty. When Blythe arrived, Ella had removed her
husband's bloody waistcoat and jacket, and asked the maid to
rinse them out. A towel was wrapped around Joseph's head, too,
presumably to prevent further loss of blood. Which begged the
question: why would Ella attempt to murder her husband and
then immediately try to save his life?

Diana Guinness had also been telephoned – why? It was as ἰ Ella was planning a party. Was she celebrating the attack? Or what she saw as a new possible future with Jim? Or was she, in her drunken, possibly morphia-induced state, unaware of the seriousness of her husband's condition? By the time Guy had arrived, the captain and other members of the crew were in the room, alerted by the doctor, and Ella was blind drunk, playing music on the gramophone player and seemingly having, to all intents and purposes, lost her mind. She was seen dancing and even trying to kiss one of the crew.

Whatever had happened, Jim had done himself no favours by going on the run in the ship, hiding in the tool room, where his panic and distress had meant he'd pushed the shelves over, knocking Guy out in the process. Guy would be able to arrest him for assaulting a police officer, at the very least.

The tool room was another conundrum. Logan had expressed his surprise that Jim had even known where it was. Any tools that were borrowed had to be requested through the Deck Department, where the senior officers were based. The return would be arranged similarly, in reverse.

The central difficulty was this: both his arrested and charged suspects were confessing to the murder, when neither seemed capable, even if the motives did fit. Why would both of them admit to it? Unless each thought the other had done it and was trying to protect them, taking the hit out of love. That led to the possibility that neither of them had done the deed.

What if a third person was responsible?

Jim had been discovered hiding in Sir Clive Montague's cabin. Why had he gone there? And had Sir Clive truly not known he was there? There was something fishy about that man.

Louisa had told Guy that Sir Clive was in love with Ella Fowler, that her husband had offered up his wife on a plate to cancel out the debt. Could he and Ella have plotted together to kill Joseph? But then why would she confess? More likely, Sir Clive had been outraged by Joseph's suggestion, and killed him for it. The problem was, although he had no alibi, he didn't seem concerned about this, which meant either he had the confidence of a supreme liar or he was innocent. Also, it didn't explain why Ella and Jim would take the rap.

What if an *unknown* person was responsible?

The logbook. Guy needed to check it. He should have been furious with himself for not doing it sooner, but he couldn't waste another minute. It was basic policing: find the weapon, link it to someone and you have your man.

Guy ran to Logan's cabin and knocked on the door. It was clear from Logan's rattled appearance that Guy had woken him from deep sleep. There was a muddle of apologies on either side, but Guy cut it short, explaining that he needed to see the logbook for the tool room. Logan grabbed his jacket and took them both down there, again down the endless stairs, through the thick, heavy doors that shut out all sound and light, until they reached the final door, beside which hung the logbook, attached by a string to a nail.

The mallet had been signed out the day before.

'I don't think this will tell you anything helpful,' said Logan, studying the initials. 'Only a limited number of people have access here, as you know. And the mallet was signed out by a man I know well and, frankly, I would put my life in his hands. He's completely trustworthy.'

'Who is it?' asked Guy.

'The initials are W.W. It's Third Officer Wellesley.'

The man who had been guarding Jim Evans in the cabin. Was that a coincidence?

'Why would Jim have asked him to sign out the mallet?'

Logan's mouth twitched. 'Jim might not have asked him. The request would have been made to the Deck Department and a message would have been left there. I would guess that Wellesley was checking over the requests and decided to fulfil it. The higher-ranking officers are required to make regular checks of the tool room; this would have killed two birds with one stone.' He looked down at the logbook again. 'There *is* something unusual, though.'

'What?' Guy held his breath. Those tiny details that people noticed at second glance were often the most telling of all.

'Well, he's worked on this ship for four years and this is the first time he's ever logged a tool out.' Logan looked back up at Guy. 'It doesn't necessarily mean anything.'

Third Officer W. Wellesley. Guy would talk to him now.

CHAPTER FIFTY-FIVE

Louisa did not know how to handle this situation. This was far more difficult, darker and plain terrifying than anything she thought she would get into when Iain had first asked her to report on Diana and Unity. She knew fascism was ugly. After Sir O's rally had spoiled their wedding day, she had closely watched the growth of the movement in Britain, as well its counterparts in Italy and Germany. The connection with Diana had appalled her, made Louisa feel dirty and guilty, merely by association. There had been an increasing use of militaristic uniforms by Sir O's followers, which were, as she understood it, to motivate the fascists and intimidate the opponents. Guy told her that the news of any gathering crowd of the Blackshirts put the police on high alert. There had not yet been any serious fights, but Guy knew that people who opposed the movement would turn up to make their voices heard, and the Blackshirts were said to be increasingly armed against them. There were whispers of knuckledusters and barbed wire wrapped around chair legs, ready to be used as weapons.

But all this was tame when it came to Nazi Germany, Iain had explained. She wasn't sure if the two leaders, Hitler and Sir Oswald, were exactly in alignment with each other, but Unity's fervour for fascism, and Diana's encouragement of it, was both unnerving and bewildering. Louisa couldn't think what it was that had cast such long shadows in their hearts. The Nazis were beginning to hound Jewish people in their own country, and while she hadn't heard Diana or Unity say anything directly in sympathy with such extremism, there had been casually anti-Semitic remarks that had revolted her.

And now she was somehow caught up in this violent, political game. She needed to talk to someone about it, but she was no longer confident she could talk to Wellesley, as Iain had instructed her to do. If he had told Wolfgang about Louisa, then he could be working for the other side. Her best hope now was to not cause serious damage. Thank goodness the ship docked within hours. If she could stall Guy from concluding his investigation before they arrived in Rome, then she could get in touch with Iain and find out what needed to be done.

Having left Diana with Wolfgang on their way to supper, Louisa walked the short passage to Unity's room and entered without knocking. She hoped she could take Unity quickly to the Blue Bar, where Diana said she would be, before the three of them went in to dinner.

The lights were on in Unity's room, even though the sun hovered above the horizon, and Louisa saw that Unity was before a small dressing table, closely inspecting her face in the mirror. She had done her hair differently, and not very well, with two short plaits on either side, pinned at the back with a mass of hair grips.

'Louisa,' mock-wailed Unity. 'I was trying to do a Germanic look, but I don't think it's worked.'

A diplomatic silence was all Louisa could manage.

Unity started to pull out the grips and undo the plaits. Her hair now had thick, uneven crimps in it. 'I don't know what I thought I was doing trying to compete with Diana.'

'What are you competing for?' Louisa asked, as if she didn't know the answer.

'Herr von Bohlen, of course. She already has the Leader, but she has to have every man fall in love with her. It's not just her. No one in my family ever lets me have what I want.'

Louisa was not going to get into this. 'Let me brush your hair; I'm sure I can fix it. You shouldn't keep them waiting.'

Unity handed Louisa the brush, and she got to work.

'What was going on between you and Herr von Bohlen when I saw you on the stairs last night?' Louisa knew this question was a risk, but it was one she had to take.

Unity's pale skin never was able to conceal her blushes. Sitting in front of the mirror and watching herself colour, she couldn't avoid answering Louisa.

'Please, don't tell Muv. We were talking, and Herr Müller was being kind, giving us privacy by being on lookout.'

'I won't tell Lady Redesdale,' said Louisa, hoping this pledge wouldn't be tested. 'But I do have to make sure that you are not in any danger.'

'Danger?' said Unity archly. 'From what? Men aren't a danger; I know how to say no. And besides, we really were only talking.'

'Really?' Louisa stopped brushing and locked eyes with Unity in the mirror.

Unity's face assumed defiance. 'There was a kiss.'

Louisa saw her own face: it showed panic.

'Only once. I had to . . . to know what he thought of me. It's not his fault, I don't want you thinking that. Besides, why shouldn't we kiss? It's not as if he's married.' A dagger in her own sister's back. 'He was so terribly nice about it and was the one who suggested that if we were to . . . talk, alone, we should go to the staircase, where no one would see us and my reputation wouldn't be ruined.'

'Very kind,' muttered Louisa.

'I thought so,' said Unity.

'Then what were you talking about?' This was as intimate a conversation as they'd ever had, but it was her chance, she couldn't let it go.

'I asked him if he knew anyone suitable in Munich that I could stay with. I don't want to go to Paris, like Diana and Jessica. I want to learn German, and I want to try to meet Herr Hitler. I feel so certain that I could do it and we could be friends. At the very least, I could admire him from a shorter distance than this one. We've so much to learn from him. I wish you could see it, Louisa.'

'Perhaps politics is not for me.' Louisa did not want to start that particular conversation with Unity. 'But I think you should be careful. He's quite a lot older than you.'

'He's twenty-eight, not so much older. Perfectly suitable.'

'Lord Redesdale would never allow it,' said Louisa.

'He can't tell me what to do. I'm a grown woman.' Unity's mouth had set with determination. 'Have you finished brushing my hair? I'd like us to leave now. Whatever my sister thinks she's doing, she's not going to get a monopoly on Herr von Bohlen.'

CHAPTER FIFTY-SIX

Louisa took Unity to the dining saloon and left her there with Diana and Wolfgang. She felt reluctant, but she also had no choice.

She couldn't talk to Guy for fear of revealing herself – if Guy knew she suspected someone on the ship of being a secret agent, she'd have to tell him about the commission from Iain, and that could endanger him. She couldn't talk to Wellesley. There was one person who was caught up in all this that might give her some answers. If she could ensure that Guy did not charge the wrong people with murder, she would have done the best by her husband, without compromising her safety with Wellesley.

Louisa went straight to his cabin and knocked on the door. Sir Clive opened it and failed to disguise his surprise at seeing her there.

'Do you have a message from Mrs Guinness for me?' he asked.

Louisa shook her head. 'I need to talk to you.'

He hesitated, then stepped aside and let her into the room.

Inside, he poured himself a whisky, without offering her anything, then sat down. Louisa remained standing.

'Will you tell me what this is about? I've had quite a day of it so far.'

'My husband is investigating the murder, as you know,' Louisa began, willing herself to find the courage to go on. 'I am assisting him, given that he is here alone and was not aboard this ship in any official capacity.'

'Go on.'

'I know that you lost money in a deal with Mr Fowler, and that you are in love with Mrs Fowler.'

Sir Clive raised his eyebrow. 'I'll neither confirm nor deny such a bold statement. But what makes you think those things?'

'Mrs Fowler told me.' His silence confirmed her earlier statement. She decided it was all or nothing. 'Do you think Mrs Fowler killed her husband?'

Sir Clive put his drink down carefully, slowly. 'No, I don't. She was unhappy and he was a bully, yet I think she was fond of him, protective, even. He allowed her to have her caprice' – his mouth pursed, as if he'd tasted lemon – 'with the cabin steward, and she was grateful to him for it.' His hulk softened, like a plum left out in the sun.

'What I don't understand is where you fit into the picture,' said Louisa.

It was strange, in the room. She could feel the cold of the night air pressing against the window. The darkness beyond, the low light in the room, somehow levelled her with Sir Clive. There was an atmosphere of intimacy and trust that she knew would disappear as soon as the door was opened. But for now, she had found her voice.

'Why were you talking to Herr Müller?'

Clive raised his eyebrows in surprise, then he chuckled. 'You don't miss a thing, do you?'

'Tell me. I've got time for the long story.'

'I see. I'll tell you, but it can't go any further.' His voice was low, gentle.

'Why not?'

'That will become clear. When I met Mr and Mrs Fowler, I was struck by them as a couple. She is someone of exceptional character. Yes, she is beautiful, but any fool can see that. If we are talking privately, and I think we are, then I will confess that I think what is often missed – especially by her husband – is her passion, her talent for music and beauty. She is no ordinary woman: she won a medal for bravery in the war, brought up her first son alone, is an artist. She is defiant in the face of British convention in a way I hope to be but never am. But she is also vulnerable to the weaknesses of her sex and needs guidance and protection. I wish she would allow me to give that to her.'

'And Mr Fowler?'

'He was a talented architect, of that there is no doubt.' Sir Clive's posture was expansive, as if he was relieved to be able to talk about his relationship with the Fowlers. 'In fact, I've seen his work in British Columbia, I know what he's capable of. But he was foolish to leave his first wife and children for Ella. I understand the temptation, of course I do. But how could he have ever thought that he could provide for and satisfy someone as extraordinary and wonderful as her? He is too dull, too failed, too embittered. I invested heavily in his proposal for Blenheim because I believed in his vision, but also because I hoped that the success of it would at last allow him to give Ella the life to which she should become accustomed. But it failed. I stood to lose a great deal of money in it, which I could just about stand, but then I heard about the potential investment by the National Socialist Party.'

'What is that?' But she knew. Louisa felt a cold trickle of fear spill down her spine. The final pieces of the jigsaw were starting to fall into place. But only she would be able to see the finished picture.

'Blythe North told me.' Sir Clive knew there would be a reaction from Louisa to this name.

'I'll exchange your confidences for one of my own,' said Louisa. 'Blythe has already told me that you paid her to check the passenger lists in advance.'

Sir Clive shrugged. 'Miss North is easily bought. She told me about a conversation she heard between Joseph Fowler and Herr Müller on the first day of this trip. Blythe heard Mr Fowler boasting of the investment he'd had from figures "high up" in the Third Reich. He believed that Hitler himself was keen on the idea of Blenheim Palace as his own residence when they take over Britain.'

Louisa did a double take. '*What*? When they "take over" Britain? What does that mean?'

'His statement was no surprise to me. Sir Robert Vansittart is a friend of mine. He's the permanent under-secretary at the Foreign Office. It's an open secret that he believes when the current government in Germany has gained the confidence to do so, they will loose another war on Europe.'

Whether this Sir Robert would prove to be right or not – and she hoped he would not – it was clear Iain had not been acting on his own hunches.

'I think there's a strong possibility that Herr Hitler, or some-one close to him, heard about Joseph's project and saw this as a way in. A peaceful invasion of the country, if you like, though everyone involved would understand that the British might not see it that way. So any investment would have to be kept very hush-hush. No one knew Mr Fowler had already spent a great deal of money – my money – before he gained the permissions he needed. What Blythe heard was Joseph trying to persuade Müller to use his influence on that Wolfgang fellow to put some money in himself. Those Nazis are thugs. I don't care what anyone else thinks or says about them, I don't trust them. It was not the debt I cared about, I wanted no association at all. And I believed that this told the real story about Joseph. He's a man out for himself.'

Louisa listened intently, desperate to understand this and ask the questions for which she needed answers. Wolfgang knew about the mallet, didn't he? Was this why?

'Are you saying it's possible that Herr von Bohlen, or Herr Müller, killed Joseph Fowler? To keep him quiet?'

Sir Clive nodded. 'I am. I can't confirm it because I wasn't there, but it's likely. If the Nazis thought Joseph Fowler had lost the money and was in danger of exposing their plans, they would need him silenced – permanently.'

Louisa remembered the gap in the curtains. Could Jim have been hiding on the balcony when the attack happened? But then why would he say he had done it? Unless he had run out through the windows when Joseph Fowler returned to the cabin, heard the row and assumed Ella had killed him. He must have been protecting Ella – as she seemed to be protecting him. She must have been in the bedroom, heard the row and assumed it was Jim.

'Why did you hide Jim Evans in your room?'

'Blythe made me do it. She was determined that he would not get the blame for something that Ella had done – or so she believed. I thought it was only temporary, a chance for him to clean himself up. It was madness, trying to hide on a ship. But I don't think any of us were thinking straight in those small hours.'

'No.' Louisa walked towards the door. She knew why Sir Clive had told her all this. Then she turned. 'One more question: how did you know I am an agent?'

'I'm afraid, my dear girl, you are an amateur and you revealed yourself with your questions. You know too much, you are too observant. And' – he reached in his pocket – 'you should not write things down.'

He pulled out a piece of paper. It was the scrap on which she had written the address at Dolphin Square to send telegrams to. It must have fallen out of her brassiere and she hadn't noticed.

She took it out of his hand. 'Where did you get it?'

'That's for me to know, but your secret is safe with me. For obvious reasons. I don't know if "pink elephants still fly in blue skies" or whatever your phrase is now, but I used to do the same for a while, after the war.'

So she could trust Sir Clive. But she couldn't tell Guy any of it. If he arrested the wrong people – Ella and Jim – he would be making a terrible, even tragic, mistake. Yet there was nothing in her power to stop him. Louisa, Guy, Ella, Jim: they were pawns in a Nazi's game, and they had no chance of winning.

CHAPTER FIFTY-SEVEN

24 May 1935
Old Bailey, Court Number One

When Ella Fowler was called to the stand, there was a palpable shift in the atmosphere of the courtroom. This was the moment everyone had been waiting for. Guy found himself holding his breath as she was led from the dock to the witness box. Her face was pale beneath her soft navy hat and even the bulk of the coat she was wearing could not disguise her thin figure. It looked too heavy for a summer's day, but presumably she felt the cold and had not, after all, had much opportunity to feel the sun on her face in some time.

When prompted, she took the oath in a voice that was almost inaudible. Guy felt the entire weight of the courtroom crowd lean slightly further forward towards her. Mrs Fowler confirmed that she had been married to Joseph Fowler for eight years and had been married twice before. Her first husband was killed in the war, and she had divorced her second. This merely confirmed the facts to the people in the public gallery who had devoured yards of press reports on her life.

Mr Manners, her defending barrister, led his client quickly to the nub of the matter.

'Could you describe relations with your husband?'

'Since the birth of our son we occupied separate rooms,' said Ella faintly.

'Were you antagonistic to each other?' Mr Manners held her gaze, willing her, perhaps, to go on and talk firmly, to try to allow no room for doubt in the jury's minds.

'For the most part, we tried to be civil.'

The barrister moved a piece of paper in front of him, signalling a change of direction. 'Could you please tell the court when you first came to know Jim Evans?'

'My husband and I travelled on the *Princess Alice* in 1930—'

'That is, three years before the murder of Joseph Fowler?'

Ella flinched slightly. 'Yes. Evans was our cabin steward. We met him then.'

'Did you become Evans' mistress?'

There had barely been a pause before the shocking question. There was a collective intake of breath. Ella gave a nod that was in danger of being completely imperceptible. Nonetheless, it was an admission.

'On our third cruise on the ship,' she whispered.

Mr Manners maintained a brisk line of questioning. 'Taking it quite generally, from that time until your husband's death, did relations take place between you and Evans regularly, each time you were on the ship?'

'Yes.'

'You were on the ship for the following dates: May 1930, October

1930, May 1931, August 1931, January 1932, June 1932, October 1932, January 1933 and, of course, June 1933.'

'Yes.'

Somewhere outside the courtroom a door banged, and everyone started.

'Aside from those first two dates, on every other one, relations took place between you and Evans?'

'Yes.' Ella's ungloved hands reached out to the front of the box and gripped it tightly.

'Did your husband know of it?'

'He must have known of it because he told me to lead my own life four years ago. I had told him I was taking him at his word and was leading my own life.' Her voice had become firmer now. She was, after all, in this situation; she had better make the best of it, thought Guy.

'Was there an occasion, in the early part of the year – the trip in January 1933 – when there was a quarrel between you and Evans?'

'Yes, I wanted to sever connections on account of the difference in age, and Evans said he did not want to.'

Mr Manners picked up a piece of paper that Tom Mitford had handed to him. 'Before you went on the *Princess Alice* in June 1933, it seemed your banking account was overdrawn. This would be about ten days before Mr Fowler died. And he – that is, your husband – gave you £250?'

'Yes.'

'How did you get that?'

'I got it as I usually did. I used to get extra money twice a year when I was overdrawn. I always had to make up a different story each time to get it.'

'Having got the £250, did you have a cheque for fifty pounds cashed on your account by Evans in Livorno?'

'Yes, Evans used some of it to get me a ring. Other money was spent on shopping. I handed Evans fifteen or twenty pounds.'

'Did you ever meet up outside of the ship?'

'Once, we met in London when he was off on leave.'

'Did you stay in a hotel?'

'Yes.'

Mr Manners gave a small cough. 'In London, at the hotel, were you living as man and wife?'

'Yes.'

The questioning and the intensity of it had been going on for what felt like a while now. Guy could feel a tension in his stomach that would not unclench. Mr Justice Hogan scratched his chin. Mr Manners, however, had more to do.

'To bring you to the day in question, the eighteenth of June 1933. Before going to supper, you were alone in your cabin with your husband. Can you tell the jury something of the conversation that evening?'

'He mentioned a book he was reading. He said he admired a person in the book who said he had lived too long and "before he became doddering, finished himself".'

'What was your reply to that?'

'I thought perhaps he needed cheering up. I said I would make arrangements for us to take an outing when the ship docked in Rome a few days later.'

'What happened then?'

'I retired momentarily to my bedroom. Evans came in. He was very angry.'

'Did he explain his anger?'

'He accused me of living with Mr Fowler that afternoon with the bedroom door closed. I told him I had not. He was very jealous of Mr Fowler.'

'What happened then?'

'Nothing. I thought he had calmed down. He left my room and the cabin.'

'Did you see him again that evening?'

'Yes, twice. There was a fight in the Blue Bar between him and Mr Fowler. Neither of them was seriously hurt.'

'Do you know how the altercation started?'

'Mr Evans made a comment to my husband, to let go of my arm.'

'Had such a thing happened before?'

Ella shook her head. 'Never.'

Mr Manners moved on swiftly. 'You said you saw Evans again that evening?'

'Yes, after supper. I returned to the cabin and Evans was there. Mr Fowler had gone for another drink in the bar.'

'What did you do?'

'I said I was in no mood to talk, then retired to my bedroom and was asleep until I awoke a little later. Some noise disturbed me.'

Ella turned to face the jury. Her skin was stretched taut over her high cheekbones and Guy could see a thin line of sweat had broken out just below the rim of her hat. 'I heard Joseph groan. I jumped out of bed and ran into the drawing room.'

Mr Manners paused, and then, looking directly at Ella, asked her the question Guy had been both hoping for and dreading. 'What did you find?'

'My husband, sitting absolutely still in his chair. I ran over and

313

only then saw the blood. I tried to take his pulse and shook him to try to make him speak.'

'Did you call for help?'

Ella shook her head. 'Not right away. I tried to make him speak; I put his teeth back in to help him. I poured a glass of whisky to save myself being sick. I drank it neat. I tried to become senseless, to blot out the picture.'

'Did you yourself murder your husband?'

Ella did not rush her answer. 'Oh, no.'

'Did you take any part whatsoever in planning it?'

'No.'

'Did you know anything about it?'

'No. I would have prevented it had I known before, naturally.'

There was a silence. Ella's breathing had become shallow.

'Mrs Fowler, why did you admit to the killing at the time?'

For the first time, her stillness broke. She became agitated, pulling at the fingers on her gloves. 'I was confused. We had been so unhappy, said such awful things. I felt that even if I had not struck him with my own hand, I must have caused it in some way because Jim—'

'Because what, Mrs Fowler?' The lawyer was stern. She had to answer the question.

'There had been a mallet in the room, and I couldn't see it any more. Only Jim and I knew about its being there, and I thought he had to have done it. But I couldn't bear for him to take the blame. I loved him then.' At last, she broke, the sobs convulsing her thin body.

Mr Manners turned to the judge. 'No further questions, my lord.'

CHAPTER FIFTY-EIGHT

~~~

Guy headed down to E-131, but Wellesley was no longer standing guard. A young deckhand was leaning against the wall examining his fingernails, standing straight as Guy approached. Guy showed him his badge and entered the cell. He might as well have one or two questions answered while he was there.

Jim, who had not slept since the night before the attack, had his head on the table, his arms used as a pillow. Blearily, warily, he sat up.

'What now? Has she been talking again?'

'Has who been talking again?' asked Guy.

'Mrs Fowler,' said Jim. Fear hummed around him, but Guy could hear the exhaustion in his voice too. Sleep deprivation was a form of torture, wasn't it? At some point, the prisoner wanted only for this all to end, one way or another. 'It's her talking too much – that's what got us into this trouble.'

'If she – or you – have anything further to say, it will be added to your statements,' was all Guy would reply to this. 'I've come in to ask one question: why did you borrow the mallet from the tool room?'

'There was a loose nail on the floor of the cabin. Mr Fowler said he kept catching his socks on it.'

'Is it usually the job of a cabin steward to fix nails in floors? Isn't there a ship's carpenter?' said Guy. He was standing while Jim remained seated. Perhaps he should handcuff him to the chair, but Guy knew Jim had enough of that sort of treatment coming to him.

'It was quicker if I got on with it myself.' Jim shrugged.

'Did anyone else, apart from you and the Fowlers, know that the mallet was in B-17?'

'Third Officer Wellesley, who signed it out.' He thought some more. 'The first officer would check the records regularly – he would have known, too.' Jim looked at Guy, his eyes glassy with confusion and fear. 'Does that mean I'm not the only suspect? Could either of them be the ones who did it?'

'Not without a further link between either man and Mr Fowler. You remain under arrest.'

Jim's shoulders dropped. 'Yeah, of course.'

Guy left the cell and, after asking the young guard outside, began to make his way up to the Deck Department to talk to Wellesley. He felt exhausted and muddled. There were mere hours until the ship docked, and he was not convinced that he had done everything he should have. And where was Louisa?

Guy changed direction and headed to deck B, where the Mitfords' cabins were situated. It was possible that she was with them to prepare them for dinner. It still bewildered him that fully grown women required his wife's services to help them get dressed, but he reasoned that most of the ways of the world were beyond him. Solving crimes sometimes seemed simpler.

As he crossed the main foyer of deck B, Guy saw Louisa. He knew she was tired, yet she looked pretty, as she always did to him. They walked towards each other, but he realised that she was taking more hesitant steps. People milled around them; no one took any notice. Guy revelled in the anonymity of it for a brief moment and wondered if he dared take her into his arms.

She made the decision for him. As Guy drew near, she held her hands out, as if in defence.

'I'm sorry, Guy,' she said.

'What for?'

'I can't really say. I'm so tired, so fed up with this ship. When we dock, I'll go back to London with you. I don't care about the Mitfords, they can look after themselves.'

'I know it's been testing,' he said. 'But it will all be over soon. I have to answer a few more questions and then I think I'll be ready.'

Louisa nodded, and he could see she was holding back tears. It had been a long time since he had seen her in such distress and he found it hard to bear.

'Would you like to come with me?' he asked. 'I'm going to see someone called Wellesley; I think he might know something.'

Louisa jumped. 'No, you can't see him.'

'What? Why not? What do you know about him?'

Louisa had started trembling, her eyes looking beyond Guy. What was she checking?

'Louisa?' Guy tried again, remembering something. 'I thought it was Wolfgang you mentioned before – you were going to tell me something. Or was it Wellesley?'

'No, not him. Guy, please, promise me you won't go and talk to either of them. I can't tell you why, you have to trust me.'

'I do but ... ' Guy had lost his footing somehow. 'Why can't you just tell me?'

Louisa grabbed his arm. 'We can't talk here. Come with me.'

She led him out of the foyer and onto the deck, where it was dark and chilly, but empty.

CHAPTER FIFTY-NINE

Out on the deck, walking together, talking so they could not be overheard, Louisa told Guy that he had to halt the investigation and wait until they got back to London to continue. But she would not tell him why.

'If I don't have this case sewn up by the time we arrive in Rome, I'm going to lose my job.' Guy, who so rarely shouted or lost his temper, was on the brink of fury. Could Louisa not see how much this mattered? 'It's not a case of personal pride. Once we are all off the *Princess Alice*, the opportunity to discover further clues is gone. If the wrong person is arrested and the real culprit gets off the boat and disappears into Italy, then there will be almost no chance of catching them.'

'I know.' Louisa spoke calmly, quietly. It was infuriating.

'What's more, we already know how this works. A man has been murdered on a ship full of rich passengers; the newspapers are going to be all over it. If I haven't done my job properly, I'm going to be found out and exposed not only by DCI Stiles and the chief of the Metropolitan Police, but by the front pages of *The Times* and the *Daily* bloody *Mail*!'

Louisa held his arm, looking up at him with brown eyes that could pull at his heart. Usually.

'If you know something, you have to tell me. What are you keeping secret from me? What is it? What is it, Louisa?'

'I can't tell you. You have to trust me that if I could tell you, I would. But I can't. All you need to know is that you have to release Mrs Fowler and Jim Evans, and wait for events to proceed once we have landed in Rome.'

'I can't un-arrest people! What do you think this is? A child's game? On what grounds did they not do it, when they have both confessed? Why would they confess if they haven't done it?' Guy had been waving his hands in the air, needing to expel the energy of his frustration somehow, but now he felt spent. He wanted to collapse into a deckchair, but if he stopped moving, he'd lose the fight. And he couldn't do that.

'I'm going to think out loud here,' said Guy, speeding up his pace, pulling Louisa along with him. He knew it was the behaviour of a detective in a penny dreadful, but it helped him think. 'I agree that it is odd that they should both not only say they each did it, but are determined to ensure that I believe the other did not do it. It looks as if they are each trying to fall on their own sword, whether to protect the other or, possibly, a third person.

'As to the third person, there are two possibilities. Sir Clive Montague, who lost a lot of money in Joseph Fowler's architectural project, and who is also, we think, in love with Mrs Fowler. It's possible he was so outraged by the proposal that the husband of the woman he loved proposed prostituting her, that it was enough to kill. But would he really risk murdering him on the ship? Surely a clever man would wait a while. Unless it was a crime of passion?' Guy's tone was more musing now. 'If he went to the Fowlers' cabin and threw himself at the mercy of Mrs Fowler, told her he loved her and would marry her, and Mr Fowler got in the way of that, he could have grabbed the mallet and hit him in the heat of the moment.'

Guy looked at Louisa, trying to see if this prompted any recognition in her, any sign at all that he was on the right track. But she revealed nothing of this, only an expression of sadness.

He shook his head at her. 'No, I'm not letting this go. With or without your help, I'm going to get to the bottom of this.' He took a few more paces. At times like this, he wished he smoked. 'The sticking points for me with Sir Clive are that he has no alibi for the time of the murder and is unconcerned about that. Surely, if you were guilty, you'd have created an alibi? Unless it's a double bluff. Secondly, why did he hide Jim Evans in his room? I'm going to come back to that.'

Louisa had let go of Guy and wrapped her cardigan around herself, hugging her arms around her waist. She remained silent.

'The other potential suspect is Blythe North. She is in love with Jim, claims Jim is in love with her, and that they have plans to marry and set up a hotel together. She told you that Sir Clive paid her to check the passenger lists for him, so that he would know when the Fowlers would be on the *Princess Alice* – Mr Fowler obviously having been avoiding Sir Clive because of the debt. There's a distinct possibility that she has been "helping" Mrs Fowler administer morphia. She's no saint, that's for sure. But I can't see what benefit she would gain by Mr Fowler's death, as it would leave her rival for Jim widowed and free to remarry.'

Guy stood before Louisa. The ship would be at Rome in a matter of hours, and all this would be over, one way or another.

'The third person has to be Sir Clive,' he said. 'But I can't

321

arrest him. I have no evidence, nothing that links him to the weapon or to being in the cabin at the right time. No witnesses, no confession.' Guy came before Louisa and bent down so that their eyes were at the same height. He spoke gently. 'What's the link with Wellesley? Why won't you let me talk to him? Do you know something that means I can arrest him? Because if you do, I am begging you to tell me.'

Louisa shook her head. 'No, I can't. Please, trust me. Wait until we get to London.'

'I do trust you,' he said. 'It's you who won't trust me, not telling me what you know.' He stood before her and said, with more sadness than he had ever known he could feel, 'I'm afraid for us, Louisa.'

And then he walked away, off the deck and through the door, closing it heavily behind him.

CHAPTER SIXTY

⁓

As the ship docked at eight o'clock in the morning, slowly manoeuvred into position by skilful steering of its hulking weight, a long queue of passengers stood by the doors, waiting to disembark with all the patience of Olympic runners at the start of a race. Lady Redesdale, Diana and Unity were not among them – they would avoid the rush of the steerage ticket-holders, but they certainly intended to leave the *Princess Alice*.

Late into the night, Louisa and a borrowed maid had packed the numerous cases and retrieved the jewellery boxes from the purser's office. There had been a long queue. Lady Redesdale telegrammed ahead to her husband and requested that he book them a night at a hotel in Rome, and they would take a train from there to Paris the following morning. Louisa had agreed to accompany them, easing the final leg of their journey by looking after their tickets and passports, tipping the porters and carrying their valuable items with her at all times. As it was, she wouldn't be able to travel home with her husband even if he'd allowed it. Guy would have to see the prisoners off the ship and into local custody, where he would take their final statements, then work with the Italian police to take them on the train home, accompanied by a further guard.

When they got back to London, they would have to work out whether they would remain in their marriage. Louisa wanted to stay with Guy, very much. She knew he was bewildered by her apparent betrayal, yet she was powerless to defend herself. She thought she was protecting Guy, but how could she ever explain that to him?

More than that, she was also upset that Guy did not trust her. That he thought she would betray him over something insignificant. That he would not realise that she could know more than him, might be seen as intelligent and able in her own right. She loved him – more than her heart could bear to admit to right now, or it would break in half – but she was not afraid of being alone. If they stayed together it had to be because they both chose their marriage, not because they chose duty.

She told herself this, bravely, but she wasn't sure if she completely believed it. Before they had even said goodbye, she began to miss him.

The last she would see of Guy would be as she watched him escort his two suspects off the ship towards the waiting Italian police cars. News of the arrests had already reached the mainland. Rubberneckers and newspaper reporters were expected, but when the dock came into view, the sight of the people took her breath away. The crowd was four-people deep, and only a line of uniformed police, their arms hooked, prevented them from surging too far forward as the *Princess Alice* lowered its steps for the third-class passengers to walk down. There were

reporters and cameramen jostling, too, flashes already pop-
ping and pencils poised over notebooks. The prurience of it
sickened her.

And then, all too soon, first off the ship and looking frighten-
ingly alone and vulnerable as he headed towards the wolves – for
that was how they looked to her – was her husband, tall and lean,
his panama hat perhaps a touch too large for his head, his glasses
reflecting the bright Roman sunshine. Before him walked Ella
Fowler and Jim Evans, and though neither were handcuffed,
their grey faces and hunched gaits left no one in any doubt as to
the magnitude of their crime and their guilt.

The sound of the shouts rose, an angry clamour that shrieked
as loudly as the seagulls that flew overhead. Their path was kept
clear by two lines of policemen, angrily shoving the spectators
back, before bundling the prisoners into the cars. It was over
in seconds, but time had slowed down. Louisa had seen every
detail, her heart tearing apart with fear and longing to be with
her husband, to shelter him from the horror.

She was standing at the railing of the first-class deck, high
above the people, so far from her beloved as to feel she was
watching him in a dream. Although it was early in the morning, the heat was already intense, lacking the breeze they had
enjoyed when out at sea.

She looked down and saw Herr Müller's stout figure walking down the gangplank, holding a large leather suitcase in
either hand, stumbling slightly as he balanced the weight on a
downhill trajectory. Several paces behind him, dressed in his
close-fitting dark SS suit, the swastika's white background daz-
zling in the sun, walked Wolfgang von Bohlen. He reached the
bottom of the steps and, without any hurry, adjusted his hat and

straightened his belt. Then he turned and looked up, straight at Louisa. He saluted her and gave a wide smile, showing all his teeth, then walked away, along the cobbled paths, until he took a corner and could be seen no more.

CHAPTER SIXTY-ONE

Two days after Louisa had returned from Rome with the Mitfords, she arranged to meet Iain. Guy had yet to make it back to London, stuck in Italy with the local police, making the arrangements to bring back not only the arrested suspects but also the body of Joseph Fowler. They had not parted angrily on the ship. It was much worse than that: they had been guardedly polite, almost formal as they said goodbye. It frightened Louisa.

On the long journey home, all four of them were quiet. Diana was returning to an empty London as Bryan had taken the boys away and Sir Oswald was still on his motoring trip in France, with Baba. No one had expected Diana's return for another three weeks, and her diary would be clear of any engagements; it was not a prospect she relished, as without the decree absolute yet in place, she could not risk being seen attached to any man. Lady Redesdale was furious and appalled by the events, wanting only to put as much distance between herself and the *Princess Alice* as possible. Unity was nursing a romantic disappointment: Wolfgang had departed without their exchanging addresses or any mention of whether they might see each other again. Louisa did not want to talk to any of them and yearned only to get home, to start to find her way back to the life she wanted with Guy.

But first, Iain.

They met on Hammersmith Bridge again. It hardly seemed possible that only a few weeks had passed since she had seen him last. The weather was a little warmer now, with the familiar damp breeze of the Thames. When Louisa saw Iain walking towards her, the need she felt to unburden herself was overpowering. She felt a terrible sense of guilt, as if she was meeting a lover, but having to keep everything to herself had been a strain.

Iain barely greeted her but propped himself up on the wall and lit a cigarette. He inclined his head a little to the side, his invitation to her to speak.

Much to her relief, as she tumbled over her words, Iain listened. She told him about Wolfgang von Bohlen, never without his henchman Herr Müller, and his admission to Unity that his family was working with Hitler on a secret rearmament programme and that he was on the ship – ostensibly – gathering information for Hitler's own cruise ship for German workers. If that was the case, why did he steal a letter from her cabin and let her know that he had done so? Why did he talk about the 'secret rearmament programme' knowing that she was listening? It could only be that Wellesley had alerted him to her role as an agent and must therefore be a double agent himself.

'Wolfgang von Bohlen works for us,' said Iain.

Louisa's temperature dropped as if she had been thrown into an ice bath.

'Then why was Wellesley on the ship?'

'Because we suspect him of being a double agent and this was the best way to catch him.' Iain calmly, too calmly, smoked his cigarette.

Louisa steadied her breathing. There were still more questions than answers. 'What happened between von Bohlen and Joseph Fowler?'

Iain threw his cigarette into the river. 'Joseph Fowler told senior members of the Nazi Party that he invested their money safely into securing the architectural proposals at Blenheim Palace, but he lost it all. Sir Clive knew this and told Herr Müller. There was a risk that Fowler would talk too much, tell people in his drunken state about the Nazi money coming into England.'

'He put his life at risk?'

Iain gave a small shrug. 'Men are stupid sometimes.'

Louisa felt a cool breeze across her face. She tried to remember more. She knew this was her only chance. 'Wellesley signed the mallet out of the tool room for Jim Evans. Did he tell von Bohlen it was in there?'

'Yes, Wellesley believed the Nazis wanted Joseph Fowler dead. They probably would have done if they'd realised, but the job has been done for them.'

'By von Bohlen. By . . . *you*.'

'Mrs Sullivan, these things are not personal. The security of our country is at stake. And who is to say that Joseph Fowler didn't attack von Bohlen first?'

'But why did von Bohlen need to kill Joseph Fowler?'

'Fowler's lips were too loose. We couldn't afford anyone finding out about the Nazi plans while we were still investigating them. And it so happened that what the Nazis wanted was what

329

we wanted too, with the added bonus of keeping Wellesley in the dark about von Bohlen's allegiance.'

'When did it happen?'

'Joseph Fowler invited Wolfgang to his cabin that night, to discuss the business deal. But when he arrived, he heard the row within. Then there was silence. We believe Mrs Fowler retired to her bedroom and it seems now that Jim Evans was hiding on the balcony. It was over in a matter of seconds.'

'What if Mr Fowler had regained consciousness?'

'That was a concern for a while, but it turned out well in the end.' Iain did up the buttons on his jacket and shifted his feet. She knew he was preparing to leave.

'Wait, someone attacked my husband in the tool room – was that Wellesley too?'

Iain wiped his hand over his mouth. 'Yes, I regretted that. He was concerned that DS Sullivan would get too close to the truth. Your husband was lucky: you prevented him from looking in the right direction, and it saved his life.'

Louisa's mind was in danger of spinning out of control. 'As well as endangering a British police officer, two people have been arrested for a crime they didn't commit, and they may hang for it. You need to intervene in the murder investigation.'

'That can't be done,' Iain said, his voice level. 'It's an infamous murder, the heat won't die down. The public want to see some-one hang for it and the police have to fulfil that need.'

'Even if that means innocent people hang?'

Instead of answering, Iain looked impatiently over his shoul-der. The traffic roared across the bridge, and Louisa felt the same noise inside her, the anger at this brute injustice.

With a small sigh, Iain spoke to her like a teacher explaining

330

basic sums to a small child. 'Wolfgang is a vital link for us to the inside workings of the Nazi Party. If we know what they are doing, and we can prevent war, then this one death may save thousands – even millions. We cannot have another European war again, and we are doing everything it takes to prevent it.' Louisa watched the water flowing under the bridge as she listened to Iain's explanation. 'It is an order from the very top that von Bohlen cannot be linked to this case in any way.'

'So that's it?'

'That's it.'

Louisa locked eyes with him now. 'I can't work for you any more, you understand that, don't you?'

'I do. But I warn you: if you tell your husband any of this, you endanger him. He must not compromise the trial in any way, and he will do that if he knows the truth. We will do our best to obtain mercy on their sentences. But again, I repeat: this is not personal, this is for the security of our entire country.' With that, Iain hailed an approaching taxi, climbed in and drove away.

Louisa walked home, afraid and crushed. She had put everything on the line – her marriage, her career, her self-worth – in order to work for Iain and the Mitfords. She thought she could handle it, but she couldn't. She was profoundly disturbed by the chilling callousness of Iain, the casual disposal of innocent people in the pursuit of something so uncertain and the freedom of those who they knew to be wicked. The pavement beneath her feet felt spongelike, her breathing became ragged and her blood rushed around her body like a speeding train. All she wanted was to find a dark corner where she could curl up and hide, but the sun was shining with careless insouciance. This pain would last, she knew, and she was going to have to face it alone, and when she finally emerged at the end she could only hope against hope that her darling Guy would still be there.

CHAPTER SIXTY-TWO

In the weeks after their return to London, Guy and Louisa had, separately, busied themselves in the complicated aftermath of the events on the *Princess Alice*. Guy was deeply involved in the case and its preparations for trial, while Louisa wrestled with her longing to talk to her husband openly about her involvement and all she knew, against the very real risk of endangering them both to forces she now knew to be black indeed.

She returned to her stenography training and the daily routine of before as if nothing had changed, desperately seeking comfort from the repetition. All the time, the fear that she could never return to the normal of their past clung to her like cobwebs.

They saw each other every day, lay together every night, yet in their cordiality they managed never quite to look each other in the eye. Louisa would sit opposite Guy at the table for supper and miss him, even when she could see and touch him. She knew it was for her to build the bridge again and determined that even if she had to do so brick by solitary brick, she would.

In the night, Louisa ducked her head down, out of the cold

air and into the groove between Guy's shoulder blades. She stretched her legs along his and slid her hand around his chest until it lay flat where she could feel his heart beat. He was warm, and he moved slightly, letting her come in a little closer.

Brick by brick.

CHAPTER SIXTY-THREE

24 May 1935

In the Red Lion pub, shabby but always busy, thanks to a constant trade from court reporters and prisoners' families, several Mitfords gathered during the lunch-hour break from the trial. Much had happened since Louisa had last seen them all together: Pamela had become engaged, and Nancy married, to Peter Rodd, a man she had met and become affianced to within months after Hamish broke off their five-year-long engagement.

'What would one call a group of Mitfords?' asked Nancy, her tiny waist beautifully shown off in its tailored jacket of black and white dogtooth check. She sat by a round table, a glass of sherry at her hand. 'A haven? A giggle?'

'A swarm,' said Tom, taking a long draught of ale. He wasn't staying for long as there were preparations still to be done for the afternoon's cross-examinations. 'Stings and honey. But don't ask me who the queen bee is.'

'I'm definitely one of the worker bees.' Pamela was about to bite into a large cheese sandwich, with extra pickle at her request.

The three of them enjoyed amusing themselves with their insider jokes, and Louisa had known them long enough not to be made uncomfortable by it, but she could feel Guy shifting with impatience at her side. Today was the day Diana was to be called as a witness and her sisters were there in support, supposedly. Not Jessica, as she was not 'on speakers' with Diana, nor Deborah, as she had been banned from attending by their parents. Only Unity was to be relied upon to agree with Diana's testimony. Pamela and Nancy no longer kept their loathing of Sir Oswald Mosley quiet, though Pamela was more diplomatic about it. Despite what they had told their parents, Nancy and Pamela were there purely for Tom, who had been both challenged and overwhelmed by the demands of being at the centre of such a notorious trial. Though his role was relatively junior, no statement could go unchecked, no evidence unexamined and no witness unprepared. While Mr Manners, defending Ella, would be the one who had to put on the display of incisive and brilliant cross-examinations and speeches, he relied on his juniors to hand him notes and information that were impeccable.

All of the sisters adored Tom. With them in court, he would feel unassailable. That, at least, was Louisa's reading of the situation. Even so, it was also true that he had seemed, as a child, to relish his freedom away from them when at school, writing letters home that taunted his sisters with his unbridled existence: long walks with school friends to sneak a cigarette, sausages for breakfast and pillow fights in the dorms. Whether he wanted his sisters beside him now, or whether they left him with no choice, was unknown.

What was certain was that Nancy and Pamela were sitting at

336

one table at the pub and Diana and Unity at another, in the back. Louisa and Guy had originally been invited to join DCI Stiles, but he was then called away to the station in Knightsbridge. Sitting with Nancy and Pamela, Louisa knew she ought to go say hello to Diana and Unity, but she hadn't seen much of either of them in the last two years and felt reluctant to do so now.

Before Tom arrived, Nancy had filled Louisa in on the recent Mitford dramas. 'Diana hasn't spoken to me since *Wigs on the Green* was published, and Unity, the loyal sheep, is cross with me, too. They've no sense of proportion. Or humour. Really, they've become too provincial for words, with Diana pretending to speak fluent German – and you know Unity met Hitler a few months ago?'

Louisa had raised her eyebrows. What was the proper response to this? Was there one?

'She stalked him. Sat in some sad little café that was his regular haunt, hour upon hour, day after day, until eventually he noticed her and invited her to have luncheon with him. Can you think of anything more revolting?' Nancy hardly bothered to keep her voice quiet. 'She wrote to Farve afterwards and told him she was so happy she wouldn't mind dying.'

Pamela, who was now engaged to a scientist, Derek Jackson – 'Debo fainted when she heard the news, she's so in love with him,' Nancy reported – signalled to her sister to pipe down.

'I jolly well won't,' her elder replied, and continued gossiping. 'Those two wretcheds have tried to claim that Tom is on their side, but he thought Hitler terrifically ordinary. He'll only have said things to please Diana because she has good-looking girl-friends he's trying to take to bed.'

Louisa wouldn't be asking him which side he was really on;

she suspected he aimed to keep all his sisters happy, to ensure peace and quiet.

'Has marriage made you so shocking?' asked Pamela. 'I hope it doesn't do that to me.'

'I hope it does,' Nancy bit back.

It was then that Tom had arrived, coinciding with Guy bringing the drinks to the table.

'Can I get you a beer?' asked Guy.

It pleased Louisa, somehow, to see her husband at ease with one of the Mitfords. The case had put Guy and Tom on something of an equal footing.

'Thank you,' said Tom, pulling up a stool. 'Where are Diana and Unity?'

'In one of the booths back there,' Nancy replied. 'Pretending to prepare for her cross-examination later.'

'Pretending?' He raised an amused eyebrow.

'It's a relief not to have to talk to them,' said Nancy. 'It's been sticky since Christmas.'

'You've only yourself to blame.' Pamela waved to the waitress carrying over her sandwich.

'No, actually. They are to blame for getting involved with those heavy-handed monsters.' Nancy turned to Louisa. 'Peter and I went to the BUF rally in Olympia last summer ... ' She deliberately drifted off. Louisa knew there had been outrage over the violence in all the newspapers, and even the *Daily Mail* had subsequently dropped its support of Sir Oswald. 'After that, I lost my sympathy for her. I cannot understand how she can remain so blind.'

'He was always awful,' said Pamela, nodding agreeably. She was in her usual country attire, with a tweed skirt and jacket, even though she had recently moved from Bryan Guinness's dairy farm at Biddesden, where she had been working.

Guy returned to the table for the second time, bearing Tom's drink, and sat down, raising his glass to each of them. Nancy didn't respond in kind and Louisa knew she thought it was common. Instead, perhaps to lighten the mood, Nancy had posed her question about the collective noun for Mitfords.

'How do you think it's going, then?' Guy asked Tom, when the joke had died down.

'Hard to say. Both pleaded guilty at the time, now both have pleaded not guilty. We always knew it was going to be difficult and the prosecution's tactics have been hard to predict.'

'Given the evidence they've got, you mean.' Guy took another gulp of beer, feeling it wash into his stomach like water into an empty bath. 'Everybody confessed, then everybody denied. We know at least one of them is lying, if not both.'

'Or someone else altogether knows the truth.'

Louisa looked up at this. Could they have guessed? Surely not.

'In the end, it comes down to the jury. Public sympathy is for Jim, but we can't know whether the jury is influenced by that,' said Tom.

'They're not allowed to read the newspapers or discuss the case, are they?' asked Pamela.

'No, but they're only human. People are talking about it everywhere. You only have to get the bus to hear people gossiping,' said Guy.

'I ought to try that sometime,' said Nancy. 'Get the bus, I mean.' She registered the response around the table. 'It was a *joke*. I take buses all the time. But it's rather nice being able to afford one's own taxi sometimes, now the books are doing well.'

'Bravo you,' said Tom. 'I'd better go and say hello to the others, then push off back.'

'Is Jim Evans taking the stand at all?' asked Guy hurriedly.

'No,' said Tom. 'If you ask me, he can't stand the heat of the scrutiny. He's an odd one, from what I can see. His statements changed several times in the last two years – I know I don't need to tell you that – and we were told this morning that his counsel has landed on the extraordinary defence that he ate cocaine before the attack and it made him go mad. They're hoping for a guilty but insane verdict.' He picked up his glass and said thoughtfully, almost to himself: 'I wonder sometimes if he didn't do it at all but is protecting Mrs Fowler.'

'Or Mrs Fowler's boys,' said Nancy. 'Those poor innocents. One father in Canada, another dead and their mother likely to be executed.'

'Justice is justice. If she did it, and I know she did, then she has to be punished for it.' Guy coloured slightly with the emotion he had revealed.

'I'm sure you're right,' said Tom. 'And I'm only a junior in this. But it's rum to me. Perhaps someone else did it.'

'We did a thorough job,' said Guy defensively. 'That evidence is there to convict them, and it will.'

Tom nodded, said goodbye and moved off to the back of the pub, to see his other sisters.

Louisa could say nothing at all. Two people were going to be sentenced to death for a crime neither of them had committed, and she was powerless to stop it.

CHAPTER SIXTY-FOUR

24 May 1935
Old Bailey, Court Number One

It was impossible for the courtroom to be any more crowded on this, the fourth day of the trial, than it had been since the start of the week, but Guy thought he sensed extra anticipation in the atmosphere, as Mrs Diana Guinness was to be called to the witness box.

Even with his lack of interest in the sartorial, Guy could not fault Diana's ability to dress for the occasion. She wore a long black skirt and a white silk top that draped softly just below her collarbone, with a wide dark belt. Her hair was honey-blonde, parted on the side and curled underneath, a little below her ears. Diana held herself straight, her face serious, her red mouth slightly parted as she waited for the man to bring her the Bible to swear on.

Mr Burton-Lands stood at his bench. 'Mrs Guinness.' He smiled at his star witness. 'Could you please confirm your whereabouts on the eighteenth of June in 1933.'

'I was on board the *Princess Alice*.' Diana's voice was firm and

341

confident. She wasn't playing to the gallery, only ensuring no juror would strain to hear.

'Would you describe yourself as a friend of the accused, Mrs Fowler?'

'An acquaintance, perhaps,' said Diana. 'On a ship one might say that friendships are escalated in a way that they might not be on dry land.'

There was an obsequious chuckle from Mr Burton-Lands.

'I had not met her before that particular trip,' she continued. 'I believe we were introduced by Captain Schmitt at the drinks he gave on the first night.'

'What were your impressions?'

'She was a good-looking woman with a colourful past. I had some sympathy for her. Both of us have been subjected to sneers because we have chosen to follow our hearts.'

Guy was surprised. It was unusual for Diana to expose her vulnerability in this way.

'Did you believe her to be a truthful person?'

'Objection!' Mr Manners had stood. 'Witness is being asked to speculate.'

'Upheld.' The judge waved a pen at Burton-Lands. 'Move on.'

'What was the first you knew of the attack on Mr Fowler?' asked the prosecution counsel smoothly, as if there had been no challenge to him at all.

'I was telephoned by Mrs Fowler at one o'clock in the morning, or thereabouts. She sounded hysterical, as if she'd been crying, and asked me to come to her cabin immediately.'

'Did she tell you why?'

'No, but I could hear the distress. I was in bed, but I went down there within a few minutes, in my dressing gown and slippers.'

'Her cabin was close to yours?'

'Along the same passage,' said Diana. 'I hadn't been to it before, but she told me the number.'

'What did you see when you got there?'

Diana adjusted her position so the jury could view her better. 'It was ... grisly,' she said, as if it had happened only moments before. 'Mrs Fowler was rushing around the room, a drink in her hand, shouting and excited. There was a maid scrubbing at the carpet. I saw Mr Fowler sitting in an armchair, but he was partially blocked by the doctor attending to him. When the doctor stood, I saw ...'

'Take your time, Mrs Guinness,' soothed Mr Burton-Lands.

'There was a lot of blood. Mr Fowler's eyes were closed. I thought he might be dead, and I left immediately.'

'What did you do then?'

'I returned to my cabin and I telephoned through to my lady's maid, Louisa Sullivan. I knew that her husband had arrived on the ship, unexpectedly, and that he was a policeman. I asked them both to come see me.'

'Why did you do that?'

Diana put a gloved hand on the front of the box, as if steadying herself. 'I had been very shocked and distressed by what I'd seen. I needed my maid. And I suspected that DS Sullivan would be required on the scene. No one else on board realised he was there, but I thought he could do some good.'

'Which was correct,' said the barrister, pulling on the collar of his robe. He glanced at a sheet of paper. 'I'd like to ask you about an event before that night. It was only the day before, in fact, when the *Princess Alice* docked at Livorno. You had made an arrangement with Mrs Fowler?'

'Mrs Fowler and I, with my mother, Lady Redesdale, and my sister, Miss Unity Mitford, were going to have luncheon together at a local café.'

'Why didn't it happen?'

'When we walked in, we saw her husband was in the café, with Sir Clive Montague, and she said she had to go, that she remembered she needed to buy some toys for her children.'

'Was that what she did?'

'She may have bought some toys,' said Diana archly, 'but the next time we saw her she was with Jim Evans. He was carrying several shopping bags and wearing what looked like a new suit.'

'Did you talk to her?'

'Briefly. She explained she'd been buying things for Mr Fowler and that Mr Evans had been helping her because he was a similar size.'

Mr Burton-Lands picked up a piece of paper. 'I believe Mr Fowler was six feet and one inch tall.' The courtroom turned to look at Jim Evans in the dock. He was sitting down. 'Mr Evans is five foot ten inches.'

'I drew my own conclusions,' said Diana.

'Which you had better keep to yourself in a courtroom,' interjected the judge. 'I remind the witness that we deal only with facts and evidence.'

If only, thought Guy.

'Later, back on board, what happened?'

'The first-class diners, or a great number of them, were gathered in the Blue Bar for the usual cocktail before going into dinner,' said Diana. 'A fight broke out between Mr Fowler and Mr Evans. It ended quickly, with the intervention of DS Sullivan.'

'Was any explanation given as to how the fight began?' asked counsel.

'Mr Fowler grabbed his wife's arm from mine a few minutes earlier. I think he believed she was about to go in to dinner without him. Mr Evans objected.'

'As everyone departed, you overheard Mr Evans say something?' Burton-Lands threw a look to the jury, to check they were listening to every vital word.

'He said something very quietly, to himself, but as I passed him I was certain I had heard correctly. I didn't take it seriously at the time,' said Diana. 'I feel guilty about that now. Perhaps I should have.'

'Can you tell the court what you heard Mr Evans say?'

Diana took a breath before she spoke. 'He said: "I'll finish him off next time."'

'Thank you, Mrs Guinness. You've been most helpful. No further questions, my lord.'

THE LONDON GAZETTE

SATURDAY, 8 JUNE 1935

'MY DEATH SENTENCE' – MRS FOWLER

Mrs Ella Fowler penned a note before she died in which she revealed that she was taking her life because she realised she could not help her lover, Jim Evans. That is my death sentence, she wrote.

The coroner (Mr R. A. Silversea) read the letters – in which she told of her anguish since the trial – at the inquest yesterday, when a verdict of suicide while of unsound mind was recorded.

It was at 3.37 p.m. on Friday 31 May that Mrs Fowler heard the verdicts at the Old Bailey, which delivered her from the shadow of death and sent the man she loved to the condemned cell at Pentonville Prison.

And at 3.37 p.m. yesterday the suicide verdict was written, which finally ended the stormy story of her life and death.

One of Mrs Fowler's final letters was written on the riverbank a few minutes before she stabbed herself to the heart. She had scrawled her last farewell on the back of an envelope, and she wrote of the beauty of the world and the spring flowers.

It must be easier to be hanged, the letter added, *than to have to do the job oneself.*

Another letter revealed how she attempted to throw

herself under a train at Oxford Circus, and then under a bus, but the crowds were too much for her.

There was only a small group of witnesses and the jury to represent the public in this final stage of the *Princess Alice* drama. The inquest lasted only twenty-five minutes.

Dr Julian Bertrand, the local doctor who conducted the post-mortem, said there were six stab wounds in the chest, three of which had reached the heart. Death, he said, was due to haemorrhage following self-inflicted wounds by a sharp-pointed instrument, and that she was dead before entering the water.

Miss Blythe North, maid and companion to Mrs Fowler on the *Princess Alice*, took the oath in a faint voice. She identified the handbag and the handwriting of Mrs Fowler. After she had finished her evidence, the coroner gave her permission to leave the courtroom.

EVANS' PETITION

A committee of prominent townspeople in Southampton was formed yesterday to help in the organisation of the distribution of the forms for the petition of the reprieve of Jim Albert Evans, the twenty-two-year-old ship's steward who is under sentence of death for the murder of Mr S. F. Fowler on the *Princess Alice*.

Mr H. S. Staines, MP for Hampshire, in whose constituency Evans' home is situated, has offered to bring the case officially before the Home Secretary.

Tables at which the petition can be signed are being

placed at various places in the streets in Southampton. Business houses are assisting, and members of their staff yesterday canvassed from house to house with petition forms during their dinner hour.

CHAPTER SIXTY-FIVE

Louisa put the newspaper down on the breakfast table. The end had arrived. Joseph Fowler had been murdered and Ella had killed herself in a brutal and horrible fashion, leaving behind her two boys. Jim may narrowly miss execution but would serve life in prison for a crime he never committed. She knew Jim believed Ella had done the deed, in defence against a bullying husband, and that he had protected her – and her sons – from a certain death sentence. But now he must lose his youth and middle-age to an institution that would spit him out the other end, a reject from society, a man with no chance to build a happy life.

Blythe North had made good her escape: she had sent Louisa a postcard to say that she would be appearing in a play in Covent Garden next month and would leave two tickets in her name at the box office. Louisa would not be going.

Sir Clive Montague had been tracked down by one newspaper reporter and, although the gist of the message had been 'no comment', it was apparent that he had retired to his country house. Louisa hoped he found his own peace there.

Since her marriage to Peter Rodd, Nancy had softened, writing quite often to Louisa, filling her in on the family's gossip. In the last letter, she'd described Unity addressing a crowd of two hundred thousand Germans at a midsummer festival near Heidelberg, and reported that she had accepted a job as the London correspondent of *Der Stürmer*. Nancy added that Unity wrote to all the family frequently, even Jessica, with jolly snippets of news about her life in Munich, always signing off: *Heil Hitler and much love.*

To Louisa's relief, Diana had broken off contact with her. She heard that Diana's relationship with Mosley was as strong as ever, matched only by their belief in the cause of fascism. Jessica, according to Nancy, had embraced communism with equal fervour. Louisa smiled to herself at the thought of Christmases at Swinbrook, but it wasn't as if the children of Lord and Lady Redesdale were fazed by raging arguments.

Deborah, the youngest, had tried two nights at boarding school at the end of last year and been made thoroughly miserable by it. She was home, said Nancy, happiest out riding and never thinking about anything so dreary as times tables or geography.

That left Tom, who had been rewarded for his part in the successful defence counsel with a case of his own – but, Nancy's letter said, he would have to fit it in with his latest affair with a beautiful Austrian dancer: *And we all know where he prefers to spend his time if he has to choose between legal chambers and a bedchamber.*

What, then, of Louisa and Guy? Soon they would be with their own child; it was a happiness that blinded her sometimes, catching her unawares with its white light. Yet her part in the

Fowler trial, however unwitting, had threatened sometimes to shut it out. Now that it was, at last, completely over, she could tell Guy the truth.

Today, when Guy got home, she would tell him. With the case closed, and Jim reprieved, she felt free at last of the danger of breaking her oath to the British government. Guy might resign from the police – if he shared her fury at the institutions that misdirected the lives of innocents and protected the lives of the guilty – but she wasn't afraid for him if he did. She already had a plan. An office somewhere, perhaps above a shop, smart but discreet, their names on the door: *Guy and Louisa Sullivan, Private Detective Agency.*

That would come. For now, Louisa put her hand on her stomach and felt the stirrings of the life within, a flutter like a silk scarf in the wind.

HISTORICAL NOTES

A warning: this contains spoilers. Do not read before you have completed the novel, unless you want to know what happens ...

All the conversations in this book are completely fictional. However, there are some elements of the plot that are derived from real-life events.

The murder trial of Ella Fowler and Jim Evans was based on the real-life murder trial of Alma Rattenbury and George Stonor. Some of the cross-examinations in the novel (with the doctor and Ella) closely follow those of their real-life counterparts, with thanks to the British Newspaper Archive. Rattenbury and her lover Stonor (who was employed by the Rattenburys as their chauffeur) were accused of the murder of Alma's husband Francis in 1935. In the trial, Stonor was found guilty and sentenced to death, but the public view was that Alma had masterminded the killing. Her treatment at the trial was criticised at the time. She committed suicide soon after, believing her lover faced execution. At Alma's burial, police had to be brought in for crowd control – over three thousand people tried to watch the funeral, with women climbing on tombstones for a better view. At the cemetery, signatures were collected for a petition to commute Stonor's sentence, which was successful. Over three hundred thousand signatures were presented to the Home Secretary and the sentence was changed to penal servitude for life. Stonor was released from prison in 1942, and died at the age of eighty-three on exactly the sixty-fifth anniversary of Francis Rattenbury's murder.

Tom Mitford did indeed work 'in a lowly capacity' on the Rattenbury murder trial (a footnote in Charlotte Mosley's *The Mitfords: Letters Between Six Sisters*, p.158), with Alma's defence barrister, Mr F. J. O'Connor, KC. Tom's chambers was 4 Paper Buildings, Temple, but his career as a barrister is not recorded as an illustrious one. There is little mention of his legal achievements in the public arena, but his passion for love affairs, particularly with the Austrian dancer and film star Tilly Losch, is information that reached me with the kind courtesy of Margaret Simmons, who holds Losch's archive.

Iain is loosely based on Maxwell Knight, the leading agent-runner for MI5 before the war. He was head of section B5(b), responsible for infiltrating agents into subversive groups, and had particular success penetrating British fascist movements. He also favoured women agents as superior in skill to their male counterparts. Maxwell is widely believed to be the inspiration for 'M' in the James Bond books by Ian Fleming.

The MI5 file on Diana was opened on 26 September 1934, so I have taken the liberty of moving that date forward by a little over a year. The file on Sir Oswald Mosley, however, was opened in 1933, with a report from Detective Constable Edward Pierpoint, who had been at a fascist public meeting in Manchester.

MI5's 'third direction', in which agents are permitted to commit illegal acts, was the basis of Wolfgang's murder of Joseph and the subsequent cover-up by Iain.

Wolfgang von Bohlen and his family fortune is based on that of the Krupp family and the money they made through Nazi support after 1933 (and, later, through use of slave labour during the Holocaust). Their steel works were the centre of Hitler's secret rearmament programme, expanding their employees from 35,000 to 112,000. In 1933, Hitler made Gustav Krupp – the only German to be accused of war crimes in both wars – chairman of the Reich Federation of Germany Industry. Jews were ousted from the company, the board was disbanded and Krupp became the sole decision-maker. (Wolfgang's character and his part in Joseph's murder is completely fictional.)

Wolfgang's work as an agent for the British is not derived from any member of the Krupp family, but there was a Wolfgang Gans zu Putlitz who was the first secretary in charge of the consular section for the German Embassy in London, where he was sent in 1934. A member of the Nazi Party and the SS, he was an agent for MI5. He consistently warned the British government that appeasing Hitler in his apparently peaceful plans was the fastest route to war.

For those who wonder if the rest of the world was alarmed by the rise of Hitler as early as 1933, the Nazi boycotting of Jewish businesses and products was in full swing by March 1933, and was government-sanctioned by Goebbels from 1 April that year. There were meetings in New York soon after – with gatherings of over a thousand people – to discuss boycotting German exports because of this anti-Jewish policy. In short: people knew.

Regarding what Sir Clive told Louisa: in May 1933, Sir Robert

Vansittart, permanent under-secretary at the Foreign Office, forecast that: 'The present regime in Germany will, on past and present form, loose off another European war just so soon as it feels strong enough ... We are considering very crude people, who have few ideas in their noddles but brute force and militarism.' Quoted in *The Defence of the Realm: The Authorized History of MI5*, p.195, by Christopher Andrew, who quotes the source 'Security Service Archives'.

Mention of the KdF (*Kraft durch Freude*) leisure organisation is real. Translated as 'Strength Through Joy', it was part of the national German labour organisation and was dedicated to instilling and strengthening Nazi ideals and unity by providing leisure and travel opportunities for the German masses. One of these was a cruise brand that began in 1934 with chartered ships operating out of German ports with cruises to the Mediterranean.

The notion of Hitler's potential investment in an architectural project around Blenheim Palace sprang from the lore that Hitler had his sights set on the Duke of Marlborough's ancestral home as his UK base, and allegedly instructed the Luftwaffe not to bomb it.

Sir Oswald Mosley did indeed have an affair with his late wife's sister Baba in the summer of 1933 (he had previously had a brief fling with the third sister, Irene, as well as their stepmother, Grace Curzon). With thanks to Anne de Courcy for these details, in her acclaimed biography, *Diana Mosley*.

Unity Mitford met Hitler in the Osteria Bavaria café in Munich, in February 1935, and went on to be a member of his inner circle. Her anti-Semitism was not hidden, and the *Jewish Chronicle* reported in August 1935 that she had written an article as the London correspondent of *Der Stürmer*, in which she declared that she thought with joy of the day when she would be able to say with authority 'out with them'. She later had boy-friends who were in the SS.

Diana Guinness went on to marry Sir Oswald Mosley in Goebbel's drawing room, with Hitler as a witness, on 6 October 1936.

READING LIST

The Mitfords: Letters Between Six Sisters, edited by Charlotte Mosley, Harper Perennial, 2008

Hitler's British Traitors: The Secret History of Spies, Saboteurs and Fifth Columnists, Tim Tate, Icon Books, 2019

Travellers in the Third Reich: The Rise of Fascism Through the Eyes of Everyday People, Julia Boyd, Elliot & Thompson, 2017

Court Number One: The Old Bailey – The Trials and Scandals That Shocked Modern Britain, Thomas Grant, John Murray, 2019

The Defence of the Realm: The Authorized History of MI5, Christopher Andrew, Allen Lane, 2010

Rules of the Game, Nicholas Mosley, Martin Secker & Warburg, 1982

Nancy Mitford, Selina Hastings, Vintage, 2002

To Hell and Back: Europe, 1914-1949, Ian Kershaw,
Penguin, 2016

A Night to Remember, Walter Lord, Penguin, 1956

ACKNOWLEDGEMENTS

First and foremost, I must acknowledge Alma Rattenbury, Stephen Rattenbury and George Stonor. One cannot know the complications of their lives, only the tragedy that caught them in a tangled web. I hope I have used the framework of their case respectfully, without losing sight of the brutality that nonetheless existed within the fatal murder.

As ever, I owe a huge debt to those far cleverer and more expert in the historical period than me. With thanks to Charles Cumming, Celestria Noel, Annette Jacot, Michael Gracy and Margaret Simmonds for their knowledge and sharp eyes. Any mistrakes [*sic*] that remain are, of course, entirely mine.

Writing a book is only one facet of the finished article you hold in your hands. For inspiration and guidance, Ed Wood and Catherine Richards are my shining beacons. Rosanna Forte stepped in as editor when COVID-19 shook things up and was exactly what I and the book needed. The teams at Little, Brown and St Martin's Press are tireless, creative, patient and excellent, whether editing, designing, marketing or selling.

Thank you Stephanie Melrose, Laura Vile, Andy Hine, Kate Hibbert, Thalia Proctor, Catherine Burke, Charlie King, Sarah Melnyk, Allison Ziegler, Nettie Finn, Helena Doree and Sally Richardson.

I'd also like to thank the many editors, translators, designers and marketers of the foreign editions of this series for their enthusiasm and good cheer in taking Louisa and Guy around the world. Not forgetting the booksellers, bloggers, literary festival organisers and, of course, readers. I love hearing from you, whether on social media or email, in any language – keep it coming! Thank you, always, for your attention and support. A book isn't a book until someone reads it, so I depend on you.

Thank you to Caroline Michel, Laurie Robertson and the Peters, Fraser & Dunlop team for their constant endeavours.

I am so lucky to be kept safe and loved by my family, enabling me to write – I couldn't ask for more. Thank you my darling Simon, Beatrix, Louis and George. Not to leave out Zola and Benson, of course, always showing us the best way to spend a working day (stretched out on the floor of the office).

This book is in memory of Hope Dellon, a giant of publishing, who I was honoured and fortunate enough to get to know over the course of several books and long lunches. Hope's love of books and writers was both generous and exacting, the perfect combination for an author, and her legacy is magnificent.

Sarah Weal

JESSICA FELLOWES is an author, journalist, and public speaker, best known for her official *New York Times* bestselling companion books to the *Downton Abbey* TV series. Former deputy director of *Country Life* and columnist for *The Mail on Sunday*, she has written for *The Daily Telegraph, The Guardian, The Sunday Times*, and *The Lady*. Jessica has spoken at events across the United Kingdom and United States and has made numerous appearances on radio and television. She lives in Oxfordshire with her family.

Read all of the
MITFORD MURDERS SERIES
BY JESSICA FELLOWES

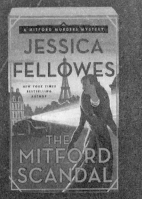

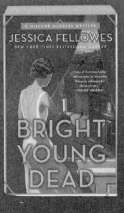

"A must-read series."
—Susan Hill, author of *The Woman in Black*